LAWRENCE SCOTT is from Trinidad and Tobago, a Caribbean Creole. He came to England to be a Benedictine monk, but after studying philosophy and theology chose to leave the monastery and study for a London degree in English. He has taught English, drama and creative writing in schools and colleges in London and Trinidad. He has travelled widely in Latin America and the Caribbean. He has worked in the theatre in Trinidad. His short stories have been published in the *Trinidad and Tobago Review*, *Chelsea 46* (New York, 1987), *The Pen*, *Caribbean New Wave* (Heinemann, 1990), *Winter's Tales* (Constable, 1988, 1989), *International Pen* (1990), *Colours of a New Day: Writings for South Africa* (Penguin, 1990), *God* (Serpent's Tail, 1992), and *Telling Stories* (Hodder and Stoughton, 1993). He was awarded the 1986 Tom-Gallon Award for *The House of Funerals*. Two of his stories have been read on Radio Four. He lives in London with his partner Jenny Green, and he divides his working time between teaching English at the Islington Federal College and writing.

Some reviews of *Witchbroom*:

'an engrossing and compulsive work of fiction . . . with a sensuous prose style . . . a vast gallery of characters – vivid, grotesque, miraculous, surprising, pathetic.'

Ken Ramchand

'an impressively written work by a very gifted writer . . . subtle but compelling . . . strange and intriguing fiction with its layers of incurable pathos.'

Wilson Harris in Wasafiri

'What a powerful writer . . . unfashionably leisured and completely self-confident. A Caribbean *One Hundred Years of Solitude*.'

Fay Weldon

'Rare and magical. The first of its kind . . . wonderful evocative language; complete emotional range; a loving, touching insight into human and family relationships.'

Sam Selvon

LAWRENCE SCOTT

WITCHBROOM

HEINEMANN

Heinemann International Education
A division of Heinemann Educational Books Ltd
Halley Court, Jordan Hill, Oxford OX2 8EJ

Heinemann Educational Books Inc
361 Hanover Street, Portsmouth, New Hampshire, 03801, USA

Heinemann Educational Books (Nigeria) Ltd
PMB 5205, Ibadan
Heinemann Educational Boleswa
PO Box 10103, Village Post Office, Gaborone, Botswana

LONDON EDINBURGH PARIS MADRID
ATHENS BOLOGNA MELBOURNE SYDNEY
AUCKLAND SINGAPORE TOKYO

First published in Great Britain in 1992 by Allison & Busby,
an imprint of Virgin Publishing Ltd
First published by Heinemann in the Caribbean Writers Series in 1993

Series Editor: Adewale Maja-Pearce

British Library Cataloguing in Publication Data
A catalogue record for this book is available from the British Library.

ISBN 0435 989332

Phototypeset by Avocet Typesetters, Bicester, Oxon
Printed and bound in Great Britain
by Cox & Wyman Ltd, Reading, Berkshire

93 94 95 96 10 9 8 7 6 5 4 3 2 1

for mum, in memory of dad,
and for Jenny

'. . . history is a fiction subject to a fitful muse, memory . . . In time every event becomes an exertion of memory and is thus subject to invention.'

Derek Walcott, 'The Muse of History'

ACKNOWLEDGEMENTS

The following writers, the complex assimilation of whose work has been a continuing inspiration: C. L. R. James, Wilson Harris, Vidia Naipaul (*The Loss of El Dorado*), Jean Rhys, Derek Walcott, Sonny Ladoo (*No Pain Like This Body*), Earl Lovelace (*The Dragon Can't Dance*), Raymond Quevedo (*Atilla's Kaiso*), Errol Hill (*The Trinidad Carnival*), C. R. Ottley (*The Story of San Fernando*), Michael Anthony (*First In Trinidad*), Gabriel Marquez (*One Hundred Years of Solitude*), Adrienne Rich (*Sources*), Caroline Griffin (*Passion is Everywhere Appropriate*); the following calypsonians whose work echoes through the book: Invader ('Rum and Coca-Cola'), Atilla ('Graf Zeppelin'), King Radio ('Brown Skin Gal'); the paintings of Michel Jean Cazabon; the following people who read the manuscript and gave encouragement and critical support: Jenny Green, Joan Goody, Nicky Paddington, Earl Lovelace, Marjorie Thorpe, Lucy and Richard Penna, Penny Casdagli, Ken Ramchand, Stewart Brown, Margaret Busby (for extraordinary faith and generosity) and Hannah Kanter. Peter Day, my editor, who from the beginning believed, my agent Elizabeth Fairbairn and Vicky Unwin from Heinemann International — without all three, there would have been no book.

CONTENTS

Family Tree

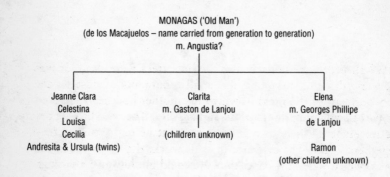

MONAGAS ('Old Man')
(de los Macajuelos – name carried from generation to generation)
m. Angustia?

Jeanne Clara
Celestina
Louisa
Cecilia
Andresita & Ursula (twins)

Clarita
m. Gaston de Lanjou

(children unknown)

Elena
m. Georges Phillipe
de Lanjou

Ramon
(other children unknown)

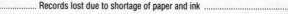

.... Records lost due to shortage of paper and ink ....

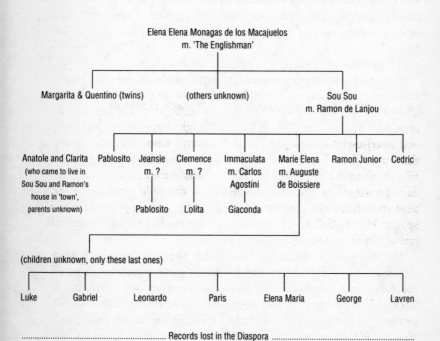

Elena Elena Monagas de los Macajuelos
m. 'The Englishman'

Margarita & Quentino (twins)   (others unknown)   Sou Sou
m. Ramon de Lanjou

Anatole and Clarita
(who came to live in
Sou Sou and Ramon's
house in 'town',
parents unknown)

Pablosito

Jeansie
m. ?

Pablosito

Clemence
m. ?

Lolita

Immaculata
m. Carlos
Agostini

Giaconda

Marie Elena
m. Auguste
de Boissiere

Ramon Junior   Cedric

(children unknown, only these last ones)

Luke   Gabriel   Leonardo   Paris   Elena Maria   George   Lavren

.... Records lost in the Diaspora ....

AN OVERTURE – FUGUES, FRAGMENTS OF TALE

THAT MORNING he noticed that the lime trees were dead. It was the same day that he found the small mountains of dust on the floor in front of the press in which his mother had neatly packed away the remaining things of his father's life. The woodlice again. He remembered them as a child. Now that he had returned they were here again. The evidence of their work, the decay, as in the doors, which were now paper-thin. He could put his fingers through them, almost, like the thin pages of a book; folding them back, there were the same rooms, musty and damp. The rains were here again. He had returned in the month of August. 'Rainy season, you come back rainy season,' Antoinetta, his old nurse, his mother's housekeeper, had said. 'So you come back? Well, I still here. You find me where you leave me, keeping your mother house, Madam house.'

On these mornings there would be no Antoinetta.

He hardly saw anyone nowadays, particularly on days like these, when the rains had been hammering all night on the galvanize roof. The ravine beyond the savannah would be flooded. He was sure of that. Maybe even the river on the plain might have broken its banks and overflowed its bridge. The Indian boys who still came to cut the lawns like when his father was alive would be stranded in the villages along the 'old road'. In the rainy season they came on brighter days to mow the lawns and keep back the wild growth of the alamanda from the gate to the yard. Long ago they would have spoken Hindi. 'Salaam, baas, salaam.' He could hear the ancestral strain. Other voices said, *Coolie people*.

The morning on which he noticed that the lime trees were dead and that woodlice had attacked his father's press and the doors to the bedrooms, he discovered an old cracked artist's portfolio. It belonged to his aunt. It had been tucked away under some of his mother's old suitcases. As he flicked through the watercolours and sketches it seemed both an extraordinary discovery and something

1

more than coincidence. That he should find these now! Was this to be part of the story?

What story? The story I had returned to this old family house to tell.

I had once started it in this fashion: neat, clipped and distanced, until after much more of that, which I beg your permission to omit, it seemed impossible for the story to hold; for me, or him or her – how did I see my alter ego? – to hold it at that distance or in sentences so always balanced like the prose of another land, the one we were taught in schools in order to write good compositions in our royal-blue exercise books with the picture of the king on the front in an oval frame and then when he died, the queen . . . it could not hold. Now neither king nor queen, but ibises, cocricoes, and the red wound in the green of the forest which is the chaconia. It could not hold.

I chose Lavren, or did he choose me, did she choose me, or did we choose each other, or was he or she chosen for me out of the bric-a-brac of history? Maybe you can tell. Maybe you can decipher, divine whether it is tragic schizophrenia or miraculous coupling or *something else* I tell you here, at times confusing and fusing my pronouns. I allowed Lavren his fragments of tale, his fugues, his first tales. I allowed him his way of telling the story. Lavren tells these tales with the help of his beloved Marie Elena, his mother and muse, and with the help of black Josephine: cook, housekeeper, servant, nanny, nurse, doer of all tasks, comforter in the darkness and in the hot stillness of noon. She it is who speaks first.

'Cric,' she says, teaching Lavren to tell stories. Not *once upon a time, in the olden days, in a fine castle*, but like an African storyteller telling anancy stories, she invites him to listen and to respond. 'Cric,' she says.

'Crac,' he replies, eager for her story.

'Cric,' Lavren, storyteller himself now, says, breaking his story.

'Crac.' Lavren hears you respond to his story and ask for more.

This was no ordinary place. Is a piece of the new world.

Where it began did not announce itself. There was no grand flourish to say this was where it had all started. The grassy fringes of the verge merely petered out down by the dairy and the black galvanize barrack-rooms in the gully. The pitch road carried on to

Princes Town, where the two English princes had planted a yellow poui tree on either side of the heretical Anglican church before they dined in Coblentz House in town, and then went back to England, where one of them died. 'One yellow poui died at the very same hour as the prince who planted it died,' Marie Elena said. She travelled to Princes Town every Friday to the market: not in a racatang Princes Town bus or in a maroon taxi fluted with silver chrome driven by a coolie man, but in a convertible Chevrolet which her sister Immaculata's daughter, Giaconda, drove like a film star, scarf flying in the breeze and lips the colour of carmine, pretending that she was still in Philadelphia. When Lavren went with Marie Elena, sitting next to her in the Chevrolet, close to her silky legs, rubbing the hem of her soft cotton dress with his thumb and index finger of his right hand and sucking the thumb of his left hand, he daydreamed as he looked out of the window, but knew exactly when they were passing the secret garden with the pond, the poisonous lilies and the staircase which led nowhere, but which he liked to climb, and pretend when he got to the top that he could see the whole world.

Yes, there could be at this point another prologue, a prologue to a swelling act and an imperial theme. This would be if you told the tales another way, if you came by another route, if you came by the Boca de la Sierpe as did Columbus and his caravels; or from the north which brought the ghost ship through the Bouche du Dragon where the isthmus is broken for the fourth time: that narrow broken-back spine of sundrenched, windblown peaks encrusted with wild forests and white orchids, the archipelago that connects the island of Kairi to the continent of Bolivar.

Cric

Crac

Bear with him, bear with Lavren, his high-flown words, his love of geography and the magic in the names of places. He will ransack the carnival for the writing of his Carnival Tales. He will dissemble: he will be man, he will be woman. He will be Pierrot, discoursing in similes, arguing in metaphor and pun, flowery extravagances. He will be Robberman: storyteller extraordinaire holding you up in the street carnival morning with stories of his origins, his travels through the nether world and the kingdoms below the sea. Lavren will rise to the heights of the Moco Jumbie, balancing on long stilt-legs, will dance the Dragon, twist and wind like the devils' Jab Jabs, beating their biscuit tins and clanging their chains. Accept it all. Delight in it. It can make you laugh. It can make you cry.

Cric

Crac

This is the one cordillera, the northern range, the Andean foothills. To come this way you would have to brave the current-eddied channels, the destiny of the middle passage between the islands of Monos; the isle of the red monkeys where Marie Elena dangled her feet in the water and went on a picnic with Auguste; Gasparee, the island of centipedes, where Lavren made love for the last time before taking the vow of chastity, an aberration which hardly lasted between one confession and another; Chacachacare, the island of lepers and nuns; Nelson, place of quarantines, where Indian children, sons and daughters of indentured labour, addicted, ate clay.

This was no ordinary place. Is a piece of the new world, boy.

Cric

Crac

Look out for the remous, the black, green vortex of currents that can take you under.

From here, at the centre of the island, where the grassy fringes of the verge merely peter out and the gravel roads are as ordinary as brown string flung down among these other peaks, humped like the back of a green iguana, running diagonally across the centre of the island; from here at the window of the turret room, Lavren, at the sill of the Demerara window, Marie Elena behind him on her deathbed telling the last tales before the end of the world as batchac ants attack the rose bushes in Immaculata's sunken garden, and woodlice eat their way through the pitchpine floorboards, and Josephine sits by the kitchen door shelling pigeon-peas: from this vantage point, Lavren can listen and write and tell the history of the new world. From here, he can see them coming with their barrels of wine that were stacked in the cellars under the gabled houses which rose from these enamelled forests, painted white and decorated with fretwork as intricate as Breton lace, embroidered with lattice as curly as crochet. From here he can survey the four points of this place of the new world. He can look myopically or can put his hand to his forehead to shade his eyes from the glare to look into the distance of history. There are the ships of Columbus in the harbour at Moruga: the *Nina*, the *Pinta* and the *Santa Maria* as clear as when

Miss Redhead, his black schoolteacher, sung their presence under the mango tree in the school yard near the walls of the Church of Notre Dame de Bon Secours, tapping the blackboard with her tamarind switch. There are the burning ships of Apodoca, the Spanish admiral scuttling his fleet to deprive the English Abercromby of the booty of surrender in 1798. There the ships whose bellies are full of black human cargo. There is the *Fatel Rozack* from Calcutta, dhotied and capraed in mourning on that fatal dawn. All come through the channels of the Serpent's Mouth and through the Dragon's teeth into the Gulf of Sadness.

Don't leap the years, Lavren hears the voices say. Eager he is to put down the record of the first genocide, then enslavement, then indentureship and then on to self-rule and independence.

No, but we must, back and forth and now, with ancient chroniclers, cartographers, cosmographers and geomorphists (who can trace the vestiges of the spirit of place, the footprints in the sand, the voices in the forests), and the others who misled the Christian, Genoese sailor Columbus, Great Navigator, to be surprised at the topography, that lying so close to the band of heat, the circle of fire, there could be such verdure, such mildness, such paradisiacal beauty, that it reminded him at once of heaven and at the same time of his own sweet Valencia in March.

This was no ordinary place. Parrots scream across cobalt skies. Eh, heh?

Cric

Crac

Down in the gully and the house high on the hill in a copse of royal palmiste, palanquins of shade – *The Governor tall tall tall, he peeping over the wall* – calypso say, their plumes like the fanfare of colonial rule.

'Pappy yo,' people shout.

'Pappy-show,' they answer themselves, twisting their tongues in irony and ridicule. The trumpets of poisonous lilies hang from the wild vines on the saman tree in the clubhouse yard which Lavren can see from the window of the Chevrolet on the way to Princes Town as he sits next to the silken knee of Marie Elena. They pass the gap, where the grassy fringes of the verge merely peter out.

Remember the house on the hill, the gabled house on high pillars with gingerbread arches, high balconies and wide verandas.

Remember the galvanize barrack-rooms in the gully, remember the clubhouse yard. This was where it had all started. Here in the canefields climbing up from the plain to the cocoa hills, the whole place an estate, a plantation to be shipped abroad to Liverpool, Cadiz, Le Havre. 'Boy, when Cocoa was King,' in the hills climbing up from the fields of serrated sugarcane leaves.

Cric

Crac

Here one sunny afternoon . . . Let us prepare the scene. Let us enter that time, that time of showers and Palmolive soap behind the ears, that time of tea with guava jelly, big chunks of yellow rat cheese, and Crix biscuits . . .

Cric

Crac

. . . rat cheese, juice and Coca-Cola. That time of pressed linen caps and aprons, that time which still smells of siesta and almond leaves falling away into the bougainvillaea hedge . . . and Josephine, sweet Josephine singing and humming a tune, leaning out of the window of the servants' room, pressing her hair with iron combs which glow on the coalpot, making her hair straight and smooth, all the kinks out with vaseline, rubbing it into her yellow palms.

'Tidy up your hair, girl. Plait it and put it away. Tuck it under your cap. Always wear your cap in the house,' Marie Elena orders.

We will sit and listen here with Lavren, in time. Her story, Josephine's story will be told. Josephine will speak. Lavren will let her speak, because of his love for her melangene arms, her breasts as heavy and smooth as watermelons, her milk as sweet and comforting as sugar-apple, her hips as comfortable as cushions, her smile as bright as the sun, her teeth as the ivory of Africa: because of these things which Marie Elena did not love: her vaselined hair, her voice as deep as the gully where the tania grows, her ears with black holes in her black lobes where she hangs gold as yellow as Benin. Her pride is the stature of a Zulu, as tall as Ashanti. She sucks her teeth with defiance. Cheups. She winds her backside with contempt and joy. He loves her for the way she sweeps her room clean and lets him sit on her bed with the counterpane a flower garden, a material from the chiney shop, for the smell of talcum powder and bay rum and her weewee in her potty under her bed which she flushes in the latrine, behind which grow the bright white

6

lilies that Auguste smells when he goes to have a shit in the morning.

Josephine will speak because no tale would be a tale without hers, no fiction a fiction, no history a herstory without hers. There is no memory without the memory of Josephine. Lavren tells a story as she would, like the storytellers of Africa, like the storytellers chained down below the hatches on the waves of the middle passage, limbo dancers passing under fire, the rod of correction, to the new world. 'Cric,' she says.

'Crac,' we answer, eager for the truth.

There is another voice: 'Josephine, Josephine.' Orders. She is called by Marie Elena and will come up from the servant's room eventually, after being called many times over. But she is not to be blamed. Her slowness to respond is not the laziness of inertia, but is a studied delaying which Marie Elena does not understand. Marie Elena wants everything done in a jiffy, is impatient with servants, with maids, ironers, washers, yardmen, marketcart men, scrubbers and women who weed the garden. She is impatient with them all, but mostly she is impatient with Josephine without whom she can't live a moment of her life.

Marie Elena is for pressing ahead with time, for forgetting, for forgetting what she wants to forget, what she does not want to remember. Amnesia ran in the family. But she is also the storer of other tales, tales no one else knows except Lavren, who sits by the window in the turret room taking it all down so that the new world will know from whence it is sprung.

Cric

Crac

Josephine remembers. Remembering takes time. She is careful that the other side gets said, is all recorded. She does not write things down. Josephine probably can't write except with difficulty. She can write her name and she can read Madam's messages on brown paper for the shop because she heard Madam read them out. She knows letters. She tells Lavren stories.

Cric

Crac

Let us enter that time. Let us enter over the scrubbed pitchpine floorboards in the soft tread of Josephine's alpagats, through the cool rooms with the high ceilings slatted with sunbeams that pierce through jalousie cracks. While we walk across the dining-room the

7

jingle-jangle of silver is laid for tea, the tinkle of china signals four o'clock, and the siren is heard in the sugarcane-factory yard, and at that very moment time is altogether altered when Marie Elena sweeps her hair into a bun and touches behind her ears and along the flutes of her neck with eau de Cologne as she sits before the mirror of the dressing-table preparing herself to descend for tea.

(Remember the dressing-table with the cut-glass powder-bowl, the silver filigree hairpin box, the varnish of the mahogany with a film of powder as pink as sand in which Lavren imprints his fingers and leaves his signature. Remember, dear reader, take time with this poetry, these fragments. Listen well to these fugues, let them work on you till the tales are told and you get the story which Lavren promises you.)

It is a time of Palmolive soap, eau de Cologne, Chanel No. 5. If it was Lent, Marie Elena would be dreaming of the Stations of the Cross and the Five Sorrowful Mysteries of the Rosary, whispering her Hail Marys and *Pater Nosters*.

Time is drenched and drunk and we can forget in an amnesia of perfume.

So, you don't water the plants in the sun. The crotons and hibiscus are heavy and green. The cockscombs in the circle bed hang their heads. There is absolute silence when the siren in the factory-yard stops. Lavren is picked up from his crib. He is puckered and wet and he wrings his face away and hangs his head over Josephine's shoulder. Let us enter that time. His cry can rend the afternoon and he can stretch his white body in an epileptic arch yearning for Marie Elena, taken away in the black arms of Josephine.

Cric

Crac

Here one sunny afternoon, this was where it had all started. The remembering.

Let us enter this idyll, this colonial time in sepia, freckled with age and the chemicals of elementary photography. The sunny afternoon that is now recorded was like many other sunny afternoons in the routine of servants and their charges. This sunny afternoon saw the procession, down the gaps from the bungalows, of black women in pressed aprons and starched caps, who generally called their charges Master or Miss in the presence of their madams but called them chubby-chubby, goochy-goochy, my white child, 'The child fair, eh?' when they were alone, and boasted to other servants of the beauty of Madam's child, mourning the loss of their own. This is the time when you hear the crunch of gravel as the perambulators are pushed down the road past the gaps, filling out the procession, the taking of the children for a walk after tea. On the verandas you can see the mothers, the madams, waving them away, trusting them absolutely into the arms and care of Josephines, Olgas, Gertrudes, Theresas, Sybils, Ernestinas, Almas, Antoinettas . . . a litany of servitude. Pray for us.

Cric

Crac

Oh, for black grandmothers who stay at home to keep their daughters' daughters and their daughters' sons . . . those sons . . . Cric

Crac

Where are the fathers? Cric

Crac

Remember the clubhouse yard, where the poisonous trumpet lilies hang from the saman trees over the gap. Stand on the green veranda of the clubhouse with its rattan chairs and look out over the red-clay tennis courts – pick pock, pick pock – where Marie Elena's daughter Elena Maria plays tennis in a short cotton skirt with scalloped hem, all in white with broderie anglaise ruffles underneath, shimmering like the curl on a wave when she leaps and serves. Her brown legs are smooth and long. Mr de Lisle, senior chemist in the sugarcane company, stands on the veranda and stares and Lavren, from his sill, stares at him and then at her. This was the distraction that lingered in the mind of Mr de Lisle on his way to the golf course, an innocent protagonist in these events, a mere peccadillo, a venial sin, in the scheme of things to come: past, present and future.

Cric

Crac

They teed off, Mr de Lisle conjuring and kissing the feet of Elena Maria. The afternoon was filled with the noise of heavy golf-bags jangling on the backs of barefoot Indian caddy boys. This was the idyll, this was the scene. This was that sunny afternoon in 1944, Lavren not quite one year old. Hiroshima, Nagasaki lie in the future, no flower so great has yet bloomed . . . *Rum and Coca-Cola* . . . *working for the Yankee dollar.*

It was into such a scene, such a colonial idyll of black servants in white aprons and starched caps, that the Holy Ghost, third person of the triune God, flew down to perform the will of God by the hands of Mr de Lisle.

Cric

Crac

The Holy Ghost hovered over the barrack-rooms, behind the screen of casuarina trees, down the rutted gravel trace – more mud than gravel – which housed, no, harnessed and shackled whole families in single confined rooms with little light, so that a child as small as the baby Lavren could upset a pot of boiling water all over his stomach and be scarred for life, and if you lived in the gabled house high up on the hill with the wide verandas and high ceilings, high above it all, the black hole of Calcutta, the fields of Uttar Pradesh in the new world, you would never have known. You might have only heard a terrible scream, and not knowing the cause have put it down to a foolish noise. Then Marie Elena or Auguste might ask Josephine, 'What is that noise? Shut the window.' What would happen to such a child? How would he see the world?

Cric

Crac

There had been such a scream, such a scar. People were dreaming in the twilight barrack-rooms, in the kerosene-lit villages for the setting of the imperial sun. That afternoon a small Indian boy ventured out from behind the screen of casuarina trees and stood where the grassy fringes of the verge merely petered out, and stared at the nurses with their white children; stared at Lavren sitting up in his pram bonneted and laced, embroidered in the bonnet and lace of his ancestors, tucked up with pillows and a delight to see, so chubby and healthy. The Indian boy from the fields of Bengal behind the screen of casuarinas stared with hands on his belly which was as white as bait, raw as white raw fish, raw like pain, no pain like this body. What delirium in his head when the boiling water splashed upon his stomach in the dark barrack-room?

Cric

Crac

The Holy Ghost hovered.

Mr de Lisle drives his ball. It has found its preordained trajectory. It is guided by the Holy Ghost, accompanying its swift flight with a flock of white doves and a hallelujah of egrets whose shadows skim the fairway to the No. 9 Green. It avoids all obstacles, crashing into the branches of saman trees, bunkers and verges, lost in the rough. *Veni Sancte Spiritu* . . . it overreaches the green and bounces on to the grassy verge which had merely petered out at the edge of the gravel road where the pram with Lavren stands with Josephine sitting at its side. The ball hits the pram. PRAM P'DAM, like steel band. Ricochets. Finds the hallowed spot at the back of the baby's bonneted head, storer of memory, soft still with the trauma of birth, miraculously protected from the stroke of death by the Holy Ghost. The ball, guided by the Holy Ghost and the illicit passionate thoughts of Mr de Lisle, dreaming of stroking and kissing Elena Maria's small feet, makes its dent which shocks the cranium and shakes up, wakes up the memory of the last of the Monagas de los Macajuelos, whose stare was at that very moment locked into the eyes of the Indian boy, smudged with the yellow of malnutrition. In this coincidence, while the tennis players continue their game, the golfers continue to stroll and Auguste and Marie Elena continue to munch rat cheese, guava jelly and Crix biscuits and sip tea, Lavren begins to remember.

Cric

Crac

Lavren entered through the black holes of those eyes, black from the black hole of Calcutta smudged with the yellow of malnutrition. He entered the white belly burnt with the pain of history. He entered this pain into a revision of history. He entered a sea of green and yellow, coppery, silted with the refuse of the Orinoco whose mouth was crammed with wrecks, festooned with skeletons, the treasure of that far-flung folly of cross and sword whose seed was sown in Genoa. Out of the empty sockets in the algae-encrusted skulls vast processions issued, performing the liturgies of Corpus Christi, the candlelit mass of Easter. Out of one skull Las Casas swam, bearing Amerindians and welcoming black slaves from the belly of ships and baptising them. The seaweed was stained with the blood of Christ and the slaves and Amerindians had their mouths stuffed with loaves and fishes from the gospels, while archbishops and nuns copulated in confessionals to the chanting of the *Salve Regina*.

Cric

Crac

In the buoyancy of the water, Lavren seemed to be without a body,

11

but had the soul at that moment wished to manifest itself it could not have done it more beautifully or wonderfully. It was the body of a young boy not quite a man, the body of a young girl not quite a woman. This was a body known only to mythology, to the pantheons of gods, a place of goddesses and nymphs in a carnival of coupling. S/he was born in the waters of the new world a hermaphrodite, a young boy who might have been mistaken for a girl. Hermaphrodite, with the breasts of a young girl, who might have been mistaken for a boy with a penis and a crack between his legs in the half-light of the coppery sea silted with the dreams of El Dorado. S/he levitated between worlds. S/he hung between genders. S/he trembled between loves and desires. S/he was pigmented between races. S/he stretched her young body between continents and hung about her neck this archipelago of islands. Swimming among these visions, Lavren was as comfortable as when s/he hung below Marie Elena's heart in the amniotic sack, or in the black arms of Josephine, cradled on her lap in the pantry, listening to her words, 'Let me tell you a true story.'

Cric

Crac

There he founds maps, undiscovered maps of Kairi. He deciphered hieroglyphs written in coral and scratched on barnacled barracoons. He opened chests as he listened to the beat of Marie Elena's heart and heard her tell her tales. There he found the Carnival Tales which told of the past, the present and the future, of which this overture contains fragments and fugues.

Cric

Crac

Monkey break he back

For a piece a

Pomme arac.

THE HOUSES OF KAIRI
THE CARNIVAL TALES OF
LAVREN MONAGAS DE LOS MACAJUELOS

1

THE TALE OF THE FIRST HOUSE

LAVREN SURFACED into the first of his tales far out at sea, where the caravels were adrift. Their keels were entangled in sargasso weed that entrapped dolphins which had gone astray. Large fish were panting to be free, or floating bloated and rotting in the sun. Whales were unable to fathom because of the sludge. Sails were hanging limp for the lack of a breeze to billow and pull taut the rigging. Lavren surfaced for air in the hot and stagnant stillness up on the open deck among the motley crew, the old-world crew: criminals set free from dungeons and prisons. Poverty had clambered aboard in Cadiz, Le Havre or up the river in London-town to make a fortune. Priests who would be saints, to make Christians of savages and extend the mantle of Holy Mother Church, matching cross with sword, abandoned their monasteries of the old world. The cocksure aristocrat, nose in the air, smelling for a breeze and avoiding the stench below, embarked on a season of adventure. These and others he saw and heard: buccaneers, pirates, conquistadors, adventurers seeking a new world, drawn by tales of El Dorado which, for some, meant a glimpse of heaven, for others, gold in their pockets and pouches, the holds of ships and the coffers of old-world kingdoms. For the poet, it was booty with which to woo a queen. Lavren was drawn to a dreamer who rested his head upon the hairy chest of his mate and listened to the itinerant storyteller, the conjuror of the future. 'Listen to this one, lads!'

They huddled in the darkness under a canopy of stars which hung from a black vault. They sought the pointers, the outline of the gods. They needed a breeze, which would come to lift them to where the constellations pointed and the new maps indicated. Lavren nestled close to Gaston de Lanjou. He will soon change that name, when he follows his imagination, set free by the storyteller's tale. 'And listen to this other one, lads.'

'Wind!' a sailor in the poop shouts, the rigging and the tackle jangle and jingle; a breeze, and sails flap. The tale of the most beautiful girl in the world, who awaited them at the next port, is interrupted. 'A wind! Set sail!' The motley crew, like monkeys, scampered and scarpered up the ropes to unfurl the sails to billow and take the breeze for the new world. They begin to move, leaving the sargasso weed of the wide Sargasso Sea.

Lavren followed Gaston as he fulfilled the future in the tale told by the storyteller.

They landed at Margarita, the island of pearls, where Gaston purchased his collection of pearls as white as blanched almonds, dived for in a sea they called Mar Dulce, later called the Gulf of Sadness. With these moons, Gaston went in search of the storyteller's most beautiful girl.

Lavren begins with the dream of Eden where it began for Gaston de Lanjou and Clarita Monagas de los Macajuelos in the convent parlour of Aracataca on the savannahs of the Monagas on the continent of Bolivar. As he begins, the nuns chant his favourite music in Saint Gregory's composition, *'Salve Regina, Mater Misericordia . . .,'* for those who live in this vale of tears.

When Gaston arrived from Margarita with his dowry of pearls, Clarita was already in the Convent of the Immaculate Heart of Mary of the Nuns of Cluny. She was put there by her father as a gift to God for favours which Father Rosario, the parish priest, had given old-man Monagas: for indulgences, days off purgatory, or a place in heaven at the footstool of archangels. Who knows? She was not yet a novice, but still a postulant, though the rules of the enclosure nevertheless applied to her, and in particular, the rule that no man was to enter the walls of the convent to visit her without a special dispensation from the Archbishop in Margarita which had to be applied for by the parish priest in Aracataca, on the recommendation of the Mother Superior. On top of that, the dispensation had to have the papal seal. So given the lapse of time that voyages across the ocean took, and the inestimable difficulties to gain audience and hearing in Rome, it would have been impossible for Gaston to enter the convent legitimately. 'No man's desire can be expected to beat that long, unsatisfied,' said old-man Monagas. 'But why Clarita?' Old-man Monagas and his wife Angustia could not understand this obsession with the one daughter who was in the convent to be the bride of Christ.

'Why Clarita?' Angustia pleaded.

'I have other daughters,' the old father said, 'Jeanne Clara, Celestina, Louisa, Cecilia. But she will be a child for ever. There is Andresita and her twin sister Ursula. There is Elena, but she is still too young, and there are three babies. I keep those for your younger brothers whom I know will come one day with bags of pearls.' Old-man Monagas laughed, but Gaston did not laugh. He remembered the storyteller's description of Clarita while he was still at sea, crossing from the old world to the new.

'A sailor on the boat I worked on told me that an old man in the town of Aracataca on these dusty savannahs had a daughter so beautiful he had to lock her up in a convent, otherwise his own brothers, the poor girl's uncles, would molest her, and even her father had been tempted to touch her where it thrilled the most.' Gaston looked knowingly at the old man. Old-man Monagas turned to see that his wife and daughters were out of earshot.

'My boy , what is it that you want? And you bring such fine pearls, yes?'

But Gaston continued the story he had been told at sea under the moon, on the loneliness of the ocean. 'Where it thrilled the most,' he repeated, 'that is what we sailors have been told, and it was only when the old man told the parish priest, Father Rosario, that they came up with the idea to put her in the convent.' Gaston winked. 'They would say it was because of some favour, in answer to a prayer, that she was being offered as a bride for Christ.' Gaston continued the tale he had been told, while old-man Monagas fingered some of the finest pearls from Margarita, which Gaston had emptied from a leather pouch on to the ledge of the veranda. He marvelled that the story told by this young man of himself and his daughters was already a legend, a story told on dark and lonely nights by sailors and travellers to fill the desire of their dreams and the passion of their sleep.

Old-man Monagas whispered with his fingers to his lips, 'Shush,' glancing round to see that none of his little daughters had crept up to listen to the grown-ups. But Gaston continued the story he had heard from the sailor, as he put more pearls on the ledge of the veranda, tempting the old man with these shadows of the moon.

Normally, old-man Monagas would have had to find dowries for all his daughters, but this was the new world and, since he had spread about the tale of their incomparable beauty, it was the suitors who had to find the dowries, and the dowry always had to be pearls. They came one after the other; Gaston, and in his wake another brother. 'If you want her for a wife you must bear my name and carry it to the ends of the world.'

Gaston ignored the old man with his plans. 'The world knew it was not because Clarita was holy. Her mama wept and railed against you, old man, but the priest quietened the sorrowing mama and reminded her of her duties to her husband. Do you say no to this tale I heard upon the wide Sargasso Sea, when our ships lay adrift under the scorching sun by day and the cold winds at night? This tale I heard by starlight, falling asleep against the hairy chest of my mate? Do you deny it, old man?' Gaston leant over to put the pearls back into his pouch. 'I must see Clarita. The storyteller said her name was Clarita.'

'Shush, man, what do you want? Do you want the confessional ears of the priest to burn?' Old-man Monagas stayed the hand of the sailor who had begun to eclipse the moons with his fingers.

'Where is that sweet-smelling priest?' Gaston had been thinking of this Father Rosario, whom he had met already, and who smelt of the rosewater he applied to his hands and face before morning mass to bewitch the women of the parish.

'Shush.' Old-man Monagas realised that this young man knew the truth, but his obsession was so great he was willing to pay for his daughter with the most perfect pearls, despite the fact that he could have blackmailed him instead. This mystified him.

But Gaston continued. He would only be satisfied with Clarita the most beautiful, in spite of the ugly rumour that Father Rosario had locked her up so that when the Archbishop came on confirmation days, there would be something to make his long journey from Margarita worthwhile. The young Gaston was even a little flattered that Clarita had had her hymen broken by an Archbishop's bejewelled finger. Cric

Crac – it broke Gaston's heart, this tale, it broke the heart of Lavren –

Monkey break he back
For a piece a
Pomme arac . . .

Now, that is the kind of comment that Lavren knows that Marie

18

Elena, his muse and mother, would not like. It is lucky she is nodding off into eternity, and probably will never see the truest history in the world of the great and pythonic family of the Monagas de los Macajuelos. It would break her heart. On the other hand, she likes a good story.

Once Lavren gets tripped up with Marie Elena's tongue, language and words of the Holy Spirit, it is no knowing where the story will go, and the tale of Clarita, most beautiful girl in the new world, precursor of carnival queens, will not be told.

Ah, she's nodded off and Josephine has brought a bowl of chicken soup into the room with the bed by the Demerara window overlooking the Gulf of Sadness where Lavren sits, sometimes at the windowsill, sometimes at the foot of the bed, depending on the light. It will settle her stomach and be a palliative to the feet and feet of intestine wrapped inside of her. If she wakes she can be given the chicken consommé to stop indigestion and keep her telling stories.

The digressionary tale has become fashionable again; the delaying of the truth, if there is a truth to be told. But it is not for this reason that Lavren uses it. He is not a fashionable writer, merely a child of the new world: educated in a parody of Albion's culture; a failer of exams; a procrastinator of tasks; a fantasiser who would have liked to have danced on the stages of the world, a creole Diaghilev; been the prince of Elsinor; the Puck of an English forest; Cesario at the feet of her Orsino; Oberon and Titania, the two heads of the same dream with their changeling boy; Ganymede, a Rosalind wooing in disguise, wooed in disguise; a creole child from a creole house; the child of a silent father and a talkative mother who told too many tales. But all must be told at the appropriate time, the time when the hints can be abandoned and the clues made clear and Lavren appears in all his contradiction, levitating between genders and races. These digressions have more to do with the indigestion of Marie Elena than with literary sophistication to charm or confound critics at the end of the century. Some little country-bookie come to town would never presume to do that. Some little creole boy from the backyards and backwaters of great empires, boy, could only hope to imitate the great users of the one thing they left us, language. But with that we go mamaguy them, Lavren thought.

There is more he would have been, more he could have been: a pope with a triple tiara, a saint, a martyr lacerated and crucified

19

upside down, Saint Lawrence on his gridiron . . . *Te Deum laudamus, Te Dominum confitemur . . .*

'Amen,' Marie Elena hiccupped, choking on her chicken soup. Lavren is reminded to avoid the tendency to digress. He must get back to the tale of history.

Gaston, in the meantime, had wavered in his intention the night before, and had almost changed his mind when he saw the ten-year-old Isabella, Clarita's younger sister, playing with her Amerindian servant girl in the yard in front of the veranda where he was sitting with old-man Monagas. Old-man Monagas detected the gleam in his eye, seduced by the beauty and innocence of the child. It was this in the end which made him think it better that Gaston go to the convent the next morning. He clapped his hands and said, 'She's too young, my boy,' and then, 'Children, go and play at the back.' The vision, which had momentarily eclipsed the beauty of Clarita, vanished into child's play, and Gaston returned to his obsession with Clarita, which was just what old-man Monagas wanted. Isabella was too young.

Mama was crying in the bedroom all that night surrounded by her daughters: 'My children, my children, is this your destiny, so rudely awakened and weaned so quickly for the desires of men?' Her voice had always been one of lamentation. Angustia, her name lives on, given to a pain that all Monagas have in their legs. They say it is because she stood for so long each evening searching the horizon for her vanished daughters. Lavren must not hasten too quickly.

When Gaston arrived at the convent, the echo of Clarita's mother's lamentation was still in his ear, to remind him, young as he was, that there was another's sorrow amidst his joy. 'I'll give your daughter heaven, old woman.' Then he put the old woman's voice from his mind and fixed his eye on the prison of the convent, as it seemed to him: this walled garden, this cloister, pretending to be Eden or a piece of heaven. The Sister Porter would not allow him to enter. She merely showed her eyes through the grille in the door and said:

'Mother Superior has not given permission, nor the Holy Father in Rome. So, off you go, young man.'

Gaston made such a racket at the door, banging and crying out, 'Clarita, Clarita,' that they eventually allowed him into the parlour, maintaining that he did not possess the official edict from Rome with the papal seal which would allow him to breach the enclosure of the nuns, and see Clarita in the garden where the fountain played among the bougainvillaea bushes and the frangipani trees. He continued to make a racket like a peevish boy, 'Clarita, Clarita.' His mother had told him how he used to lie on the floor and kick his legs in the air in order to get what he wanted, and she would always relent. One day he even did a shit in his pants. Gaston knew he would eventually have his own way and so began to bang on the door. But then he grew strangely silent, and this seemed to have more power than the noise to terrorise the nuns. Intermittently, he would cry out with a great lamentation as before: 'Clarita!' – which made the poor postulants who were scrubbing the corridor overthrow their buckets and run away to the scullery.

'Diabolus!' they screamed, letting their divine reading concerning the Prince of Darkness take hold of their imaginations.

Gaston spent most of that day pacing the parlour whose walls were adorned with murals depicting the overshadowing of the Virgin Mary by the Holy Ghost. These had been painted by one of the nuns, who was famed for her calligraphy in gold lettering and was an illuminator of extraordinary beauty in the new world. She had inscribed the words, Maria, integra et casta: without stain and unbroken.

Even after a special meal of vegetables cooked in herbs and spices which the nuns had prepared for Gaston from the convent garden, he would not relent, and vowed to spend the night on the floor of the parlour. 'I will root myself to the ground and grow like a strong vine against your walls, until I see the face of the most beautiful girl in the world. Clarita!' The name of the most beautiful girl in the world echoed through the vaults of the cloister.

After compline, when the nuns, in the darkness of their choir, implored that they be saved from the diabolus, their adversary like a roaring lion going about seeking whom he may devour, the Mother Superior opened the grille and spoke to the impetuous young man who had travelled from the old world and came with stories heard upon the ocean of the most beautiful girl. 'This young girl you seek, my man, has been given as a bride for Christ, but since you have come from so far and persist so strongly, I will give you a glimpse of heaven, but then you must leave our town of Aracataca and go on your travels. And you must not be so noisy, young man. Come back in the morning.' The Mother Superior spoke with a wisdom often gained by women who live for a long time without men. She was not sure, however, that Gaston would agree to come in the morning, have his glimpse of heaven and then leave. After admonishing him again for his behaviour, she said he might see Clarita through the grille in the morning after lauds.

Gaston went off cheerily into the town, feeling that he had won the first round. He caroused at a neighbouring hacienda with the servant-girl Cigale, so called by her master and mistress because she had such a piercingly high voice like a cicada crying for rain.

Marie Elena used to raise her eyebrows at this point of the story when she admitted that Cigale was half Amerindian and half Spanish. 'Mestizo, mulatto,' she would say, tapping her wrist and indicating that she meant the girl's colour. It is reputed that this became such a habit of hers that no one paid any attention when on her deathbed she tapped her wrist, and her family kneeling around the bed thought she was either hallucinating or wandering in her mind, giving expression to the one overriding obsession of the Monagas, the colour of their skin and of the skin of black people, yellow people, Indian people. People were the colour of their skin except if they were priests; then they were let off.

There are still some who never let anyone off, priests or layfolk: everyone for them who was not a Monagas, or carried 'de' before their name was beyond the pale, as the verandas reverberated with, 'A damn blasted nigger, a damn coolie. Give us another punch, there.' This was in the last days, told in the last of the tales when the verandas rocked on their rickety stilts, corrupted by woodlice and history. Lavren must resist the future.

In fact Lavren, who was an expert at the slightest variation in mood and gesture of his muse and mother, realised that she was indicating the time of her death. The gesture was the common one of indicating a wristwatch which she never possessed, always wearing her watch on a little gold chain pinned to her dress like a brooch; but then she always acted with ambiguity. This meant she would die at the time of the Angelus. He knew that Marie Elena, in nearing her death, had been asking forgiveness of her God for the whole world, and for the discovery of the new world, for the conquest, for the destruction of the Amerindians, for the enslavement of Africans and for the indentureship of the Indians. He was proud of her for this.

She smiled when she was dying because she knew that he knew. Of course Marie Elena surprised everyone at the time of her death and did the completely unexpected thing, or expected thing, depending on how well you knew her.

Lavren must not leap like a salmon to his death, spawning his pearls. He must resist the future and return to the convent in Aracataca.

Gaston arrived the next day at dawn. He was refreshed by the night he had spent with Cigale, and she had brought him a fresh change of clothes and a bowl of coffee. All the small children who were out on errands for their mothers abandoned their duty and followed Gaston down the street to the convent. They skipped and played around his feet calling out, 'Gaston, Gaston, pearl thief and nun-snatcher.' He ignored them at first, but then he called a little boy and girl who looked weaker than the others and were lingering behind the crowd.

'Go to the nearest shop and buy me a dozen tamarind balls.' He gave them money and off they went, soon to return with the sugary purchase. He gave them the change. 'Now go and find what you want the most.' The other children, still chanting, continued to follow him till he got to the convent gate.

The Sister Porter again showed her face through the grille. When she saw him she opened up the side door and let him into the parlour reluctantly. She shooed the children away. 'Off, you urchins, little devils.' She crossed herself, believing Gaston to be the devil incarnate. Marie Elena would often say of someone she disapproved of, 'He is the devil incarnate.' Lavren uses her words, but must not digress.

Clarita, being only a postulant, appeared in a simple cotton smock without a scapular. Her head was covered with a short veil which did not enclose her forehead, so some strands of black hair shone from beneath the white linen veil. She knelt with her arms tucked into her sleeves and she rested them on her banded breasts. Her head was lowered, her eyes downcast but not shut. She whispered her rosary while fingering her beads within the folds of her sleeves. *'Ave Maria, gratia plena . . .'*

It must be remembered that this Clarita, reputed to be the most beautiful girl of the new world and precursor of carnival queens, was not here from choice. She was her father's gift to Father Rosario, to be kept by the nuns, rumoured, a nuance omitted by Marie Elena, as a solace to the visiting Archbishop. Ha! Marie Elena dribbled her chicken consommé.

Behind Clarita stood a young nun dressed in the full habit of the Nuns of Cluny. This nun was Clarita's guardian angel, Sister Luke, and responsible for showing Clarita the ropes of the convent. She was extraordinarily tall and was in her youth as famed for her intellect, as Clarita was for her beauty. She was reputed to have had the most fiery crown of auburn hair, which of course would now be a crop of bristles barely covering her scalp. She had an encyclopaedic memory, an index of authors and manuscripts in theology and philosophy, both sacred and profane, which she expounded upon at the drop of a veil. 'In 1022 Boniface of Turin completed the manuscript on the heresy of . . .' and quite soon her audience were lost by her erudition. She could tell the dates of the earliest manuscripts from the times of the early fathers of the Church and the monks of the desert. She specialised in the theology of the Virgin Birth, the varying diameters of the Virgin Mary's hymen, and had written a treatise called 'The Proof of the Unbreakable Hymen'. Sister Luke was not beautiful at all, though her high brow, stretched in the constraints of her tight skull-cap and veil, shone with a kind of beauty that indicated spiritual enlightenment, if it did not speak of sensual pleasure, which was written all over the face of Clarita and curled in her full lips. But somewhere in that tall frame, crowned with a stubble of auburn, burned a desire insatiable. Would she be able to withstand Gaston herself, far less defend Clarita from the seduction of the Prince of Darkness, as the postulants and novices called him, gossiping about the events in the front parlour?

It was hoped by the Mother Superior that Sister Luke's severity would dissuade Gaston from his desire to deprive the convent, and as Lavren thought wickedly, the Archbishop, from such a prize as Clarita, his solace after long journeys.

Gaston, slightly awed by the situation, was nervous, but this did not last very long. He belched his morning coffee and the memory of Cigale. He wrenched open the convent door and was met by the silence of the room and the two nuns. Clarita jumped, immediately disobeying her Mother Superior and glancing up, a mere flicker. 'Oh,' she gasped, and then was immediately quietened by Sister Luke, who put her hand on the kneeling girl's shoulder.

'Shush, my daughter. Say a Hail Mary.'

Being in the grilled and high-ceilinged room was like being in a chapel, and being in the presence of the two nuns was like being in the real presence of the Blessed Sacrament. Here was Clarita, whom he had heard of on dark nights under the moon, listening to a crazed storyteller in the stillness and heat of the Sargasso Sea. He could hardly see her face and he had to admit that he was a little afraid of Sister Luke, whose deep voice was a legend in the town. 'In the year 1220, Gaulbert of Paris wrote a treatise on the Trinitarian Mystery which was to confound the Blessed William Saint Theirry in his belief in the sacramentality of human friendship.' The poor girl had to keep saying anything to keep her passions at bay.

This parlour was not as claustrophobic as the one in which Gaston had had his first interview with the Mother Superior. He stood at the entrance and surveyed the scene. He had not all this time moved very far from the open door. Sister Luke did not seem to be looking at anything in particular, yet he had a feeling of being penetrated by her scrutinising stare.

Doors in convents are closed and opened as if by a thief in the night. The only sound announcing someone's arrival was the swish of a nun's habit along a draughty corridor. Clarita had been instructed, 'My daughter, you must not raise your eyes to the man.' She was to fight the temptation to look at him, even if she was from necessity forced to speak to him. She should leave all the speaking to Sister Luke. 'Keep your holy silence, my daughter.'

Gaston was in a room that never before had heard the voice of a man. The Archbishop had his own suite, and officially no nun was allowed there except accompanied by the Mother Superior or with her express permission. Sister Luke had not heard the voice of a man for twelve years, apart from the inner voice of her lover, Christ. Clarita had not heard the voice of a man since she last said goodbye to her father. Of course this discounts the spoken words of the mass in Latin by Father Rosario, who as well as parish priest of Aracataca, was chaplain of the convent, uttering the words of the liturgy and the admonitions of the confessional.

'Sister, leave the young girl to me,' Gaston spoke softly, brave enough now to look into the eyes which had previously scrutinised him. Sister Luke was immediately disarmed. It was the unexpected charm and quiet in the deep voice, when she had expected a gruff voice that would speak angrily. This was not what the Mother Superior in all her wisdom had described, and hence her strategies of defence fell. She was prepared to meet violence with the power of prayer. She did not know what to do with the charm of chivalry. Indeed, it was a command but it sounded like a request, something that Sister Luke had dearly wanted in her life. She longed for someone to ask her to do something rather than, as had happened to her all her childhood, be commanded. 'Leave the young girl to me, Sister.' It was a command of love and passion which had not even entered the dream life of Sister Luke.

When they were alone, Gaston knelt at a prie-dieu next to the grille opposite where Clarita knelt.

Lavren puts his story down as one of the most sensual moments in the history of the new world, a moment matched only by the day that a young man, removing the tiles from the roof of a bathroom in the town of Macondo, tried to enter and make love to Remedios the Beautiful in the garden of the Buendia house. That day in the future spawned a host of yellow butterflies. Today, in Aracataca, on the savannahs of Monagas, on the continent of Bolivar, white ants coated with sugar, and tamed by the indulgence of glucose, crawled over the walls and the panelling of the convent parlour and gently tickled the arms and necks of the two lovers who knelt facing each other.

Lavren, of course, is quite aware that Marie Elena has not told him any of this, and that within the power of a hermaphrodite to collapse the stringencies of gender, he has penetrated the primal moment of the new world: the seduction of Clarita, the most beautiful girl in the world, the precursor of carnival queens, as white as milk tinged with the coffee of Tamana, seduced by Gaston de Lanjou, the pearl thief, as the children called him.

Clarita wished to do everything her Mother Superior wanted her to do. Gaston did not do anything at first, not even brush off the sugar-coated ants that were crawling up his legs and over his arms and down his neck. He could see the procession of insects, sweetened with his desire, crawling towards the young girl, the young postulant, novice of the mothers of Cluny. Gaston, in spite of these ticklings and sensations, knelt as if in prayer, in adoration of her sweet young face. Clarita felt the silence all around her and she kept her eyes downcast. The ants had still not got to her, though she was startled out of the corner of her eye by their encrusted backs shining like diamanté. Coming out of this long silence was a voice as gentle and coaxing as the cooing of a turtle dove in the eaves of the convent's cloister which had come to live there out of the Song of Songs written by King Solomon. 'Clarita, Clarita.' At first it was just her name, utterly familiar, repeated several times at discreet intervals allowing the familiarity of herself with him to grow. In his simple male way Gaston had thought: call her by her name and she must surely respond. He said it again and again, 'Clarita, Clarita,' He could see the relaxation in her shoulders.

Gaston had learnt the art of love from a young aunt who had always liked the way he used to pronounce her name. It was his voice she liked and she would take him to bed with her at siesta saying, 'Whisper my name,' and he would put his boy's lips to her ears as she fell asleep with him in her arms.

'Bianca, Bianca.' Bianca was the aunt's name. Even Marie Elena intimated this. Now the older Gaston whispered, 'Clarita, Clarita, sweet Clarita,' remembering the cicadas that scratched the air at noon when he was in his aunt's arms at siesta.

'Your sisters send to say hello, your mother sends you these,' and out of his pocket Gaston took a sugar-coated tamarind ball. He handed it to her with an outstretched hand, but she did not at first respond. She did not stir. She obeyed her Mother Superior.

This was trickery. These were lies. This was wooing. The outstretched hand, the tamarind ball which she had peeped at, tantalised her. The tickling sensation she could feel between her toes, up her leg and in the nest of hair between her legs, as the first sugar-coated ants carrying the desire of Gaston got to her over the stone floor, crawling over the sticky fingers of his outstretched hand, broke down her resistance and her obedience to her Mother Superior. She sighed at his voice, 'Clarita, sweet Clarita, your mother, Angustia, sends you these.' That this warm voice was telling her about her mummy and her sisters, and had only just spoken her own name so deeply and gently, could only herald something good. This was what Gaston hoped she would think. She heard his whisper again: 'Clarita, Clarita.'

Clarita bent down to scratch where the ants were tickling her. Then she lifted her eyes to the dreamer whom her Mother Superior had said wished to look at her face. There were no mirrors in the convent and Clarita had not seen her face for six months except for her reflection in the pool into which the fountain spilt. In the instant of her looking, in the instant of her sin, or should we say, *felix culpa*, Clarita was met with the eyes of Gaston. She saw her face reflected in his eyes. 'Oh,' she gasped, suddenly bewitched by her own beauty. His were large and brown and his face was in the shadow of a crown of black curls. Hers were the same pools of brown. We are twins, she thought. He wished he could uncover her head. *'Abyssus abysum invocat,'* as the psalmist says. One depth called to another. In the moment of her temptation, Clarita could hear her sisters at choir in the convent chapel intoning the *Salve Regina*. She knew they were praying for her, but the beauty of the chant seemed to lull her more into Gaston's lure. She smiled, still not saying anything, but giggled and smiled as she licked the sugar off the first tamarind ball which she took from his outstretched hand, pulling at the stickiness of his fingers. Then she bent to scratch the inside of her leg where the ants were tickling her.

Gaston took another tamarind ball from his pocket and brushed off the ants which crawled over his arm in search of the sugar on the confectionery. 'Here's another,' he said. Clarita took this second one almost greedily, continuing to lick on the first tamarind ball, but hurrying it, excited with the anticipation of the second. Then Gaston continued to feed her more of the innocent childhood sweets, which she liked because of the mixture of sweet and sour. 'Here, take this'; he went further, picking up the crystals of sugar from around her mouth with his fingers. If she were a butterfly she would have fallen asleep, drunk with the nectar of the fruit balls.

This seduction is not recorded in the legends, or in the teatime stories of Marie Elena, but in the transforming memory of Lavren. The truth that is transmitted tells of an extraordinary series of events which took place while Gaston and Clarita knelt in front of each other in the parlour of the Convent of the Immaculate Heart of Mary, in the little town of Aracataca, on the savannahs of the Monagas on the continent of Bolivar. If one had been a fly on the wall one would have seen very little. Lavren immediately disputes his own assertion, but offers no description of the events which followed in the inner sanctum upon this sweet and sour seduction. It was not what occurred inside the parlour, but rather the repercussions outside, that announced to the world that the most beautiful girl in the world had decided to taste Gaston's desire. Signs were soon noticed outside the convent walls in the streets of Aracataca, in the haciendas and in the wild parts of the savannahs where tiger cats lived. Later, astronomers and meteorologists put together a number of coincidences and constellations that gradually emerged. Much later, other stories of signs in the heavens and under the heavens, in the waters and under the waters, arrived at the shores of Bolivar and were brought from Margarita to Aracataca. When these were interpreted and other facts divined as simultaneous, people remembered that these events had taken place at the very same time that Clarita and Gaston had been in the convent parlour sucking tamarind balls with the grille of the enclosure between them.

Gaston had relaxed and was himself nibbling at one of the tamarind balls from his pocket. He restrained from screwing up his face because of the sourness. Clarita continued to lick at the sugar-encrusted jaggery. Gaston thought he had purchased only a dozen, but there now seemed to be an endless supply of the innocent sweets; Clarita herself had lost count now. Both were unaware of the disturbances they were causing in the world.

So much was going on at this moment that Lavren's memory ran the risk of being jammed. He forgot, dare we say it, how the events in the cloister were concluded, at least for the moment. Lavren was too distracted by what was going on in the streets of Aracataca.

All the children, a greater crowd than the one which had followed Gaston to the convent at dawn, were in the streets buying up all the tamarind balls, to the joy of the confectioners, who managed to get rid of all their stock before lunch time. These same young boys and girls, some of whom were themselves destined for the convents and the priesthood, had been sent out to collect eggs. They were subsequently detained because of the unusually large lay of eggs that morning, and they also found it difficult picking up the eggs because of their sticky fingers. Their parents were worried and wondered what they were up to, imagining the worst: that they might be looking at each other in the bushes, taking off their clothes and feeling for the first time the wonder that lay in the nests of hair between their legs. For the pubic hair of the children had suddenly sprouted and grown like some mysterious fern in the dark forests. A comet appeared in the sky.

The women who had gone to mass had not come home yet, detained by the music which continued all day, coming from the convent chapel. That was one reason, but it was secretly rumoured through history afterwards and confirmed by the reliable Lavren that Father Rosario had overslept with his mistress, the mestizo Olga.

A storm which had been threatening the banana crop in Aracataca had exhausted itself out in the Caribbean Sea. A rare orchid bloomed on Point Galeota on the neighbouring island of La Trinidad. At the very moment that Clarita consented to have another tamarind ball, the Pope promulgated an edict for the reform of the Order of Cluny, The Edict for the Safeguard of the Hymen, in memory of the unbroken hymen of the Blessed Virgin Mary. This was prompted by reports that men had been discovered breaching the walls of the enclosure in the new and the old world. What was good for one was good for the other as regards hymens. This later proved to have been the only repressive sign manifested in the universe at the time. Of course it didn't work. All others revealed a delight and rejoicing in nature at the consummation of Gaston and Clarita's desire, as they gorged themselves with the sticky tamarind balls.

The Mother Superior had her hands full with a revolution in the cloister, so forgot the couple. The town was trying to cope with the apparent disappearance of the children, the fear that the confessional would be overcrowded, and the glut on tamarind balls. There was deep relief at the exhaustion of the storm and the rum shops were overflowing with revellers and gamblers. Father Rosario's peccadillo was ignored and seen in itself as excusable, given the times people were living through.

By evening the main street of Aracataca was like carnival. Old-man Monagas came to the convent with his wife Angustia and her brood of daughters to find out what was going on. People began to wonder what had happened to Gaston since he had entered the convent. The town began congregating outside the convent walls. The vigil went on all night. In the morning, when the Mother Superior had quelled the passions of her nuns, she entered the parlour, apprehensive of what she might find. She asked Father Rosario to accompany her, with acolytes carrying cross, candle and incense to commence the liturgy of exorcism. She felt she would have to ask the Bishop in Margarita to come and reconsecrate the convent after its night's defilement. They entered, chanting first the *Dies Irae* and then the *De Profundis*. At the door they were wrapped in a great silence and peace which intoxicated them with the fragrance of wild lilies, which usually grew by the river banks in Kairi because they liked moist places, such as, centuries later behind the latrine, where they revealed their prophetic quality.

These lilies were now growing in vast profusion in large earthenware pots that no one had noticed before. Their leaves were green, thick and glossy, and the white perfumed lilies had yellow stamens dusty with pollen. Because the room had been locked up all night, the scent was trapped and was so powerful that some of the young acolytes immediately fainted into a deep sleep. Father Rosario was so relieved by this vision of beauty that he did not notice the clatter of the thurible on the tiled floor, or the emptying of the coals which continued to glow red against the red tiles. The acolytes with the candles had sunk to their knees, holding on to the large candlesticks for support, leaving the candles spluttering and flickering. Father Rosario, resisting the tendency to faint, intoned the *Te Deum*. The Mother Superior knelt, supported by a young novice. The nuns who had hoped for a glimpse of Gaston and their sister Clarita were secretly disappointed. They had vanished. But the legacy of beauty they left behind, suggesting the quality of the resurrected body, was so gratifying that they all gave thanks, and consequently the lilies became known as thanksgiving lilies, or eucharist lilies. They became a special concern of the Monagas family.

As the world grows older, look out for the eucharist lilies and their prophecy behind the latrine of the future, Lavren says.

It was not until the next day that the nuns, and the people of the town who had remained all night as if at the altar of repose on Holy Thursday night and Good Friday, found out the couple had eloped. Clarita had left her mother a note explaining that they had taken a pirogue to the island of Kairi across the Mar Dulce. 'Dear Mama,' it began. 'I have gone to heaven with an angel.' They were rowed across from the port of Guira, then up the muddy river to the plains beneath the Tamana hills. 'You are my Eve and this is our Eden,' Gaston said to Clarita as they sat in the shade of the arching bamboos on the river bank. She smiled and lowered her eyes, as a Monagas daughter is taught to do on her honeymoon. She bowed and said yes, mostly with her eyes which she raised for a instant.

The savannahs of Paria, of which the plains of Kairi form the western coast on the shores of the Mar Dulce, reminded Clarita of her own savannahs on the continent of Bolivar. When she woke on that first morning of her honeymooned elopement, she felt that she was still at home as she tiptoed to the window across the bare earthen floor of the ajoupa Gaston had had built for her. She wished to be fooled by the mountains in the north which were changing from blue into pink and becoming the strong green table of Mount El Tucuche. She wished to hold on to her childhood. She did not think of the convent but of the old house on the savannahs of the Monagas. 'Mama, tell me a story,' she heard herself whisper.

Two centuries later, geologists were to prove that Clarita's instincts were not coincidental. The savannahs of Paria, the plains of Kairi on the shores of the Mar Dulce, earlier called the Gulf of Pearls and even once, by the Great Navigator, Golfo de la Ballena, were the primordial river-bed of the ancient Orinoco which now emptied itself, clutching with its many fingers in its estuary at the tongue of the Serpent's Mouth. Kairi had indeed been part of the continent at the beginning of the world. To the very tip of her toes Clarita was a child of this hemisphere and could divine accurately the geological strata through feelings that were transmitted through her toes, the touch of her fingers, the smell of her nose, the whorls of her ears, the echoes on her eardrums, the down on her arms and on the side of her smooth brown face. 'I've been here before,' she said, 'I know this place. This is home. This is heaven.'

The breeze that stirred each morning through the grasses of the plains raised the down on her arms and her face and made her remember, and in that remembering, divine that this very land, on which the house Gaston had had built for her stood, was the same land of her birth. 'I can smell the place where I was born.' She plummeted its origins, diving back to the year of the comet, to the year the volcano diverted the great river, sunk the river-bed and created the Mar Dulce, opening the Bocas to the ocean of Atlantis, letting its cruel sea through the Dragon's Mouth and the Bouche du Serpent where the Great Navigator's caravels had foundered.

Once the sun had risen, Gaston would come to her. 'I've smelt your body,' he said. He came up silently behind her, licked the beads of sweat off the nape of her neck. He licked the whorls of her ears and whispered to her, so that she thought it was the crash of the wave she had heard on first arriving at the shores of the Mar Dulce;

the sweet sea, called so because of the mingling of the sea water with the fresh water from the rivers whose sources were the ice-capped mountains Lavren can now see from the window of Marie Elena's turreted room on Kairi's horizon, the continent of Bolivar. 'Clarita, Clarita'; she was comforted by her name, whispered as she had heard it whispered in the parlour of the convent at Aracataca.

Lavren, as he turns the leaves of this tale, and as Marie Elena turns in her linen sheets, dreaming of her death and the heart of her son Leonardo which is to be pickled as a testament of his love for her, does not want to digress or leap forward to the sadder times, but would much rather stay with this love of Gaston for Clarita, this passion of his fancy, in the realm of heaven.

He was tender at night as his aunt Bianca had taught him to be; as now when in the morning he came and kissed her and licked her ears and the sweat off the nape of her neck. She closed her eyes when she heard him behind her. She dared not look at him. He lifted her and took her to the bed, still a tent beneath the mosquito net. He took her into the bed in her cotton chemise and laid her on the pillows and lifted that chemise; all the time her eyes were closed. He entered her still fully dressed in the clothes he wore in the fields. She could feel him through his hands. They scraped up the inside of her leg to the hair which had only recently grown there and which she herself, on the advice of Father Rosario in the convent, pretended she had never looked at. The nuns had told her never to look there. 'That is the house of the devil, the door of the incubus,' Sister Luke, who had written the treatise on the unbroken hymen of the Blessed Virgin Mary, said.

'Clarita, Clarita,' he continued to breathe in whispers. His rough hands were tender but still she closed her eyes. Later, she lost her shyness and she peeled the clothes off his back and nestled between his legs and lay in the grass where the tamed serpent lay and where the tree of knowledge grew. They were in a garden where the tiger cat lay down with the agouti and the jaguar licked the flanks of the wild deer.

Did history take this path because of the myth or did the myth grow out of the history? Lavren wondered. But now in the beginning of time, in this Eden of their love, this heaven, Lavren is content to stay and tell of the carnival of innocence.

In the simple wattle ajoupa laced with bamboo and twigs, smeared with mud and the dung of animals, they continued to live without being found.

There were no towns, no monuments, no churches. The green of the plains and the blue of the hills were disturbed only by the seasons of rain and dryness; by the flowering of trees and the passage of birds, and the change which came with their excitement. Kairi: the sound of its name tells of its people, and the humming of small birds, because while some said it meant 'the land near to the mainland', others said it meant 'hummingbird'. It drew Gaston with other stories he had heard on the dark hot nights when he and his fellow sailors lay adrift in the sargasso weed.

The two dreams had become one in Gaston's mind and imagination: one the winning of Clarita from the convent, and the other the island of Kairi, which sounded to him like a piece of heaven. The earliest adventurers had said it was like Valencia in March.

Here he was with Clarita in their ajoupa, amidst the fields of corn, cassava, bananas and cabbages grown along the rivers which were full of fish and had crabs crawling along the banks. They lived like the ochre people who were adorned with gold and jade. Their loins were wrapped in dyed cotton as smooth and fine as silk. Here they stayed, and because they came without gunpowder they were received and allowed to live on the plains. But they were pulled further inland by stories of the city of El Dorado, and moved to the centre of the island which was called Tamana. Here the stories of Gaston and his beloved Clarita fade into myth and legend whose light is sepia.

'My dear, she looked lovely in her white chemise. She was like a child. They say she was always like a child, but of course no one knows because so few saw her. But they say it was remarkable how everyone still remembered her. Everyone thought they had seen her. Must be because everyone has a memory of their own childhood, and think it is like everyone else's.' Many years later, an old aunt, Marie Jeanne, whom Lavren met on the road to Tamana, told these stories to another young couple who came seeking El Dorado, not for its glimpse of heaven but as the city of gold.

The voices of Gaston and Clarita echoed. But what people can see is the blur of hummingbirds hovering and then scattering in flight, overwhelmed by the hysteria of parrots.

Lavren cannot remember the dates of these legends and beginnings.

They fade as Marie Elena fades away. They fade like the dry almond leaves that crinkle like the papyrus of ancient manuscripts. They evanesce with the incoming tide, a sponge which erases the entablature of the sand, inscribed with the heron's hieroglyph from where it has just taken flight. They cannot even be deciphered in the sepia of the register of births and deaths, penetrated by moths in the sacristy of the church of San Jorge de Monagas. The time of Gaston and his child bride Clarita Monagas de los Macajuelos, the most beautiful girl in the world and precursor of carnival queens; their love story and disappearance into the Tamana hills fades and is retold as myth. Think of these as fairy tales, stories upon which the beginnings of a world are founded. 'Nancy stories, yes, Master Lavren?' Josephine asks.

'Indeed,' Marie Elena says.

THE TALE OF THE HOUSE
ON THE PLAINS

LAVREN NOW ACCOMPANIES Georges Philippe de Lanjou, the younger brother of Gaston, on his journey from the old world to the new. The story which Lavren hears on the ship which brings them to the shores of Bolivar is a quite different story from the romantic tale of the most beautiful young girl in the world. That tender tale was Lavren's fancy: to begin with love, because of his desire for love, his belief in love. It tells of his search for the meaning of love, caught between the yearning of women and the silence of men. What he hears now of the Monagas is quite different. It is a cruel tale. But first he hears of their origins.

There is a legend in the eastern provinces of the continent of Bolivar, the mainland on Kairi's horizon across the Gulf of Sadness, that tells the tale of the arrival of the first Monagas in the new world, from the town of Valencia. He was attacked by a large python in the Orinoco forests. Being a Monagas, handy with sword and large of stature, he killed the python, to the utter amazement of the Amerindians. He then proceeded to cut it into pieces on the banks of the river. On cutting it open, a small cow was found inside it, which had been crushed and partly digested through the labyrinthine intestines of the python. This was a sign, surely, an omen. They barbecued the python, as well as what remained of the cow. Monagas and his company thanked God for the cow that had saved them. Because the python had recently eaten − at the side of the river where the cow had been drinking − it was lazy and could not attack, or fight back with its accustomed strength and alacrity. If it had been able to, it would have crushed them and this history of the new world would never have been written, Lavren reflected.

The Amerindians, legend continues, called the python Macajuelos, or Macajuel. The exact derivation of the name is lost in the mists and swamps of the Orinoco, but what did come down to successive generations was that the first Monagas became known among the peoples in all parts of the old and new world as the Monagas de los Macajuelos. 'Monagas rode next to Bolivar,' Marie Elena had said, but no one knew which one. This naming was to commemorate for the rest of time that act of killing and the baptism, as it were, by the Amerindians of this intruder into the enamelled forests. The apocrypha of Marie Elena, into which Lavren delves, also relates that the Amerindians were astonished by the digestive capacity of the Monagas, which was akin in their minds to that of the python itself. Hence they decided to name him after the python.

'He eats like a python,' they said. Conquistador and conqueror, digester of peoples did not escape the analogical imagination of the new world. The view is also held, according to the apocrypha of Marie Elena, that this is the first known metaphor made in the new world. To this day the people of Bolivar say what they said then, 'Man, it big like a Macajuel. It big for so.'

'More nancy story, Master Lavren?' Josephine asks again.

'No, this is the truth.'

It was the power of this name, with these origins, which took possession of Georges Philippe when he married Elena, the eleventh daughter of old-man Monagas, giving him the customary dowry of pearls from Margarita. Elena was a mere child, whose only bridesmaids at her wedding were her dolls.

After the wedding, this couple too left the shores of Bolivar for Kairi, with a band of adventurers. Elena left everything behind her except her dolls. These she took with her in the pirogue, and as they crossed the Mar Dulce her tears would not stop. Georges Philippe took her roughly because he was in a hurry. He broke the cup and licked up the syrup. He had not taken the advice of the African woman in Margarita, who had sold her body to him for a pearl. He forgot her advice, 'Wait till the fruit is soft and ripe like a dou douce mango.' It seemed as if Elena's tears would fill the sea and from that day the gulf was no longer known as the Mar Dulce, the sweet sea, but as the Gulf of Sadness. She cried for her Mama and her sisters, and now, as she crossed the Gulf of Sadness, for her sister Clarita who had vanished in the blur of hummingbirds and the hysteria of parrots.

'I can hear her crying,' she said to Georges Philippe, 'take me to her.'

'What you are hearing are the parrots. Look, look up there. Can you see green against the blue?' As he raised his hand to the sky, the parrots seemed to cry even more, and it was even more that Elena heard the screams of her sister. *Elena Elena Elena*.

'I must find her, she cries for me.'

'We will go,' and he lay with her and silenced her with his mouth on hers, forcing her to drop her dolls.

But this time not only honeymooning lovers came to Kairi.

Lying between the long muddy river that springs from the Tamana hills and the mudflats of the Baie des Crabes is the wide green plain of the island of Kairi. The plain grows from the mangrove swamps in the west, on the shores of the Gulf of Sadness, to meet the sand's edge with filigreed manchineel in the bay of Manzanilla in the east. Georges Philippe and his adventurers were told, as their ancestors had been told, that the land was fertile; their coming was like the first coming of the conquistadors. He knelt, Elena at his side with her dolls in the mud, while he and his brigands sang the *Salve Regina* and blessed themselves with the Trinity: Father, Son and Holy Ghost. They looked about them because of the shimmer in the forest and then Georges Philippe shouted for the world to hear, 'Where is the gold?' The forest screamed back with the hysteria of parrots and then became unusually silent. They bartered costume jewellery with the few who ventured out of the forests in their innocence to meet them and who pointed to the interior for what he asked. Then the invaders crashed into the forests. They came with horses, and were believed to be centaurs. They came with dreams that soon became nightmares.

They pushed on up a muddy river to where the stones in the river are smooth and prehistoric. Here Georges Philippe founded a town in his own name. He proclaimed himself Governor, and the town San Jorge de Monagas.

The sadness that swelled up from the depths of the gulf was not only the sadness of Elena and her dolls, but also the sadness of a dying people. The shores of the Gulf of Sadness were constantly being dredged for the drowned and exhausted bodies of Amerindian divers, forced to dive for the last of the pearls on the sea bed. Fishermen dragging their seine with hope and expectation of a large catch were more often than not disappointed by the dead weight of a corpse – the dead of a dying race that gave up the wealth of the new world to the conquistador who rode his horse and seemed like a centaur.

They gave up their spirits to the baptising priests, with their gourds dipped into the waters of the Gulf of Sadness. 'I baptise you in the name of the Father, the Son and the Holy Ghost.'

Georges Philippe was a soldier. He too sought El Dorado, like his brother before him, though not as a glimpse of heaven, not as an Eden, but as a mountain of gold, a horizon of fractured crystal. He was no dreamer of heaven. His child bride was already big with his first child. His folly was grand. Was it not he who had founded the ancient city of San Jorge de Monagas, where the first church was built amidst the first ajoupas and where he made himself Governor? Governor Monagas de los Macajuelos made soldiers of his motley band and prepared them for the first of his expeditions in search of El Dorado up the Orinoco where the ancient maps indicated the gleaming city. But soon pirogues were found by fishermen, holding the bloated bodies of soldiers. Their adventure had foundered. They did not find Arcadia and, like Raleigh, they caulked their boats from the same lake of pitch and planned to go again, persistently obsessed.

While Georges Philippe was away, Elena kept hearing her sister, now calling out her own name – 'Clarita, Clarita!' – telling her, as it were, that she was there. Yes, and it did sound like the hysteria of parrots.

Georges Philippe came back from his first expedition to find his first child born, and his wife a little older, but still preferring to play with her dolls and leaving the small baby-boy Ramon to the servant girls. 'My ears, my ears are full of her. Can't you hear her crying? When will we go to find her?' He stayed long enough to make her pregnant again and ordered his Amerindian slaves to build her a house, on the plains where he was told that Gaston and Clarita had built their first ajoupa before disappearing into the forests of Tamana. The floors of the new house creaked with their voices and the rain on the carat roof whispered their secrets. 'You see, I can hear their voices even here. They need our help.'

'You are hearing beetles. That whine is the violin of Anopheles.'

Georges Philippe did not stay long enough to listen. He was busy with another expedition up the Orinoco, but he ordered soldiers out of San Jorge de Monagas to go into the Tamana hills, bringing him back news of what they found. It was a part of the island to which no one had yet ventured.

While Georges Philippe was away on one of his expeditions – he seemed always to be away, the number of children indicated the number of expeditions – Elena began to inspect the stools of her children and herself. It became an obsession. She believed she could divine the future from the shape and particular aroma of the daily faeces. So each day, with her dolls beside her, and her children sent out with the servant girl, she would get the Amerindian slaves to line up the used chamberpots of all the children. Georges Philippe on his return wished to put a stop to this; but could not succeed, because no sooner had he gone away than Elena would begin her morning ritual again.

In the present day, as Lavren knows only too well, there is still evidence of the gigantic stature of the Monagas. The mysterious circulation of their blood and the perplexities of their digestive system continue to baffle even the doctors, priests and politicians within the family. The servants who have continued to work for them, out of loyalty the family say, have wasted away as the Monagas have grown larger. The evacuations of this digestive system became a means by which the Monagas traditionally sorted out the signs of the times, working on the logic that since where things come from determine their present state, so the residue of the present should tell of the future. In the modern age we may wish to write this all off as a whole lot of shit. Lavren would ask you to postpone your judgement. The Carnival Tales seek to explain a great deal about the new world.

The interpretation of fact, the history of event, is in the end a fiction. On the other hand this fiction is history. The memory is a muse that is continually fretting and changing. This muse is Marie Elena, Lavren's muse, Marie Elena's memory; this is the history and fiction of a hermaphrodite, a spirit of mythology with the power to mythlogise, to levitate between fact and fiction, reducing opposites to a mixture of genders and races. Lavren's digressions or intrusions come from the distracted mind of his muse Marie Elena, and her art of telling stories while they eat Crix biscuits, rat cheese and guava jelly together in the turret room overlooking the Gulf of Sadness.

With the failure of his expeditions and the arrival of more bloated bodies in pirogues, Georges Philippe began to divide up the island for crops and drove the Amerindians into the fields. On the plains he planted sugarcane and in the hills, cocoa. When Georges Philippe came into Elena's bed the screech of the parrots was at its most extreme and she could also hear the lash of the whip on the backs of the Amerindian slaves. She clung to her dolls even though she was now a young woman. Her dolls and her daily inspection of the chamberpots kept her sane.

It was in the year of the comet, when the first crop of cocoa was planted, the first ratoons for sugarcane crop, that the disease began and spread. There was froghopper, the perennial plague of the sugarcane, but worse, much worse, was the appearance of the parasite that was to grow in the mind of this first Monagas governor and between the forks of the cocoa trees. The encroaching witchbroom had lodged itself in the brain of Georges Philippe. The comet, whose coincidence with the arrival of the centaurs the Amerindians held responsible for the spread of the parasite, could still be seen in the skies of the new world. The Amerindians said that the shamans had long prophesied the appearance of the flying light, as they had the arrival of the tall ships.

Father Camillo, whose parish included both the plains of Kairi and the missions in the Tamana hills, with its largest mission at Arenales, came to speak to the Governor Georges Philippe. 'The reason the witchbroom has appeared has nothing to do with what pagan Amerindians think, but with the fact that they and the Governor and his family themselves refuse to pay tithes for the upkeep of the church at Arenales, and for the indulgences that will be bequeathed to them and so afford them the possibility of a place in heaven, or at least a few hundred days off their suffering in purgatory.'

The Governor grasped at the opportunity to enforce tithes on the Amerindians, though long nights in the Orinoco delta and the upper reaches of the river had long dissuaded him from a belief in purgatory, hell or heaven. If heaven was not at the top of this river then it was nowhere. 'Father, I will assist you in getting the tithes from the people, but don't pester me and my family with your illusions. Work with the poor.'

The appearance of the witchbroom and its continuing presence in the life of the family prompted Lavren to go to the shelves in the room which had been used as an office, to get down the dusty tomes that had been passed down and updated and told of the problems of agriculture in the new tropical world. The first volume was riddled with woodlice and smelt of dry and rotting leaves. He looked up the chapter on parasites. He read where the eyes of many generations of Monagas had read and become engrossed in the development of the disease that had lodged in their brains and was responsible, along with their greed, which was lodged in their pythonic intestine, for the destruction of their wealth. This first tome shed no light on the parasite in question. Here was a world whose terror grew as vivid as it might be to a chemist or biologist under a microscope. Lavren, with power bequeathed to him by the Holy Ghost through the instrument of Mr de Lisle, read, equipped with this heavenly wisdom. He read of warbles, minute microbes that could ravage the stomach. He could feel intestinal parasites growing inside him. He read of sheep with fluke, horses and cattle with intestinal strongles. In the days and nights when he carried out this investigation, his dreams became inhabited with arthropods, worms and protozoa. He began to scratch himself, came out in a rash and wondered if he was picking up some fungal disease as he turned the pages of the book that was itself infested with minute parasites living on the paper of the centuries. Lavren detained himself in this microbic world and delayed his incursions into other tomes in search of the family parasite, witchbroom. He was almost convinced now that through his imagination he had become the psychosomatic victim of *sarcoptes* which burrowed and tunnelled their way into the canals and galleries of the skin. Marie Elena said he had eaten too many oranges. Here too he found out more about Anopheles who hummed and pestered him in his sleep, so that he always had to have a mosquito net. He learned of tick fever. At one point he wondered whether he would be able to extricate himself from his microscopic visions, from the haemoglobinuria that was infectious to cattle and other intra-corpuscular micro-organisms whose names were as much magic to him as the terror of their infection. He rapidly turned the pages away from the bloodletting parasites and the ones that lodged themselves in the corpuscles of the blood. His was not an age to dwell too long on the terror of blood-borne diseases. He decided to leave the chapter on tapeworms and nematodes which attacked the respiratory, circulatory and digestive apparatus. Diseases known to attack only animals in centuries past could now attack the human race. Marie Elena's cure, like the Pope's, was the sacraments and a pure life. All this decay, reflected in the animal world, was too near the bone and mythology of the Monagas de los Macajuelos. This was too near the pain of the century, which was nearing the end as Marie Elena lay dying in the turret room overlooking the Gulf of Sadness.

Lavren rejoins his tale where he meets the first expedition to Tamana.

Elena's neglect of her children, her dependence on her dolls, her obsession with faeces, and her desire to see her sister Clarita, persuaded the tiring Governor to make the expedition into the hills where it was said that his brother, seeking a glimpse of heaven, had gone with Clarita, the most beautiful girl in the world.

Elena and Georges Philippe left the plains, travelling on horses as centaurs. The Amerindian guides were on foot. Georges Philippe pondered the life of his brother. The story of the wooing of Clarita was already mythology. All Gaston managed to do with his life turned to myth as it passed from mouth to mouth through the family of the Monagas de los Macajuelos, the stories emanating from Tamana no less so than any others. Clarita had been seen only once since her arrival on the island, so there was a natural concern for the young girl who had been abducted from a convent and had left in the train of her departure a shortage of eggs and tamarind balls in the town of Aracataca. The delineations of this myth were sketched in the mind of Georges Philippe, and irked him as he rode along with Elena.

Elena herself knew little, as she always found herself falling asleep when an old nurse sitting on her rattan rocker told stories to the children. No one knew for sure whether what she said was true or not. If asked to be specific, she would say, 'What does it matter, dear? It is the truth as I know it, and who would you rather believe, your old nurse or one of the fellas on the estate?' They would laugh and ask for more stories. Elena would fall asleep because she did not want to be reminded about her sister. She did not want to remember. She would rather go out on the veranda at the side of the house and play with the dolls she had brought from Aracataca.

She took her dolls on all the journeys she made with Georges Philippe through the island, even on the long donkey trips to Paria, and as far as Galera where the land looked like the prow of a ship. He took her everywhere for he could not let a day pass without making love to her, something she did not remember, except that she awoke next morning having dreamt she had died.

They would leave the children with servants and then take off with Amerindian guides like those who now led the expedition to Tamana. Georges Philippe's only regret was that Elena was growing up so fast. The little girl whom he had brought with him was no longer a little girl and now had little girls of her own. He savoured the memory of her as he savoured the taste of almonds dipped in sugar. It was essentially a matter of taste. When he was younger the black woman from Margarita had reminded him of molasses. When Elena did not play with her dolls on the side veranda she played with the cats because she liked to stroke their smooth black fur.

Georges Philippe no longer knew if what he was journeying towards was there, was truth or myth. Were they becoming story themselves as they entered the forests, which closed behind them to the cry and hysteria of the green and yellow parrots? One of the soldiers had brought back a report of children who been seen running about in the yard, naked. They had been playing beneath the citrus trees newly planted on the edge of the decimated cocoa, which looked as if a spell had been thrown about it. A vast forest entangled in the witchbroom. These stories came and were told at the same time as the story of the comet and Father Camillo's tithes. The revolt against the church was accompanied by a revolt in nature. This was the word on the lips of the travelling soldiers who went out from San Jorge de Monagas. Revolt.

The forests were thick and Georges Philippe felt that many eyes were watching himself and Elena. These many eyes were the pinpoints of light pricked out in the leaves. These were the eyes of the ones who cried like parrots. Some had come in the early days to the beaches to meet the arrivants. Some came to the plains, but others remained part of the forests, and their skin melted into the shadows and their adornments were the leaves of the forests and the feathers of the birds that lived in the forests. The most secret ones lived in the Tamana hills.

But this first expedition to Tamana was curtailed by the arrival of a soldier in hot pursuit from San Jorge de Monagas to report that the town had been burnt to the ground, every building except the porch of the church. Georges Philippe ordered the immediate return to the house on the plains of Elena, while he went with a band of soldiers to the burnt town. A week later there was a mass execution of three hundred Amerindians as punishment for the burning.

All the early records were burnt and, as Lavren reflects, all the writing paper and ink destroyed. The province of Kairi became cut off from the rest of the world. Now, Governor Monagas could do what he wished. The expeditions up the Orinoco continued no longer, since they only foundered and sent pirogues back as coffins, back into the Gulf of Sadness.

Marie Jeanne Monagas de los Macajuelos, whose origins no one had any idea of, had built the small town of San Raphael, named after the Archangel who was reputed to have brought Joseph of Arimathea and his house on his wings all the way from the Holy Land to the new world. A statue of the Archangel which stood in the middle of the town had been brought from Cadiz.

This was not a place of monuments. The Amerindians had built in leaves, twigs, wood and wattle. Their habitations were fragile and cool. The Monagas had a memory of monuments and wished to build. Georges Philippe was turning his mind from the Orinoco to Tamana. 'Maybe it's true, maybe the gilded one is here,' Georges Philippe said. This, and not Elena's desire to go on a second expedition in search of her sister, persuaded Georges Philippe to gather his horses and soldiers and make for the town of San Raphael, where they were to spend the night with Marie Jeanne.

Before telling of the second expedition in search of Clarita and Gaston, Lavren cannot rest at San Raphael without telling the tale of the remarkable Marie Jeanne, though Marie Elena does not approve of what he tells. He rocks in his hammock to the strumming of a cuatro and the singing of the town's music, parang, and tells you this tale, a tale which mixes the cruelty of the time with the desire for love.

At night, the moon shone on the statue of San Raphael, and on some nights the people swore that it got down from its plinth and walked through the town until it came to the door of the priest's housekeeper, Marie Jeanne. There it entered and did not leave again until dawn. Those who thought they were the more discerning, and could distinguish between the miraculous and the natural, said it was not San Raphael the Archangel who had gone into Marie Jeanne's house. It seems to Lavren that the story of the ambulating statue was put about by the priest. 'No one had ever heard of this walking statue until Father mentioned it in his sermon on the Feast of San Raphael,' said Renaldo the apprentice shoemaker, who was in his cobbler's shop earlier than most of the other townsfolk. His old father Felice was blind so he had to be there early, even though he might have been carousing until the early hours of the morning.

'Renaldo, we have always known that the Blessed Raphael likes to take a walk. I've known that since I was a boy.'

'Since you were a boy? That means that those priests have been using this story for a long time. But you didn't believe it, Father, surely?'

'There's not much to believe in, son. So, hold on to these things, they don't do you any harm,' and the old man smiled. 'And the Blessed Archangel Raphael brings a lot of people here for the harvest festival, which is good for the town and for the sale of shoes.'

'Yes, but who is doing the walking? Surely it's Father . . .'

'Shush'; old Felice put his fingers to his lips and then instinctively placed them on the lips of his son. 'Don't tell our secret, and besides, what else has that poor woman got?'

So it was that the discretion of an old man, the faith of women, and the loyalty of sons to the wishes of their fathers allowed Father Bernardo to disguise his passion for the saint of the Monagas family, as his predecessors had disguised theirs for other women in the town since the old cobbler Felice was a boy.

No one had ever heard of an angel without wings. No one had seen Father Bernardo with wings, though some of the children at the catechism class used to giggle and say that his hunchback was where he tucked his wings during the day. The rumours did continue. Marie Elena says you can believe what you want, but she would have nothing to do with these nancy stories, as they came to be called. Marie Jeanne's sainthood depended on the fact that she seemed to have children without having a husband. Were these immaculate conceptions?

Stories were told of Marie Jeanne, but Marie Elena says that they were definitely nonsense and that Lavren should not even entertain the idea of them. 'Marie Jeanne,' said Marie Elena, 'knew only how to grow gladioli and anthurium lilies for the church. You mustn't write things like that down. She used to keep fowls so that the priest could have eggs in the morning. She was an extraordinary woman. She milked her own cows and grew her own cassava.'

In the end Lavren understood, and could see her clearly in the large and first of the houses in San Raphael. He saw her sewing and mending the cassocks for Father Bernardo. She was an insomniac and spent the night embroidering altar cloths for the San Raphael church and the new chapel at the mission of Arenales. She had black circles under her eyes all the time. This was put down to sewing by candlelight, but still the visits of the statue that left its plinth continued. On the other hand such zeal and devotion towards a priest was never to be found again in the Monagas family, according to Lavren, until the present century. The tendency towards sainthood is yet to be rewarded by an official canonisation of one of the family. Lavren himself thought to try once, but doubt overtook him when the zeal ran out in his twenty-fourth year.

'Read on, dare I say, dear reader,' says Lavren.

Georges Philippe and Elena were relieved to have a bed for the night in Marie Jeanne's house. They were stiff from riding, something which continued to mystify the Amerindians who, believing that the horses were an extension of the riders' bodies, ran away when they saw such a creature divide itself in two and one half step down to the ground and walk upon its own feet.

Legend repeats itself. Truth lags behind.

Georges Philippe and Elena had a meal with their cousin which she served, but she ate nothing herself. She ate only on Sundays, she said, 'Publicly'. She would have liked to be a nun, but there were no convents at that time in the new world, the Convent of the Immaculate Heart of Mary in Aracataca being the first. She never conceived of a voyage back over the ocean to where she had come from. It seemed an impossibility to her.

Elena and Georges Philippe were thankful for the meal. When they went to bed they could hear the insomniac Marie Jeanne, moving about the house. When she settled down to her embroidery they fell asleep, with Georges Philippe still inside of Elena and the dolls on the floor, so that Elena woke a few minutes later with the sensation in a dream that she was drowning. Georges Philippe rolled over on to his side and began to snore. The next morning neither of them could decide whether they had dreamt it or not, but they were sure they had seen Marie Jeanne peeping through the wattle wall at them, when Georges Philippe was still inside Elena. But Elena had dreamt all night that she had been climbing a greasy pole in order to reach heaven, but she never arrived there. Then she was overwhelmed by a flood and was being taken down a brown river in a strong current. She was saved when she held on to a log which was floating down to the open sea. In the midst of it all was Marie Jeanne peeping through the wattle wall.

In the morning Marie Jeanne made a noise banging down utensils in the kitchen to rouse the couple for breakfast. The Archangel had not come that night. She became so annoyed that she swept the kitchen three times and shooed all the fowls from the kitchen and decided not to take any eggs to the presbytery that morning, knowing that she would have to go to confession. The fowls ran out and got entangled in the ankles of Elena, who was splashing water over her feet in the yard.

Marie Jeanne could not understand how the couple could stay in bed so long. She had left the house at four in the morning to open the church and dust the bat droppings from the altar and the sanctuary floor. She put out the vestments and arranged fresh flowers and put out the wine and unleavened bread. All this she did with a passion that went beyond the ministrations of a sacristan. They had to be careful with the unleavened bread and the wine. There was shortage on the island and things took so long to come from the old world. The wine and hosts had to come from Rome. Marie Jeanne experienced these shortages as God taking away His sacrament from the new world. Father Bernardo had to prohibit communion at times, and then Marie Jeanne and the congregation, mostly of women, would make a communion of intent. That morning at mass, Marie Jeanne made a special intention because it was not a dream which Elena and Georges Philippe had had. The insomniac had seen them through the crack in the wattle wall. Georges Philippe thought he had had a hallucination of passion. He thought he was having a vision of the future face of Elena. 'Don't grow old,' he had said, 'my little girl.' She was reputed to look as Marie Jeanne had when the saint was a little girl. This was the first time Marie Jeanne had seen a man and woman in this position since she had come upon her parents when she was four. It had seemed worse because it was her parents, but she vowed she would never find herself in such a preposterous position. From then on, she viewed her mother and father with a certain cynicism. She had turned away at Georges Philippe's voice, 'My little girl. Elena, Elena.' There are not so many instances of this tradition, viewing copulating parents, as there are of the tradition of peeping through keyholes at parents and grown-ups having a shit. Lavren surmised that this was because of the fascination children have with the source of the truth.

Marie Jeanne never remembered when the Archangel visited her house. But she knew that she was in a bad mood at times, as on this morning when Elena and Georges Philippe were staying.

Marie Jeanne was scarred by a plague that was to infect many Monagas women and some of their sons. The plague was called scruples by Marie Elena, and Lavren himself was to inherit them. To be scrupulous meant that you paid attention to each little sensation, each thought, each daydream. They all nibbled away at the brain like piranhas in the Orinoco, and eventually drove one to the brink of the Soufrière volcano, as to the brink of hell. Marie Jeanne had all her life been nibbled at. If she were a modern woman, and were to analyse the source of these persecutions, she would trace them back to a siesta when she had been lying in her hammock out on the veranda, and on one occasion had been stroked by her brother, and on another, by her father. The shame she had felt, and the silence that had been put upon her, meant she pursued this new-found pleasure on her own. Her hand used to stray to the crack between her legs and eventually found there the stamen that grew at the centre of her purple rose. This guilt had spread to everything else. Now in the town of the new world, she found herself trapped by the secrecy of the visits of the Archangel Raphael. She herself was well aware of what the people of the town were whispering, but she could cope because in her heart she believed that it was the Archangel Raphael who had chosen her in his loneliness in the new world. She felt that the saints must feel much more at home in the old world. She could always believe these things because she always kept her eyes shut.

Each morning, after she had prepared all that was necessary for the early morning mass, she would wake Father Bernardo by calling out his name under his window, so that people of the town, those who were up that early, could see she did not go into his room. 'She had no need to,' they said. She did sweep his room, but only when he was far off in the mountains catechising the Amerindians at Arenales.

On this particular morning her scruples got the better of her and she went and waited for Father Bernardo in the confessional. He came into the church rubbing his sleepy eyes. 'Bless me, Father, for I have sinned. It's me, Marie Jeanne.'

'My child'; Father Bernardo always adopted his priestly role with the rigour of a schizophrenic. She told him what she had seen through the hole in the wattle wall, and he blessed her: 'Say as your penance one decade of the rosary for the souls in purgatory.' The custom of counting Hail Marys and *Pater Nosters* on beads, the Dominican friars said had been given to them by Our Lady who had descended from heaven on the backs of chubby cherubs. She knew she had peeped into the room because she had wanted to see love which was free and open, but she had seen an older man pretending to love a little girl.

'My little girl, my little pet.' These words reminded her and drew her. Then she had lain with herself the night the Archangel did not come and had found again, as she did when she was a little girl, the stamen at the centre of her purple rose. Marie Jeanne did not give Father Bernardo all the details.

Marie Jeanne hoped that these young people would go on their way. 'Let them go and take their foolishness,' she said to her servant girl when she came back from mass, after having given Father Bernardo his breakfast; she regretted she had not brought the eggs. 'Take their sheets out and wash them immediately,' she told the girl. 'They're bound to be dirty, stained.' Not with blood, she said to herself, not with blood. 'Filthy little girl, filthy,' as she tied the leather belt tighter round her waist.

The Monagas were obsessed with bloodstains and their significance, because, just as they divined the future in coprolites, so they divined it in the patterns of blood on the sheets of brides. Blood always meant the blood of Christ and then it meant blood from bruises and grazes and then it meant most of all blood from menstruation. The young girls were never instructed in these spontaneous outflows of blood each month. They were seen as connected with the Passion of Christ and the shedding of his blood.

Once Georges Philippe and Elena had left the town, Marie Jeanne went each night to the wall of the bedroom where Elena and Georges Philippe had lain. There she looked through the hole in order to keep alive the vision of their passion. She kept hearing Georges Philippe's voice, while remembering her father. 'My little girl'; she fell asleep, sucking on her cracked thumb until the servant girl woke her before dawn to open up the church. Apparently the Archangel had not come that night either. Marie Jeanne would have kept her eyes closed but the young Renaldo saw all from the window of his cobbler's shop.

As Georges Philippe and Elena rode out of the town to complete this second expedition Elena could hear the scream of the parrots and in their hysteria, which screamed green across the blue morning sky, and disappeared as a lighter green against the deep green of the forests into which they were climbing steadily, she could hear the cry and voice of her sister Clarita. It was so clear that she turned in the saddle in front of Georges Philippe, who was now carrying her. The voice called her name twice and then kept repeating the refrain, 'Elena, Elena'. All she saw were the pricks of light which danced on the leaves of the forests, and the deeper caverns of light which she could glimpse in the even deeper recesses of the forests. At her turn, her gaze and her listening were met by an almost impenetrable silence, a silence which later Marie Elena was to hear. This was silence more silent than a honeymoon. The silence also reminded the world of the silence which came after the hysteria of the parrots at the arrival and first footsteps on the sand at Moruga. It was the silence in the drone of Anopheles.

A runner, out of the forests, brought the news that Gaston and Clarita had heard of their coming and were on their way to meet them and would do so at Mundo Nuevo, at the heart of the island. Elena had never travelled so far into the interior of this new world. This was a long way from the savannahs of Monagas, a long way from the Baie des Crabes. She longed for the open plains and the mountains that reminded her of the mountains on the horizon of Aracataca. They were now deep in the valleys, which were the valleys between the humps of the iguana, the diagonal cordillera at the centre of the island. Georges Philippe said that the runner could not be believed. 'Yes, he speaks the truth,' Elena cried. 'I keep hearing her, all these years I've kept hearing her.' The forests began again to hiss and cry with the scream of birds and the movements of insects. They passed a procession of Amerindians, being dragged by soldiers to San Jorge de Monagas to be baptised.

They stopped at Talparo, where the first village shop of the new world would be built. This was a serene place, and they rested in a small savannah in the shadow of saman trees and drunk the clear water from the Talparo river. Lavren speaks of this place with affection, because he only visited it himself for the first time while writing the tales and awaiting the death of Marie Elena. When he got there he was on the trek to Arenales himself. He imagined this moment with the inspiration of the Holy Ghost, as it were: his ability to levitate and hover like a dove over the new world and create again the moment when Elena wept, as the rain came down from the mountains and soaked them on the savannah. This heavenly blessing made Lavren realise now that this second expedition had also failed. Clarita and Gaston were not there.

He wondered now, like Georges Philippe and Elena, what was truth and what was myth as one narrative was found inside the other. Who could they believe? They had waited at Talparo, and Gaston and Clarita had never come. After final research, Lavren realised that this visit, that is now drawn up from the palimpsest of his memory, was the moment when things became much much worse. Georges Philippe was wasted by searching and malaria. He had insisted on making one last expedition up the Orinoco, but had to retreat because of the fierce attack he met at the gate to the interior.

Elena spoke in repetitions. She had begun to speak like a parrot. She never initiated anything new in conversation. She merely repeated her children's voices and whatever Georges Philippe said. Her mind became filled with the idea of the parrots, whose hysteria had first drawn the early conquistadors' notice to the forests and to the presence of the people of the new world.

It was from after this time that Monagas women decided not to be silenced. The spell of silence began to fall on the men. The silence which took hold of them usually began on their honeymoon. It was initially caused by the shock of refusal. The women would not be dolls as Elena had been. They would do their duty, pay the marriage debt, but the rosary beads would never be far from their fingers. As Marie Elena continually said, 'It was a time when I felt closest to God.' Women decided to transcend themselves. No one could ever say that Marie Elena was short of words. Indeed, Lavren himself feels the silence descend on him as she speaks her last words, fading into eternity, and he decides that this talk must be preserved. But he is so enchanted that he takes licence at times, for which he must be forgiven. As you see, his inspiration was not altogether to do with the Holy Ghost.

Elena and Georges Philippe grew apart. Georges Philippe, wasted with malaria and with neither money nor authority for more expeditions, had only his memory in which a parasite was lodged. He stayed in the canefields attacked by froghopper, and made incursions into some of the cocoa estates to rescue what he could from the witchbroom. And even though there were no more pearls in the gulf, and it had truly come to be known as the Gulf of Sadness, he continued to have young men dive deeper and deeper. Those who survived came back with hallucinations of the future. Most didn't. The tide kept delivering corpses.

The witchbroom was hacked away and burned. They had to keep burning and burning. They did not understand this plague, and Father Camillo kept insisting again and again that it was because the family as well as the Amerindians were not paying their tithes. The comet did not appear in the sky this time, but the memory of it remained and the Amerindians believed that it was retribution from the sky for what was being done upon the earth. They kept dredging the mouths of the rivers for corpses, where the tides had dragged them from the green depths of the gulf.

It had always seemed to Elena, who had the feel for the hemisphere at the tips of her fingers like her sister Clarita before her, under her skin as it were, divining through her senses the feel of the new world, that it never stopped raining on the plain, and because it lay beneath the level of the gulf, and was in fact an extension of the mangrove swamps and oyster beds, it was always damp. But in this year of her growing silence, the continent and its island peninsula experienced a severe drought and dry season. Elena moaned as she swung in her hammock, 'What a dry season; what a lenten hold the heat has upon the earth.' This was the first original statement she had made in a month, and the rest of the household fell silent for the remainder of the week pondering her meaning. No parrots were kept as domestic pets, in order to discourage her tendency towards repetition. It was around this time that stories began coming out of the jungle, stories of crucifixions similar to the crucifixions that had been performed in San Jorge de Monagas after the town was burnt down in a raid from Guaico. But Elena did repeat herself, in part: 'What a lenten hold the heat has upon the earth!'

As they got on with their normal life, Elena and her family forgot about the ships which came through the Bouche du Dragon, or which were eventually reported – news travelled slowly even in this small piece of the new world – as having foundered in the Serpent's Mouth. One day Ramon, one of Elena's sons, discovered an old anchor on the sea bed when the tide had gone out in the Baie des Crabes. The old men, who had gone on the very first expeditions up the Orinoco with Georges Philippe and survived, said that it was one of the anchors belonging to Raleigh's ship, the English poet who was seeking Arcadia in the jungles of the Orinoco. He had once stopped nearby to plug his ships with the pitch he had found in a lake which had no bottom, and when Lavren went to school Miss Redhead taught him that it was a wonder of the world, and they had to learn Raleigh's name and that he had discovered the pitch lake.

As time went on, Elena persuaded Georges Philippe that she must see the sea again, and that he should let her take the donkeys and mules and go to the beach to swim and watch the horizon. The horizon she wished to stare at was not the one which would eventually reveal, when the glare lifted, the coast of the continent of Bolivar. No, the horizon she sought was the one where there was absolutely no danger of seeing anything, so that she could imagine what the rest of the world must be like. There was nothing except clouds that looked like continents and ships, and the heart would surge when a real ship came out of nothing. One day, when she went through a place whose name indicated that a lot of blood had been spilt there in the last massacre, Sangre Grande, she reached the sea and found that a ship had run aground and was being lashed against the beach, and the sea was strewn with lots of little apples. The place became known as Manzanilla, the seashore of tiny apples. Later historians say it is so named because of the manchineel, which grows there in abundance. Lavren is attracted to this theory, but is also taken in by the story of the little apples.

One morning Ramon, who now became known as the little discoverer, came running to Elena who was on the back veranda in her hammock doing some mending, an occupation which was passed down to all Monagas women. 'Come, come,' and the whole family, as well as the servants, had to go down to the small river which entered the gulf in the Baie des Crabes. There they found a small pirogue; a man was blindfolded and tied face down at the bottom of the boat. No one knew who he was, but some old fishermen said that he looked like one of the men who had gone looking for El Dorado.

Elena made a second statement sitting at the evening meal: 'We live in a world which is slowly being destroyed.'

'Not having the parrots is really working,' the children said as they sat at table.

But Georges Philippe looked at Elena as if she were a ghost. He had returned from Mucurapo that day, where he was told that in the old town of San Jorge de Monagas they were busy with more crucifixions because of the fire, and getting through the latest list of baptisms. Marie Elena said that this was the first ironic gesture of the new world. Georges Philippe did not tell Elena the news, but she had picked up what he had said to the family. She spoke again: 'They take their faith too literally, those priests in San Jorge, the fire of baptism, salvation by crucifixion.'

Stories of this kind were either more common, or Elena had begun to listen to them, because now she had given up any hope of seeing her sister in the Tamana hills. Even the cry of her voice, which she used to hear in the hysteria of the parrots, seemed to have faded away. This fact, and the increasingly common stories, kept her saying, 'We live in a world that is being slowly destroyed.' They were called out on to the mudflats in the Baie des Crabes to see a ship which had entered the gulf and seemed to be heading for the rocks on the island of centipedes. When some of them went out in pirogues to see what was the matter, they found that the ship was completely empty, except for one man who had a long grey beard. He was a raving lunatic.

He kept shouting, 'Gold, gold. Where is the gold?'

'What does it mean? Gold?' Elena asked at dinner.

The family all laughed; even the little ones, the grandchildren, giggled. 'Elena,' Georges Philippe leant over and touched her arm, a gesture not performed in years. 'You live in a dream. What do you think I've been doing all these years when I've left you for the Orinoco?'

She stared at him. 'This is not a dream. It's a nightmare.'

'Kill all the repetitious parrots!' the children yelled and Elena left the table and stood on the veranda, hoping there would be nothing on the horizon to interrupt her imagination.

In the end, to satisfy her obsessions, Elena persuaded Georges Philippe to take her back to San Raphael to spend the night with Marie Jeanne, who was now one hundred and four and was still visited by the Archangel, though these days she freely admitted that it was Father Bernardo, who came now for comfort and warmth from the damp nights, and not for passion. Moss had grown all over the statue of San Raphael. People joked that it was because he had not got down off his plinth for so long.

It was here that Lavren has brought them, to Talparo again, on the final expedition to meet with Gaston and Clarita, whom Elena still imagined to be a child. A raving soldier said, 'Yes, they still live and are as young as the day they first went up into the forests'; the forests which were believed to be heaven at Mundo Nuevo. Immediately the voices in the cry of the parrots returned to Elena. The hysteria was noisy with 'Clarita, Clarita, Clarita,' repeated with the madness and regularity of a catechism question. Then she heard another voice which she did not understand.

The forests were as unreal as the ones described by the Great Navigator in the ancient writings of the sailor from Genoa. Elena saw them as if she were seeing them for the first time with the same wonder and awe, the same terror. Far away she could hear the crashing of the waves at Manzanilla. *Manzanilla . . . Manzanilla*, and the little apples were like golden baubles being scattered by a gilded god from a golden calabash.

As they rode on, Georges Philippe said, 'No one has seen Albujar.'

'Who is Albujar?'

'No one has seen his golden beads or his calabash.' Elena realised that Georges Philippe was in the past, talking of the first man reputed to have been taken to the golden city blindfolded and then shown its wonders. She marvelled at how lucid she was becoming. She wasn't sure. Was this dream or waking life? Truth or story? The soldier with wounded feet and hands said that Clarita and Gaston sat on golden thrones and were themselves gilded, and walked about naked like in the first Eden at the beginning of the world. They had grown old, but they had stayed young. They lay down together with serpents and wild cats. All was harmony at the heart of the forests at Mundo Nuevo in the Tamana hills.

On the road from Talparo, Georges Philippe asked another soldier coming out of the forests where they were going with the young girls and boys, who were chained together and being dragged along the jungle floor. 'To San Jorge where the crosses are.' And he laughed.

The two old people dreamed of a former time.

'The world needs its innocence,' Elena said.

In a clearing off the road from Talparo at the mission called Tamana, their journey was aborted. There had been fewer and fewer chaingangs as they approached the spot. The screams of the parrots were at their most intense, and the corbeaux were circling and swooping. Then they saw why. The cry which Elena could not previously understand cracked in her ears. *Massacre.*

The gibbets stood in a circle. When they descended from their horses, diminishing their divinity, they stood at the foot of twelve crosses. They were told later that they were meant to represent the twelve apostles, so thoroughly had the executioners been schooled in the teaching and the analogy of sacrament. There were ten friars, made out by the fragments of their grey habits still flapping in the wind. The other two were Clarita and Gaston. Their Eden had become a Golgotha. The corbeaux were swooping in and pecking the remaining flesh off the legs and torso, near complete putrefaction in the heat. The corbeaux tugged at the clean bone in parts. In the distance Elena could hear the parrots and thought it must be the cry of her sister's departing soul. Georges Philippe stared and then howled. This howl was taken up by the forests, the plains and the far distant mountains on the horizon.

When Elena awoke she was in her bed at the house on the plains. There was a deep silence and she no longer heard the parrots. But it was one day soon after that she discovered that she could never get rid of the scream in her ears of many people wailing and lamenting. She was unsure whether they were lamenting the past or the future. She often, in those days, came across Georges Philippe cleaning out his ears. 'Have you been bathing in the sea? You're too old.'

'No, I keep hearing someone screaming. It sounds familiar, but I can't remember.'

Near the church in San Jorge de Monagas where the first ajoupas had been built, there was a mass crucifixion all along the road down to the river where there were prehistoric stones and where the washerwomen bleach their clothes today. 'You see this place, this is a Calvary, yes, they crucify people here, yes. Is Golgotha for truth.' The soldier in charge was young Ramon Monagas de los Macajuelos who had discovered Raleigh's anchor, and the old soldier from the Orinoco blindfolded in the pirogue. He gave the order on the authority of the Governor his father, the King and the Pope, and those from Tamana, who had been deemed responsible for the massacre, were given the punishment of Christ by Christians. The spirits of All Souls linger in the molten wax on the grave stones against the walls of the San Jorge de Monagas church.

Those who believe in martyrdom hear the friars chanting the *Magnificat*, 'My soul doth magnify the Lord and my spirit rejoices in God my Saviour'; but those who do not believe in martyrdom consider that the monks and the deluded Gaston and Clarita were justly executed by innocent people who saw them as emissaries of a conquering God with a conquering faith. Those who do not believe in martyrdom do not see the blooming of orchids, but hear only the scream which started in the ears of Elena and Georges Philippe, who lived the rest of their lives in a silence which forced them to hear nothing else. As they neared their death, they realised that the screams came from the future as much as from the past. Kairi became a place of ghosts forgotten by the rest of the world.

In order to comfort herself Elena believed that the orchids, which were reputed to flower spontaneously, miraculously, on the graves of the priests and the Monagas, were the soul of her sister growing out of the ground, but really she knew better, being the wife of the first planter in the new world, that it was because of the incontestable fertility of the Montserrat hills. She never ventured to Tamana again, not even for the funeral of Marie Jeanne. She decided that things had happened so long ago that it no longer mattered now what happened to the world, so long as she could wake in the morning and see the mountains from the window at the back of the house on the plains which in a later century her cousin Immaculata would paint and leave to Lavren. She couldn't even remember when Georges Philippe had died. 'He has died such a long time ago,' she said. Her children roamed the continent of Bolivar and the archipelago. Then she died. But before the priest anointed her with the little bit of holy

oil that was left in the island, she wrote a very long poem entitled
A Very Sad Story, in which she told of all these events which are
deciphered by Lavren Monagas de los Macajuelos, the last of the
Monagas, who levitates between centuries, races and genders in the
interstices of time, understanding the yearning of women and the
silence of men.

THE TALE OF THE HOUSE
IN THE COCOA

THE SILENCE that forced Elena and Georges Philippe of 'The Tale of the House on the Plains' to hear nothing else but the screams and hysteria of the forests was inherited by their children and their children's children. It was inherited by Elena Elena, the last of the child brides. See how she bears the ancestral name, doubling its hold on the generational progress of the family of the Monagas de los Macajuelos. Since she was sent to play in the turret room of the great house in the cocoa hills by her husband, the Englishman, to keep her as a little girl, dressed in her cotton chemise for his pleasure, she has hoarded paper under the floorboards there to write down her memories of his visits when she does not speak to him, but sees only the ghosts of the past creeping over her bed, coming into her as he lies with her. 'Helena, Helena, my poppet,' always mispronouncing her name. She never understood, especially, poppet. It is in these fragments which Lavren dredges up that we glimpse and feel this time. The silence in which hysteria grows, grew as tall as the silk-cotton trees and as broad as the saman in the hills of Tamana. This silence grew hard and deep and knotted itself in the lianas which tangled themselves in the bois canot. It bewitched the cocoa. It lived in the parasite, witchbroom.

This province of ghosts, which had been Isabella's and Ferdinand's, holy monarchs of Holy Mother Church of Rome, had become a grave for the last of the feathered and ochred people of the gilded one. Their lungs had expired in the diving for pearls to satisfy the desire of the Monagas in their search for child brides. They died of malaria, syphilis and influenza from the snotty noses and dribbling penises of Cortes and Pizarro, the spittle and puke of Monagas' babies. They choked on Holy Communion weighted on their tongues, and grew drunk and alcoholic on the altar wine. They drowned in the baptismal waters, renouncing a myth they did not understand; seeing only pomp and power in those who came like centaurs to ravage and rape their men, women, children and

60

land; forcing them to leap to safety in their deaths where the waves crashed on the rocks in the bay at Balandra, and where golden bodies still leap at Sauteurs. Their spirits inhabited the rocks and their screams flew into the forests and became the hysteria of parrots and the sad cry of Clarita, the sister of Elena, in 'The Tale of the House on the Plains'. 'Why don't they stop those parrots? I hear them calling my name and the name of someone called Clarita.' Elena Elena had only the house slaves to talk to, since the Englishman was often away in town on business, returning only for the pleasure of his poppet, as she thought, but spending the late hours of the night in the barrack-rooms, or having the young girls brought up to the house.

Elena Elena, unable to sleep alone but frightened of the Englishman's creeping over her body in the night, had to wait for the one night in the week which he allowed himself to visit her. He was unable to resist the child who continued to bear her own children. 'Helena, Helena,' mispronouncing her name as he made his way into her and she thought that there was another in the room whom he called. It was alone at night, under a hurricane lamp, that she wrote of the ghosts who visited her from the plains and the Gulf of Sadness. All the time, names, in the voice of parrots.

After the massacre of the ochre people, Kairi was depopulated, and the ships that arrived in the Gulf of Sadness were either empty, or full of ghosts. The Franciscan friar, whose name suggests many mansions, invented a new terror, too late to save the feathered ones and just right to line the pockets of the merchants and rulers of Europe to build their cities and churches. He flung his rosary beads around the continent of Africa and chained its people with Our Fathers for forgiveness and Hail Marys for purity, in this vale of tears, this lacrimarum vale, at the bottom of ships which rocked their way across the wide Sargasso Sea, the middle passage, to this ghost town, this port of Spain, at Mucurapo, under the silk-cotton trees. So they passed under the limbo stick of their cages like the spiderman Anansi into the new world. From this very first moment they pressed for their freedom, for the blue air of freedom above the green land of Kairi, haloed with the blur of a thousand hummingbirds.

The silence of hysteria hung in the memory of the strange black fruit which Elena Elena saw on her visit to the town, hanging from trees along the avenue stretching from the carenage near the cathedral to the front garden of the Governor's house, where the Englishman had taken her on a visit, through the gridded city at the edge of the gulf. They travelled through the savannah which to this day is a calendar of the seasons, dry as the Sahara, a carnival of dust in Lent, a Mardi Gras of thirst on Ash Wednesday. In the rainy season it became rank and vegetal. While she sipped tea with her husband, the Englishman, on the balcony of the Governor's house she asked: 'Why?' Why the Passion Play enacted over and over again? 'Why the crosses; it isn't Lent?' Then she remembered the hangings on the estate, supervised by the Englishman, which she saw from the window of the turret room. The Governor and her husband answered her with the silence of Kairi's rivers. The silence of the hysteria was as golden and silted as the Orinoco with its mouth jammed with wrecks, festooned with brigands, buccaneers, pirates, in the country selling human cargo in overcrowded barracoons, between whose bars the young and lithe creole hermaphrodite, Lavren, swam and levitated between genders and races in the infested seas which rocked the island of Kairi off the shelf of the continent of Bolivar. The very same silence bloomed in the sunset over the Gulf of Sadness, which Elena Elena could see from the Governor's balcony.

As the decades unfolded they came again and again, each time as conquistador. Lavren watches where he reads Elena Elena's memories and the stories she was told by Ernestine her nurse, and nurse of her babies. Ernestine administered at their births and their early burials when they died of typhus or malaria. In her pain, Elena Elena hallucinated the ships entering the Dragon's Mouth, and on a moonlight night sidle past the island of centipedes, the jagged outcrops of Gasparee. She woke, crying for Ernestine. 'My little girls, why are they putting them in a hole? Who takes them from my belly?' Looking out of the window, she dreamed of the ships entering the Gulf of Sadness with the slaves, their masters escaping revolution, religious persecution or the revolt of slaves in the north of the archipelago who follow the style of Napoleon with their own dream. They escaped the massacre of Haiti, the general, Toussaint, the citadel of Dessalines. The waves on the sea brought his name, *Toussaint, Toussaint, Toussaint.*

'Ernestine, who is Toussaint?'

*

Now, they are landowners like the Englishman with his estates, wanting more land, and come to manage crops to fill the coffers and bellies of Europe with sugar, cocoa, pimento, nutmeg, ginger and bananas. Lavren conflates history. The statistics only get worse, a litany as regular and repetitive as the litanies of the church, changing nothing but enforcing resignation. House of Gold – pray for us; Tower of Ivory – pray for us; Mother of Pearls – pray for us. 'Ernestine, my back, someone is whipping me.'

'Mistress, I know; they beating old Moses down in the yard. That is what you feeling. Is your husband's whip you feeling.'

The gabled house, the great house in the cocoa, sprung on pillars out of the enamelled forests. Cocoa was King. The old and new world bowed to King Cocoa. House of Cocoa – pray for us.

Lavren giggles and wakes Marie Elena who drops her prayer book and tarot pack of holy pictures.

It was about this time – Lavren cannot always see through the sepia mists of memory, cannot always dispel the seaweed before his eyes as s/he swims between the ribs of the watery barques encrusted with barnacles; cannot see as well as s/he would like – that the place was wild with rumour like the tangle of wild yams and corilli bushes on the fences of the estate. Those who hung each day over the balustrades of the verandas in muslin and lace, and played on the sloping lawns beneath the jacaranda trees, those children of the last of the child brides who had not died of typhoid or malaria, had to depend on rumour to know what was going on in the barracoons beneath the hill; beneath the high-pillared house which jutted, cantilevered, and spread among the saman trees, almost as tall as the immortelle which gave shade to the cocoa, whose flowers sprinkled the green of the forest with the colour of cinnamon. In the day, the wooden house was a jigsaw of filigreed gingerbread cutouts which filtered light, so that it splayed its shadows with shifting symmetry on the polished floors that mirrored the burnished faces of Guinea women. They scrubbed the white floorboards where more minute shadows of pots of angelhair fern, seed fern, fan-shaped fern and the fern that was powdered on the underleaf, which children stamped on their innocent skins, trembled. In the day the house rocked like the hammocks strung across the verandas, gently, and then rumour began to rock it more harshly, and fear convulse that house when fires raged on the plains, sabotaging the crops of cane. CANBOULAY CANBOULAY! The fires burnt the cane, the drums shook the night, the dance shook the ground. Fear entered the bedrooms; one added to another, doors opening one into the other, creating an openness belying the secret that the household kept from themselves and from each other, as the children were born and soon died. The secret was mercantile, fiscal and the colour of black skin, harnessed first by the indolent Spanish and then by the victorious British administrators, put in while Apodoca's ships burned in the harbour, scuttled with their own fear. Cultivated by the French. Did it matter – British, Spanish, French, Dutch, Portuguese – if you were harnessed to a new world stretched across an ocean into whose deeps your brothers and sisters were dropped, because they hadn't made it to this market on the shores of the Gulf of Sadness?

Lavren meditates on the nightmare, but Elena Elena, the child bride who bore children for death, became a woman with too much bearing. Still, the Englishman kept coming to her once a week with his itch. Still, she did not speak to him. 'That man. I know why I can't learn his language to speak to him. He tells me he is a cocoa planter, but he is always smelling of saltfish when he gets into my bed naked. He must be a fisherman.' In each century the women understood the horror. They knew, but they turned to the porch of the church. They turned from their husbands to the consecrated hands which soothed troubled hearts. They turned to hands consecrated and smelling of altar wine, hosts and incense, that could comfort when the hands of husbands had been elsewhere, fingering smelly saltfish crutches on the carenage. They would not have thought it of priests. They chose to forget the story of Marie Jeanne of San Raphael, and the priest who was like the Archangel in the night, and who grew moss in his groin.

The century jangled with the throwing off of the iron chains, the manacles which clasped the ankles and wrists, the muzzle on the mouth, the bit between the teeth. The century howled with a voice which Lavren hears, and goes towards its power in a small board-house on the road to Moruga, where an old man sits with his family, as the memories of Elena Elena bleed through her writing paper and come up through the floorboards of the great house in the cocoa.

'Why does he keep putting dead children in my belly? Ernestine someone is whipping me.'

'Mistress, is the master. Old-man Moses bleeding down in the yard.'

Canefield and sea: river, mountain and forest. Lavren cut his way through the serrated leaves. S/he swam through the blades of the waves, climbed mountains to the top of Kairi, cutting through forests loud with the hysteria of parrots. In the rain, drumming on the roof of the small board-house on the slope that crumbles away from the road in heavy rain, running runnels into the gully, dank and dark with tania and other ground provision with large green leaves splayed with rainwater; in a small board-house of an old man with a brain wrinkled like old parchment, s/he listened to the voice of Africa. S/he listened to the voice, which was a preacher's voice, a Shango voice, the voice of Africa lodging itself in the tongue of the conqueror to crack it, listened to the voice in the whips on the backs, the murmur of the trapped tongue, bitten lips, the tongue trapped in a bit like a horse with its head caged and mouth gagged, tongue entrapped. Lavren listened to the unmuzzled voice. Lavren put an ear against the old black wrinkled lips cracked by the sun, and listened while the rain drummed and the wind sighed, and s/he wondered whether s/he would be able to decipher the code, the language of the old man whose voice became the voice of the rain and the wind, the voice of the waves and the breeze through the serrated sugarcane leaves; became the voice of the groans of the drum, a groan beaten on skin in the belly of England's caravels, mingling with the castanets of Spain, Parang! – Parang strumming the cuatro of the continent of Bolivar, the sound of the rain dripping in the cocoa which put Marie Elena asleep as a small girl in her hammock and as a young bride in Brasso Piedro. Lavren listened to the voice of Africa. Lavren listened to the voice of Congo. S/he listened to the voice of Guinea, to Guinea woman with the etiquette and grace of Martiniquaise, her head tied in the cloths of the rainbow, her flower-garden skirts ruffled with the lace of the waves, bouyant with petticoats of cotton, bodices of broderie anglaise, lifting her douillette with fingers as slender as okros to free her naked brown feet, tilting her breasts polished and purple as melangene, dancing to the music of Africa, mingled and changing, dancing to the music and voice of Joropo, the castanets of Castillian in the mornings by the river, Manzanares, in the evenings of Serenal, Galeron, Vieux-Crois, Fandang – Parang!

All this, Lavren heard in the voice and drum of the old man's voice, in the beating of sticks between the stickfighters in the gayelle, in the drumming of the rain and the sighing of the wind. In this voice was the fire and the fear that the children of Elena Elena heard, in the house cantilevered over the plains of Kairi on the shores of the Gulf of Sadness, guarded by the Serpent's Mouth in the south and the Dragon's Mouth in the north. All this he heard resting his head on the breasts of Josephine, listening to the beating of her heart.

The fires burned the cane on the plains of Kairi, *cannes brûlées*. The voice in the drum drowned the whispers of Wilberforce in his parliament. The fear of fire and the fire of fear were scratched on the dispatches and written in family letters. The drums, the sabotage, the riot, the fires, the dance and the music; the language lodged in the language of the conqueror broke the chains, shattered the ledgers belonging to the merchants, the Cocoa and Coffee Growers' Association. Freedom! Emancipation!

'My grandfather belong to the land of Africa. I can't remember the name of the real place he was born. When he left that place where he was born, coming down to the Caribbean, he came to a place called Muluwanda. This place is now called Angola. When he left Muluwanda he went to Portugal. From Portugal he came to Trinidad. That is what my grandfather told me. The year he reached Trinidad was 1832.'

'What was his name?' Lavren put his lips to the old man's ear and spoke into the conch, his tongue to the whorl of the black ear.

'Which of the name you want?'

'Give all the names.' The rain drummed and the winds sighed with the voices of his wife and daughter and granddaughter.

'His name, home in Africa, was Matundo. My grandmother's name was Yobendo. Down here they call him Frazer. After a certain time my grandfather leave and she find another partner. My grandmother married a next man. This man called Captain John Pierre.'

'How they get those names?' The voices in the drumming of the rain and the sighing of the wind whispered into the conch, licked the whorls of the old man's ear with tongues of questions.

'Somebody, as godfather, stood up for them and change their name.'

The world of green trees outside the board-house with the drumming rain and the sighing wind and cock-crowing betrayal in the yard, shook against the old house of the old man.

'My grandfather told me this. My grandfather born in Africa. His real name, they put it aside. They put it to one side. English people would not tolerate these things. When he reach he was taken to Picton Estate. Twenty-six sugar estate in the place. He spent his time on the estate.'

Lavren's mind saw the serrated sugarcane fields named after the English Governor. He saw the twenty-six estates in the burning sun under a clear blue sky: Petit Morne, Golconda, Corinth, Malgré-Toute, Union Hall, Williamsville, Reform, Retrench, Savonetta, Monkey Town, Tarouba, Spring, Embarcardier . . . the names ran out in the silence of the drumming rain.

'They meet many hard times. During the time at Picton they had to work night and day with whip on their back. But while flogging them, plenty trouble come.'

'What kind of trouble?' The voice of a granddaughter.

'That you would like to hear? Well, I'm telling you. If you wait I'll tell you.

'They like to dance, the country dance. They don't work so they flog them. But a wheel in a wheel of the licks, something not natural in the licks. According to my grandfather. When they don't feel to work they go and dance. But a wheel in a wheel. Science work there too. A man who work in the sugarmill put his hand on something, some machinery, and the mill stop working. They go and dance. Dance skin music. They flog them, but when they go to flog them, a wheel in a wheel. When they beating, say John, they hear the manager wife bawling, "Let him go, let him go." A wheel in a wheel, something more than natural.'

Rain fall. Rain silences the voice of the old man. In the silence, Lavren heard him say: 'They run away. They fly. They mount the hoe in the field and fly, fly back to Africa.'

Lavren pressed his ear against the old man's wrinkled lips to hear the truth.

*

The fires which destroyed the canefields whipped the pillars of the great house. They stung the bannisters of the great staircases and cracked in the rafters of the great house in the cocoa, till all that was left was a shell which got patched up, and Elena Elena had to watch her step as she climbed to the turret room where she had played as a young girl, but now took refuge as a woman who had already buried nine children, dead of malaria and typhus, and borne three others well beyond the wisdom of bearing years: Quentino and Margarita, the twins, and her last child, Sou Sou.

Elena Elena had saved the charred fragments of her memories which Lavren has given you. Now she had these and in her solitude, deserted by her husband the Englishman, she tried to keep the estate going, while he has moved into the Planters' Club on Plaza de la Marina to be near the child prostitutes of the orange market. She tried to keep things as they were. But, after freedom was won, many had left the estates for the town or for their own plots of land, or simply refused to work any more. Time, change and pain had taken its toll on Elena Elena, who had been the last of the child brides. Left on her own with her ghosts, the voices of the parrots naming names, she found that she had to divine her own future much in the way a clairvoyant reads the patterns at the bottom of teacups. She began to read the future in the pattern of her daily stools, not only the pattern on the side of the porcelain bowl, but the size and consistency, the odour: they all told by their different signs the shape of the future. The administering of the chamberpots was a task she was very particular about, until Ernestine refused to comply with the service she had grown accustomed to give in the bad days. In her defiance, one day, Ernestine who had been midwife, undertaker and comforter, announced to Elena Elena, 'I am a queen. I don't do this kind of thing any more.'

Elena Elena was so shocked at her assertion she said, 'Very well, you're a queen, you're a queen, well, be a queen. Go and sit on the latrine outside with this mosquito net over your head and that pot you refuse to wash. Let that be your crown. You think you are a queen, well, be a queen.' In the bad days Ernestine would have had to do this, but not now. She left Elena Elena having a tantrum, but she had to fetch, empty and clean her own pots.

'I am Queen of Africa and I'm not emptying your shit and pee.' Of course, like all Monagas, Elena Elena was horrified that anyone would refuse to do their service. In the end, she had to accept the times. She had to empty her morning's evacuation which she eventually found gave her more time to study the consistency and the variation in the aroma of her daily move. Her Englishman husband was dismayed when he found out what was going on, but as long she continued to play her piano and give him his rights when he was home from the Planters' Club, he was not too worried.

There had been little else except her beauty and compliance as a child, and her beautiful piano playing. He had had the piano especially brought from London. She would not speak to him, even after bearing him twelve children, nine of whom were buried under the mango trees. When she thought he was not there she would have an outburst, forgetting the times, and insist they have slaves: 'There are so many free people now, we must have a few. Not only for the estate but for the house.' And she laughed. 'I want a peepee slave, a shit slave.' This she said in English, by mistake, and giggled. But then she remembered and insisted that her potty was not to be removed from under her bed. She put it on the windowsill, but removed it eventually because of the stale stench, and when the turds began to dry up and were no use to her in divining the future.

Why had she always refused to speak English? 'It is barbaric. He is barbaric. Look at me,' she said, tethering her tiger cat to the foot of her chair imagining she was a Cocoa Queen, the Countess of Couva, or Marchioness of Tortuga. She had not had a new dress for years. To her dying day she held her tongue within the music of castanets and her laughter within the strumming of the cuatro. Her laughter was fabled. The people said they could hear her from the bottom of Pepper Hill. She would not speak the tongue of those who had forced her Admiral, Apodoca, to burn his ships in the harbour of Chaguaramas in 1789. Her reasons were lodged in a past beyond even the scratches on her charred fragments of memory. 'I saw Apodoca today, did you see him? I spied him walking on his deck,' she asked Father Eugenio who had come to see her.

'No, my dear, but don't worry about it. God allows his chosen ones to see the impossible.'

'Oh, yes, Father, I see the impossible all right. I see what's going on here. But what do you want? You never come and see me now unless you want something for that church with your miraculous madonna. Why doesn't she help me? Why doesn't she help my children? Why doesn't she marry off my Sou Sou? Have you seen her lately, how pale she is, how silent? It's not right.'

'She is a good girl, my dear. I hear her confession. She takes communion when I advise. But you know we have to ration it. The shortages. This is what I want you to see the Archbishop about.'

'The Archbishop! Look at me, Father! How can I impress him?'

'Wine, unleavened bread. The sacraments. If we run out of these things what will become of the world?'

'Why? Is he Christ, now? Can he change water into wine for blood, and out of nothing, make bread for his body?'

'But your eloquence, my dear.' The parish priest appreciated her Spanish and brought her Cervantes to read. 'And he has money. It must not all stay in the cathedral.'

'Father, you flatter a poor woman. I will do you this favour. But you must ask that madonna of yours to marry off my Sou Sou. And my twins! My twins! What kind of world is this?'

So, Ernestine and the other servants went with panniers and donkeys down the road to the plain, carrying Elena Elena into town to see the Archbishop. The piano too had to be taken into town to be tuned by Monsieur Girot, so it was also packed up at the back of the cart. They slept in the house on the plains, though usually she found this too damp and the place reminded her of her ancestors Elena and her wretched sister Clarita. The piano had to stay outside, otherwise it would crack the floorboards. 'We'll soon be sinking into the swamps with the oysters and mangrove. Poquito, poquito?' This was all she said as she rode across the plain. She would stay in Mucurapo in the rundown house by the silk-cotton trees.

The Archbishop lived behind the cathedral and she had not liked making the journey there because of the young girls and boys who sold their bodies in the grass market. She pretended to herself that they were only selling oranges and mangoes. But this was only up the road from the Planters' Club on the Marina, so she knew it was more than just oranges and mangoes.

'Your Grace,' she said, in Spanish of course. The Archbishop of

70

Holy Mother Church of Rome was Spanish, but left to his own devices would only speak Latin as he had no intention of being understood at all by anyone in the island. 'Your Grace,' Elena Elena said, smiling. She could be charming. She could speak softly and carried herself with an air of being the most important person in the world; she was not going to shove it down your throat, but would not let you not think it so. 'Your Grace'; it was her habit to ..ddress three times people who thought they were more important than her. She thought that when the day came and she stood before the triune God, this was what she would have to do, so she had better get used to it. 'I come on a matter of great importance, never wishing to take up your important time with anything else.' Archbishop Gaspar Grande de los Angelicos, no less, smiled. He didn't like women, but he had to think of the tithes and the collection boxes. After all, they did not want another attack of the witchbroom and collapse of the cocoa. He looked at the woman who read her future at the bottom of a chamberpot.

'Yes, my dear? Yes?' His rhetorical questions became more than a silent thought, and their sibilance disturbed the room, creating the slightest flicker of annoyance on Elena Elena's face. She could not bear to think that anyone being addressed by her was not completely taken up with the expectation and excitement of what was to follow. The Archbishop's sibilance – most of what he spoke was flavoured with a sibilance, an affectation customary to cardinals whose college he wished to join, privately dreaming that he was the most suited person in the world to be Pope – revealed that he had other matters on his mind. Elena Elena knew well what occupied the flatulent brain of Archbishop Gaspar Grande de los Angelicos. She would never verbalise it, but she was not stupid, and the proximity of his palace to the orange and mango sellers seemed more than a coincidence of municipal planning. These thoughts filled the intervals between their mutual arrangements as they seated themselves in the vaulted room overlooking the carenage.

'It's a matter of the altar wine.' At this point she unfurled her fan which depicted a floral triptych of the hanging gardens of Babylon, some dusty old thing from the attic in the turret room. In surprise, he blew his nose with a lace-edged handkerchief that seemed more ornamental than functional.

'Altar wine?' He said this with such surprise that you would think he didn't drink it every day, so that it was as usual to him as the wiping of his arse.

Marie Elena jerked in her sleep at Lavren's thought and irreverence.

The Gulf of Sadness, whose waters filled the carenage and almost lapped the foundations of the Cathedral of the Immaculate Conception and the palace of Archbishop Gaspar Grande de los Angelicos, crinkled like crepe de Chine in the blinding light and the sizzling heat of the afternoon when the dog-shit outside on the pavement was curling and growing white as the coral on the reef of the neighbouring island. Elena Elena Monagas de los Macajuelos continued to fan herself, furling and unfurling the triptych of the hanging gardens of Babylon, her tiger cat from the Amazon tethered to the foot of her chair. 'Yes, altar wine and unleavened bread. These are your responsibilities, Your Grace, not those of a poor woman with children and a husband who philanders under your nose.' She put forward the point that the parish priest of Tamana, Tortuga, Montserrat and Gran Couva was at his wits' end because he could not get any altar wine from the Monsignor in San Jorge de Monagas. 'And Your Grace, has not been up to our hills for a long time.' She slipped it in that the Archbishop too had not been up to the cocoa hills for years, and even now she had prepared a confirmation class for the parish priest. Though this was something the parish priest did not want to see repeated, given Elena Elena's growing instability, the future divined at the bottom of a chamberpot.

This woman reminded the Archbishop of his mother and he didn't like it. What did altar wine have to do with it? Only the priests drank the wine, the people had to make do with the bread alone. Rumours had gone around that Archbishop Gaspar Grande de los Angelicos had instructed the priests to water down the wine so that it could go further. The wine in the cathedral was kept at the right alcoholic levels. The parish priests were in a crisis. 'Was the wine changing into the blood of Christ?' She put the point to the prelate. Elena Elena did not bother to add to the lists of shortages. She could see that she had sufficiently disturbed the holy man. A crisis over transubstantiation was no small affair. It could mean that the new world, without knowing it, was bereft of salvation.

'Salvation is really in jeopardy, Your Grace, no transubstantiation in the new world and the wrong man hanging on the cross.'

'What do you mean, my dear?'

'When last did you see a white man hanging from a tree in this place?'

That afternoon Elena Elena left the Archbishop pondering her question. She refrained from going to visit her cousin Iseult in the Cascade hills, where they had an estate. As she began her return journey back to Pepper Hill, she saw the corbeaux were all over the sky and sitting on all the low flamboyant trees in the vicinity of the big savannah. 'What, after all this time, still feeding on the dead?' Then she remembered why she had never wanted to come back to this town. She remembered the voices then: 'Madam, you mustn't go there; if you see dead people . . .' The Governor was punishing people because they had decided to take their own lives, rather than live in the cages that had brought them from the kingdoms of Ashanti and Benin. 'Poison, Madam, they poison themselves and the other ones get hang.' There had been a gibbet in the Governor's garden. Spanish law had been thrown out of the window by the Governor's children, not that it was much practised anyway. Who knew what went on when there was hardly any paper to write anything down?

Elena Elena knew when she got back to the mountains she would have to get her papers out from under the pitchpine floorboards to read what she had written then on that last visit. Along the plain she met her old ghosts.

When they got to the bottom of Pepper Hill they had to rest because of the piano. They had to push the last two miles to the top of Pepper Hill, called so because of the vast number of pepper trees that seemed to grow wild, but might have been planted in a previous century by people who no longer lived there, people whose spirits lived in the branches of the enamelled forests and in the screams of parrots. These peppers were called bird pepper because the birds seemed to like feeding on them, and the children thought that since the pepper was so hot, the birds screamed with pain. Halfway up the hill, the procession of servants and carts had to stop for a rest. Elena Elena herself was exhausted, but suddenly, with the exuberance at times evident in her character – she had had to be so controlled with the Archbishop – she got off her donkey with the panniers, and was helped to the top of the cart with the piano.

'Bring me a stool;' and the velvet upholstered piano stool was brought for her; 'now rest in the shade of those cocoa trees while I play you an adagio. Do you know what that is? Or a fandango?' And she threw back her head and laughed so loudly that it disturbed the parrots in the high branches of the immortelle, which took sudden flight and circled the company twice, and then settled again at the top of the cinnamon-flowering trees. 'Take care, the piano!' Elena Elena shouted as they pushed her, still playing, towards the house in the cocoa, a charred relic awaiting its mistress of the turret room, where Ernestine and Sou Sou met her on the veranda with the twins Margarita and Quentino, who had been made to dress properly by Ernestine for the return of their mother.

Elena Elena decided to wear muslin dyed black, with black lace: to shroud herself in black mantillas and hang about her waist a long rosary like a cloistered nun. She said that, in spite of her young children, there was nothing she could think that did not tell her to mourn. Like Elena in a previous century, she kept saying, 'We are slowly destroying the world.' But Lavren knows that when she returned from her trip to Mucurapo she had to bear all the filthy rumours of the giggling servants and the overseers. When she was away the Englishman, her husband, had of course been spending the night carousing in the barrack-rooms, and she knew that already there were three children with marmoset eyes who came to the house asking for food, as if they had a right. Once, when the Englishman was drunk, he even wanted Elena Elena to take them in. Father Eugenio said it was her duty to respect her husband. She decided, therefore, that she was a widow and wore black. 'I don't have a husband,' she said; 'you don't call that Englishman a husband.' But she continued to play the piano when he came to the house, secretly trying to charm him. She knew he stayed in the Planters' Club to be near the carenage with its carnage. She knew he had tea with the Governor on the balcony which overlooked the garden where the gibbet had been, and was one of his men. The *Courant* had told the story of the young mulatto girl tortured in the upper room, and she had wondered at her husband's absence that week, that dreadful week long ago.

Elena Elena was the first of the Monagas women to cultivate the eucharist lilies that had bloomed in the parlour of the Convent of the Immaculate Heart of Mary in Aracataca during the seduction of Clarita by Gaston. Once she had her potty, her piano and her eucharist lilies, she was satisfied and could spend the rest of her time speaking to her husband in Spanish, which he didn't understand, and trying to keep his hands from under her skirts when they were alone. She did not succeed and he got more than his hands under there. Father Eugenio said she was made for this: 'My daughter, this is what God meant by obedience.'

'Yes, Father, but I'm a big woman now. I think I've done my duty to the cemetery.' Elena Elena maintained a secret, but healthy, disrespect for clerics.

Elena Elena stayed more and more in the turret room overlooking the Gulf of Sadness. She left the care of the children to Ernestine. As time went on, Elena Elena would not allow anyone else up to the turret room except Ernestine, even though she knew it was she who had stolen all her babies' lace and muslin dresses and had developed the habit in little Margarita of going about the house stark naked and standing by the window overlooking the barrack-rooms and showing the spider which lived between her legs. This became a traditional afternoon pantomime that no one could put a stop to. 'The mother mad, so the child going mad too,' is what the people in the barracks said, and what the house servants whispered as they giggled behind their fingers while serving dinner and bringing the dishes back out to the pantry. Elena Elena knew exactly what was going on because she had her telescope. From the turret room, she could look down into all the dark secrets of the estate, but also, she could keep a watch on the ships which came through the Dragon's Mouth into the Gulf of Sadness. Sometimes she sat so long looking out on to the gulf that she fell asleep, and dreamed the history she had been told about. She witnessed the anchoring of the ship in the Bay of the Turtles with Count Lopinot and his slaves, whom he said were loyal to him and took them to a remote but fertile valley in the northern cordillera. Elena Elena casually went to the window of the turret room in her dream and picked up her telescope and aimed it at the Grand Bocas and saw the caravel that brought Roume St Laurent from Grenada with his bunch of rag-tag-and-bobtail, penny-a-bunch aristocrats, moored alongside the Island of Eggs. When she was bored and the bay was empty, she could dream them up, navies of plunder, charnel galleons.

The turret room was her lookout for seeing which flags the ships were flying when they came through the Dragon's Mouth so that she would know whether the sale of their crop of cocoa was safe and would reach the merchants at The Hague, Le Havre, Liverpool and the basin of London under the tower of Elizabeth. She would sit there, and with her telescope – the first ever to be used by a woman in the new world – would keep watch on the goings-on in the Gulf of Sadness. She instinctively knew which ships were laden with lace, muslin, brocade, silks and satins, and she would at once begin to plan a wedding for Sou Sou, but then remember that she could not afford the splendour which they had once had.

She now no longer told her English husband about the activity in the gulf, the reason why he had bought her a telescope, though the one concession she had made in spite of his betrayal had been to inform him of the mercantile trade, so that he could get the offices on the wharf in the port of Spain ready for the imports and exports. She tried to be an accomplice to his wealth, for her children, but now that her husband spent his money on his courtesans and concubines in the barracks, she kept the knowledge to herself.

Since she had fulfilled her part of the bargain with the parish priest, doing him a favour and going to see the Archbishop in town, Elena Elena wanted her own favour returned. She was not sure whether the Archbishop would do anything about the shortage of wine and un-leavened bread, but she was sure that she had left him with a thought about sacramental salvation and the question of crucifixion. She wanted her prayers to the miraculous Madonna of Tortuga, La Divina Pastora, to be answered. She wanted a husband for her Sou Sou.

'But, Madam, look at the twins – who is going to come to this house looking for Miss Sou Sou with those two going around the place as naked as the day they born?' Ernestine said, as she brought up Elena Elena's lunch-tray with a bowl of chicken soup. Yes, already we see where this habit of drinking chicken soup came from.

Elena Elena's anger at the Englishman's betrayal, right from the very beginning when he had taken her as a child, made her now even forget her own children; it was not only Margarita who was going around showing herself naked to the servants in the barracks, but also Quentino. They were carrying on a double-act nudist pantomime on the back veranda. One day, when Ernestine came down from the turret room with Elena Elena's empty lunch tray, she found the brother and sister at siesta time in the hammock together without any clothes on, innocently involved in the business of copulation. What amazed Ernestine was that the young Margarita had so soon realised that she could increase her pleasure by lying on top of the young Quentino; it made her wonder how long this had been going on to make the young girl so aware of what could afford her the most satisfaction. She guessed that the young Quentino, bless his little prick had, like his father and father's father, like most men she knew, no idea that little girls, child brides whom they had taken as wives, could experience any pleasure at all from this business. Ernestine felt that she had to report this to her madam. 'Those children not up to any good, you know, Madam.'

Elena Elena listened in silence and then said, 'Call the priest. I've done his business with that prelate. He must work something for me with his madonna, his La Divina Pastora.' Ernestine went that afternoon to the parish priest and asked him to come and see her madam, because she wanted him to hear her confession. Father Eugenio was the only man whom Elena Elena would allow up the steps to the turret room to sit with her. It was not that in the silence of her soul, where not even the parish priest could enter, she had any illusions about this man of God. She knew quite well what they could get up to, just as she had the full measure of Archbishop Gaspar Grande de los Angelicos. At least the sacrament of confession obliged them to listen. She had not found many men who would listen to what she really wanted to say. They heard, indeed they had grown silent, and as time went on became utterly speechless, but that did not mean that they listened, listened to what she was really feeling and thinking. She usually ignored what the parish priest had to say.

'My child, my child, what is it? What can we do for you on this feast of our holy brother and fond father, Thomas of Aquino?' The Dominican friars had come to the new world and brought with them the memory of their saint and angelic doctor, whose body was so fat that his fellow friars had had to cut out a bay from his desk for him, to fit his stomach. His logic had confounded the world by its dismissal of the celestial ideas of Plato, and imprisoned the world within the ethics and logics of Aristotle until this day, when philosophers can only pretend they have broken out of the prison the humble friar put the world into. Even Lavren to this day is mesmerised by the beauty of the fat friar's 'Tantum Ergo', even though he would not be seen dead at benediction. He loves to hum the tune in the bath and even sing the words, with the most reverential intonations and remembered devotion.

'Come, come, Father,' the title stuck in her throat almost, 'none of your priestly, sycophantic obsequiousness.' The priest flinched at her bitter dismissal, but knew well her sharp tongue, sharpened over the years on truth, as she sat in the turret room presiding over the mercantile expansion of the new world. Though cutting through his ceremony, she nevertheless wanted his advice about what she should do, given that her husband had left his house and only visited it intermittently to give his concubines their periodical stipends. 'My children are running around the place naked, exposing themselves to the world and copulating with each other incestuously in hammocks.'

'Hammocks.' This interested the parish priest and he made a mental note to exploit its pornographic possibilities when he was next lonely, depressed and deprived of any comfort alone in his presbytery.

'Come, come, Father. I'm not talking about hammocks. I'm talking about the salvation of my children. I'm talking about the salvation of my husband, about my own salvation and the salvation of this darkened world on the edge of the Gulf of Sadness.' The parish priest knew of her eloquence and had himself pinched some of her words for his Sunday sermon, particularly as she no longer came to mass. 'Father, I must leave this gaol. My children need me and Sou Sou must get married. I've been sitting here and thinking about who her husband should be and I've decided I must leave it in the hands of your miraculous madonna *negra*, La Divina Pastora. Remember that the pearls which adorn her dress are the original pearls which came from Aracataca with the first of the Monagas child-brides. A fitting madonna to find a husband for this bride-to-be, my daughter, Sou Sou.'

'Of course, I shall certainly pray for the child, and for a husband who will bring her celestial happiness.'

'Don't ask for too much, Father; a husband will be sufficient, as long as he's not an Englishman.' The priest knew what she meant.

'Poor child, she must think I want her to be a nun, I've neglected her for so long. Margarita can be the nun. That should shake up the convent, from what Ernestine has told me. But it's only puppy play. And Quentino, he can be the priest. We need a pope in the family. We need a pope to put this family straight.' Elena Elena picked up her telescope and spied it upon the island of Monos. 'One day I will build a house there and go and live like an anchorite. I hope you get your wine and your unleavened bread, priest. Find Sou Sou her husband, and there is no knowing what else I might do for you.'

Father Eugenio, a Capuchin who came from a good family he said, well born as his name signified, said he would begin a novena, starting with early morning mass the next day.

'Let's hope it's nine days, or at most nine months, Father, not nine years to marry off this daughter of mine.'

When Father Eugenio left with his mission to the mediatrix of all graces, Elena Elena took the sheets of paper from under the floorboards and wrote down her thoughts, and then secreted the paper beneath the pitchpine floor again. 'They'll find these one day and know the kind of woman I was.'

That evening, after the parish priest had gone, wondering at her eloquence and wisdom even though she had deprived herself of the sacraments all these years, Elena Elena, using her telescope, was the first to see the reappearance of the comet in the sky over the Gulf of Sadness and her elation dropped. She nearly swallowed her heart. She could not believe her misfortune, that just when she had decided to emerge from her solitude, God should let her down. That just when she had decided to sew new clothes for her young naked children and darn some of their old clothes, just when she had decided to marry off her daughter Sou Sou with the help of La Divina Pastora, the heavens should herald the parasite that had enmeshed her family since the beginning of this new world.

But then she noticed that the sunset was saffron, and the blood which bled that evening over the mountains of the continent of Bolivar was the colour of paprika, its flames the yellow of cumin. The clouds over the Gulf of Sadness were a cumulus of muslin, turbans for Muslims, dhotis and capras for Hindus. That sunset, as it flamed over the archipelago, jangled with the bracelets of Indian women with gold in their ears and noses, bangles around their ankles, their brown arms braceleted from wrist to elbow. They walked with all they possessed in the splendour of their poverty, the women saried and veiled with orhnis, the men capraed in the cloth of the subcontinent, off the *Fatel Rozack*, which brought them from the black hole of Calcutta, from Bengal and the fields of Uttar Pradesh, clasping in their hands the papers of indentureship as they stepped ashore on to Nelson Island to be quarantined and disinfected before the march into the canefields of Kairi, the Gangetic plain of the new world, the river-bed of the ancient Orinoco. 'You see, Ernestine, you people don't want to work, you want freedom, yes, but how are things to work, how am I to cope with this estate, again overrun with the parasite? Well, take a look, here, take a look through this telescope. What the Lord takes away with one hand he gives with another.' Ernestine, the black woman, put her eye to the glass and came face to face with Madoo, who was to come to be a gardener on Pepper Hill, and later factotum of the house in town. Madoo Krishnasingh, Madoo, son of God.

'Salaam, salaam, salaam baas, salaam mam!'

'Madam, you people can do anything! Just so, you bring these people all this way to cut cane. Cheups'; Ernestine sucked her teeth in defiance.

'Not only cane, Ernestine. Cocoa! Child, you see him, my little god, Krishnasingh. My son of God. Maybe that La Divina Pastora is listening to Father Eugenio. Maybe he is well born after all, that priest.' Elena Elena threw back her head and laughed with that laughter which the people on Pepper Hill had come to recognise from the woman in the turret room. 'Maybe that little genie you see through that glass, maybe that little Gungadin' – Lavren gives to Elena Elena the benefits of his colonial literary education – 'Gungadin is going to work a miracle right here in this house.'

While Elena Elena laughed and the drumming of the tassa drums rocked the archipelago and the music from the sitar and flute drifted from the minarets with the prayers of the imam, and echoed in the domes with the pujah of the pundit, Madoo Krishnasingh, son of God, little Gungadin, came up to the house on Pepper Hill bringing the smell of freshly cut grass and the smell of cow-dung mixed with mud and the sticks of wattle, the smell of garlic and curry and the mysteries of sanskrit. 'Salaam, mam, salaam!' And then the barrack-rooms proliferated like witchbroom around the grounds of the great house, still bearing the scars of emancipation. They bred malaria, typhus, hookworm and internecine murder in the cramped hatches.

While Elena Elena takes Madoo down into the estate to show him the parasite, Lavren again leaves the turret room to consult the dusty tomes on tropical agriculture that Auguste had consulted in the last battle against the witchbroom. Elena Elena did not have the benefit of these tomes, but she now had the wisdom of of her Gungadin, her son of God, Madoo Krishnasingh. 'Wait till Father Eugenio sees how his prayers have been answered,' Elena Elena chuckled. He had elicted the prayers of other parish priests and the nuns, but the church used the appearance of the witchbroom to cash in on the people's superstition and again said it was because they did not pay their tithes. Archbishop Gaspar Grande de los Angelicos decided to promulgate a special edict on the appearance of the witchbroom and its significance as a curse on those who did not pay their money to the church.

Elena Elena told Father Eugenio that she would go into town again and give the Archbishop a piece of her mind, but in the meantime she had to fight back the parasite which again threatened her family's existence. The Englishman had shifted his concern to coffee and tobacco, and used the excuse of business to go up the islands on a sloop to Grenada, on the pretext of an interest in nutmeg and ginger, when it was in fact the nice Martiniquaise who interested him more. Elena Elena said to her cousins in Cascade that she didn't give a damn: 'Let him go, let him populate the archipelago. I have my little Gungadin dhotied and indentured to Pepper Hill.'

The fungus had come on the wind from Saramacca, in Surinam on the continent of Bolivar. It conceived itself in the wild Theobroma in the dark forests of that corner of Bolivar's continent. It spawned and multiplied in the wind troughs which eddied the waves on the Atlantic Ocean along the coast of the continent, and like all else that had conquered here, it blew through the Serpent's Mouth into the Gulf of Sadness and settled on the plantations in the mountains of Kairi, till eventually it settled on Elena Elena's cocoa estate at the top of Pepper Hill.

When, in the solitude of her turret room, Elena Elena first saw the comet in the sky over the Gulf of Sadness, she knew she would have to make the journey, like her ancestors, into the valleys to inspect the galls, the abnormal and deformed outgrowths. The presence of the comet had again thrown a net about the island to ensnare the family and their wealth. Elena Elena wondered if it was because she had retreated to the turret room and neglected her responsibilities. This fear, and her nightmares – the same ones which the little girl in a cotton chemise had had of the mass suicides and poisonings on her cousins' estates – returned to terrify her. She saw them again from the window, harnessed like cattle in their grotesque iron contraptions. By a coincidence of history she now saw other people in the barracks near the silk-cotton trees, Madoo and his breed of felons. Yes, he worked like one of his water-cattle which slouched in the canals on the plain, caked in mud, preyed on by egrets, but you couldn't trust him. 'Never trust a coolie' became a favourite Monagas statement, as they sat on their verandas in the evening, while the sun set like abeer on muslin in the Phagwa of a Chowtal springtime.

While the tassa drums beat in the barrack-rooms and the flambeaux flickered in the early evening, Margarita and Quentino performed a macabre pantomime on the back veranda even now, though she had darned their old clothes and was fast making some new tunics and frocks for the boy and girl; they confused even her by wearing each other's clothes, pretending to be the gender opposite to their own. 'Puppy play,' Elena Elena insisted, if any of the family saw anything amiss, or Father Eugenio found one morning that it was Margarita who was his acolyte at the morning mass, and not Quentino.

The condition of the trees, Madoo found out, was further irritated by insects. The web which was forming was fungoid and bacterial. No sooner had Elena Elena and Madoo entered the dark, dank, leaf-strewn path near the river, than they saw the first tufts and mass of interlacing twigs. Elena Elena's instant reaction was to ask for more sun and air. The Englishman had imported the immortelle trees from the region of Aracataca on the continent, to shade the cocoa trees, but this was not helping, and what they needed was light. Elena Elena ordered the immediate cutting down of the immortelle that sprinkled the mountain sides with their cinnamon-coloured flowers. Even though she had sent a letter to the Englishman at the new Planters' Club near the Marina rebuilt, after the recent fire, another riot, near the Cathedral of the Immaculate Conception, he did not bother to answer or come. She took more stringent measures than just letting in the sun and air. In order to halt the spread of the hypertrophy of the young shoots, and the effect it had in hardening and malforming the pods, the trees were severely pruned. This would, she was sure, nurture further growth.

The curse of Saramacca infected the imagination of the family and sent Elena Elena back to her turret room for months, making her forget the macabre ceremonies of the twins, making her forget her request to La Divina Pastora. Obviously this little god, Krishnasingh, her Gungadin, was not going to solve all her problems. Quentino, as would a future cousin, had begun to eat grass and decided to be a horse. The children were often found on the back veranda, with Margarita, herself naked with fresh young breasts, riding bareback the naked Quentino. Ernestine had given up hope and would simply raise her arms in despair, one day in the process dropping Elena Elena's lunch tray of clear chicken soup, a luncheon which became the custom of any member of the family with Elena in her name.

This is why, as Lavren is at this moment checking on the research of the bacterial epidemic, Marie Elena is sipping the chicken soup that Josephine has brought up to the turret room overlooking the Gulf of Sadness. The women of the family had discovered a way of placating the chronic indigestion that occurred in the pythonic labyrinthine intestines of the members of the family. Lavren was an exception, being so close to Marie Elena and often finding himself finishing off the soup she had left. Being a hermaphrodite, he partook of the best of both genders and usually had a look of total pleasure on his face because of his natural prolixity, though he could be saddened by his visions and the discomfort he constantly had in writing down all these things about the family. He finished the soup, mainly so as not to upset Josephine, who would have been offended if her soup had not been drunk completely. He burped and farted. The Monagas men belched a lot and tried to forget their pain in frequent copulation, masturbation and, though strenuously denied, sodomy.

In her newly elected solitude, Elena Elena invented a method of inoculating her cocoa trees to try to rid them of the epidemic. She believed her discovery was the result of an intervention by the Holy Ghost. She still wore black-dyed muslin and black lace mantillas in the evening. In daytime, wearing a black linen veil like a nun, she went about the estate. 'Madoo, Madoo Krishnasingh, come, let us go and fight this pestifirous pest of the Ganges,' an expression which Elena Elena invented one day when in a tantrum with Madoo himself, accusing him of being a pest. She never divulged the formula of the antidote she was using. While small changes in the deformed trees were detected by those who knew the worst, in the long run little changed, and though Elena Elena believed that the formula for the antidote she used in the inoculations was divinely inspired, she also believed that its ineffectiveness was because of her and her retreat to the turret room away from her family and her husband. God was punishing her. It was as simple as that. The disease that had racked her ancestor Marie Jeanne at San Raphael, took control of her, and she too believed that almost any act she committed or omitted was a sin and brought her to the brink of hell. She began to identify herself as the main reason for the upsurge of the witchbroom. It was clear that the inoculations were not working, had no effect on the corrugated twigs or the furrowed contours of the humps. All was turgid and malformed. The leaves were soft and flimsy, their colour darker than should be. The stalks were blighted and covered with curly white encrustations that turned the yellow of limes. The usual purple and golden pods became blotchy, blackened and hard. The estates were rotting. This epidemic was as bad as the one that had heralded the crucifixions of Arenales. Nature was revolting at what was being done upon the earth. The days were spent in vast expeditions overseen by Madoo, pruning and burning the limbs on which the parasite had lodged itself. Where there was no space for another fire, lest the whole estate go up in flames with high winds, they buried the diseased limbs in huge graves.

In the evening Elena Elena returned to the turret room, deciding now to allow the children to come and hear stories before they went to bed. She tried to make up for lost time with her love. She hoped to save Margarita and Quentino from their aberrations by giving them some of the love they had been deprived of. She kept an eye on the Gulf of Sadness and the plains of Kairi laid out before her, the view clearer because of the extensive demolition of the estate on the gulf's edge. The children were afraid at night because of the fires on the plains, as the sugarcane was being sabotaged yet again, and now by indentured labour. They were afraid too of the drums from the plains, the beating of the tassa drums, and while they felt somewhat safer in the day with the servants and Madoo, whom they knew, about the house, they were often witnesses to conversation and rumour which told them that all was not well. Elena Elena knew that the situation was no longer tenable; they would not be able to control it. They would be killed. Above all, as her husband kept saying in the Planters' Club, the situation was no longer profitable. Cocoa prices were dropping and there was a glut of cocoa from other dominions. Sugar had taken precedence, but even that was now becoming unprofitable.

Elena Elena decided, that before all the world as she knew it finally collapsed, she must marry off her daughter Sou Sou.

As we know, Elena Elena had sent Father Eugenio to his miraculous madonna, La Divina Pastora, to mediate on behalf of her delinquents, Margarita and Quentino, but also on behalf of her Sou Sou whom she could see turning into a spinster, marooned in the old estate house as the families from the other estates moved into town, leaving the dying cocoa trees. But, so far, all that La Divina Pastora seemed to offer her was Madoo and his breed, in the barrack-rooms to take the place of the slaves. With Madoo she could eke out a living, but she needed to get Sou Sou out of this place and launched on her own life. 'Poor girl.'

'Madam, what I tell you is, that no one going come to this house for a bride with Master Quentino and Miss Margarita going about the place like they were children, and what children!'

'So, what would you have me do, Ernestine?'

'Madam, is the house too, and – excuse me if I say it – well, Madam, is you.' Ernestine was taking a chance, but Elena Elena was willing to try anything, even the advice of a servant. After all, it was Ernestine who had been here since the beginning of time and knew everything there was to know.

'Go ahead, child.'

'Madam, people fraid you. You up here all alone by yourself, people talking.'

'Talking? What are they saying?'

'Madam, I don't exactly want to say, but as you ask me. Well, you know, they say you up here, eating nothing but chicken broth, and the children running wild and the house falling down. Well, they laughing.' Ernestine was looking down at the floor, afraid herself to see how Elena Elena, her madam, was taking this.

'I know all of that. Very well. What are we going to do? You tell me.'

'Madam, we have to make the house nice, pick some flowers, tidy up the yard. That old piano, is so long now since I hear you playing it. If we make the place nice and cheerful, maybe some of the mister and them from town, or the overseers from the other estate will come and call and maybe, you never know, take a little fancy to Miss Sou Sou.'

'Ernestine, I think you are the answer to my prayers all along. You, right here in front of me. We'll try it. Tell Madoo to sweep out the yard and then start scrubbing and polishing floors. We're going to invite people.'

So it was, as it had proved on so many occasions in history, a black woman saved the day; a black woman and an Indian man, indentured to the old run-down cocoa estate of the Monagas de los Macajuelos. The place was a hive of activity. The brass was cleaned with sand and sour oranges, the pitchpine floors were scrubbed with bicarbonate of soda, the old mahogany furniture was polished. Madoo oversaw his wife and children dusting the crystals in the chandelier, polishing the silver which Elena Elena had to count before it was given over to those coolies: linen was darned and ironed, and fresh water put into the tins in which the tables stood to prevent ants from climbing into the sugar bowl. 'Ernestine, I want you to keep a sharp eye on those coolies.'

'Yes, Madam.' So, Ernestine fussed and managed her madam's affairs.

Then Madoo had to take the buggy and go into town to pick up Miss Metivere to come and make Sou Sou some evening dresses, to show her off to those young men Elena Elena began to imagine would be clamouring for her daughter. Elena Elena could not afford to buy any new materials, so it was a matter of opening old trunks and cutting up dresses she hadn't worn since she had decided to wear nothing but black. 'That old priest. I haven't seen him for weeks, but maybe his madonna is performing some miracles. Miss Metivere, you are certainly performing miracles here with all this sewing.' Sou Sou was shy at first, but then she began to fill out into the dresses which little Miss Metivere conjured out of Elena Elena's old rags.

In the evening, Elena Elena still insisting on her widow's weeds, 'Because, you know, Father Eugenio, I don't have a husband. He died on the first night of our marriage. And I've never even spoken to him.'

'The madonna, my child, have faith, can change even that.'

'We'll see, Father, but while I wouldn't like you to lose your faith, I would like you to use your influence with the priests and nuns in town. Margarita and Quentino, I can't have them here when I entertain Sou Sou's prospective suitors. See what you can do for an old woman who has had to bear far too many trials. And all your madonna has sent me is a little Hindu God from Calcutta. Bless that little man. I can't trust him, but he can work like a slave.'

'I will see what I can do, my daughter. They may very well have vocations. All that passion of theirs maybe has been going the wrong way. Let us direct it upwards. Yes, I think you may be right. I will see if Quentino can't go into the monastery and Margarita into the convent with the enclosed Carmelites.' Elena Elena shut her ears to their pleading the day Father Eugenio came to fetch them for the journey into town.

Marcel de Pompignon called for cocktails. He could hardly climb the stairs to the veranda without falling asleep because of the soporific feeling which suffused the old estate house, lit with its candles in the newly cleaned chandelier and full of the piano playing of Elena Elena. As it was the first visit Sou Sou, in one of Miss Metivere's creations out of nothing, sat demurely, while Marcel was forced to repeat his genealogy to the persistent questioning of Elena Elena. She had been a recluse for so long she could not remember who the families were, and she did not want to take the risk of being landed with one of the bastards whom they used to leave up on the estates to keep them out of town society. Also, she had to be sure about the pigmentation, the texture of the hair. She didn't want any little nigger boy for a grandchild, any of the outside children masquerading as family. So by the time Elena Elena was finished with her inquisition, Sou Sou and Marcel had had a chance to view each other for only an hour.

'No, my dear, you couldn't possibly contemplate the sacrament of marriage with that. It is obvious why his parents have left him up here in the hills. That look, you can see that look. This has been our problem all along, intermarrying. His parents are first cousins: not even the papal dispensation could prevent the curdling of his brain and that mongoloid look. No, my Sou Sou, we are not that desperate.'

'Mama, he was nice, kind looking.'

'Yes, my dear, that may be so, but let's look to the future. We have to provide the next century with a change, fresh blood.'

By the end of the year they had vetted every possible eligible bachelor up on the old, run-down cocoa estates. They had invited the overseers from the sugarcane estates on the plains and beyond the hill of San Andres. The story which went around the place was that by the time these young men were finished with their cocktails they were wondering whether it was the mother or the daughter they had come to look at. Elena Elena could not believe that the families had become so degenerate. There had been no new blood for years. Either they were mongoloid like Marcel de Pompignon, or a fairy, like Jean-Marc Agostini, or uneducated like the fifteen or so de Verteuils who came, all pretending to be charming and bringing messages from their mothers whom Elena Elena had forgotten. 'No, my dear, this is ridiculous. Well, I suppose I have my Margarita and Quentino; imagine if I was trying to marry those two off.' Lavren marvelled, in his own ambisexuality, at these specimens of intermarriage. He suppressed his laughter so as not to wake Marie Elena and have her vet what he was writing.

Then one day Elena Elena's favourite cousin, Iseult, from Cascade Estate outside town, sent a letter by messenger that a young man, a distant cousin, had just arrived by boat from France, a de Lanjou. The name sent a thrill through Elena Elena's spine. That madonna was performing miracles after all. This was like the ancient days, a de Lanjou of the de Lanjou from the Basses Pyrenees in the Mazzerolles had arrived in Kairi like a suitor of ancient times, when the de Lanjou had come to Aracataca for the child brides of the Monagas de los Macajuelos. She noticed that morning that her eucharist lilies on the veranda had suddenly bloomed. She had been getting Madoo to water them for the last few weeks to no avail. This must be it. She immediately sent the messenger with a reply which was written on her special note-paper, which she still kept under the floorboards, perfumed with tonca beans. It was a short message: 'My dear Iseult, send him. E. E.' Then she went herself with Sou Sou to the shrine of La Divina Pastora, the divine shepherdess, and bestowed upon the already weighed-down madonna three of the pearl necklaces which the Englishman had given her, in attempt to woo her into his hammock the last time he had visited.

Ramon de Lanjou, his very name a contradiction and mixture of events, visited the house on Pepper Hill on a Sunday morning when Elena Elena had organised a picnic for the young cousins, who came up from town to go bathing in the river at the bottom of Pepper Hill. It was at the bathing party that the suitor from the old world, miraculously transported to this place of the new world by the power of the divine shepherdess, La Divina Pastora, first encountered the last daughter of the Englishman and Elena Elena Monagas de los Macajuelos. Iseult, the cousin from Cascade, who had first announced the arrival of this new blood, did not tell Ramon about her niece in the cocoa hills and the mother who was desperate to marry her off. The picnic was an innocent Sunday frivolity; the cousins in the cocoa hills were family. And, neither did Elena Elena say anything to Sou Sou about the young Ramon. Of course she had exchanged more letters with Iseult and knew now that he was a doctor. This surpassed her expectations, thinking that she would have to be content with a planter's or a merchant's son.

Sou Sou had grown in confidence after all the practice of receiving the leftover sons of the creole families, whom Elena Elena called reprobates. It was as if no one was good enough for her. She was almost ready to reject Ramon de Lanjou herself, and at first she could not understand her mother's charm and acquiescence all through the picnic by the river pool, hanging on every word of the young doctor, trained at l'École Normale and the Sorbonne.

Soon he was calling every other evening at six. Here, in the tradition of the creole families which was passed to all members of the family of Monagas de los Macajuelos into the next century, they sat on their veranda in the magic twilight when the fireflies, caught by the servants, were placed in calabashes with cutouts, glittering like lanterns and hung in the eaves, lighting up the place as at Diwali, and sipped cocktails, as they were called, punches made of rum, lime and sugar cooled with handfuls of crushed ice, aphrodisiacs for some, sleeping pills for others and the cause of insomnia in Elena Elena.

Then they sat on the rattan chairs on the veranda. The large rocking-chair was left for Elena Elena. When Ernestine had brought out rum punches on a tray and they had each had one, Elena Elena went into the drawing-room to play the piano. The old house began to imitate some of its past grandeur. Elena Elena's departure from the veranda allowed the travelling doctor Ramon to woo Sou Sou. They sat and sipped their punches slowly. This was quite a different seduction to the one that had taken place in the Convent of the Immaculate Heart of Mary in Aracataca. Ramon did not bring tamarind balls and there were no ants encrusted with sugar glittering like diamanté. Ramon wooed Sou Sou with words, with the poetry he had learnt when studying in Europe. He wooed her with small presents. He bought her a comb, a silver pin, a shawl embroidered with English flowers and some black lace, which made the black-lace dress afterwards given to her daughter Marie Elena, that later bewitched Lavren. He developed in her a taste for things from away, wooing her with stories from his travels around the island of Kairi and to different parts of the world on ships. He wanted Sou Sou to be able to travel with him and make him comfortable when he was working. Sou Sou was glad he was a good man. She did not want to live with a man like her father. But, being Elena Elena's daughter, she was a little suspicious and knew, from stories of past Monagas women, that she had to look out to see what men would do. But like all Monagas women she kept these things in her heart like the Blessed Virgin Mary. There she pondered them.

Lavren could see through the sepia of time, through the jaundiced, malarial time, to when Ramon the travelling doctor would grow thinner than he was now. He had already suffered two bouts of malaria. This affliction sunk his cheeks and emphasised his cheekbones, giving him a gaunt but haunting beauty that Elena Elena told her daughter reflected inner beauty. 'Look into those deep-set eyes, my child. I see the promise of tenderness. A tenderness I did not receive.' At times Ramon got confused, wondering if he was being wooed by the mother and not the daughter.

Lavren could see through the moth-eaten time to when the beautiful Sou Sou – her beauty was in evidence now that Quentino and Margarita had been sent to the monastery and the convent, allowing her paleness to disappear, her fear to subside – would become the regal woman whom Ramon took to Queen Victoria's Diamond Jubilee. Lavren could see, through the dark shadows of nitrate negatives that haunted his middle life, the flounces on her gown, the flowers on her bosom and the scalloped ruffles of her skirt as she sits poised for a royal occasion, her right arm of porcelain arranging the stem of a flower while her left lies along her silken lap, holding a closed fan in her hand. This apparition is crowned with her black hair swept to the crown, a nimbus of softness. Lavren can see, through the torn edges of time, this paragon of Pepper Hill, whose real name remains forgotten even to Lavren and history and, time eternal, is left with the sweet diminutive Sou Sou, which a child might call her cat, but was the affectionate diminutive the Englishman always whispered to his daughter when he had her on his knee, claiming her as his favourite pet in order to make his wife jealous.

Lavren can see through troubled and changing time to when Sou Sou is not the diminutive given by an incestuous father to his little pet, but the affectionate cry of children for their stricken mother; she whose first child was snatched away by malaria in the mosquito-infested swamps, who became the mother of many children and grew fat with childbirth and inertia, sitting in comfortable armchairs mending the dozens of pants and dresses of her children as she served tea on a veranda suffocated with the perfume of the eucharist lilies, that reminded all the family of the first seduction of the family at Aracataca. But these things were to come and change them utterly.

It is unfair of Lavren to herald events in this way. Excuse his obsession with history, the future of the world and the images that spring from his fertile memory. Let us listen here to this young and innocent couple in the restraint of their passion and love, as they sip rum punches prepared by Ernestine and brought in on a silver tray.

'My dear, you must understand that you can always come back to your mother any time, when you want to. But we won't be going too far and there will be a buggy for you to use and a groom to drive you. You mustn't worry, I insist.' Ramon tried to quieten the fears uppermost in Sou Sou, in this woman who seemed like a child but was nearly twenty-five, and had been thought destined for the shelf for ever. Sou Sou's fear was passion.

Lavren says passion. But what passion was there? Ramon was almost completely debilitated by the malaria that kept recurring, and Sou Sou, who had witnessed her mother's retreat to the turret room from the Englishman, had a fear of passion between men and women. She was not like her sister and brother Quentino and

Margarita, who were ruled by passion, as she had heard Father Eugenio tell Elena Elena one day.

Ramon's assurance was to Sou Sou's plea: 'Mummy says you are a good man, but I don't want to leave my Mummy and my home and Ernestine.'

Ramon understood a sign he had seen in other members of the family and which Lavren knows gets repeated down the centuries, that members of the family had a deep reluctance to leave their mothers and the mothers had a deep reluctance to give up their children, be they boys or girls. Lavren, through Ramon's insight, understood that this was because the women of the Monagas family found love in their children when they could not find love in men.

Sou Sou continued to be wooed with words: words from medicine, philosophy and theology. She did not understand, but she allowed herself to be seduced by the sound of them and what she imagined they meant, which was not very much. But she felt that her husband was clever. Ramon wrote philosophical and theological essays in his spare time.

Elena Elena was adamant that before they left the house on Pepper Hill, a move forced upon the family by the collapse of the cocoa price and the spread of the witchbroom, she would marry off her daughter to the travelling doctor, Ramon de Lanjou. While the plains of Kairi burned with the sabotage of indentured labour, while the drums and dancing filled the night, the Monagas de los Macajuelos prepared to marry off their daughter, in the last of the days when cocoa was crumbling. King Cocoa was dead. The Englishman came home and behaved himself with the young girls in the barracks, and visited his bastard heirs to prevent them from coming up to the house to embarrass him. By this time he had populated almost half the village.

Elena Elena decided to come down from the turret room and share her marriage bed with the Englishman. No one dreamt that they would share the Savannah, as the family called this bed, which was reputed to have been built by Georges Philippe for his child bride Elena. Other members of the family hold that it was built by Gaston for Clarita. Elena Elena felt that it was right that she should be in her marriage bed with her husband on the day her daughter got married.

Ernestine organised the young girls in the back. Madoo, with the young fellas from the barracks, erected a huge tent made from bamboo poles and the branches of palms and coconut trees, which extended out from the front veranda and around the side of the house. They tried to recreate the splendour of old times. More servants were brought in from the villages, given a bath and a change of clothes – white livery – to serve as waiters and cooks, and as nurses to look after the innumerable children who came from the other estate houses and from the house in San Jorge de Monagas and from New Town. Though Elena Elena had fallen out with Archbishop Gaspar Grande de los Angelicos, he sent a personal emissary to insist that he come to the church in Gran Couva to perform the nuptial mass. More servants to assist the aunts were detailed off to the church to pick and arrange flowers in the sanctuary and down the aisle of the church. Elena Elena sent Madoo down to town to fetch Miss Metivere to make the wedding dress out of the last moth-eaten remnants of her own. The Count of Couva sent crates of Champagne and Sauternes. All the families were invited with their sons and daughters; descendants of Roume St Laurent, the cousins of Count Lopinot, the haut aristocracie, cousin de Lapeyrouse, Vessiny, Agostini, Salvatori, Cipriani, de Verteuil, Farfan de los Godes, Lange and other lesser families of Irish and English descent, Knox and Fitt, all arrived. They came in their numbers and swelled the house on Pepper Hill in the passing of the age when King Cocoa was bewitched by the witchbroom and world prices. The comet made a freak appearance over the Gulf of Sadness, and the turds on the morning of the wedding foretold what Sou Sou in her middle age was to deplore: how everyone was getting like any Portuguese shopkeeper and setting up import and export on the wharf.

The five tiers of iced wedding cake, each tier given by a different family, rose like a cathedral spire crowned with a small silver vase of orchids. The mahogany table gleamed beneath the lace tablecloth edged with asparagus fern and rosebuds. Asparagus fern trailed the arches between the room and the entrances to the verandas. Ramon's parents sent expensive presents from Paris and London and these were displayed on mahogany side-tables to remind everyone of former times, when Cocoa was King. The first photographer to work on Kairi, Monsieur Felix Marin, came in a special carriage with all his equipment, which he had brought from Paris, to record the last of the great marriages, as witchbroom entangled the fortunes of the Monagas de los Macajuelos.

After this chaotic extravagance had taken place while the canefields burned on the plains of Kairi and the gayelle was lively with stick fight and cock fight, Ernestine hung out the marriage sheets the next morning in the sun to bleach out the bloodstains of the broken hymen of Sou Sou, who nine months later would give birth to her first son Pablosito, who was quickly snatched away by a malaria epidemic.

'Salaam baas, salaam!' The latest voice of the century echoed down the years, stumbling upon its own solution to the new world.

A JOURNAL

1 September

AS THE TALES of Lavren unfolded, I found myself inextricably, almost insidiously, seeking out the conclusion of a quite different story. This I must return to tell. I must take over from Lavren. I keep it within my journal. This house told me another tale, or hinted, leading me on a wild-goose chase of clue, sensation, memory and feeling, the torn edges of a sepia photograph, an old daguerreotype, a bundle of baby's clothes, a black lace dress, a mother-of-pearl crucifix and the items of my father's press. His voice, now that he is dead. I itemise and it seems a list set out in positions of priority or importance, but that is not what happened at all. I was led and made to progress, a word suggesting far too absolutely a forward movement, when in fact this story was not to be told by linear progression but rather by a process of simultaneities: yes, I think that's it.

Lavren, my narrator, demanded more: more space for his tales, his history, his digressions, his exaggerations and fantasies. You've seen his fragments of tale, his fugues. He revels in the grandeur of carnival, its noise and colour, like he was playing mas in a historical band with his storytellers Pierrot and Robberman.

I have a plainer style. I have the sentences of my colonial education. Secretly, I envy him his creole loudness. He would paint in oils, big canvases in oil. I would paint in watercolours like my aunt.

I need the specific moment. There, the sky as it is now, this instant, there, that egret as it turns pink in the setting sun. I need to get back to the immediate, to the fleeting. Lavren works at permanence. Setting up his solid structures, his tales. I merely take notes, keep this journal. I expect we've got digression in common.

3 September

Sometimes in the photographs, one of the ones I find in the house, the edges blur and I see that the pain which is this body, this heart, seeks out the black face in the background, the woman in the white starched cap and apron who stands to assist her madam, or holds the baby, and I say, 'My pain is not like your pain, but the edges blur.'

Antoinetta says in a voice I give her, speaking with a love that I remember, 'I know your pain. I live and serve in your houses. I love you as my own when I yearn for my own black child body near my skin in the bare room, alone at night beneath the house, and I can't even bring you into my bed to comfort me. Madam never give she child away. I miss my own child.'

She knows my pain but how do I approach hers, that double century of ancestral pain? How tell it? How presume to tell it? Yet I must not forget. I must keep the remembering.

There were stories I could not tell, and I hoped their voices in Lavren's preposterous narratives would speak out from where they stood.

Both stories were of pain, mine and hers, autobiography and herstory. They both began to merge as stories I could not go near, but would have to wait in this house for them to approach me. I would have to listen to their voices. If there was method in this it was the method of memory. The clear balanced sentence, the sequential paragraph would not always do, the linear logic would not hold. Lavren would have to take hold.

But as I look back, read over that distanced piece, the way I once began before I allowed Lavren his tales, the 'he' is I. I notice even there the elements of the story. Even there, there were clues and hints: decay, my father's press, my father, my mother, voices, Antoinetta, the portfolio of watercolours, the Indian boys, the plains and the river. I lay them out like artefacts in my museum. Here was a skeleton of place, people, and one or two things. Later, I would go down river or, leaving the gulf, enter the river mouth from the Gulf of Sadness into the tales. Here was a plot. Semblance of plot.

I begin with these, and with dreams, in a place where both remembering and forgetting are inventive. I must listen to the story which approaches me in a dream.

Cric, Lavren says.

Crac, I urge him on.

10 September

I work at this journal, this chronicle of my heart, in the evenings. Lavren takes up all my mornings; in the afternoon I'm at the museum. Acting Curator. It's leisurely, administrative but easy. There's not much there. It's a matter of supervising the women who dust; I put it like that. We have ideas for the future. I like it most when there is, believe it or not, a dig; then we return to some old midden, and even undertake new ones. More recently I've been visiting old spots whose names echo, but the ground yields little which is immediately relevant, though unsuspected things emerge. Recently I've been in the Tamana foothills. I am prospecting to see what can be done to conserve, create interest, give a sense of history; actually it's an adjunct of the tourist industry, picnic spots. But I've found myself alone at the end of the day in the presence of something else.

Today, the others, the museum assistant, the diggers, had left earlier and I had not quite finished taking notes and measuring out a square where we thought we might put up a signboard with details of the place. They gave me such a fright. All of a sudden, a terrifying screech, and it seemed as if all the trees around the clearing were alive with green parrots. The hysteria continued long after they had flown off. It was getting dark and all the way back down to the plains I could not get their hysteria out of my mind.

Lavren would tell his tales, I would tell mine. I allow him his metaphors. What would be my metaphors? Can I have my own carnival? Wear my own mask?

12 September

It's a rather shabby place where I work, the old Royal Museum. Three floors. On the ground floor, glass cases of Carib and Arawak pottery, sharp points, artefacts, and then there is a miscellaneous collection of old estate-yard reliquaries: a piece of an old plantation water wheel, a copper, iron contraptions which manacled wrists, shackled ankles, subdued the writhing torso, bits to silence the tongue, weights to bow the head, whips. A logbook of one of the ships with numbers, the markings of one from Bristol, another from Liverpool, that port where the bricks are cemented with the blood of Africans and Negro heads stare from the walls of the Custom's

House. Schoolteachers tell the parties of children, who come to learn history, that they are reminders. You could make something of this, but we haven't the resources, they say. On the second floor is a small gallery: old prints, watercolours and oils by local artists. My aunt exhibited here. I think there is one of hers here permanently, *Immortelle Glade*. In the far corner there is the great nineteenth-century master, Cazabon. There are a lot of still lives of fruits, mangoes, pawpaws, starapples and bananas, amongst the seascapes, landscapes and forests, not many portraits. And then, in an annexe off this small gallery, another room for carnival costumes collected over the last couple of decades or so. Very dusty and peculiarly dead. They live and move when inhabited. You can see why I prefer to be out and about, instead of being on these floors or in my hot little office off the second floor when the still air is pushed by the whirr of the ceiling fan and the papers on my desk flutter. My glass of lemonade sweats. The third floor is empty. I go up there sometimes just to get a sense of what might be. I call it the museum of air. Who will fill the museum of air?

So there you have it. That's what I actually do: in the afternoons. At dawn Lavren sits at this desk. I need to state these things categorically for myself, so that when I return, I know who I am. As dawn approaches I lose hold, I lose myself.

3 October – morning

I'm up early by myself, finishing last night's notes before my mother rises and Antoinetta arrives from the village where she now lives. My mother will leave this month, following the departed family. Still the old fear remains: miscegenation. I'm here to help, but have my own reasons. I wish to witness the end. This is the last haul. Blank spaces are edged and squared with dust where pictures once hung upon the walls, portraits of grandparents, the picture of the Sacred Heart. In this house the furniture gathered to the centre of the drawing-room is for cousins, in the dining-room for sale. Antoinetta has chosen her pieces. There is hardly anywhere to sit. I use one of the upstairs bedrooms.

Will I have an hour before she stirs? I sit with memory and I keep this record, this chronicle of the heart.

I sit at the oval table, shrunk to a round by taking out one of its leaves. My place used to be at the edge, at her side, not quite having a proper place. Here I could have my meat cut, my rice shovelled. My father sits at the other end and they, brothers and sisters, sit around, and Antoinetta is at the pantry door, is at the correct side where vegetables are served. We are the protagonists of this tale, which comes to me in this house.

Peace. The Indian boys mowed the lawn yesterday. The rains have abated. Dawn can be a crash of machinery through grass. Funny how some of the old ways continue. Boys come up to the house to mow the lawn. *Salaam, salaam* . . .

I wish to hold this room in perpetuity for me, for them, before the removal trucks, before they, the family, that breed of blood cousins, all come for the bits and pieces. Nothing precious here, not to them. But still they come just in case: a linen tablecloth, lace, a jewel. Corbeaux, over a dead thing.

The house sweats. It breathes. They are still here, the others. I draw back the frayed and faded curtains which gives me the savannah, and just, almost imperceptibly, my aunt's watercolour mountains. I notice the rust where the curtain rings have bled on to the faded yellow. Why can't I let go? Yes, these things will be dispersed and still I won't let go. Still I hold to them, to this especial scene. Once more . . . I will describe it, once more. I haul them like the rest of the bric-a-brac through the centuries, through these houses, through the forests, hysterical with amnesia.

Here, I place them here, as reminders.

When I come down the pitchpine stairs and leave her upstairs sleeping her snoring sleep, a woman with almost as many years as this century of pain, I stand and stare at the room below, in this last of the houses, in the last estate bungalow. This was a manager's bungalow. Managing. They managed. They managed very well, didn't they? They were all that I have to look back on: ancestral entrepreneurs, planters, managers, merchants. It took them a while to realise that they were no better than any Portugee, coolie, or Chinaman with his shop. *Lazy niggers, never did any work.* This is one of the voices which speaks in a simple little bungalow on the plains, the last of the houses. *Can't trust a coolie.* We grew that way, locked up at the top of a hill, looking down, sloping lawns, and beyond the bougainvillaea hedge, the other life. Then, some dispersed, the diaspora, the desperate flight from black people. As far as the antipodes.

Yesterday was the beginning of the dig, as it were. This bungalow, a midden. The results of the excavation, the retrievals and the piling up of the keepsakes are on the floor in front of the linen cupboard. I have agreed to assist with this task as a daughter might, but not quite. No, not quite. My father had wanted a daughter. I know that. No, I dreamt that.

My life is folded here like linen or freshly laundered and pressed clothes. I don't wish to open the pages of this book. I resist Lavren. I have my own story. Maybe, when I open the doors of this linen press, dead leaves and the dust of moths' wings will fall out, accompanied by the alleluia of archangels, on to me and her sitting there patiently. How lucky for Lavren. He can fill his presses with dead leaves, moths' wings and the song of archangels. His doors can be battered by the wings of a devil. I envy his imagination, his metaphorical element. What are my metaphors?

I hold the silver key threaded with a piece of blue ribbon, always blue. Blue is the colour of Our Lady. I've pulled a heavy mahogany chair for her to sit on.

'Fetch me down those linen mats, dear,' she says.

She's been planning this task for weeks. I stand like a servant (or as I said, a daughter). I stand as I saw young black girls stand and wait for her instructions. How could someone I love be at the same time immortalised as Madam? I look out of the window into another time; in the yard under a mango tree, a groom is standing beside a horse, handing the reins to him whom I longed for in khaki and white and a cork hat, 'Gee up . . . whoa.'

'Madam?'

'Bring those clothes, girl.' The young black girl raked in the dirty laundry of the family. I handed her the pile of linen mats, the open pages of a book.

Here are written all our lives. She begins to read here, in these embroidered hieroglyphs, the story of her children and her ancestors. She will name names. I leave the names out. Lavren will play old mas with them all. I put it another way in this chronicle of my heart.

'Darling, those mats with the forget-me-nots (those English

flowers); I so remember when she did those. They were her first work on the Singer sewing-machine. I must keep them . . . my only daughter's work.' Only daughter?

As she turns the linen in an old pair of hands, I turn the pages of Lavren's tales. At last he has his way with me, as the last egrets leave the swamp to forage on savannahs . . . the elation of morning.

Cric, he says.

Crac, I say.

15 October

She's gone. Flew off by jet, beating the tarmac, roaring, rising slowly above the foothills, soaring aunty's watercolour mountains sprinkled with cinnamon and saffron, immortelle and pouis. The rains are going to come soon again. Now is *Petit Careme* – the little Lent. It's like an Indian summer, they used to say.

She reaches through the clouds to a blueness that I can hardly imagine. She disappears, a silver line speeding through blue up the archipelago, the one chain which is our only hope. Already I miss her, but I am relieved at her going.

I can now write without interruption. Her presence in the next room was a censor. I can still hear her mind, sounding like the keskidee in the almond tree, my conscience outside my window. I can hear her French on the telephone to Aunt Marie, *Qu'est ce qu'il dit?* when I was a little boy and she didn't want me to understand what she was saying. And I sought the silk of her hem to suck my thumb. Now she wants to know what I'm writing, *Qu'est ce qu'il dit?* she asks herself. I can't tell her, but I want to. I want her to understand. I need her to understand before she dies, or I do, and then there is no more time and only regret and guilt following behind forever, till Lapeyrouse Cemetery where my father is buried claims us with the rest.

Maybe there will be a way in a future, contrived by me in a fiction, to speak plainly to each other without regret or guilt.

Secrets kept for a lifetime. 'Later, not now.'

Because she would only blame herself and say, 'It's my fault.' You see what I mean. 'I shouldn't have let her play with you. I shouldn't have let her dress you up.' My innocent playmate. Or then she goes on with the blame, 'I didn't love you enough. In the right way.' Not enough! Imagine! Imagine a love like ours and think that it was not enough. Should I reach here for the letters, quote your letters, evidence of that passion?

I hear her saying in an early letter when I used to be away. She hears my voice in the breeze off the savannah. She calls out when a door opens and slams shut, or a window bangs. She's alone with my father. 'Darling,' that's me, 'I miss you. The house is empty without you.' But it was her passion that I followed. I left home for the cross, for the cave in the mountainside, the celibate's retreat. I retrace these steps back down the mountainside to the house on the plains in order to understand what happened.

'I want to be a monk.' She turns to look at the picture of the Sacred Heart. Then I left the house in the heat of the afternoon with the car tyres crunching on the gravel down to the gap.

Now, the creak on the stair is my step. She calls out when she's lost something or left her glasses on her dressing-table, 'Your eyes are so good. You are my eyes.' My eyes fade now, they dim. I remember having to look between the pitchpine floorboards for needles which she had dropped off her lap when she was sewing, mending, darning.

The creak on the stairs are her footsteps now. I call out, 'Mummy.' She is not here. I detect that it is a leak from the rusty guttering, drip, drop, on the awning over the kitchen window, like the creak on the stairs. Desire and fear.

It is three o'clock in the afternoon, the sun burning the gravelled road; the sugarcane grass swaying along either side, swishing, blown by the wind, which blew with heat. Bits of the asphalted road, hot, sticky now, burning, stuck to the soles of my feet, soothing cold on the green and spotted white veranda tiles. I run on to the polished floor of the drawing-room. Anthuriums, standing stark pink against the creamy wall. The door against the gale blowing through the window, in the room my mother lying on the bed. I lie, put my arm across her breasts, and inadvertently hurt her, pushing her spectacles against her tired face. Yes, I retrieve that. Love and hurt.

I have driven back over the plains from the airport. My eyes are blinded as I drive into the setting sun, going down over the gulf. There, in V-shape formation level with the mountains, are the white egrets flying back to the swamp, turning pink then yellow as they flap into the sun after a day of foraging on the savannah of Aripo. They punctuate my day. They decide its beginning and bring it to a close. My father loved them. Sometimes I think I've become him. Now that my mother has gone, it's his voice I hear, him that I feel just beneath my skin.

There is time to put all this down, then, when she returns we'll have to close this house, end the chapter, put an end to this life. Close the estate.

1 November – All Saints' Day

palimpsest *n. & adj.* [from Latin *palimpsestus*; from Greek *palin* again + *psao* to rub smooth] Writing material, manuscript, original writing on which has been made room for a second; ∼ *adj.* so treated.

. . . the plains remain, the gulf, the mountains and the bungalow breathe and whisper to me . . . of passion . . . they have not gone . . . the linen-cupboard door hangs open, and folded there in her best linen are the leaves of my book embroidered into the tapestry of conquest, the history of cruelty in all its grandeur . . .

palin – again
psao – to rub smooth

. . . upon each fiction another story is written, other chronicles of the new world, documents of the heart . . . *palin* – again, *psao* – to rub smooth the pain from the crimes of passion on the shores of the Gulf of Sadness.

This entry follows the above etymology (a note to myself, a guide to you?) to help you with this tale, this other tale I find myself trying to tell. Lavren is a good storyteller when he keeps to it and does not digress to give you his own views or his distortions of poor Marie Elena's stories. Though I must confess to liking these flights of his. Marie Elena can hardly defend herself now, but I trust his love for her. Then there is his or her conflation of history, the way decades elide. Must be to do with this living between elements, all this swimming and surfacing, so much more bouyancy and ease in the water. Anyway, I can promise you an easier diversion from the extravagances of Lavren's tale. This time at least. I try to keep to my plainer style.

2 November – All Souls' Day

The house is empty. Now that she's gone away, it is he whom I hear in his silence. His silence draws me. The silence we must keep.

10 November

After the trip to San Raphael I kept wondering about the passion of parents, their lovemaking. Tomorrow afternoon the Minister of Tourism and Culture wishes to erect a plaque in that ancient place, so I won't have to go into town to the museum. I'll take the old road and reach San Raphael through the backroads. Foothills and savannah. I will go again to the place at Tamana where I heard the hysteria of the parrots. The Catholic Church wants to make it a place of pilgrimage and erect three crosses.

Yesterday, one of the women, dusting a piece of Carib pottery, dropped it, and it immediately became a heap of dust, not fragments or recognisable pieces. Dust.

I close the tales to open them again in the morning, elated by egrets.

8 December – Feast of the Immaculate Conception: dreaming

Last night, coming in through the back door in the darkness, trying to find a candle, the house smelt of old candle grease, dead anthuriums and the new flame burning a new candle in my hand. The smell of altars. I knew where to put my hands; leaving my body in the flicker, they reached out to touch what they knew would be there, the familiar feeling of the things of this house, that safe feeling of having been here before. Then in an instant everything would switch, and *déjà vu*, the questioning would return. Had I been here before? Or, was I this instant remembering so vividly and with such deep going back, with historical recollection, the very things that were unmistakably beneath my skin, in the palm of my hand?

I took my shoes off and now was walking with that feeling of childhood. Always childhood. The things in this house: childhood.

Why I had come back: childhood. What I had taken with me: childhood. Driven by childhood. What was it in this childhood?

I felt shifting sands beneath my feet, and could immediately hear the sea in my ears with its own peculiar thunder. It was the rain on the galvanize roof, the shifting sand to the touch of my fingers, the grainy deposits left by woodlice from the bannisters on the stairs.

I turned on the stair and looked back at the room beneath me in the last of the houses, the pink bungalow on the plains.

The rain was coming down hard and I could hear the thunder of the waves and feel the sands shifting beneath my feet. The silent industry of woodlice. The noise of the rain cut off the rest of the world and I felt utterly alone. It took a moment to realise that the screams I was hearing were the dogs screeching and barking in the village. I imagined the worst.

In that moment I had imagined the worst, thinking this was the last and whole of my childhood shrunk to a single flame with all the love and anxiety, all the guilt, regret, remorse; all the grief for never having grieved, for never having had him to myself to love. I ran up the remaining steps of the staircase leading to the bedrooms and burst through the weakly locked door to the lost bedroom, the last of the bedrooms, where they had made love and I had not known what their passion was, or if it was. Was I born of passion, necessity, duty, the law of Nature and the Pope's injunctions?

I was convinced that these screams in the thunder of the rain and of the waves which broke and broke to remind me of everything and nothing, were the screams of an old and anguished woman dreaming her last dream or her pain at my birth, or his cry of passion, which at another time I had imagined to be a whimper, and her receiving of him a silence.

In the flicker of the candlelight I could see nothing. I could not see his face. Beneath him I could see she whom I loved. They were caught in an act I could only surmise and which she had said brought her closer to God. He was fucking her and the screams in the waves were hers; pain of passion. The thunder was a voice of his I had not heard, except in a fiction of my own making.

When the wind abated, the flame grew strong and in its steady light I saw that the mattress was bare. There was nothing there except the bare mattress on which I had been born and the old mosquito net which Antoinetta had forgotten to take down to launder in readiness for my mother's return, hanging, the colour of tea, against the cream wall.

There was nothing except the things of this house. They were left to speak as I stood and looked at the empty bed and the room filled with her things.

Dust palled the beauty of her dressing-table. I put the saucer with the candle on the mahogany top of the Singer sewing-machine. Shadows grew on the walls, intermittently lighting up and darkening the picture of the Sacred Heart, with its own red flame curling at the centre of Jesus's chest. Jesus's skin was yellow and I thought of malaria. I remembered how once I had said to my mother in the old estate house that it was easier for her to love Jesus because He was a man. The sickly portrait is one of the things in this house, glossy and waxen with a weak smile.

I sat on the stool at the dressing-table. They were all still here. They had not left. The grasses on the plain whispered their names. The creaks in the house were their cries. Lavren's characters mixed with the protagonists of my tale.

I felt that the dust of woodlice was covering my feet and would soon, like the sand dunes at Manzanilla, fill the room, come up to my neck, choke and smother me completely. But I was fine sitting here as I had so often sat when the house was empty and no one knew and I could bare my own secrets.

Someone had left a window open. Mother? Antoinetta? No, she had left. Antoinetta had not been for days.

The flame was wild again and the room was inhabited with large and looming shadows. The looking-glass had become stained and mottled, and looked speckled and misted as if someone had just breathed upon it on purpose to deceive, to shut out what I already knew, which drove me to reveal clearly, maybe too clearly; but through suffering was the way. Had we not learnt that: through Calvary to Tabor, through transfiguration to crucifixion? I could see the mother-of-pearl crucifix hanging from the railings of the brass bed as big as a savannah. She had kissed this and pressed it to my lips still so small.

I tried to rub away the years from the mirror. *Palin*, again, *psao*, to rub smooth; lift off the fiction, one story written over another. I stretched one arm across the dressing-table, the other planted a hand in the dust, a print . . . a footprint on the beach.

At the centre of the dressing-table was the doily embroidered with blue forget-me-nots. To the left of the dressing-table the Singer sewing-machine, singing. I felt the enormity of what was here, and what was to be revealed. I felt sure it would be revealed here, with all the things of this house, now that I knew they had not left. The doily took me to the linen cupboard on the landing, which I had passed in my eagerness to breach the door, to discover the source of the screams in the rain, in the waves and in the thunder of the waves on the beach. The rain was still pounding on the galvanize roof. Galvanize. This place is made of galvanize, the shacks along the road, the rusting roofs, the barrack-rooms, the memory of the barrack-rooms.

I swivelled my body on the stool. Sideways in the mirror I saw he was still there on the bed with she whom I loved. Fucking. His bottom humped and pushing in and the buttocks opening and the hairs of his anus curled and glistening in the candlelight. I saw him inside the rain and the waves of rain against the bungalow on the plains whispering with the voices of my fiction; I could hear the straining and pleasure, the pleasure of his passion which I had never known. Never known him naked, but longed for that nakedness; longed now for him to turn away from where he had buried his head, in the linen pillowcases fluffed up by Antoinetta in the morning. I wondered whether he cried when he was finished, or whether he cried because of the loss of himself to her. Not to me; kept me yearning all my life, a whole life of yearning.

This too was part of the record to be kept. A chronicle of the heart. The quest of a son for a father. Is this the story, the fiction?

I wished he would turn and smile and say, 'Come'; take me down there on the bed and with a complete fatherly embrace, make me feel everything I had ever wanted to feel with him.

Then I saw she whom I loved turn beneath him, push against him and cry out, with her face smothered in his chest, against the black hair that grew there and was wet with tears of joy in her vision of her God who was crucified in pain.

I was sure that when I entered the room at the first cry, the face I saw was possessed. He had forgotten her and everything else except himself. This was where he found himself. Here only, in this amnesia.

I turned to get up and to go to the bed because I felt sure he had turned over and was lying there almost alone, because she whom

I loved was asleep on her side, peaceful and with her fingers strung through her rosary beads. I remembered she had said it always brought her closer to God. I had not thought then that this was about guilt and pain but solely about goodness. They had kept the secret from themselves. They could not speak what they felt. They had not reassured me. But when I got up to go near, to go towards him as he lay there naked and completely at ease and smiling so invitingly with one leg drawn up relaxed, looking so open and vulnerable, completely lovable with his penis not erect but lying against his leg, not small, not hidden by its foreskin, I realised that the bed was empty and that the mattress was bare. Far away . . .

Far away I heard a dog bark and a child scream. I was not sure, because of the rain. The whole yard was transfigured with lightning and the thunder which followed later as it always did when I was a child. I could feel the low-lying land of the plain filling up, swamping. The candle had almost burned down.

After I had put a new candle in the saucer I felt more peaceful myself. I opened the press with my mother's things . . .

9 December – 1 a.m.: still dreaming.

I return again to the night before, unable to sleep, fever. One day becomes the other in darkness.

The smell was of cuscus grass. This smell was mixed with the smell of polish and eau de Cologne. The shelves were lined with old Christmas paper and tissue paper. She did not hang her dresses here. There were four wide shelves in front of me. The first was waist height and was for odds and ends, my toys when I had ventured here alone. There was a bottle of smelling-salts. I unscrewed the stopper and inhaled deeply. It refreshed me, I was revived. But soon the fever returned.

I didn't want at that time to turn around, though there was a strong pull to recognise him again on the bed. I had forgotten for the moment my disappointment at not being held by him as he lay with her whom I loved after fucking her, she lying curled next to him with her fingers strung through rosary beads. The rain was now falling gently like needle-pricks on the tin roof, a new music, one that didn't terrify me, or take me with the force and pull of the sea at Maracas which sucked me to the bottom so quickly that I thought

I was drowning. I would have to take this more easily, more slowly, carefully, before I lost myself, all passions spent. I closed one of the doors of the press and kept the other open because there was a half-mirror in it. It was once a full mirror but my mother had had it altered by the man from the estate yard, or had it been Mr Callender, who sold mirrors in his hardware store? These facts were a respite. I could write down a litany of them and make one of her digressions, never wanting to come back to the truth or the road that would lead there. She made lists.

Desire. Passion. The only passion allowed and recognised was the one of suffering. Pain. A naked man hangs from a cross with nails driven deeply through his hands and feet. He has been pierced with a lance where his appendix would be. His head is bleeding profusely because a crown of thorns has been pressed firmly down on his brow. Hours before that he was whipped savagely by other men. He was spat upon, urinated over. They called him vile names as in drinking brawls, shouting as men do in their denigration of each other. This is called that man's passion. The chalice of blood he had to drink. He would not refuse it in the garden during his agony before the betrayal and the crowing of the cockerels. This was done for love of men. This we had to celebrate. This celebration I had a passion for, a desire that cassocked and surpliced me in linen and lace, embroidered in satins and silks and entranced me with the antiphonal breaking of the waves of Gregorian chant. This was passion, my sublimated passion . . . *Cantate Dominum canticum novum, cantate Dominum cantica canticorum*.

What of the passion that had begotten us all? They were the cries I had heard on the stairs.

There was the passion of wild grass, corilli vines, bush in the wet season to be cut back, brushed back. There are the girls in the barrack-rooms, the black girls in the village, the naked Indian boys in the secret garden, kisses on the Hollywood screen. Such passion is whispered through the confessional screen for the burning ears of priests.

How old was I when I stood on the stairs and decided to follow the sounds and screams of she whom I loved? How old was I?

Mirror, mirror on the wall . . .

How old?

The door was always locked. Now I had opened it. Breached it and saw them. The two whom I loved. And I turned from the tabernacle of the press that housed the true presence of her: her smells, her feel, her relics, the chaplets given at first communions, the broken beads of our childhood, horn chaplets, mother-of-pearl, black jet, filigreed silver which children's fingers had fingered as they whispered the Hail Mary for purity and the Our Father for forgiveness before they knew what either meant and their innocence was confounded by priests. 'Hail Holy Queen, mother of mercy . . .' in this lacrimarum vale.

Salve Regina . . .

The true presence of childhood fell out of the press, the black lace dress folded in tissue paper, the aquamarine petticoat slippery like water, soft as her touch. Clothed in her I walked barefoot across the pitchpine floorboards, white with Indian women's scrubbing, jangling with silver bracelets. Indentured to my memory. Floors that were brushed with cocoyea brooms by black servants enslaved to my memory. I undressed in front of the mirror, undressed my boy's body, fractured and broken; I could hardly reassemble it from memory, from the fragments I saw in the mottled yellowing mirror. I remembered the vision the hermaphrodite Lavren had had of the middle passage and this memory told me how mixed was the personal with the historical, and how uneasy it would be to separate them in this hallucinated history, how uneasy it was to forgive one another across the races of the nations for the cruelty of the races to each other. How difficult to forgive, across the silence of the years which had separated a family nurtured in this dangerous place, this family house. In the flicker of the candlelight my boy's body was stretched to breaking upon a tree in the forest of their making, in the garden of their Eden, a fiction of their mythology blurred by the green of parrots and noisy with their hysteria; a serpent crawls upon a fallen branch, reaching its own goal, in its own skins varied and coloured like the rocks in the face of the cliff. A coral necklace of fear. Upon my boy's head the crown of the Infant Jesus of Prague, jewelled with earrings, pendants and bracelets, my mother's opal ring set in the middle of the crown and my boy's arms braceleted with the silver bangles and mail of indentured women, with gold like that gold that shines among the white teeth of black women who told me stories on the kitchen floor and hung in their ears the gold of Benin. I was their child. The child they could love freely and were paid to love, paid the price for leaving their own children to love me so much, folded in melangene arms, resting on breasts smelling of ginger.

My fiction was true.

In the flicker of the candle I could see my boy's body heave with a desire for comfort, and in the thunder of the rain that had begun to fall again I could hear his young cry for forgiveness. 'Father, I forgive you because you do not know what you do.' I at once turned at the word 'Father' to look for him again on the bed. At first the mattress was bare and I looked again at the mirror for the vision of my boy, my self that had always loved me and that I had forgotten to love, but instead punished and sought forgiveness for over and over again. Now I wished to write it down so that it would be known, read for all to understand, so that all would be liberated to a history of true feeling. I could see him clearly now. In the thunder I said:

'Father, I forgive you because you do not know what you do.'

I thought these words must bring the tablets of Sinai to the ground, shatter the cross of Golgotha, melt the words of the sermon on the mount. I wished them to unhang the lynched from the mango trees of the Boulevard Fondes Amands. I wished them to unhang the Indian men who had hanged themselves in Hangman Alley for tabanca, the suffering of their unrequited love. I wished for all crucifixions to end: the chambers of Auschwitz, the drowned nuns of Buenos Aires, the untrue eagle which sits on Capitol Hill riddling with bullets the poor, stigmatised; the hysteria of religion and power and, in my fiction, amidst the burning city, the gibbet of Governor Picton.

I turned again to the bed and my father was lying there naked and whole on his back, his arms in cruciform, his penis neither long and thick with sex nor small and quiescent, hidden in its foreskin, but as before, lying vulnerable against his leg and open to the sight of his son to enjoy and know to be good. This would not bring forth the wrath of a God who had made an Eden to fool men and women. I walked towards the bed as big as a savannah, a family joke, and saw that she whom I loved was lying curled on her side with a chaplet strung between her fingers, sighing and breathing. I thought of what I had first seen when I came through the door, first entered the house. My boy's voice was still in my ears: 'Father, I forgive you because you do not know what you do.' My boy's words were on my lips as I neared the bed. I realised now that my man's body was naked too. I was not dressed, a boy in my mother's image, so that I might be loved by him. Not loved?

The first thing I did was to take his arms from where they hung in cruciform and bring them quietly to rest; one casually on his chest, the other at his side on the leg where his penis lay in its own hair and the hair of his leg. Then I walked over to the other side of the bed, to she whom I loved. I took the chaplet from her fingers. Still holding them in the palm of my hand I stretched to the centre of the bed and untied the mother-of-pearl crucifix from the railings of the brass bed. With both the crucifix and the chaplet I returned to my mother's press, the tabernacle of the true presence of childhood. I put them in there with other relics of the past. I laid them on the shelf with the odds and ends of a life. The back of the shelf was pasted with a portrait of St Thérèse of Lisieux, who carried in her arms a bouquet of flowers among whose blooms lay a heavy wooden crucifix. The other side of the shelf was pasted with a portrait of the Virgin Mary, the Immaculate Heart of Mary (companion to the Sacred Heart), its flame curled between her breasts. I turned from these icons of childhood and closed the tabernacle of the press. As I did that, I thought I would have to put away the offending relics as I found them, in my research among the things of this house.

I woke next morning having dreamt that my father was not dead. The morning breeze from the window overlooking the savannahs of the plain shook the mosquito net. Mother? Antoinetta? I found my damp clothes from the night before, over the mahogany rocker. I remembered the rain and saw that the dawn was rosy. The manuscript on my father's desk fluttered.

At work I read that a traveller in the nineteenth century had said that the remnants of the first people lived in silence. 'Silence is their dwelling and idleness all their ways.'

25 December . . . and the Word was made flesh.

At the foot of the cross at three o'clock in the afternoon.

I embrace my oppressor who has colonised my imagination. I kneel down. I kiss the flesh of his leg. I press my desire against his crotch where testicles bulge, penis cocooned in a loin cloth. I sniff there the perfume of his passion. I inhale my oppression. I look up, my cheek hard against his leg. I scrape with my fingernails, adding injury to injury. I look up. See! See! How I adore you, crucified one. Back . . . back down the corridor to my nursery:

Snap: sun-suited four years old I step out in my mother's high-heeled shoes, my mother's wide-brimmed hat. I am dressing up.

Snap: sun-suited three or four years old, crying, alone. I have shitted myself. I feel the weight of it between my legs. I can't walk. I feel the moistness of it, the stickiness of it. I smell it, smear it on my fingers, smell it (I remember this, always remember this). Wipe it off. I can't.

Snap: she leaves me, not knowing I'm dragged through the gravel by the small black Austin at whose bumper I hang on, bruised and bleeding.

Snap: the lacerations of the afternoon. Three o'clock in the afternoon sun, the English boy with the pale white skin, freckled nose, uproots the long whip-stalks of the cockscombs, heavy and purple, scattering the fuzz of petal seeds. He whips my naked legs. His pale white cheeks are flushed. I feel, pressed into my small bare knees, the sharp stones on the gravelled yard.

Snap: a tamarind switch, a father's punishment. Is God a father?

Snap: I find myself at this moment in a bright space, surrounded with shadow and secret. I would hide in the shadows. Gravel, like when I was much smaller with a softer skin. My skin is still soft at this moment. Gravel is sharp. Knees get grazed. Abrasions on small hands. Did I find a patch of grass for my face, to press my face, or was it gravel too that scratches and cuts my lips? And my tears, were there tears which got mixed with wet lips and dirt? I don't remember. But I can feel that pain as if it were now at the foot of this cross. I imagine. I have imagined it all. No. Stop. Don't punish me.

I will imagine no more. I don't accuse. I ask to know. Did you love me? Love me.

Snap: the cool forest path on the way to the reservoir. Hot afternoon. Across my path a sleeping snake, hanging from the low branch of a fallen tree. I wake it. I attack it with sticks and stones with fear in my stomach, blood rushing. The silence of the afternoon forest screams in my ears with the hysteria of parrots as ancient as this island. Green against blue, swimming before my misted eyes. Like electric shocks. My whole body behind each blow. I killed it, battered it with a stick, crushed its head with a stone.

> Sweet Virgin Mary
> *Integra et casta*
> Star of the sea
> Miraculous mother
> Standing on top of the world
> The green globe
> Encircled by a red serpent
> Crushing the gold and black head
> With your small white naked feet. Pray for me.

Snap: I am fourteen. I am kneeling in front of this shrine, at the foot of this cross on a forest path. This could be ordinary and usual with classmates to say the rosary. I am alone this afternoon. No watering of flowers, singing of hymns, lighting of candles, the devotions of the innocent and pure. I kneel, not at the stone prie-dieu but on the gravel path. It hurts. I try to pray. Pain fills me, excites me. That from which I flee I embrace. That which I pray to deny I indulge. Such pleasures as the battle rages. I unbuckle my belt.

My fairy tales have been the lives of saints. My fantasies, martyrdom. Scourged, tied to pillars, pressed upon by heavy stones lowered into raging waters, submerged beneath boiling oil. Tied to crosses, crucified with nails, transfixed with arrows and raised on high. My imagination has been enslaved and indentured.

> Sweet stigmata
> Man of five wounds
> See the petals, stamen
> Of the passion flower
>
> O Sacred Head ill-used
> Crowned with thorns
> Reviled
> Spat upon

These acts I seek with unquenchable thirst, the thirst of the desert.

I unbuckle my belt. I use the end with the buckle on my back. The buckle does the work with the strap. And I hope that the high winds blowing in the tall trees, the water rushing in the valley below over the rocks and stones, the screech and scream of parrots in the blue air will deafen the world to the lashes of my leather buckled belt upon my naked back of skin and soft flesh.

New Year's Day

. . . the skeletons of this world are not found in attics or cellars but, as the saying goes, in the cupboard; in the press, a Victorian word we use to this day.

I had removed the mother-of-pearl crucifix from the brass railing of the bed as big as a savannah and put it away in my mother's press. Hadn't I? To this day if there is anything I need to find from the past it is to the press I look, with the same excitement that ran through my young limbs as I approached my mother's press or my sisters'; it was with a different excitement, then, that I approached my brothers' or my father's. Which costume would fit a growing child best? I knew what was in my own press, though I could be surprised by what I had forgotten I had hidden there.

The linen press was more communal, less private, though my mother saw it as her domain when she sat in front of it on a Friday afternoon after the ironing was done and the clothes pressed; each piece with its own creases, lying in a large wooden tray like neatly folded pastry and brought up on the head of Antoinetta through the pantry and the drawing-room to the linen press outside my parents' bedroom. We children – my father would not have thought of doing anything so domestic, and the servants were definitely barred – were not to go to the linen press for anything without permission. The proprietorship of my mother over these six shelves of cedar, locked in varnished panels with a brass key, with its piece of pink ribbon for identification, saddened me then. So I learned to know the feeling which sadness brings. I smelled sadness. It smelt first of all of faded cuscus grass from Dominica, sewed into organza sachets in bulging little bundles, which were laid between the old linen sheets and the newer cotton ones. My mother checked the labels methodically, counting each one with a hand ringed in marriage, a gold band and the encrustation of a diamond, later stolen which led to another moment of betrayal and accusation: 'Antoinetta, that young girl, I can't trust her, you know.'

'Madam?'

Each piece of laundry was counted early on Monday morning when the soiled linen was put out in bundles on the floor, and my mother wrote each item in a ledger. 'These people steal anything: they run off like goats with anything they can lay their hands on.' So the ledger was filled week after week, year after year, in her indelibly strong hand with a Parker fountain-pen with Quink ink from the bottle that used to stand on this desk I now write upon. Then each item was ticked off on Friday afternoon when the ironer laid the tray at my mother's feet, clothes still smelling of sprinkled water before ironing and the steam rising off the damp linen, and stooped each time to hand her the items which she checked, opening and closing along the creases before the ironer laid them in the press, her black hands on the white linen. My eyes focused on her hands, and on the hands of my mother, each in their sphere doing the deeds their world instructed them to do. Then I did not reflect.

Now I remember. But then I smelled the sadness of washed clothes sprinkled for ironing, steaming under hot irons, pressed with precision and skill by black women who were paid by the piece. My sadness smelt of Antoinetta's sweat, the perspiration she wiped with a side of her hand over her brow, trying to do the impossible task of preventing beads of perspiration from falling on the freshly ironed linen and having to stoop each time, this woman, no young girl, but my mother's age, to pick up each piece for inspection. The scene is arranged in my memory. The smell of sadness: I smell it now in the words they broke to pieces as they negotiated this transaction of labour.

'Hmm.'

'Madam?'

'Hmm.'

'Madam?'

'Hmm. I don't know nuh, Antoinetta.'

'What, Madam?'

'Hmm.'

'Cheups.'

Silence.

'Cheups.'

'Is no use nuh, Antoinetta. Is no use cheupsing. Look at these clothes.'

I too could see these clothes. I was witness to this crime. I did not reflect then: I insist, I did not reflect then. I did not see the linen or the clothes, I saw the hands, one pair black, the other pair white. My sadness smelt of my mother's eau de Cologne. Perfume from a foreign city in a golden bottle with a special label she kept on the waist-high shelf of her mahogany press. When I stole some, sprinkled on my hand and forehead as she used to do to me if I had a bad feeling, like when I fainted after I fell from the flamboyant tree and she gave me sugar-water and sprinkled the linen pillowcase with eau de Cologne and I felt better with her pressing the bed down with her weighty girth, the girth and comfort of cushions, the comfort of my only love and safety: when I stole some, my guilt filled the house. Somewhere between those shattered words it was difficult to tread, because of the feelings like shattered glass-bottle. I placed my own words of double allegiance, never knowing whom I betrayed the most. I insist I did not reflect then. If memory serves I ran away to play, to sink into the currents and tide of play. If memory serves, I tried to forget. Taking my words even as I offered them, laid them between the pairs of hands. 'But Mummy, I don't see nothing wrong with the clothes.'

'Child, run away and play.'

'But, Madam, he right, you know, he right, yes . . .' A woman my mother's age seeks corroboration in a child's statement: her words broke and I felt confused as I ran away, avoiding the broken glass-bottle feelings but wounded by not knowing where to turn, how to love them both and be loved equally.

I did not reflect, I insist. I smelt the sadness, leaving the inspection to continue. She left her own children to love me with her time; that needs to be recorded in any chronicle of the heart as remembered history.

So one day when she told me, 'You get a lot of loving, yes,' I cried.

6 January – Feast of the Epiphany

Difficult to avoid, the voices in this house.

'Morning.' She pushes the old gate which scrapes on the gravel and shakes the dew from off the trumpeting alamandas. 'Morning.'

I never answer at once. I hadn't noticed when the Indian boys who had been mowing the lawns had gone. The lawns had been mowed. I had conditioned myself not to be disturbed by this weekly interruption of my solitude, with the boys coming from the village. Where had I been? 'Where was I?' my mother would say. She would mean that she had lost herself in herself, in her thoughts. 'Where was I?' I had adopted this way of talking. Are these the signs of death's last stages, when we take on the idiosyncracies of those who are dying, old and dying? Yet, when she is away I feel I'm becoming him.

I shut the door of the linen press on the landing, noticing the boxes of old photographs.

In the kitchen downstairs: 'You not going to work today, Sir?'

'Maybe later. I'm working here this morning.' The lawns are shorn and shine like green enamel. I can never get her to stop calling me 'Sir'. I am her baby, her recalcitrant child, a negligent housekeeper in my mother's absence and for this she will take me to task, but still call me 'Sir'. She knows that nothing has changed for her, essentially. She knows the boundaries. She could overstep and with that bunch of keys left her by my mother has access to any press, theoretically to any secret, but she knows the boundaries. 'Sir' means: don't come any further. I understand the contract. We have not negotiated a new world. We have learnt to live in the old. When black friends come and sit in the morris chairs, sip rum and coke on the veranda, I can hear her in the kitchen.

'Why you bring these blasted dirty nigger people them inside your mother house?'

'But, Antoinetta . . .'

'Don't speak to me, go and attend to your guests them, don't ask me to serve out any food for them dirty nigger people. Hmm, Madam, if Madam . . .'

Indeed 'if Madam', oh, Madam, you have a good guardian of your domain in this old black woman to do your dirty work, to keep guard, to keep her own 'dirty nigger people them' outside the gate. The schizophrenia of a servant. But once they were inside, if you had come down, Mummy, as you've done, to find them at the dining-room table you would be sweetness self, charm of centuries, grace and elegance, a plantocrat. Do I see you sweep up your train of muslin, and do I see you descend and with the gesture of a duchess unfurl a fan, a triptych of the hanging gardens of Babylon, and stir the air about your powdered, rouged face and the flutes of your neck, where your hair has been swept into a bun. My anger breaks into fiction. My love will be a tantrum. My guilt will stop me. Allegiance and betrayal.

'Book. You writing book. You room in a real mess, you know. Madam not going to like that. I not tidy in there for weeks, dust or mop the floor.'

'Leave it, Antoinetta. I'll do that. Madam gone away,' I smiled.

'Madam gone away. You not shame? Is your mother, you know.'

'Antoinetta, you don't have to come when Mummy not here. Why you coming so far in the morning when you could stay home?'

'You don't tell me nothing. I come because I come. I come because I tell Madam I go come.' She fixed her hair with a hair-clip behind her ear. 'Who else will look after this place? Not you, upstairs thinking about nothing but book, book, book. You not shame? Come sit down and eat your breakfast before you die on me hands and Madam say I not feed you. Come, child, come, Sir, sit down. Is not that you like? Is not so you like it?' She ran her fingers through my hair. Then pressed her hand on my shoulder. 'I weary, yes. I weary for so.'

'Antoinetta, what you doing all this for? Come and sit down. Have some tea.'

'I going sit down right here and drink my green tea.' She settled down by the kitchen door, just inside the kitchen. Soon she had dozed off with the green tea going cold.

Shame. I wondered what that meant. Shame. What should I be doing? They'd all gone. She was right. No one came back, now that my father had died, and my mother could not live on her own. So she kept going away. Writing letters and leaving things to Antoinetta and myself. I felt now that I was working against time. There were hardly any of them left now: a crippled aunt in town and a shaky uncle and one cousin going mad without knowing it. Another planning and selling out the land, plot by plot, like graves. *Rum and Coca-Cola . . . Mother and daughter working for the Yankee dollar.*

In her last letter she had said, 'You do exaggerate. Mad? What do you mean?'

They are obsessed. They are obsessed with the colour of their skin, with the colour of other people's skin. They are obsessed with blackness. It is a kind of madness.

My mother would leap into history or fiction. She would tell the tale of the uncle who spent months in the dusty archives of the Cathedral of the Immaculate Conception endeavouring to find the first marriage certificate of the first member of the family who had come to the island. The story at the tea table was that he had found the certificate and it had said that we were white people. We were let off the hook. But it hadn't got rid of the obsession.

'Rubbish. Rubbish,' she would say if she were in the next room eavesdropping and would come in here during siesta and peep at what I was writing and want to put her mark on it, write her book, to put the record straight. 'Rubbish, you weren't there. You don't know what you're talking about. It is all your imagination. Something is wrong with you. Why don't you let me write a chapter in that book and tell the real truth?'

They were all still in the house. I felt safer when Antoinetta came. Though I also preferred it when she did not come. It was an interruption. Always felt that I had to go and talk to her; how could I not after all these years? Coming all that way in the hot sun.

'I sure Madam wouldn't like all this thing you write here.'

'How do you know?' Antoinetta insisted on mopping this morning. I sat on the bed pulling up the bedspread so that she could get under the bed with the mop.

'Look at dust. Dust like peas.'

'What did she say? I didn't know you talked about what I was writing.'

'Yes, hmm.'

'What did you tell her?'

'I know what Madam thinks. She thinks you should get a priest and get your soul wash out clean.'

I laughed. It was true. 'She told you that?'

'Madam does talk to me, you know. All the time you up here

clicking away like a beetle, Madam does talk to me downstairs. When she here. Since the boss gone, Madam can't keep sheself quiet.'

'Madam?'

'Is your mother, you know.'

'And you? What about you?'

'Look, don't make joke.'

'Joke?'

'You is a big man now, Sir. You don't find you should do something with yourself, except all the time with this book and all this paper?'

I am a child again up on the bed, following her all over the house in the morning when she did out the house. Talking, talking all the time. That's how it had always been. And she, now an old woman and me in middle age up on the bed, was still sweeping, talking about Madam. Then it was more complaining.

'You know, they don't come and see me now. Besides, I wouldn't have them come and see me at all. They want my money. I not letting them get one black cent.'

'Who?'

'My niece and them. They want my money.'

She was thinking of these things because I had said, 'And you?' Meaning what she was to me.

'You is a real big baby. Come get off the bed. You know, you should do something with yourself. Look at these clothes. How they get so wet? And all them clothes belonging to Madam? What they doing on the floor in her bedroom? I find the press door open and she black lace dress on the floor. How that get there, Sir? And your father press open too. Sometimes I wonder what going on in this house, yes, and I think is best if Madam come back soon and everything go go back like it should be. I don't find that Madam should be going away all the time. I don't know what you does get up to when Madam not here. You is a big man now, you know.'

When Antoinetta eventually left with her questions, poor old soul, I realised that it had not rained as I thought it would. The rosy dawn had held its promise and the Tamana hills rose out of the plain, reminding me of my fiction. The wind off the savannah was beginning to turn the leaves of my book on my father's desk.

2 February – Carnival season

I return to the cracked artist's portfolio which had been found at the top of my father's press under some of my mother's old suitcases. Over the last months, while she has been away, and Antoinetta does not come up to the house as often, I have taken the liberty of sticking up some of the watercolours and sketches on the dingy cream walls of the bungalow. I can see that the sun will quickly fade the colours, and that the extremes of damp and heat will crinkle and corrupt the paper. The light is pernicious. Already they are altered and have been attacked by insects and termites, even inside their cellophane envelopes, concertinaed within the covers of the portfolio. The sense of decay is relentless. I am weighed down by it. My respite from this ennui is a sketch pad, a brush and a box of watercolours. A jam-jar full of water, in which I rinse my brush and change my colour, stands on the ledge of the veranda overlooking the savannah. This is not my art, though art is what she, my aunt, offered by example, both through these instruments and the relentlessly written record which she kept from the time she was a young girl. Both I have emulated. I am left with the pen, these tales and this record of the heart.

I went to her in the mornings, school vacation, after mass, a neophyte at the feet of the small lady.

She too is here, as I open doors in this house, listen to voices and now, with her sketches and paintings on almost every wall, her presence fills both me and the house.

'They change so quickly,' I hear her say, stamping her foot a little in irritation and flicking her brush away from her into the wind which sends the water back off her brush as a drizzle over my face. 'They change so quickly.' She raises her spectacles off her nose and bends to peer more closely at her box of paints. 'I think I've got it, and then I turn away for an instant and there – it's completely changed.' Her gestures are expansive as she takes in the whole view of canefields and sky in front of us, pointing it out to me with her brush, as a conductor might wave a baton.

'What?' I'm at her side on my knees. She is big-hipped on an artist's stool before an easel.

'Sky.' She waves her extended arm in front of her and uses her hand as if it held a thick brush for the expansive liberation of oil on a huge canvas, instead of the finicky concentration of a watercolourist to catch it all before it changed. 'Skies, they change so quickly.' Oils! – slapped on, applied layer on layer, Lavren's way.

At another time it was the mountains. My mother had immediately made of these, those mountains found in the psalms: 'I have lifted up mine eyes to the hills, O Lord, From whence comes my help.' So that the part of me which was her, transposed my full reality into biblical mountains, deserts, inland seas. A garden was the Garden of Gethsemane and every hill was Golgotha with a gibbet at the top. I remember that my aunt had her devotions too and some would refer to her as a saint. There was that part of me that was hers, also wanting to be a saint. But the her which now fills the house is not about being a saint, but about being an artist, transposing life, metamorphosing, organising the arbitrariness of reality into one imaginative whole, one narrative within another.

I never took skies for granted and noticed their changing quality, defying representation. Art had to interpret. It could not represent. This was what her little tantrum of stamping feet and flicking brushes had been about, the conflict, because the instinct was to represent, yet one was forced to interpret.

Metaphor, story, interpretation, truth.

The mountains too, in themselves, were defiant. At sunrise, when still suffused in mist, they could be the pink of a rose, but as the mist lifted the green began to show, then turn blue and never from this distance be green again, though we knew they were green. Things were dependent on the distance from which you saw them. Didn't that ever allow for them to be something which always was, and never changed? Change came suddenly, and as the mist lifted almost completely, leaving only some wisps, shafts of strong golden light would penetrate from sky to earth and suggest canvases by Italian artists who tried to represent, or who gave us their interpretation of creation. It was when these were offered not as art but as life that everything ran amok and our concept of God became Italianate, finite, uninteresting.

The gulf was never just that bit of sea, and across its metallic surface she searched the horizon from the terrace of her home for the outline of the mountains of Venezuela. The mountains appeared like a mirage, only to disappear by the time she went into the house to get her materials, set up and begin her painting.

Sky, mountain, gulf, sea, the wide green plains and undulating hills of the island. These were her subjects. These, yes, but above all, light.

As a child it bathed everything so generously. It wasted, but too, it was unconsciously imbibed and then made particular at her knee. Now I watch that same light fade her work, crudely and roughly stuck about the house: in memoriam.

She drew close to subjects nearer home: the orchids which hung in her orchid house, or in the shade of a calabash tree growing from its branches or encrusting the barks of logs. She drew close into the velvet touch and smooth gloss of their vulvas: purple, pink, carmine and puce, fading like dye does at the edges where the petals curl and scallop. A bloom from a golden shower startles with more light its goldenness. The white which is in orchids with a sheen like satin, taffeta or silk, the edges of petals like gathered lace, undone.

This woman, who painted and reached beyond the confines of colonial womanhood for some passion, sewed: and I here mix my metaphors purposely, horticulture and couture, haute couture in the wedding dresses and dresses for débutantes, brides and their maids. The shimmer in the garden is of those daughters dressed in light, carrying orchids. She too remembers herself leaning back with the crowd on the balustrade of the balcony at Government House, laughing, their laughter light, tinkling like the ice in their drinks and the echo of the laughter from the other dancers in the cars on the lawn between dances.

That other art keeps her within her role, remembering illusions. Painting liberates.

27 February – Carnival Tuesday

After independence a gesture was performed. The Governor General was moved out of the nineteenth-century Governor's House and housed around the corner in a modern sprawling bungalow. The nineteenth-century house became an art gallery. The paintings which now live in the annexe of the second floor of my museum were moved there with others which artists loaned.

She took me to see these paintings. But also to see the gallery, the house where she had gone as a young girl, a débutante, when the Chancellors were hosts.

I recall the afternoon and the visit. I had never been in a house as large, and the staircase and the way I was forced to walk up it and then down into the hall and into the ballroom opening on to the gallery and balcony allowed me to inhabit that grand past. It enveloped me.

She had come to see the paintings and to show them to me, but had become distracted by the vandalism (she said)which had been perpetrated upon the house. When we left and she met my mother they both lamented the passing of the furniture, the panelling and the curtains. They lamented the absence of the chandeliers. And, I dare say, the Chancellors. They lamented the passing of their past.

I remember the few portraits. Black faces, black torsos, black shoulders, legs and muscles. I had not seen many paintings, but I had never before seen a painting of a black person.

I remember the portraits.

'My dear, the panelling, all ripped out, the chandeliers taken down, the . . .'

As I walk about this house and look at each of her paintings and sketches I can still admire the effort, the skill, and feel the desire and passion for more, but now as I peer into them, inspecting where the termites have penetrated, they are empty, consistently empty. She has not put any of her people into them, nor has she painted black people as they are. A smudge in this corner is the bandannaed black mammy, carrying a basket on her head to the market. Picturesque poverty: that shack, the fisherman's hut, the old Methodist school for Indian children on the Canadian Mission, this pink bungalow on the empty plain; saying nothing about it, but its loneliness.

That is not without perception. That was their loneliness, up on their hill, not noticing what was going on in the gully. Their loneliness was in their desire to live in large houses set on hills with beautiful views and gardens sloping away. It was part of the illusion they created, an eighteenth-century *folie*. What you see is not what is there. Here for instance are the black iron railway trucks which take the cane from the loading depot to the factory. They are a blur in the gully, or are they her effort to try to erect a symbol that mars the landscape? A menace, a cruel smudge. But she dares not approach that symbol to show more, to show the people loading the cane. How show it? Would they be jolly and black?

I don't blame her taking solace in landscape, in natural beauty. As I write now, the mountains are changing once more and the savannah is a shimmer of green and early morning wetness. I take solace from writing by trying her medium.

I thank her for her landscapes, but I am forced to people them. The paintings leave out everything that has happened here, except the smudge in the corner, a parody, like in the photograph: at the back the white aproned and starched cap, the black woman who holds the child.

Smoke rises from the villages and an Indian man walks across the savannah to tether his cattle, which follow dragging their chains, while an egret picks ticks off the back of the cow and another pecks for worms where the turf is uprooted near the cow's mouth.

Savannahs as empty as these pages to be filled – across which a man strolls with cattle following. Cazabon's Eden.

15 March

The fictions close in, press down. They get nearer to this time as I try to lift the chronicle of my heart out of its forests, from beneath the contours of its plains, the swamp, the clogged rivers and the wet sand, where herons and crabs inscribe their hieroglyphs, their fictions, which are pulled away by the incoming tide and the force of the moon. I wish mine to remain, to be read as part of the truth. What I choose to lift here from this palimpsest is what I can manage. This morning in the house, the bungalow, I lift out that piece of the past. I circle it. I describe it. Not for nostalgia, but because it exists now, as part of this time, to be looked at as affecting how I see the history, the tales. I lift it as I lift the cut-glass powder-bowl from the dressing-table of she whom I love, leaving a clear space encircled with dust.

It is a bright space. Shade at the edges. An open gravel yard, the edges are shrubs, shade trees: flamboyant before flame blooms, all masses of overlaying feathery branches under the tamarind trees, all shadow and filigree of shadow. This past is all sepia which I find in the drawers of his desk. This very desk on which I write and keep a chronicle of our love. I find him and find myself in the same light, penetrated by moths.

*

I find us at this moment in that bright space surrounded with shadow. I hide in the shadows, where I am sent to pick a tamarind switch. Gravel, like when I was much smaller with a softer skin. My skin is still soft at this moment. Gravel is sharp. Knees get grazed. Abrasions on small hands. Did I find a patch of grass for my face, to press my face, or was it gravel that scratches and cuts my lips, and my tears: were there tears mixed with wet lips and dirt? I don't remember. But I feel that pain as if it were now and as if it had been, though I must say I cannot remember. I imagine. I have imagined it all. I offer him the tamarind switch. NO. STOP. Don't punish me . . . love me . . . punish me . . . love me.

I will imagine no more. I don't accuse. I ask to know.

Can a father be God? Can God be a father?

16 March

This morning I go to his press in the empty bungalow, and there on the shelf-slats of pitchpine, as bright as sunbeams through pleated jalousies, are the few discreet things of his life which have been left. This other tabernacle which I must venerate.

Are there those who would say I desecrate, dishonour name and the hallowed place of parents? I hear those voices. I say, did you know how much I longed for his love? Do you know now the cost? This is no revenge. This is the chronicle of a heart.

The varnished door falls away into my arms. It has come away at the hinges. Woodlice. I remember the sand shifting to the touch of my fingers, the grainy deposits of woodlice on the first night I re-entered the house. This last of the houses. This bungalow. Now it falls away. It was special to have the key to come here. To be sent to fetch a box of matches, a packet of cigarettes. I leap on too quickly. Too quickly to mention each one of those hallowed things placed each in its own, and very own place, not be disturbed. Each in its place of brightness and shadow on the shelf-slats of pitchpine, as bright as the sunbeams through pleated jalousies.

'Don't go to your father's press without permission. Did he send you there?'

And when 'Yes', the excitement to run along the varnished floor of the cream corridor, with the flat silver key in the sweaty palm of my small brown hand. No ribbon identifies this key. The hole over which I place my fingers to insert and turn it in the lock is a clear round of nothing. This is his key. The key to his press. Now there is no lock. The door falls away into my arms and I have a responsibility to take care of what is left of his life. The things which lie in their stillness and dust are relics now, remnants of a life, but I won't yet treat them so.

I recall the press. It is how different it is from hers that always strikes me. It is uncluttered. I speak of what it is not. There are four shelves of pitchpine slats. They are all used, with a few things on each. This is his very own arrangement. I smell tobacco. A carton of Raleigh cigarettes with the cellophane torn, but not removed, is on the top shelf with a box of Ship & Anchor matches. He smelt of this tobacco, it lingered on his breath. My boy's cheek against his unshaven cheek, scared to kiss him good-night.

'Daddy.'

'Your father is not a demonstrative person.' And that excused everything. All her life she protected him.

I remember when I had to climb on to the bottom shelf to reach for the packet of cigarettes on the top shelf, or matches, when they had run out in the kitchen and we had to ask him.

On the second shelf are the sacred vessels: the monogrammed silver cigarette-case, a father's wedding gift to a son. He grew in the shadow of this absent father, admired from afar, who wore white linen suits which Daddy later wore until they fell out of fashion. The insidious circle repeats itself with intent. The other smell is Yardley's shaving soap. Standing next to the wooden bowl is the horn-handled horsehair shaving-brush. The Yardley's bowl of soap is scooped and smooth, the colour of ivory. When he was finished with it he would clean it out with his penknife and what remained was a small wooden bowl fashioned by a lathe. It occurs to me now that this indicates something quite significant about his character. This keeping of bowls and little boxes, each with their hoard of gentlemen's secrets. In the now empty clean Yardley's bowl are kept gold studs for his starched collars, gold cufflinks for his starched pressed white shirts, monogrammed with initials, a gold tiepin. He never wore jewellery, not even a gold wedding-band. There is the rosewood cigarette-case with two medals won for rowing kept inside. There is the gentleman's toilet-case, round leather, in which he keeps brown and black laces for his shoes, and Gillette razor-blades for his silver Gillette razor.

On the third shelf are the shirts, all white. I never saw him wear colours – unless grey, black, brown and khaki are colours. They are the colours of a colonial gentleman. One pile of shirts is pressed and folded, best of cotton. The other softer, a pile of white cotton Aertex shirts. Here there is another smell, something she managed to insert, secrete. This is a pocket made of cuscus grass from Dominica. Into this are placed the white linen handkerchiefs folded like the linen corporal used at mass for resting the chalice and host on. Embroidered here are his initials. These shelves of bright pitchpine are altars. On the bottom shelf, socks and folded khaki pants.

I could have chosen this identity. Could I? I have not reached for these. I have not entered here to play to be a child.

Black lace, black lace covers my boy's body stretched upon a cross.

Now they are relics and they are not all here, even though I see each one clearly. She has given his clothes to the poor. Some poor man walks in a dead man's clothes.

Each thing now in its circle of dust. The Yardley's shaving-bowl, a clean wooden bowl, holds my little odds and ends standing on this desk, his desk: odds and ends, different, accoutrements of writing; paperclips, an eraser, the stub of a pencil, a pencil sharpener. I just like to have it on my desk, open it when it is empty and put my face to it to inhale him who never touched me. It's faded. I remember there was another smell. The smell of Palmolive soap when he had showered or washed after the lavatory, fresh soap where there was sweat. The whole house scented with his presence.

17 March

But today, while the almond leaves rustle, lizards scuttle and the keskidee asks its question, *Qu'est-ce qu'il dit?* . . .The yard opens up into another yard along a gravel drive lined with palmiste. There is the round bed of cockscombs and behind another screen of casuarinas are the barrack-rooms, indentured to my imagination. My motive now is selfish. This is not Lavren's ironic fiction which tells you about the nightmare of history. It is to ride with him to see the estate, not as the place of enslavement and indentureship, but the place it was before I understood guilt or knew its uneasy feeling. It is him. I return here for him. I take the clothes from the press and clothe him as he was then. I take a white Aertex shirt and pair of khaki pants through whose loops at the waist is laced a brown leather belt (discipline of a father who had to discipline sons, though afraid to touch them). He wears brown shoes and white socks. Neat, discreet. Clean, well combed. He stands to mount a horse called Fortune. I am lifted once he's mounted, helping myself, one small leg in the silver stirrup, levering and allowing myself to be lifted by his brown bristly arms and put between his legs, seated close against him; when he bends to hold the reins, his unshaven cheek brushes the nape of my neck. We ride the estate on Fortune. I am happy here. Held and allowed to share the reins, to guide the horse by a tug to the right or to the left. His right arm is lifted, holding one strand of the rein with that posture which is agile and can turn and be still, can allow slack and then hold taut. I move within his control of the animal and feel free. I feel free to lean forward on its neck, to brush the mane, to lean along the side of its smooth, brown sweaty neck resting my cheek there, patting and talking encouragingly to this animal, tamed by my father. From this height I see the world through his eyes. I see a sea of green waving sugarcane – which is simply green waving sugarcane – cut into fields by the hard, rutted mud traces we ride up and down. I am lost in this world with him under the sun. So far he's not spoken. There has been the monosyllabic 'Up you get,' as he pulls me up to him on the horse. And, 'There. There you are.' Established, given an existence.

I see my world from this height as we mount one of the traces to an escarpment above the fields, on the horizon the Barackpore hills. I don't reflect on the meanings of names, the history in names. I am with my father as a son, excited because he shows me attention and involves me in his world through his eyes which see the world before us. I see the square concrete bungalow on the hill; behind the high hedges of hibiscus are the barrack-rooms encircling the house. I see this with the eyes of a child, with the eyes of innocence. I see them now and wonder whether for us too innocence existed only in the womb, as it did for those huddled in the barrack-rooms and in the shacks above the city. There, over there, is the 'yard': the estate yard with its stables, the office and the bookkeeper's house. And dotted here and there on pieces of higher ground, the houses for the overseers. This is an unquestioned world: it has no idea of how it came about. But we don't dwell on the architecture or social stratification.

'Ah, young cane. Must inspect the ratoons.' We sidle through on saddle the wild grass which grows on the edge of the trace, to stand firmly on the bank and edge of the field. Ratoon, the word rings today. Ratoon. I see the young shoot springing from the sugarcane root after cropping. 'A good field.' This means it will yield a good crop. There are bad fields too. There were fields that were burnt when they shouldn't have been. Sabotaged. This is Sunday morning inspection, after we've been to mass. He didn't worship with us at first. The inspection continues until eventually we trot back up the gravel drive lined with palmiste. I am lifted and lowered; one foot finds the silver stirrup, the other is dangling and stretching for the ground. There is a terror as I stand unheld at the foot of the tall animal, my father high astride. I reach with my short brown arm to pat the sweating flank, too short to reach its forehead; it shies away from my surprising arms' trying, and then he steers Fortune away to the waiting groom.

She's given his clothes to the poor. Some poor man walks in a dead man's clothes.

18 March

I repeat: it is a bright space. Shade at the edges. An open gravel yard, the edges are shrubs, shade trees: flamboyant before flame blooms, all masses of overlaying feathery branches under the tamarind trees, all shadow and filigree of shadow. The past is all sepia which I find in the drawers of his desk. In this very desk on which I write and keep a chronicle of our love I find him and find myself in the same light, penetrated by moths . . .

I can leave it here. NO. STOP. Don't punish me . . . love me . . . punish me . . . love me.

I will imagine no more. I don't accuse. I ask to know.

Can God be a father? Can a father be God?

12 April

I remember Antoinetta long time when I was small. I remember her defiance in this family house, her defiance of my mother. This defiance, rebellion I say, showed itself as much in her silence under the correction of my mother's tongue, and with her obstinacy in continuing to do a piece of work in a way that ran contrary to my mother's wishes, as in her disarming smile and apparent loyalty to my mother. The way she let my mother know, for instance, her admiration for my father. As I observed this from long time, not quite up to the level of the dining-room table and then growing taller, seeing more, Antoinetta's admiration for my father was charming. This was trickery. My mother would be flattered that Antoinetta loved my father. 'Is the boss you like, isn't it, Antoinetta?' As she served the vegetables from the right side, or the wrong side, Antoinetta's reply was a mouth of teeth, smiles and chuckle, which from small always sounded to me like saying two things: 'Yes, Madam,' simpering, giggling; and, though I might not have conceived it so from the start, 'You bitch.'

My mother probably saw it as good house-management that she could employ someone who would be approved of by my father and also show such respect to him. Because though Antoinetta had been in the family since long, she had come and gone on occasions to have her babies, and had even been fired once by my mother. There were scars which had not healed. Antoinetta did things for my father with joy. I detected almost in my mother's milk, and Antoinetta knew, that my mother was jealous. My mother would have liked to have been loved by her servants. Indeed, I think she thought she was. In my judgement she deserved to be more than my father, since he did nothing but on his brief appearances or in a smile at table seem to be the complimenting, pleased boss. The hard work needed to get Antoinetta actually to perform at times was never seen by him, though my mother sometimes complained to him about it. You see, my father never corrected Antoinetta. And he teased her. This made her smile more, but a different smile, almost colluding against my mother, the two of them. My mother never teased Antoinetta. So they both worked to pleasure my father, and for this had to be against each other; but (and I say it intuitively, because that's the way I came to it at first) they were allies in this world: a madam and her servant.

The most extravagant form of defiance Antoinetta showed my mother was the way she carried herself, carried her body. My mother often remarked on Antoinetta's body: her hair was a source of contention. 'That hair,' as my mother thought of it, was to be kept under cover. 'Antoinetta, you must wear your cap.' A blue cap in the day, a white cap in the afternoon and evening. 'Where is your cap? I want your hair plaited and tucked under your cap.' This was the battle after, say, a day off when Antoinetta had probably had her hair ironed out and worn it not in plaits, but bouffant. 'Antoinetta, child' – Antoinetta was my mother's age – 'your hair sticking out like two horns, child.'

'Madam?'

'You better go downstairs and plait that hair and put on a clean cap.'

After lunch, when Antoinetta had freed herself of blue apron and cap and her black body moved freely under her dress, loosened, she would go down the gap to the Chiney shop by the main road. My mother, too, had loosened herself into a petticoat for her siesta, and as she lifted off her cotton dress and caught sight of Antoinetta going down the gap from the window of her bedroom, she would exclaim, 'Oh, my God, how *can* Antoinetta!' I would look, and Antoinetta almost for sure, knowing my mother's eyes were on her back, would swing her hips and backside even more than usual to say, 'Yes, is me, I free, I off down the road, you bitch, you.'

Antoinetta's bare arms, her loose body under the dress, her backside, her shoulders in the sun, her breasts free without a bra, scandalised my mother. 'That woman's body.'

My mother was scandalised. I was enchanted, and when my mother had fallen off to sleep I crept down to Antoinetta's room, smelling of vaseline and bay rum. When she came back from the shop I would watch her tidy up, rest on her iron bed until time for the white cap and apron. She performed for me, lifting her petticoat and showing me her panties, screaming with laughter. I smell it all, soft and enchanting, that time in the servant's room. And then in the bacchanal of the backyard, when the half-day girl came up to put down the mosquito-nets and the watchman came to watch.

These noises reach me here, these voices. 'Come down here, you little scamp.' I am at the kitchen window. 'What you peeping at? What you smiling at? Come let me hug you up, come let me hug you up. Is only your mother you like to kiss you, now that you think you is a big man?' Antoinetta turned to the half-day girl and the watchman down in the backyard. 'You see this child here, this is my boychild, Madam little dress-up-in-she-dress child. I like you so.

This is my white child, you know. You don't like to hear that now. Is I that bathe you, you know. Is I that wipe your backside, feed you, take you for a walk, tell you nancy story in the night when you couldn't sleep, stay with you when your mother gone out. Is I. Me. Boy, you get a lot of loving, yes.'

These noises reach me, these voices and old Antoinetta will be here in the morning. I'm sure she's forgotten all of that.

I hadn't forgotten her red earrings, little red baskets with yellow flowers, plastic, from Woolworth's. They flashed against her black skin. I was not taught to find Antoinetta beautiful. Everything I heard told me that she was ugly; and a part of me thought Antoinetta herself thought she was ugly. But the feeling and the taste of her, how she spoke of her love for me, tells me different.

I never knew what my father thought of her body. He never said, but he smiled. And in extravagant anger Antoinetta once told me how she could make my father feel sweet even if Madam, my mother, couldn't. She knew how to make a man feel sweet, and this was when she took me in her arms as if there and then to make me a man. but then, in the stillness of the under-the-house-siesta-time-silence, while my mother slept upstairs shackled to rosary beads, she showed me by moving her body in circles, playing the role of the man against a pillar of the house and then against my boy's body as a girl, how to pleasure a woman. I did not resist her pleasure.

When I see her now she is an old woman, Antoinetta, who comes to clean, calling at the gate, 'Morning, morning, all.'

Her body was her defiance, her black body was her rebellion when she had to use silence and the sabotage of contrariness. She was mother, manager of the kitchen, maker of pumpkin soups and all delicious food, coquette, play-play courtesan to the fantasies she knew she spun in my father's brain. I don't know if he would have touched her. To imagine it! Almost a cliché, a history of interference, but true. True as my fiction. Mother, who left her own children to mind my mother's children. Me. 'You see me here, I has children too, I does have to leave them and come to work for other people, mind other people children, when mine needs the minding, needs the minding bad. I have children too, mine. Boy, you get a lot of loving, yes.'

Her voice is at the gate. 'Morning, morning, all.'

*

15 July

Rainy season really here. Time flies. Lavren takes my time.

Cocoa died. Witchbroom. My father moved into sugar.

In two simple sentences and a word is a history of a place, the loss of a fortune, a family story and the task of both my fiction and these chronicles of the heart to unravel, to say: this is how I see it; this is my need to put it together, hold it so it is not all a meaningless list of disjointed memories, but a pattern with a meaning.

16 July

My father's first task on retiring here, when the land was still land and he could eke out the time he still had to plant, pasture animals and oversee the planting of grass for grazing, was to plant lawns and trees. When the pastures became plots and when the selling started he grew bored with the figures. He retired into himself. The rhythm of his world had stopped. His was the rhythm of a planter. The last of the plantocracy, their code refined into an ideal of fairness and justice, words used when dealing with the men, provided the order of that world remained unaltered: the house on the hill encircled with barrack-rooms, the overseer's house in the gully, the bookkeeper's house down in the yard with the stables. An estate: be it cocoa, coffee, bananas or sugar. Here in retirement it was pig farming and pangola grass for cattle. The world was crowding in, the land was needed for houses and it was profitable, much more profitable than any crop might be. Sell up and leave.

There were other trees. He had planted poui, cassia, king of flowers as well as the almond tree. Croton hedges screened the house from the farm. Palms enclosed the veranda. Lawns encircled the house, then beyond the fences pastures fading into the savannah of the plains and the mountains rearing in the north.

I have longed to see the weeds growing in the cracks of this stone floor. I watch the industry of ants in the pitted craters of the pebbles set in concrete. I feel the house breathe around me as the breeze comes off the savannah. I hear it tell me stories giving up smells of memories. One or two egrets flap by. Stragglers.

'Look,' he points, but he has no words left. He has returned to that time before the world was named. 'Thing.' Yes, he is left with *thingness*, but retains some initial pleasure which must be sensation, maybe even understanding, as he points, but no words. The egrets punctuated the beginning and ending of his day. Dawn, and twilight when they turned orange as they flew into the setting sun. We sit and look out on to the front of the house. He points at the trees, 'Look'; he wishes me to notice and wishes to mourn their going. I have noticed the blight crinkling the branches. I don't say. I don't speak many words and when I do, I speak the ones he grabs at but cannot snatch, and then I speak my own. He hears. I don't know what he thinks.

'Yes, the egrets, lovely the way they fly in formation.' This is not an original or a new perception. It is stating the obvious and the remark is one he has made and I've made for him now. This does not detract from the beauty of the birds and their flight. 'The trees – there are still some flowers.' I notice the persistence of flowers blooming on half-dead branches.

The morning after we took him to the nursing home we woke to the poui, which had known the fullness of yellow glory, blown down, cracked at the base. The branches pushed against the glass windows of the bungalow, darkening the room. The roots were forced out of the ground.

'Like there was a strong wind last night, eh, Madam,' Antoinetta began as she opened the gate beneath the alamandas. 'Only the other day the boss looking at them trees and pointing. He know something.'

Now, as I go towards him where he lies dying, I stop and turn and am in another room, in an earlier time. I'm in the drawing-room of the bungalow. That room, there, which I see as I sit here on the veranda, on that chair at that table. Fixing it. Locating the time. At times this need overwhelms. I wish to recover each part of him. Like the way I pinpoint each object in his press. Like how I know each smell, like when skin peels from dry hands. I know how I am held, how I was held. I know the unshaven cheek on the nape of my neck.

Is there invention in this remembering?

'We have a boy who is away who looks like this young man, who looks like him,' he says to my mother, pointing at me opposite him at the dinner-table. She remembered me and looked at me with understanding, wanting me to believe in his love for me.

'He loves you,' she said.

But I knew that now I only reminded him of someone like myself. For him I was no longer me. The reunion would be impossible and I would have to make do with a love which was expressed in continuing anonymity.

This was how the last weeks were spent, before this hot afternoon at two o'clock when I found myself at his deathbed. I remembered as I looked at him, his breathing pulling on the oxygen mask, the concrete drain at the side of the road outside the nursing home. I noticed it as I came in after getting out of the hot plastic-seated taxi which had dropped me on the main road. I had to walk up a suburban cul-de-sac to an old colonial house which was now the nursing home. The drain was bone dry, but in a crack where the earth had collapsed was a stagnant pool which had grown moss, and mosquitoes had spawned larvae there. My shirt was sticking to my back with perspiration, aggravated by the plastic seat of the taxi. Instead of being caught up in the throes of a momentous event, my father's death, I found my mind focusing on these facts and realities: moss, larvae, plastic seats, sweat. Then I went over the last weeks as we waited for him to give up or for the oxygen to be turned off.

'Could you not turn it off?' my mother said to the family doctor and friend who had delivered her babies, stitched cuts.

'He will go in his own time,' he replied, sounding professional and comforting and then leaving us to witness each last gasp.

I had missed the anointing of his body by the priest.

What I salvage from the last weeks is his body, old now and so easily allowing me to hold him, different from the past when he shut it away from me. I had no fear now of the unshaven cheek on the nape of my neck. I took it gladly in my hands to shave. Lifting him up from the bed into the wheelchair he would have to embrace me. I steadied him by his shoulders, fixed his feet on the rest, pushed him on to the veranda, where I sit now, looking and remembering everything that has changed. I salvage his nakedness, an old man's quiescence when he did a pee, had a shit and I had to wipe his arse, feeding and cleaning up after feeding, and finding the words he snatched at in his pointing, 'Look, thing.' Soaping his nakedness, towelling, powdering the creases where he might develop bedsores.

I was grateful for that time.

Time now was concentrated and focused around a hospital bed. Still he gasped. I watched the plastic tube which connected the mask to the cylinder which stood at the head of the bed. I watched the saline drip from the plastic sack from which a tube hung and was inserted into the vein where the elbow was bent; another entered the nasal passage. He breathed. A fly buzzed infuriatingly against the glass of the window in a mad effort to be free, to reach for the open air. A black nurse in a white uniform dabbed his brow with a folded hanky to blot up the beads of sweat. My mother whose knuckles were shackled with rosary beads, whispered her own prayers. I did not pray. I no longer prayed. One of my brothers stood and watched. To imagine what was in his mind would be another fiction, not this one. I held my father's hand, bending towards the bed awkwardly, until he almost sat up struggling with the exertion to keep breathing, and found that he could not, and fell back with all the exertion spent and a startled look which remained fixed on his face: all four of us at the same time realised that he had died.

'It is the end. May he rest now, poor dear,' my mother said, almost inaudibly. He was dead. We hardly lingered. The nurse lowered his eyelids with her black fingers and shut his mouth after she had removed the respirator. My mother turned and we followed her, my brother and I, as if we were following my father out of the room, so definite was the sense that he was no longer in that room, in that body.

Outside, the sun was hot and blinding.

'Eternal rest grant unto him, O Lord, And let perpetual light shine upon him, May he rest in peace. Amen.' I no longer prayed, but I repeated the formula three times, instinctively.

> *Requiem eternam dona ei Domine*
> *Et lux perpetua luceat ei*
> *Requiescant in Pace*
> Amen.

I did not pray. I no longer pray, not knowing what it means to speak to a father. It is not a metaphor that holds much power or meaning. Can God be a father? Can a father be God? But the formulae and the antiphonal beauty of Gregorian chant can still lap around me like the waves on the gulf and bring peace, though without the illusion that anything is eternal.

Much that followed did not touch me. I could not find in myself reasons for grief or mourning. There was some regret that we had never managed it. All I had was my invention to use to expurgate, to exorcise, to make myself free. I would never know if I spoke the truth.

The requiem mass, the funeral procession across the plains and along the gulf to the city, the burial in Lapeyrouse while the women recited the rosary, all these were gestures made by a family who supported a widow.

Weeks later, for no reason that I could easily see or with any sign that it was to happen, I began to shake uncontrollably. I stopped the car I was driving across the plains going into the city, to the museum to work, and at the side of the road, where an old shut rum-shop stood in rusted galvanize, I sat with my feet on the ground with the car-door open and gave myself up to my grief and loss. My whole body shook, my shoulders in particular rose and fell and I sobbed (sob, I use it for the sound); I uttered words that came from a cave in my chest. At first there were no tears but all sound, and waves of shaking as if possessed, as if inhabited, another body moving inside my own, so that we wrestled for control continually. I let the fight go on and on until it no longer seemed a fight but a passionate embracing and searching both painful and sweet, in a union that was unknowable, till in the end tears bathed my cheeks and comforted my spirit. I knew then that he had departed from my body and would let me rest in the knowledge that if there was invention in my remembering, it was because forgetfulness can also be inventive. Through both, I came to acknowledge my love for him, and his love for me.

8 August

I could describe the light, rather than go on with this story. I would prefer that. Light which is filtered through a misty haze and which hangs over the savannah and is the light of the Mayaro sun which I have described before. Easier to do that, to stay with words which are like paint, delineating landscapes which you hope speak metaphorically – watercolours like my aunt's. Their light which is this same light. The ochre bush she paints around the pink bungalow, her orchids I have stuck to the cream wall. Light corrupts. That would be one way of putting down this history, herstory, which speaks of another time, in another house, another life. The history of light.

Easier than to dip into the drawer through sepia and the perforations of moths which hold the ennui which can fall on me in the afternoon, after work, after trying to disentangle myself from the skein of betrayal, treachery and crime. Light.

Tropical contemplation. That was once an ideal, I have to admit, before this epistemophilia, this story. It was part of the story.

My heart was in my mouth. She sat, where it seemed she always sat when a special word was sought, a special word heard, confessional-like, at the edge of the bed. 'I want to be a monk.' Those words sear through me now. Like these. 'I want to enter the monastery.' I remember her back as she walked away from me along the long corridor to her bedroom, shaking her head, looking up as if to heaven, whispering a prayer of thanks as if a prayer, offered since when, had been answered. She sought the icon of the Sacred Heart. She had shaken her head as if her assent was not to me but to God. He had asked her for this offering and she had freely given it to Him. Her eyes filled with tears and I remember that I could not swallow. I left the house for school.

I had never seen the villages so transformed, so lit from within with pain and want. Their passion.

My passion was the cross. It cassocked and surpliced me in fine linen trimmed with lace. This was a divine ballet moved by Medieval chants. *Salve regina, mater misericordia . . .*

A new name. My habit folded me in safety. Hooded, arms folded in the folds of a cowl. A sacrifice. I lie outstretched, cruciform on the floor of the sanctuary. A mother's love. Yearning for a father. Can God be a father? Can a father be God? I had to leave and make another kind of search.

I return to how it had been.

That morning: early. First Communion morning. Is a morning of starched whiteness, starched white pants, starched white cotton shirt, a satin tie as white as the embossed satin quilt of tabernacles. First Communion morning: as fresh and white and pure as starched clothes, as white washing on the line in the breeze, as white as my soul the day before, cleaned and cleansed in the confessional where I took the long list of my seven-year-long life of sin to whisper each and every secret wrong, each and every secret sin, each and every betrayal in the bamboo patch; allegiances of sin, each and every dart of pain pinned to the crucified Lord like the spears stuck into the naked body of Saint Sebastian in the Book of Saints.

First Communion morning: as white as my new white socks slipped into my new white shoes, as white as the satin white rosette pinned with the gold pin and the gold medal to my breast pocket. All resplendently white.

First Communion morning: the wind rocked the house and threw down the statue of the Virgin Mother on top the globe of the world, crushing the head of the serpent. The wind blew her down and cracked her base. First Communion morning: marred.

First Communion morning: practised for by kneeling at my mother's knee, practising to take the white wafer, host, Jesus, the real presence, the transubstantiated presence of a man's flesh into a crumb of bread, practising to take this upon my tongue. All ready. A saint for a day. I have done deeds of goodness, brought each hour to my mother's attention, each deed a new and little flower to be pencilled in a little notebook, a bouquet of intentions and deeds offered in this month of May the month of the Virgin Mary. Then the church and the kneeling in the front pew clasping my soul as white as the white plastic prayerbook embossed with the good shepherd. First Communion morning: the hymns – 'Sing to Mary . . .', 'O Sacred Head ill used', and the Latin benediction hymn, a child's faith in Aquinas' logic 'Tantum Ergo Sacramentum, Veneremur genui . . .'

I have starved myself from the night before, no drop of water has passed these lips, no food touched this tongue. I am ready. It is my turn. I am squeezed up against a little black girl from the First Communion class held on Miss Violet's back veranda, learning hymns on the old harmonica, learning catechism with the green parrot in the cage by the sapodilla tree repeating after us as we repeated after Miss Violet.

'Who made you?' Miss Violet.

'Who made you?' The green parrot by the sapodilla tree.

'God made me.' The First Communion class.

'God made me.' The green parrot by the sapodilla tree.

'Why did God make you?' Miss Violet.

'Why did God make you?' The green parrot by the sapodilla tree.

And so on and on, until we and the green parrot by the sapodilla tree knew the little blue penny-catechism by heart and by parrot. The little black girl's tulle veil tickled my neck and my new shoes gave me blisters already. I failed the test. 'Mummy, it's stuck to the roof of my mouth.' I cannot bite this transubstantiated presence. Lest it bleed? Miss Violet didn't tell us.

'Leave it there. It will melt away.' What? Like ice? Out into the sunshine – 'AVE, AVE, AVE MARIA' – to be kissed and embraced by aunts and handshaken sternly by uncles. I manage to curl with my tongue the last fragment of the real presence from the roof of my mouth into the saliva to slip down my throat, to be digested and become me and I become it, Him. How did my imagination hold such a wonder? At seven? Even now.

First Communion morning: warm white bread from the Portuguese shop by the railway line for First Communion breakfast. White vanilla ice-cream and black cake encrusted with white-sugar icing, rosettes and scalloped edges: in the afternoon, party for cousins and presents of white plastic prayerbooks and mother-of-pearl rosary beads.

I remember the dust by the railway line and passing the barracks and seeing the little Indian children half-naked and black, dirty and poor. I saw the small boy who always stood at the end of the gap with the burnt stomach as white as white fish-bait, white as my First Communion day.

'Poor people,' my mother says as we pass in the car. Where did my allegiance lie, where the betrayal? I kept looking back through the rearview mirror as we turned into the gap and could no longer see the barracks behind the screen of casuarina trees. Could no longer see the boy. Where had I read about him?

I remember the dust by the railway line, and the dust is in my eyes as I move these well-placed things, each in their circle of dust on the top shelf of the linen press.

I have returned knowing that what had led me to the altar, to think of being an *alter Christi*, a priest, was my passion for her. That had not been possible, so I had sublimated those desires, surpliced and cassocked that passion, girded up my loins with the girdle of chastity. Now that I had returned, not knowing what I could be or do other than retrace the steps, decipher and decode, invent, I was here again, the family curator.

I had taken my guilt, my love for her, my yearning for him, into the cloister. All that passion was spent.

I return for the last rites.

A letter came this morning from her. Now it is no ennui. It is guilt, tears. She still has the ability to spin a web, a web of illusions, a web she hopes will hold when she dies, a web in which we will all be held, the family.

So the words that describe the landscape, the light that furs the hill, is easier, instead of questions that accuse, statements that admonish in their kindness. Insinuating herself, intervening, never being able to relinquish. Can I relinquish?

She let me know the saint day that I had forgotten, a day we had both been fond of; letting me know it so that she could let me know that she knew that I hadn't remembered, had forgotten yet again . . . our passion was at the foot of an altar: *Introibo ad altare Dei . . . Ad Deum qui laetificat juventutem meum*. She wants me to be still there, squeezed into the edge of the chair listening to the lives of the saints: Saint Andrew taming the wolves, Saint Lawrence burnt on a gridiron and asking to be turned over, Saint Augustine who met an angel by the sea trying to empty the sea into a small pool, the impossibility of understanding the Trinity.

I turn to the light, not to the gnostic sense of illumination, but this simple brilliance, this Caribbean sun, which, yes, can corrupt, but, too, can mingle with foam, be lace to surplice these shores, surpliced and cassocked with clouds of white linen. Metaphor in a novelist? Oh, for the plain style in a poet to ease the solitude of middle-age still in love . . . turning these pages as she sorts through the linen.

15 August – Feast of the Assumption

This is the last day. I return here where I began with the empty spaces on the walls. Now most of the furniture has gone. When I come down she is sitting on the couch fully dressed, a small neat woman, without the extravagance of the past which is somewhere but not here in this small room, shrunk to an empty space. My mother. She faces the empty veranda and the lawn with the dead stumps of the dead trees which my father had planted. I stand at the foot of the stairs and look at her. I take it all in, she in the empty space. At the door of the pantry is Antoinetta, sitting on her chair with her back to me, looking into the kitchen. I hear her slop and wet munch, as she dunks buttered bread into her tea and slurps on it with her toothless gums.

Yesterday, we had gone for a last drive through the cocoa hills, my mother and I, and she had showed me the last of the old houses on the old cocoa estates, blight on the branches of the cocoa trees and some still entangled in the witchbroom. We had a drink together on the veranda in the evening and she told me about my birth. Then we went to bed early.

I woke suddenly to the sound of a nightmare, the voice of a dream. It was my mother in the next-door room. She was breathing heavily and crying out with a strangulated voice. I went to her. I was naked because of the heat. I pulled out the tucked-in mosquito-net and sat on the edge of the bed next to her and took her hand. She woke startled, crying out and relieved presumably that it was me and not some phantom of her dream. She turned over. 'I was having a terrible dream. Go off to your bed now, dear.' I sat on the edge of the bed and stroked her frizz of grey hair as she fell back to sleep.

Early this morning: 'Your dream?'

She was a little girl dressed in a thin cotton chemise. She was standing outside at the back of one of the large estate houses in the middle of the quadrangle of outhouses and barrack-rooms. She was looking up to the galvanize roofs of the barrack-rooms, and rising up out of the barrack-rooms was a huge tall black man dressed in breeches. He was bare-backed and his black skin gleamed. He was bearing down on her with a whip.

She said that when I woke her, she was crying for help. 'Stop! Don't punish me!'

I never asked her to interpret her dream for me. I thought of the journey the previous afternoon through the old estates and I thought of the centuries of accumulated guilt and fear which had taken hold of her in that dream that night in the pink bungalow on the plains, near the swamps and the oyster beds, now that she was closing house, leaving the estate.

This is it. I'm bereft of words. I am bereaved. These are the last rites.

Within an hour the last bits will be loaded up and taken away.

My mother watches as the Indian and black men lift the heavy mahogany pieces and shoulder them out of the house into the yard to the back of a truck.

I must help Antoinetta with the odds and ends she's collected from the kitchen; so little, after so long. When I put her down at her small board-house with the cardboard boxes full of old saucepans and Pyrex dishes, she can hardly reach the top stair to her little veranda. It has come to this.

We part and I know I will visit. 'You go come soon, eh, Sir?'

I keep holding that picture of my mother on the couch (later, the Indian and black men came back for the couch when we had left, and took it for Antoinetta), in the empty room looking out on to the empty veranda and the lawn with the dead stumps, as we sit in the airport lounge and await the announcement of her flight.

'Darling.'

'Yes?' and we don't finish our words.

'My pet.'

Did she have some last thing to say?

I stayed till the end and watched the fuselage disappear into the blue and cloud over the mountains. I turned and left and then made my way, leaving the plains and the mountains for the north-east coastal road. I was finished with the museum, and now had a small house by the sea. It was while I was there, completing this journal, that I came upon the last tales.

THE HOUSES OF KAIRI
THE CARNIVAL TALES OF
LAVREN MONAGAS DE LOS MACAJUELOS

2

The Tale of the House in Town

LAVREN WAS STIRRED once more by the tales of Marie Elena, muse and mother, to leave the turret room and to descend the staircase, where he met his beloved Josephine whose memory he took with him. He dived beneath the corrugated waves of the Gulf of Sadness through a saffron light, and resurfaced at a time when one century tottered towards the horizon of the setting sun, bleeding over the mountains of the continent of Bolivar. Another rose with the morning over the beaches of Manzanilla and shone down on the indentured from the Gangetic plain, the last of whom Marie Elena remembers having seen, brought in boats to the island of Kairi from Nelson, the island of quarantines, with their children whose mouths bled with the dirt they chewed from the haematite cliffs.

As he emerged from the waters of the Gulf of Sadness, the previous generations fell from him, from her, and faded into the sepia of memory and tale. Elena Elena had died of a grand old age back in Aracataca, guarded by her tiger cats and saying, 'Take the crucifixes away from me, old priest, and paint them black.' The Englishman had died of syphilis in the Planters' Club on the Plaza de la Marina, and was buried quietly in Lapeyrouse Cemetery.

Lavren found himself under the old silk-cotton trees at the water's edge on the mudflats of Mucurapo, where the tide had once strewn the beaches with the charred flotsam and jetsam of the fires of emancipation; the wreckage of indentureship that had destroyed the cities of San Jorge de Monagas, the old and founding town, San Andres in the south and the New Town which now rose above him. He looked towards the Laventville Hills, where the sun came down upon the new streets and squares, the new avenues and boulevards of the Belle d'Antilles. This is what the sailors called her, shimmering in her basin of green hills, circling above Santa Ana, Maraval, Sainte Claire. He looked with the eyes of the master of colour, the art master, Monsieur Cazabon.

Lavren turned the pages of his tale, eager to reach where he was

149

being drawn. The heat delayed him. He made his way slowly, following where he was led by the murmuring of water as of a fountain playing over rocks and falling into itself. The murmur of the water was like the murmur of a voice. It came to him on the breeze that descended from the green hills. Wafting on this breeze was the scent of cuscus grass, which he had first met in the port near the walls of the Cathedral of the Immaculate Conception with its twin towers. It was mixed with the scent of the market and the orange sellers. The murmuring of the water was mixed with the laughter and shouts of the market criers.

At the corner of Prince and Queen Charlotte Street, Lavren stopped by the Rosary Church gleaming in the morning sunshine, built of limestone from the Laventville Hills. Here, the cuscus grass which pervaded the grass market and the smell of fish from Petite Pointe where the sloops and pirogues from up the archipelago were moored near the cathedral wall, were distilled into a single scent. It was mixed with what he learned later at Marie Elena's dressing-table was eau de Cologne. This distracted his desire which had been to linger in the new town. He had to pull himself away from the pavé beneath the balcony of the Hotel Colombie where Uncle Anatole had recently taken a room. He'd moved in there to be near both the vaults of the cathedral (to investigate whether or not the Monagas de los Macajuelos were black), and to be near the spot where it was easiest to procure small boys for pleasure for a modest sum: easier even than outside the Planters' Club on the Plaza de la Marina. Most of what he had found so far was dust, as he inspected marriage certificate after marriage certificate. He was more successful with the small boys. 'What will you do when you find out that you are black?' the concièrge of the Hotel Colombie asked him one morning.

'I cannot believe that we are, but if there is some touch of the tar-brush I shall do my best to erase it from the history of the new world,' Lavren laughed as he pulled himself away from the Hotel Colombie, its mahogany staircase leading to the powdered and perfumed boudoirs with the lace curtains. He will return to suffer his first disappointment in love.

He followed his obsession. He followed the gurgling sound of water, the murmur which sounded like the chatter of a young girl. He followed the scent of cuscus grass from Dominica and eau de Cologne. He turned towards Brunswick Square, thinking that there must be a fountain there, and that this was where he was being led. He enjoyed the auditory and olfactory sport as he rested against a stone wall overgrown with purple bougainvillaea. He was drenched by the perfume of the frangipani trees. The square was a further distraction from his journey to the north of the town.

While it was partly the breeze which brought the sound of the murmuring water and the scent of cuscus grass and eau de Cologne, it was also love. Love drew Lavren. His desire was to love and be loved completely, to know the open hearts of women and the silent hearts of men. He walked this city in the full knowledge of his ambisexual nature, which gave him the knowledge of what lay within different genders. He laughed again at the words of Uncle Anatole as he went in search of she whom he knew was born here and lived here, in search of he whom he had been destined to meet. Betrayal was not in his mind.

The fountain in the middle of Brunswick Square was dry. It was dry season, the time of the flowering trees. The hills encircling the Belle d'Antilles were golden with the poui and sprinkled with the cinnamon of the immortelle. Like springtime blossom in Valencia.

He had become a young man on this journey. He had descended from the turret room as the nearing-middle-aged person that he now is, a Tiresias of the new world, who from the beginning of these tales has been sitting at the foot of the bed in the turret room or at the Demerara window, depending on the light, overlooking the Gulf of Sadness and retrospectively and clairvoyantly spanning the centuries, writing down his Carnival Tales. 'Farewell,' he says, 'farewell' – to her and to her world which is passing away. But now as you meet him, leaning against a wall on the main street of Puerto de los Hispanoles, he is a youth who shows in his features the beauty all youth has of mixing genders and attracting similar poles and opposite polarities.

He was eager for all experience. He bought a small brown-paper bag of pistache from a marchande who sat at the gates to the military barracks near the Municipal Council Chamber, and nibbled on the nuts as he watched the British soldiers practise their parade on the gravel yard while he stood in the hot morning sun. It had taken since dawn to amble up from the Cathedral of the Immaculate Conception, savouring every sight and every smell, eager for a knowledge of this place as the century tottered towards its end with black people, free people. But the calypsoes of the recent past were not far from the lips of the old, and the marchande, stooping, selling pistache on the pavement, sang the old calypso. 'Under the Marabella Bridge, is there I lost my grandmother.' The riots and the massacres that had forced the emancipation were not far from her memory. The same soldiers marched out of the gates this sunny morning to change guard at the Governor's House, in the garden where Picton had once erected his gibbet. The city changed before Lavren's eyes. The age came with the brush-strokes of Monsieur Cazabon.

Now the Governor was Lord Chancellor. Lavren hears the calypso – *The Governor tall tall tall, he peeping over the wall* – he knew that name. He tingled with anticipation. He had heard of the Chancellors, of Lady Chancellor. He had heard the old Marie Elena talk of them. It had to be admitted that he had clues. He had more than clues. He had heard Marie Elena's tales. But in this moment of re-created youth, he suspended belief. He stepped into the shoes of a young lover eager for the sight of his beloved. He placed himself in her time. He frocked himself in a white linen suit and donned a Panama hat for the sun, and awaited with eagerness the moment when his beloved would be on his arm, a sylph in white muslin, he a suitor in white linen.

He eventually stopped journeying around the city, going into the Laventville hills to see it laid out in front of him from high up, by the hilltop shrine to Our Lady of Sorrows from where he used to look down at the new and shimmering Belle d'Antilles spreading into the canefields of Mucurapo on the edge of the waters of the Gulf of Sadness which rippled like tin foil. He is pulled to a crowd which is gathering in front of one of the large houses on the Savannah, the centre of the basin in the north of the city, where the rich live. He goes there with ears filled with the sounds of the criers in the market, the pulling of carts in the dirt streets of downtown, to these pavements and gateways of limestone erected with wrought-iron gates, and fences tumbled over with bougainvillaea and trumpeting alamandas.

He approached where the crowd pressed against the gates of No. 18, Cipriani Boulevard. He noticed their faces, the sallowness of yellow fever, the anaemia of malaria, these victims of Anopheles. Though a freedom had come, poverty and sickness remained, emancipation had become indentureship, and they had brought their suffering to the gate of Dr Ramon Monagas de los Macajuelos, itinerant District Medical Officer, his title engraved on a brass plaque set into the limestone of the gate post.

Lavren peeped through the wrought-iron railings into the garden of flowering shrubs and at the veranda screened with asparagus fern, from whose steps the queue of patients stretched; some on crutches, others brought on thin pallets and still others, old men and women, using young sons and daughters as supports. The scene reminded him of descriptions in the gospels. They had come from far and wide bearing bundles of ground provision: yams, eddoes, dasheen, sweet potatoes. Some had callaloo bush and cradles of crabs and pots of lobsters, buckets of oysters from those who lived near the swamp. Having no money, they paid in kind. A young boy had brought a turtle from Rampanalgas; there were others with chickens and ducks and even one old woman with a goat. The profusion of vegetables, fish and livestock was laid on the floor of the veranda and on the front steps.

'All you, hush. The doctor working. He go see all you, but hush. The madam inside and she can't stand the noise.' Lavren pushed to the front of the queue.

'Excuse me, excuse me.'

'What is this, for truth? What this white man doing in the street? Sir, you can't see is poor people here?' An old woman touches Lavren on his shoulder.

Lavren was transfixed at the gate. The murmur of water was the generous fountain in the middle of the garden, and for a moment the scent of cuscus grass and eau de Cologne was diluted by the pungence of ginger and bay-rum, the scent he knew from when he used to bury his child's head in Josephine's woman's breasts. It was Josephine. She was young and taking complete charge of all affairs going on in the yard. She was a mere girl. He wanted to call but she turned and went back inside.

Lavren, storyteller at the foot of Marie Elena's bed, had taken the lorgnettes resting on Marie Elena's bedside table, which had once belonged to Sou Sou. He has them now in the top pocket of his linen suit, raises them inquisitively to his nose and magnifies the garden of Dr Ramon Monagas de los Macajuelos. The queue of sick crush upon him, but he stands and surveys the garden. The scent of cuscus grass and eau de Cologne emanates from the house and comes with the laughter of young girls whom he cannot see even with Sou Sou's lorgnettes. But within the laughter there is pain, a pain reaching up from the former century, a guilt choking at the throats of the children as the witchbroom chokes the cocoa estates. Shadows move beyond the veranda doors . . . Lavren enters a former time.

'If I eat another cockerel,' said Sou Sou, 'I shall be crowing morning and night.' Josephine had a job to collect all the produce off the front veranda where it was piled up by the poor who came from the surrounding districts to see the District Medical Officer, Dr Ramon Monagas de los Macajuelos, the miracle worker.

'Madam, these people really like Doctor,' Josephine said to Sou Sou, who refused to come out during the hours of the clinic and would rather have gone and shooed them away, so that she could have had some peace, and also have had her husband to herself.

'Look, Josephine, we need some peace around here. After the next one shut the door and say the angel has flown back to heaven.'

The fame of the District Medical Officer, Dr Ramon Monagas de los Macajuelos, had been spread through the century by none other than his daughter, Marie Elena.

Deciding to seek some balance to this history, herstory, Lavren came upon some interesting information when he went to Savanna Grande, led by Josephine. He was becoming lulled by these stories of goodness and miracle-working, and he wanted to get the record straight about this land flowing with milk and honey and everyone living like one big happy family. He took off the lorgnettes belonging to Sou Sou, which at least had showed him her dissatisfaction with marrying a husband who was an angel. Lavren surfaced from beneath the gulf through the wrecks of Apodoca, and came at last across the plains to the great savannah, near the swamp on the other side of the island, where the great rebellion had singed the grasses. He came with Josephine as his guide. He came again to the board-house on the road to Moruga, the road now bumpy pitch because of the mud volcanoes spluttering away in the devils' woodyard. He pushed on to the board-house below the crumbling red dirt road where he had been told stories of Africa and the middle passage before, by the old man with a face wrinkled like parchment, who had heard stories from his grandfather and was now supported by his wife, daughter, granddaughter and great-granddaughter all living in the board-house above the gully where the tania grows.

The rain had stopped falling since s/he was last here and s/he noticed the palmiste that almost touched the sky at Indian Walk in the yard of the Doctor's House. This was why s/he had come, to ask about Dr Monagas, his revered grandfather, writer of essays, miracle-worker and angelic lover. He knew the place, pointed to out of the car when he was a baby hermaphrodite and sat sucking his thumb on the silken knee of Marie Elena. 'That is the Doctor's House at Indian Walk.' The name stuck in his memory, like other words — Barackpore, bungalow, ratoon — indentured and enslaved now, not only to his memory, but to his imagination.

At the board-house, the old man, grandson of Matundo whom down here they called Frazer, whose grandmother was called Yobendo and married Captain John Pierre, was sitting on the small veranda that looked out on the road with his daughter, granddaughter and great-granddaughter. He remembered Lavren and smiled.

'Did you know Dr Monagas?' The old man leant forward to hear better.

'Who you say?' he shouted, in order to hear himself.

'Monagas, Dr Monagas.' The women attended to the telling of the tale. 'You hear of him? He' (these women are unaware of the hermaphrodite nature of the apparent young man in front of them, so therefore use the masculine pronoun) 'ask if you know a Dr Monagas. Is so he call?' The women turned to Lavren for assurance. He nodded.

'Yes,' he said.

'Oh-ho, Dr Monagas, Indian Walk? Yes? Indian Walk.' The old man straightened himself in his rocker and looked at them all and spoke solemnly. 'You know why it call Indian Walk? You know why it call so?' He bent towards Lavren and the women.

'Tell us, tell us, we don't know.' The women attended to the telling of the tale with their chorus of voices and Lavren attended to the meanings, his memory still of salt and the wrecks of Apodoca.

'Indians, Indians from India. This is the way they come, they pass here to the estates.' Lavren knew he was right and his memory conjured the repetition of cruelty. The old man told the tale of the

155

Fatel Rozack to get the history straight. 'Indians,' the old African said. 'They bring Indians when we say no more. We march off the estates and we say no more.' He told again of the sabotage, the rebellion to the whip; the whip on the back of the manager's wife bawling because of the whip on the back of the man, or the woman or the child in the sugarcane field. Lavren saw the cruel repetition, the murder and exhaustion of the Amerindians when there were no more pearls left in the gulf. He saw the folly of the priest Las Casas who had thrown a rosary about the neck of Africa and chained its people to the middle passage and the overcrowded barracoons. He saw the addiction to clay in the children, who stuffed their mouths with dirt, and now he saw another lot coming in the *Fatel Rozack* and put on Nelson Island, every name an echo, quarantined and disinfected and put on the trail to the plains of Kairi which they made their India in the new world.

'Trail,' the old man whispered.

'What you say?' the chorus of women asked.

'Indian Walk, a trail, a trail of blood beneath which is the trail we walk and the trail the first people walk. They come here from the *Fatel Rozack*.'

'But he ask you about Dr Monagas?' the women piped in, suitably impressed with the sermon of the man with a voice of Shango.

The afternoon sun lowered its lances to where the tiptop flowering plumes of the palmiste told of the governors to come, and the rise and fall of empire still too far away to imagine. Lavren picked a tune from out of the calypsonian's hat: *The Governor tall, tall tall, He peeping over the wall . . .*

'But tell him about the doctor. What you say his name is? Morgan?' The women resumed the tale.

'No,' Lavren interjected, 'he was a pirate.'

'Well, this one was a murderer. Yes, you hear what I say. The man was a murderer. They call him l'Diable. You know what that is, eh? Monagas l'Diable. That is what they call him. He was a devil, yes.'

'You sure?' Lavren asked. 'I know a Monagas l'Diable who lived in another valley, the valley of San Martin. This one I asking you about was a miracle-worker. He was an angel.'

'Is him: we drive him from here.' The old man was sitting bolt upright in his rocker and was again in the possession of his Shango voice. 'Is him, Monagas l'Diable. He is the one that cut the child throat. Angel, devil, is the same man. You know they have some angels fall from heaven. Well, this one was one of these.'

'Cut the throat of the child?' Lavren spun in his memory, using both hindsight and clairvoyance to scan the centuries for evidence. He settled into the teatime tales of Marie Elena for corroboration of this astounding fact. Never had it been mentioned. He could not find an inkling of it, not an insinuation, not a glance of the eyes, not a flicker that might betray the hidden secret. Lavren wondered the impossible, whether Marie Elena never even knew? He found it difficult to accept that *he* had never even had an inkling. Mr de Lisle's golfball had obviously not shaken up memory as much as he thought it had. To find another hermaphrodite was a perpetual desire, yes, as yet unfulfilled, though he suspected quite a few were locked away in the closets (those presses), but to find a murderer was a real coup. He was a little disappointed that he had not known about it. He was taken aback. He really did believe the tales of the angelic lover and the miracle-worker. He believed the mountains of chickens, fruit and vegetables left on the veranda were not so much payment for the cure as votive offerings to the saint.

'Which child it was now?' The old man turned to his wife over there where all the women sat staring at Lavren and wondering at the old man's telling the white fella these things about his own people, his own family. 'Not Miss Gertrude boychild? Yes, he it is that get the fishbone stick in his throat and the doctor say he go operate. Operate – he cut the child throat and the child dead.' He smiled at Lavren. 'That is what the people say.'

The women smiled too. Lavren smiled.

'L'Diable, Monagas l'Diable, a real devil from heaven'; the old man rocked back on the wooden rocker and laughed and laughed and laughed.

Lavren chuckled so loudly that it woke Marie Elena as she lay on her bed dreaming of her funeral. 'What did you say, dear? Is that you laughing? You always giggled as a child. I thought it was the undertaker, but I couldn't understand why he was laughing when I was asking him to see that the grave was tidied up.' She raised herself on her pillows and they both looked out of the window of the turret room at the Gulf of Sadness, full of blood in the setting sun. 'There are some things I've not told you and there are some things you have not told me. I'm too tired. One day you will know everything.' Lavren raised her back slightly and fluffed up the pillows to make her bed fresh for the evening, before Josephine came up with the bowl of chicken soup and some dry toast.

The laughter of the old man was to bring the world down round about their ears. It continued to echo in Lavren's ears as he returned to his tale. The laughter of the old man and his wife, daughter, granddaughter and great-granddaughter shattered the memory frame of this creole hermaphrodite and made him descend beneath the waves of the Gulf of Sadness to resurface again where his passion and interest had always been, with his muse and mother Marie Elena. Here he is, in the last days, where these tales get written, sitting at the foot of her bed or at the wide sill of the Demerara window, depending on the light. Here he is with her old wrinkled body, kept alive with chicken soup, dry toast and the thin wafers of Holy Communion.

Lavren, self-styled youthful lover, debonair in white linen suit and Panama hat, returned to his tale and to his city, the Belle d'Antilles. He returned to find there had been another fire, another riot for freedom, and downtown near the lighthouse on the carenage the walls were charred. He returned to the city trembling with excitement of riot and the sound that filled his ears was more than the murmur of water, but now the rush and gush of it. The *Gazette* warned of flooding as the newly laid water system was constantly sabotaged by the people who were angry at the taxes. Instead they allowed the water to flow wildly and waste. Lavren did not need Sou Sou's lorgnettes to magnify the time, to magnify the change as he walked among the fallen timbers and the still-sizzling city. The music of drums filled the ruins and the people came out to see the drummer Johnny Zee Zee, father of Gumbo Lai Lai, the mighty stickfighter. Lavren stopped in the square behind the cathedral to see kalenda dance with Johnny Zee Zee as tall as a Moco Jumbie. He hears the cry and the shout: 'They break open the prison. Greasy Pole come out the jail and he big like Lolotte Borde.'

He pulled towards No. 18, Cipriani Boulevard, where the sound of water was loudest. Here he picked up the scent of cuscus grass and eau de Cologne once more. Once more he tingled with the excitement and expectation of Josephine in the garden. But what of those other shadows behind the veranda door, behind that scrim of lace, the laughter of young girls, the pain?

This was a morning when Lavren had again left Uncle Anatole in his room on the first floor of the Hotel Colombie, about to descend the stairs after a night of clandestine passion to continue his investigation concerning the pigmentation of the Monagas de los Macajuelos. Miraculously, neither the cathedral nor the hotel had been touched by the fire. Too many political reputations were at stake in the rooms on the first floor. It provided work too; the unemployed around the markets of the Petite Pointe and those from up the archipelago, come by sloop from Grenada and Santa Lucia, were all too grateful for work carrying buckets of water to the upper floors of the hotel.

This was a morning when the sky was eggshell and the stillness of the gardens in the north of the city was interrupted by the questions of the keskidee and the shimmer of butterflies competing for pollen with the hovering hummingbirds which disappeared in the blur of their wings. But on this morning it was also shattered by the crash of buckets and the gush of water, not only from the fountain in the middle of the garden, but overflowing the steps of the veranda so that Lavren could only imagine, standing as he was at the gate, the pandemonium in the house. This pandemonium drowned the laughter of the girls and the shadows behind the scrim of lace tangled with others rushing to and fro.

The house in town was convulsed and this flooded the backyard. 'There is no water; we don't have enough water even to wash our skins,' Sou Sou complained. 'We need more water because we keep ourselves clean. They stand at standpipes wasting the water and then we cannot fill our baths.' Sou Sou, as she grew older and neglected by Ramon who kept on being the travelling doctor and writing theological essays, asserted herself by demanding several hundred gallons of water daily for her own personal plunge bath. 'Celestine, is it that little child of yours who turned the tap off in the bathroom?'

'No, Madam, the child don't come in the house.'

'You know the tap must be left on all night to fill the plunge bath. How else can I bathe? And the girls have to bathe when they get back from the convent.'

'Madam, you not hear, you don't listen to the message people send you? People have no water. People waste out the water. Right now the girl next door tell me they burning the government building down by Brunswick Square.'

'Waste out? Fire? Burn?'

'The people them deliberately turn on the tap in the place. They say if they can't get water, all you must stay without.'

'People?'

'We, Madam. Soldiers, Madam. Soldiers in blue jackets come off ships in the gulf and they killing people. Police.'

As Lavren waited at the gate, the tune of the passing calypsonians looking for a couple of pennies for a song plaited their tale into the story of the century:

> Wrightson wouldn't give us water
> Maloney don't want us to enter
> Vincent Brown make an ordinance
> To tax us without humanity.

Then as he waited for the pandemonium to end in No. 18, Cipriani Boulevard, he watched the Lancashire Fusiliers march past on their way down to the south of the city to quell the riot. The day after the riot was quelled, Lavren was again at the gate of 18, Cipriani Boulevard. The fountain had been restored to its usual quiet burble, and Sou Sou was calmly mending on the front veranda, assured of water for her plunge bath. There was a smaller than usual queue for the miracle-doctor.

At first Lavren did not notice anything different. The scent of cuscus grass and eau de Cologne still tickled his nose, and at such an early hour of the day he was almost swooning at the gate with the pot-pourri of scents arising from the frangipani trees and the oleander bushes with the blush of rouge. There was not the same laughter behind the lace curtains, nor were there the same shadows. There was Sou Sou in the armchair mending, and Josephine was directing the daily sick to the side of the house where Sou Sou insisted they go. 'If I wanted to be treated, do you think he would have time for me?' Lavren heard his grandmother. It was his focus on her, with the lorgnettes he had borrowed from a different time expertly placed at the tip of his nose, that was still preventing him from noticing anything different.

The thud on the ground of a falling fruit from the low-hanging jolie mango tree to the right of the fountain momentarily shifted his focus to that side of the garden. It was here that his glance was immediately arrested by the figure of a young girl sitting on an artist's stool in front of an easel. Her back was arched, her hand holding a paintbrush at the end of an arm expertly extended to touch the paper ever so lightly with a drop of blue for an eggshell cloud, in the sky of this morning above all mornings which she was endeavouring to capture; a changing sky above the circle of hills overlooking the Savannah at the heart of the Belle d'Antilles. Emanating from the cloud of muslin in which she sat, gathered in at her slender waist with a sash of satin, was a mixture, a tincture, of eau de Cologne and the cuscus grass in which her frock had hung to protect it from the nibbling moths that left their dust in the night. It was for this apparition that he had come up from the wreckage of the ages which lay beneath the surface of the Gulf of Sadness. It was for this figure of beauty, as delicate as a porcelain figurine on the dressing-table of Marie Antoinette or Josephine Beauharnais, that he journeyed each morning from the Hotel Colombie, refusing to be distracted by the absurdity of Uncle Anatole's investigations into the pigmentation of the Monagas de los Macajuelos. Lavren was aware only of the expertly poised body, the intermittent lifting of the girl's head with its brown curls tied in a white taffeta bow at the smooth nape of the neck to the subject of the painting, the sky above the circle of hills, and then to its representation and interpretation on the easel.

But as Lavren became accustomed to the focus of Sou Sou's lorgnettes, the picture began to grow. The cloud of white muslin was tainted. It was not the light. A stain began to grow at her right side and seep through the satin sash gathered at her slender waist. It was as if her right side had been pierced. The red stain grew. She visibly held her side, and as she moved her hand, putting down her brush, he noticed the back of her hand bleeding as bright as a ruby. The idyll had changed. She took a linen handkerchief trimmed with lace from a small purse encrusted with seed pearls and dabbed at her brow, which was ringed with ruby beads that threatened to drop their blood on to her skirt.

'Immaculata!' Her name is called by her mother Sou Sou from the open veranda where she sits mending. 'Immaculata!' Her name is unstained and as pure as the white muslin she wears. Her concentration does not allow her to hear her mother. In her concentration there is modesty and the demeanour of a novice of the Nuns of Cluny. 'Immaculata!' She stirs and turns, holding her side.

'Mother?' As she rose to respond to her mother, Lavren noticed the wounds bleeding from her feet.

'My child, I've dropped a needle and I know what good eyes you have. You must be your mother's eyes.'

'Let *me* be your eyes.' The morning was suddenly transformed. The painful idyll of the stigmatised artist was broken, and Lavren was torn between this first vision of Immaculata who was to instil in him a love of the spirit and art, and this new voice which he recognised to be the sound in the murmur of the fountain which he had followed. 'Let me, let me.' This other young girl was dressed as a gypsy, obviously an old costume from the carnival trunk which the children liked to play in when they were small. She jumped up from the floor of the veranda where she had been playing with the Braganza tea-set, an intricate Victorian picnic one fitted into its velvet-lined case of lacquered walnut decorated with marquetry. Each teacup and saucer of the finest china, each tea plate, the milk jug, the sugar bowl with silver tongs for the sugar lumps, and the most minutely fluted teapot with its delicate spout, all were tucked away into the lacquered box with its silver handles, locked with the tiniest of silver keys. It had been a delight to Marie Elena since she was a little girl to unpack, display and pack away again for the sheer pleasure of its beauty. It had been a gift from the Count and Countess de Braganza who had honeymooned on the Gulf of Sadness on their yacht and had come to the house for lunch with the Doctor and Sou Sou. They were so enchanted by the girls and the doctor and his wife, that they left them one of their wedding presents. Up Marie Elena got, picking up a tambourine. Her jet-black hair was caught up in a scarf the colours of the rainbow and behind one ear was a full-blown red hibiscus. 'Let me, let me, let me be your eyes,' she continued to chant to the rhythm of the tambourine as Immaculata picked her way across the lawn.

'Marie Elena, behave yourself, and take off that ridiculous dress. Take care of the Braganza. You are supposed to be trying on your début gown upstairs and standing still for the seamstress to pin the hem. What are you doing in that ridiculous get-up?' Lavren, at the gate, has sensed the mischievous glint in Marie Elena's eyes. He realises he is now at the source of the opposites which have torn him in half, the freedom of the saint and the freedom of the gypsy.

'Mother, you hear what happened to Mother Philomena in the middle of the history lesson? I was sitting there, quite calmly as I always do . . .'

'As you always do?'

'As I always do.'

'Marie Elena! Mother, she is not telling the truth.' Immaculata looks up from where she is searching for the needle.

'Yes, but it is a much better story than the true one. Who likes true stories?'

Lavren smiles. Where has he heard that before?

'Now, girls. You both need to try on your dresses. And you need to change that muslin, Immaculata. What a mess you're in.' As the girls went into the house, Sou Sou whispered under her breath, 'It is wonderful to be favoured by the Almighty, but this is going too far. What am I to do if she starts bleeding on the night of her début in the middle of the Princes Building dancefloor?'

Behind the mother and her two daughters, through the open door panelled with jalousies, the grandeur of the past loomed in the shadows of the interior. The mahogany morris chairs, the saman wood side-tables, the Victorian lampshades of clouded glass, the oval dining-room table with its six high-backed chairs, all rang out, like the china in the cedar cabinet, and told of a fading grandeur. *Folie des grandeurs*, the ideas that grew inside their heads. Over these polished surfaces black hands moved and black faces saw themselves reflected in the passing glory of others, the paraphernalia of a previous century brought down from the house in the cocoa. Lace curtains began to breathe their last breath in the house of the District Medical Officer, Doctor Ramon Monagas de los Macajuelos. The sick continued to queue, despite the story of Miss Gertrude's boychild who had had his throat cut for a fishbone, and Josephine continued to collect the votive offerings from the steps of the veranda. But this morning, the District Medical Officer had gone to visit his clinic in Cumana. Hence the quiet, the presence of Immaculata at her art lesson in the front garden and Marie Elena playing gypsy.

The time now retrieved by Lavren is a time retrieved by desire. Desire brings him to stand at the gatepost of No. 18, Cipriani

Boulevard. In this former time he can only be an observer, but he comes with clues gleaned from sitting at the foot of Marie Elena's bed. She is a fitful muse and Lavren must follow his imagination, follow that desire which has brought him here, so invention may fill the gaps where memory has been forgetful. He must combine both the exertion of memory to be inventive and the forgetfulness of knowing to be equally so.

As he leaned against the limestone gatepost, still intoxicated by the perfume of cuscus grass and whiffs of eau de Cologne, he was also drenched with the scent of the frangipani hanging over the garden walls. In this miasma of scents, his desire conjured the question, 'Why so nun-like, so compliant and obedient in demeanour, why the pain of the crucified one when your beauty moves so, like your own body under your muslin?' And then, as he asked himself this first question, he wanted to know what lay behind Marie Elena's mischievous nature and her desire to tell stories that were untrue. 'Why so tempestuous, so talkative, so flirtatious, and opposite from your sister?' His answer lay in the tale he now tells: the tale of the two sisters. Here again, as in a former tale of the other two sisters, he surfaced in a convent. Now his desire leads him into the cloisters of the Nuns of Cluny round the corner from the second-most important brothel, known popularly as 'The Garden of Eden', which was trying to compete with the girls and boys on the first floor of the Hotel Colombie patronised by Uncle Anatole.

But first, what has been going on in the house of Dr Ramon Monagas de los Macajuelos, republican, District Medical Officer, miracle-worker and writer of theological essays? Angelic lover! In the early days, when malaria took their first child, Sou Sou herself was still compliant and obedient and used to sit mending and darning his socks while Ramon read her poetry and theological essays; then her patience snapped. 'Ramon, I don't understand a word you're saying. You might as well be speaking to a keskidee – who at least can ask you questions, even if the same one repeatedly. What is he saying?' Ramon withdrew and kept his poetry and theological writings to himself. He put a barrier between what he did and what he thought. So he never remembered what went on in bed with Sou Sou. It was a surprise to him that the house seemed always to have another child. Then he would go to his clinic and work with the sick and the poor. He would not attend to Sou Sou or the children.

Ramon wished to make recompense for the former century of pain. As the indentured came across the plains of Kairi from the sugarcane fields, Ramon felt that he was making recompense for the past by opening his clinic to them, and for this he was called a socialist by the Third Most Intelligent Man in the World who was yet to write the definitive history in the second half of the century. While he found a way through silence, poetry and theological writings, Sou Sou grew fat and obsessed with the maintenance of the correct water levels in the tank outside for her plunge bath. She did not care for his reputed republicanism. Celestine and the young Josephine looked after the growing children till Celestine's death, and then Josephine had to look after them on her own. It was as if the children erupted and bloomed like wild and exotic flowers in a magic jungle. When Immaculata began spontaneously to bleed from her hands and feet, and the wound in her side, not to mention the beads of blood on her brow, Ramon pronounced that it was haemophilia. But Lavren takes you, dear reader, to the murals in the cloisters of the Convent of the Assumption around the corner from the brothel, 'The Garden of Eden'.

Indeed, it was a kind of haemophilia, a love of blood. Bear with Lavren. He has left the two sisters trying on their début gowns, which have come from Paris and are being altered by the seamstress Miss Metivere from Charlotte Street whose mother and grandmother had sewed for the family in the past. He will return. But he enters the childhood of his muse.

In the street that runs parallel to the main street and is named after some English Duke or other, the Nuns of Cluny, coming from Aracataca, built their convent opposite the priest's house which had its main entrance on Fredericstrasse, as it was always known. Here they had a college for the sons of the families, and now the nuns started a school for the young girls; here, each in the appropriate institution, Quentino and Margarita had been all this time. Lavren must not digress into the tale of their antics. It is at three o'clock on this particular sunny afternoon that he is awaiting the sisters.

The afternoon reverberated with the excitement of after-school. It rang out with the end-of-school bell, clanged along the echoing corridors by Mother Philomena. This was the signal for the popsicle man to ring out his ices for the young beauties of the Savannah houses as they crowded out of the classrooms, making into the streets to buy snow-cones, popsicles, coconut ice-cream, toulum, pistache and more and more goodies from the string of marchandes along the sidewalk. Lavren was caught up in this excitement and knew from his history that many of these treats would not have been possible without the coming of ice.

He waited for her whom the century welcomed. Her arrival was inaugurated by the coming of electricity, trolley buses, trams around the Savannah, the sacred telephone, newspapers and trains. Lavren clung for dear life at the gates of the convent. He was brushed against, stared at, even had his white linen suit soiled by the sticky fingers of smaller girls unable to control their melting confectionery. His Panama hat was knocked off in their play. He pressed against the railings, and there again, in the shadows of the trees that bore her favourite fruit, was his muse whom he had hunted through these terrible centuries. A schoolgirl: he lingered upon her as she lingers to pick the forbidden fruit. He lingered on her bowed torso in blue and white cotton with a white bow pulling her jet-black hair back to a bunch on the nape of her neck. He lingered at the nape of that neck, knowing it in a way that she herself now does not yet know it. He kissed that nape, placing his lips where it was as tender as the white of a young chicken. In the shadows she moved with her brown legs showing where she hitched up her skirt to collect her mangoes quickly, before Mother Philomena came to lock the gate. He lingered and longed to touch her arms, her face the colour of olives.

'Marie Elena Monagas de los Macajuelos, have I not told you it is forbidden to pick jolie mangoes from those trees?' Mother Philomena's voice accustomed to catechising, echoed about the school yard and down the corridors of the cloister. Marie Elena, scattering mangoes, escaped the cloister and detention in the linen room where she had spent weeks on end in the past for her mischievous behaviour. Lavren was bereft of his beloved muse as she ran past him, faster than Diana on the hunt, and his second and brief vision was eclipsed by Mother Philomena's fluttering veil. Marie Elena escaped down the side streets to No. 18, Cipriani Boulevard.

It was now, as Mother Philomena forgot to lock the gates, that Lavren was allowed to understand Immaculata's plight or favour. While one sister, his muse and mother, grew up impervious to the illusions of the nuns, driven only by marriage to their conclusions, the other, Immaculata, was deeply affected from youth. As Lavren entered the corridors, he was enveloped by a world of mystery and fear. The corridors were lined with murals painted by the young novices of the Order of Cluny. The murals depicted the host of fallen angels floundering in the flames of hell, and pulling down as they fell the unsuspecting figures of young girls who dangled their feet over the brink of the fiery pit. It was from these visions that Immaculata fled, having been found one day in front of the murals in a faint. Some days after that, the bleeding began.

It was this passion which actually ignited the beams of the convent and made of the cloister an inferno in which Margarita was trapped and burnt alive, as she sang the *Salve Regina*. The supposed martyrdom of the aunt enflamed the niece, so that she bled the red of roses and burned with the flames of red-hot coals. (It was soon after this that Quentino was posted as parish priest to the nuns on the leper colony at Chacachacare where he stayed until his death of leprosy, after years of ministering to the sick.) Lavren amazes himself at the reparation which he, or Marie Elena, has allowed these two.

'She must be kept at home,' Ramon, doctor and miracle-worker, ordered. 'She is suffering from religious mania.' It was after months of fainting, thinking that she was dying and was in a state of mortal sin because she had seen her body in the mirror one morning before going to mass, that Ramon decided on the idea of inviting Monsieur Cazabon, the old art-master at the boys' college, to teach Immaculata to paint. And so it was that she was painting when Lavren first came upon the young girl at the easel in the front garden. Painting was supposed to ease the bleeding, but her passion for beauty often brought the blood rushing to her wounds.

As the weeks went by and the début approached, Lavren lingered at the limestone gate beneath the frangipani trees of No. 18, Cipriani Boulevard. As time went by and desire seemed fulfilled, Lavren hardly noticed the changes, thinking, fooling himself that it could stay like this. He had hardly even been reading the *Gazette* or noticing what had been happening in the world. This had been all of the world to him, here on the edge of the Savannah with his muse and mentor. He had developed such a leisurely and serene pattern to his day, even staying as he was at the Hotel Colombie. He was on the second floor, not the first, but was well aware of Uncle Anatole and his secret passions. So far, Uncle Anatole had not come up with anything concerning the pigmentation of the Monagas de los Macajuelos, leaving the more obsessed of the family in dreadful uncertainty about the colour of their own skin, and refusing to linger in the sun longer than was absolutely necessary, lest they be mistaken for being black. Lavren's day was shattered and calypso brought the news: *Run you run, Kaiser William, run you run . . . Hear what Kitchener say . . .* Calypsoes threaded the world into his memory. The next time he arrived at No. 18, Cipriani Boulevard the pandemonium was worse than during the Water Riots. War. The First War, they called it.

But that morning, before he made his daily pilgrimage to No. 18, Cipriani Boulevard, he was forced to stay within the Hotel Colombie. It seemed as though the whole population had come to town and was massed on the Plaza de la Marina like J'Ouvert morning at carnival time. Lavren watched from the balcony of his room, whose railings were covered with pigeon shit. At the end of the plaza, a huge ship reared up high above the shops and the old houses with Spanish balconies, towered with its masts above the twin towers of the Cathedral of the Immaculate Conception. While he watched the march-past and the Governor take the salute, the band playing 'Land of Hope and Glory', white, black and creole pressed together by the catastrophe that awaited their sons, he picked out the two sisters in the bandstand with Ramon and Sou Sou. They were here to see Jeansie the oldest brother, and other boys of the families, join the black boys of the West Indian Regiment going to war. But Lavren, where he stood at the railings with the pigeon shit, was distracted by a sailor who had just entered the front entrance of the Hotel Colombie.

Lavren immediately left his room. He began his descent to the lobby of the hotel, which was filled with sunlight off the dusty street. The sailor was from the crew of the great ship towering above the buildings at the bottom of the Plaza de la Marina. He stood with the sunlight behind him. Lavren paused on the last flight of stairs. He could not continue. He was fixed to the ground here while a part of him wished to run out and find the two sisters in the Plaza. For all his other desire, he could not leave the view of this tall blond sailor who stood nonchalantly in the lobby near the steps to the dusty street, asking for a room. His skin breathed snow and the pale light of the north. It had been tanned by the sun up on deck. His eyes were the blue of lapis lazuli.

Lavren allowed himself to indulge the moment, to suspend his own disbelief. He did not use his gift from the Holy Ghost to traverse the centuries to retrieve information to make sense of this particular sensation, fascination with this Norwegian sailor. He had discovered his nationality from hearing him speak to the concierge and realised that he had been given a room on the infamous first floor with Uncle Anatole. He must intervene. He must protect. He must guide. He wishes to savour the moment without using hindsight or clairvoyance to interrupt the plotting of his tale. In other words, dear reader, he will not spoil it for you, by letting you know quite how much knowledge he really is in possession of.

'Room Ten, Sir'; the concierge directed a small boy to take the sailor's luggage up the stairs. And it was on the fifteenth stair, where the mahogany bannister twirled to take the next flight, that Lavren Monagas de los Macajuelos, visitor himself in the city of Puerto de los Hispanioles, met the Norwegian sailor face to face. On the fifteenth stair they turned and looked into each other's eyes as the sailor ascended to the first floor. Lavren was almost metamorphosed in the instant, feeling within himself the transition from one gender to the other, feeling the ascendancy of his female self. He checked the fluctuation. Where had he met that face before? Where?

He put out his hand, standing in his white linen suit, his skin the colour of olives, his eyes the black jewels of jet. Opposites collided: 'Lavren Monagas de los Macajuelos.' The flaxen-haired sailor took his hand and smiled.

'Lavren Undsett.' Their breaths commingled and the syllables of their names entwined as one. Lavren knew that this was him, but he will not tell you, dear reader, who must still guess. While the sailor rested in his room, Lavren kept guard and shooed away the boys and small girls whom the concierge sent up to the first floor, as she would do to any other sailor to pleasure their desires.

It was the wont of Lady Chancellor, the Governor's wife, to leave her card for all foreign officers of Royal navies along with an invitation to come to her 'At Home' at six o'clock at Government House, to stay for supper and then to dance with young girls of the best families. Lavren contrived for the sake of his tale, his romance and his sojourn in the Belle d'Antilles, to protect this beautiful sailor from the designs of the concierge and the secretive taps on his door by the small boys and girls from the grass market around the Petite Pointe. The calling-card was delivered and Lavren contrived a cab to transport his sailor safely to the drawing-room of Lady Chancellor without the least compromise to his propriety, at least not at this port of call.

Lavren knew himself to be the Tiresias of the new world, but a Pandarus too he will be for the sake of destiny. Once he knew that his namesake, Lavren Undsett, officer in the Royal Navy of the North where the ice melts in May and the fjords are as deep as his own memory, was drinking rum punches with the Governor and his wife and the other officers out during the war, he could make his pilgrimage, later than usual, to No. 18, Cipriani Boulevard, where sadness lingered after Jeansie's departure for the war, but where too, another story interrupted Lavren's romantic indulgence.

It was not just an ordinary 'At Home' at Lady Chancellor's. It was an 'At Home' before going on to the Princes Building, where her very favourite young friends Marie Elena and Immaculata Monagas de los Macajuelos, daughters of Dr Ramon Monagas de los Macajuelos, District Medical Officer, and his charming wife Sou Sou (never known as anything else, except possibly the duchess of the Savannah houses), were to make their début. Lavren arrived in the middle of the excitement of dressing for the ball. But the day had been marred and Lavren must interrupt his indulgence, must interrupt this teatime tale of Marie Elena's, savoured with rat cheese, Crix biscuits and guava jelly, the tale of the two sisters and the sailor called Lavren Undsett. He twirled the name on his creole tongue. Lavren, Lavren he whispered.

Josephine breaks through with words of another life.

'Celestine was buried quietly,' Marie Elena said.

'That is a lie,' Josephine interjected.

The voices Lavren hears now, breaking through his ears, are louder than the voice of the old man on the road to Moruga when he told of his grandfather. He hears a great lamentation, a great wailing of women in the house. The little board-house is so full, it breathes with the breathing of the big women who hold each other up in their clouds of white cotton, bearing up their sorrow with their melangene arms, holding their watermelon breasts. Lavren knows this through Josephine, as he rests on her and sees her now, a young woman at her mother Celestine's wake.

Lavren goes to the wake, surfacing from the Gulf of Sadness into the gully of the voice of his sweet Josephine. Lavren has promised her voice. Her voice has been trying to break through the lines of this fragmented narrative, the Carnival Tales of Lavren Monagas de los Macajuelos, last of the Monagas before the diaspora and the departure from the island. Lavren has promised her voice since no tale would be a tale without her voice, no fiction a fiction, no history a herstory without hers. There is no memory without the memory of Josephine. 'Cric,' she says.

'Crac,' he eagerly replies.

'Is night-time, yes. People know the dead reach up from town. You could hear people feet slap on the pitch road. They did have pitch road even then, must be the first pitch road. Mammy dead right there in the kitchen of Madam house, where else she ever be all these years, you know, Master Lavren? She dead right there standing up in the kitchen by the sink. Myself, so, was in Mistress Elena room cleaning out. Madam, she where she always is, on the veranda in she rocking-chair mending clothes. She mend so much clothes she eye get small small. Madam say, "Josephine, what is that noise?" Like someone put down a heavy crocus bag on the kitchen floor. Not so she describe it, but so I imagine what she tell me. At first I not answer. If you answer everything Madam say, you spend the whole day back and forth to the veranda for nothing, she does forget what she say by the time you reach, you never get no work done. And that is the one thing Madam pass on to she daughters them, Mistress Marie Elena and the one like a nun, Immaculata, is to keep the servant them working, working. You see Mistress Marie Elena, she particularly following you everywhere from small, inspecting how you turn up the sheet, smooth out the bedspread, dust down the bureau. She have real jumbie eye. She coulds always find Madam needle when it fall in the crack on the floor, like yourself, Master Lavren, your eyes does look for your mother needle in the crack between the pitchpine floorboard them. What I telling you this for, Master Lavren, and you know these things? Is we thing I want to tell you about. Is Mammy I want to tell you bout. I go, yes, to see what it is Madam hear in the kitchen, because I know nobody expect to come and put nothing down that I don't know bout. So I say I go go and see. She slump down right there, you know, Master Lavren. Mammy slump down right there. The water was running from the tap, cold cold. Mammy hands still wet from rinsing wares and she fingers still smell of the red fish she preparing for Madam, Mister Ramon and the children them. Master Lavren, I ent bawl, nuh, the sight of Mammy get me so quiet I could hear Madam sew on the veranda out in front. You could hear angel passing in the sky. I turn off the tap. I look at she and she look like she sleeping, but she face twist bad and that is what tell me is she heart. What I see in she face is the pain she feel in she heart. I know that, I feel my chest full up, me throat like a man strangle me and me eyes cloud over. I ent bawl, you know, I kneel right so next she body and let the tears fall. I kneel by Mammy and I want to dead with she. Mammy see things, you know, Master Lavren! Mammy come from far and she see a lot of things, things she tell me that I wouldn't tell nobody even if they ask me. Time pass, yes, because I think was Mistress Marie Elena self who find me, yes, slump over Mammy slump-down body, and all the time Madam had been calling, but Madam does never come out in the kitchen once she give instructions for lunch. She does call you out in the front where she sit down and sew. I ent know who cook the red fish that day. You hear the women bawling, Master Lavren, I ent bawl yet, nuh. Come, leh we go in. Cric.'

'Crac.'

'That night, wake night, is full moon and the wild lily them down by the ravine, white and shining like satin. I did want some satin to line Mammy coffin, but it too dear. Miss Clementina from up there so, line the coffin with some plain white cotton. You see me here, Master Lavren, I get so that I would have put she in the coffin with the plain wood and call that George, but is Clementina who say that is the cloth of we sisters. Mammy self, they lay she out in a white cotton dress and they tie she head in white cotton. That is how I remember it, Master Lavren. Is so you remember it?' Josephine smiled when she asked the question.

Lavren nodded, his head against the breast of Josephine smelling of ginger. In the gully of her voice he could hear the singing, the wailing and the great lamentation.

'Is when I enter the house where the sisters them lay out Mammy when they bathe she, that I bawl. Is the first time I bawl. I throw myself on the ground and bawl. Miss Cleotilda and Miss Olive hold me, and I hang between the sister and bawl for the life Mammy give me. You know I never think of the man, the man they say is my father, because I never did see him in all my life. I bawl for the life Mammy did give me and the life she live. Mammy never did come on no boat from Africa, but she born right here in a sugarcane field. She tell me that is what she mother tell her. She mother begin to bleed right there in a field one morning early when dew still on the ground and she mother was out with the gang them. It was crop-time. That was the way things was then. Is better to work in white people house. That is what Mammy decide, and that is why she have me in your grandmother house. All the time so the sisters singing "The Lord is my shepherd, I shall not want", but underneath that song I could hear the voice of the old people, and the sister right there next to me by Mammy coffin, catch the spirit. "By the rivers of Babylon I lay down and weep." She tell me Mammy say I is a good daughter and I must live a good life. I must fight the good fight. I remember when I pass in, the yard was full of men playing cards and drinking rum. They bring me some black coffee and soda biscuit. Is so we stop the whole night with Mammy, the men in the yard playing card and drinking rum, children running about like is Christmas time. The women in the house with me, bearing me up as we make a circle there, a circle of women round Mammy. The next day when we take she in the church for the service, I see Leo come in the car, you grandfather had the first car I ever see. Madam send flowers with Leo, and Leo self dress up in one of Master Jeansie old suit, looking spruce up. I take the flowers Madam send. She must have get the little coolie boy, Ram, Madoo son, to pick them before sun-up. I put them at the foot of the coffin. I say inside my heart, when Mammy rise on the last day the trumpet call, the first thing she go do is stand right on top of Madam flowers. Is time Mammy take she stand for she self. Not she not teach me to stand for myself? I telling you these things, Master Lavren, because things a little different. Each year things does get a little different. But things still bad. You understand?'

Lavren wept on her smooth breasts and nodded his head into the valley of her bosom.

'Master Lavren, if Madam should see you. You is my little white child. What kind of child you is, Master Lavren, that you find yourself here?'

When Lavren dipped beneath the corrugated waves of the Gulf of Sadness, he took with him the voice of his sweet Josephine; this young lithe body, streaked with the light which the ocean allowed to filter to this depth, lifted itself upwards, pressing nubile breasts and pert nipples against the force of the sea, beating with legs like a fish's fins. S/he stirred within herself the sensations of that secret crack between her legs and wondered whether history would give her time to deal with the contradictions of this body. (Lavren can never settle on the appropriate pronouns when talking about herself, and so himself writes in a confusing way about himself, but never wanting to deny herself.)

The insistence of his narrative drew him back to the Belle d'Antilles, the city of his love, Puerto de los Hispanioles; knowing that in the drawing-room of Lady Chancellor, the Governor's wife's drawing-room, was his young friend, the sailor Lavren Undsett. But it is to No. 18, Cipriani Boulevard that Lavren goes, to his favourite spot at the limestone gate under the frangipani trees, to await the glimpse of his beloved muse, Marie Elena, and her sister Immaculata.

Ramon's car is in the driveway; the parents will chaperone the girls. Lavren, Pandarus of the new world, is arranging a rendezvous. His fancy and indulgence force him to keep an eye on Lavren Undsett.

The scent of cuscus grass is overpowering where Lavren is settled by the limestone gatepost, as the débutantes' dresses are taken out of the tissue paper in which they were originally packed in Paris. Since when, of course, Miss Metivere, from down Charlotte Street, has altered the waists and hemmed the length. But Sou Sou is insistent that other alterations are made to Immaculata's dress. 'Miss Metivere, now, you have been coming up to the house for years. You helped with Clemence's trousseau. You know our business.'

'Yes, Madam.'

'Now, you've seen the child. I'm talking about Immaculata, you understand. I don't really worry about Marie Elena. She'll have the heads of those young men turning before they can say Lord Kitchener. But Immaculata, poor dear. What will I do, if in the middle of the governor's drawing-room, she starts to bleed through the sash from the wound in her side, or if at dinner, she starts bleeding all over the white linen napkins and on Lady Chancellor's best linen tablecloth?'

'Madam, you could trust me, you know. I hear the nuns saying she is a saint. We must pray she don't bleed at the dance.'

'Yes. We can pray, and we shall, but just in case those prayers are not answered quite how we would like them to be, we must do something else.'

'Well, Madam, I've got an idea, because only yesterday I had to take precautions when Miss Immaculata was trying on the dress. I made a kind of bandage, a kind of poultice, and made her hold it by her side. I tell her not to press hard in case the pressure make the wound open up. Though I hear it don't work so. It quite spontaneous, I hear people say. She like the Blessed Francis Assisi, yes, Madam?'

'Come, Miss Metivere, carry on, tell me about these bandages. She will wear gloves; that will take care of the hands. The poultice you're talking about is for the side and we are going to have to give her a nice headband. I will carry spare gloves, spare headbands and spare poultices, and at the slightest sign of bleeding, she will have to come to the ladies' room with me. I think it's a miracle, Miss Metivere. God will reward you.' Sou Sou had quite developed the idea as if it was her own in the first place.

'Well, Madam, it look like we well organise. But, you know, is one thing still worrying me, and that is when she well dancing with a young fella, and you know how some of them like to squeeze you.' Sou Sou couldn't help smiling at the middle-aged spinster, Miss Metivere, who must have often wanted to be squeezed, poor thing.

'Miss Metivere, don't worry your head about that. Her father is going to dance the débutantes' waltz with her and I will instruct him carefully how to hold her at the waist, because even though you are right, and it is a matter of spontaneity and not necessarily any pressure, you never know what Immaculata's feelings may bring on. After that she will be sitting beside me, and not go out of my sight for a second.'

'Well, Madam, that will be fine. It bound to go okay. I mean, is the Lord Himself that choose she for His own.'

'Well, her father thinks it's haemophilia.'

'I see. Well, I don't know about them things, Madam. I sure the doctor right if he say so.'

'Well, I myself think it's damn nonsense and those blasted nuns and all their commesse. Excuse me, Miss Metivere, but at times my patience runs out with Immaculata and her phobias and ideas.'

By this time Miss Metivere was busy with the poultices and bandages, and a lovely headband encrusted with seed pearls.

Lavren was quite drunk with eau de Cologne as evening came on. He had digressed and time had been almost forgotten in the best of traditions. His sense of history had been quite overpowered by the inventiveness of his imagination. It was his precious responsibility to make sure that not the slightest embarrassing blot be made on Immaculata's character. Miss Metivere contrived to insert her poultices and bandages well so that Immaculata did not look as if she had suddenly put on weight – something which Sou Sou and Ramon, when he thought of his own children, would have liked as she seemed to live on so little these days but soda water, dry Crix biscuits and the wafers of Holy Communion. Marie Elena was constantly having to stop her secreting her food on to her lap when no one was watching at supper or dinner. It had started when she was a little girl and used to roll her meat into little balls and plug them into her ears. Sou Sou begged her to try the chicken salad, which Lady Chancellor was renowned for.

Lavren will certainly keep an eye on Immaculata, and already, as Sou Sou had suggested and indeed had been partly arranging for some time with her third cousin Yvonne Agostini, for her son to be a suitor. (Beware of first and second cousins, though it was getting difficult for the families to avoid each other, as the number of white people got less and less – Uncle Anatole's investigations having not yet proved anything.) Carlos Agostini had come up to Immaculata almost as they entered Government House and been received by the Chancellors, to have his name put on her dance card. Sou Sou whispered him away, saying to come after the débutantes' waltz. She was procrastinating because, while she wanted to encourage Carlos in his attractions (she had to get this daughter off her hands), she did not know what she would do if the excitement of the evening were to encourage a spontaneous emission of blood from these wounds of Christ with which poor Immaculata appeared to be inflicted, whatever Ramon's diagnosis might be.

Marie Elena in the turret room interrupts: 'I don't want any chicken soup or dry toast and I'm not up to Father Sebastian coming with Holy Communion either. Tell Josephine to bring me a pot of strong tea, some cheese, Crix biscuits and guava jelly.' Lavren descended to the kitchen in order to avoid Josephine having to climb all those stairs with the tea things. Once the great chunk of rat cheese and the Crix biscuits and guava jelly were arranged on the tray and brought up with the tea, Marie Elena got out of bed to sit by the windowsill herself. 'You take a rest,' she said to Lavren, 'I'll tell this part myself. It's my favourite part.'

'Dear reader, take it with a pinch of salt,' Lavren says.

'You know that's not fair. How else would you be able to say anything? Now let me tell you. Wonderful jelly this. Just like Mother used to make it. As I arrived at Government House I was immediately surrounded by all the young lads. Most of them were my cousins; I had played with them as a child. We just had fun. My card was filled up before I knew it. Of course Mother had arranged for dear Uncle Anatole to dance the débutantes' waltz with me as Father was dancing with Immaculata.'

'Because of the stigmata,' Lavren interrupted eagerly.

'The what? Darling, I have no idea where you've got that from. Your imagination, dear, is quite extraordinary. Father danced with Immaculata because she was the eldest. Anyway I was fond of dear Uncle Anatole. I was his favourite. He always said this and would take me on his knee and bring me special sweets, bonbons, from downtown. He worked down in the town.'

'You mean . . .'

'Now, who is telling this story? And I won't have anything terrible said about Uncle Anatole. Why do you want to say these things? Of course, my dress, which was from Paris, was white with the softest crepe de Chine around the bust and off my shoulders. Mother said I could show my shoulders. Immaculata was so nervous. She was always nervous, I give you that. She was highly strung. But I had done the most stupid thing in booking up my card with all these boys I knew, all the cousins. Because when I entered the dining-room for supper – after the débutantes' waltz, of course – I was introduced, called over by Lady Chancellor to meet the boys off the boat which was in port. Of course, it was the war, and Lady Chancellor was like a mother to those lads, and she knew she could invite me and Immaculata, girls from good families, to meet the boys. Of course my card was all booked up. I was so inexperienced. I never did that again. But I decided there and then without a second thought to tear it up.'

'Tear it up?' Lavren had heard the story so often he was practically miming the telling, as Marie Elena told her favourite story. But he liked to ask the same questions as a prompt, to take the story in the direction he wished it to go. Also so that he could see the excitement on her face, the face of his muse and mother.

'Yes, I simply tore it up. And I gave the pieces to one of the negro butlers. Get rid of this, I said. He said, "Yes, Miss," and then I was as free as a bird. Before I knew it I was surrounded by all these young English boys.'

'But . . .' Lavren interrupted, seeking to guide destiny to create a different future.

'But then what? Take these tea things away, dear, I must get back to bed, I'm too old to be doing all this remembering.'

'No, you must tell what happened next.'

'What happened next. What did happen next? I danced all night, even going on to the Princes Building where I was escorted . . .'

'Escorted by whom?'

'Come, come, freshen these pillows for me. I'm an old woman.'

'Why didn't you?'

'Darling, what are you talking about? Now take these tea things away. I must rest. Phone Father Sebastian, tell him to bring me Communion in the morning.'

After Lavren had cleared the things away he went back to the windowsill of the Demerara window and looked out over the Gulf of Sadness. The story rose from inside of him, rising out of the gulf whispering: *The sea. The sea . . . The sea is history.*

She was escorted from Government House to the Princes Building (called after those same princes Lavren told you about in his opening overture who planted the poui trees in Princes Town), by none other than he whom Lavren has contrived to enter the Hotel Colombie so that they can meet on the fifteenth stair. It is to him that Lavren has had the visiting-card delivered from Lady Chancellor. It is he whose virtue Lavren has protected from the temptations of courtesans and nubile prostitutes on the first floor, whose name is his own name, and is the reason for his name. Of this he is sure. Let's see if Lavren can construct his destiny.

From the very moment he came up asking for a dance she flirted with him; she teased him on to the veranda overlooking the botanical gardens. She told him that her card was empty and danced all night with the tall nordic sailor with flaxen hair and the eyes the colour of lapis lazuli.

'Darling, I hope you're not writing down anything silly. You've been getting me to say lots of silly things this afternoon. Holy Mary, Mother of God . . .' Marie Elena returns to her prayers.

Lavren Undsett's ship was departing the next morning, and after the ball at the Princes Building, he asked Marie Elena Monagas de los Macajuelos to accompany him on the officers' launch out to the ship in the stream of the harbour. Her father gave permission. Anything to calm things down; Immaculata had had to be rushed home with severe bleeding after Sou Sou had relented and let Carlos Agostini dance with her, since he had been sitting patiently at her side trying to brighten the occasion for her. 'He will make a good husband. He is a gentleman,' Sou Sou whispered to Yvonne Agostini. Ramon and Sou Sou also knew that Clemence their eldest daughter and her husband would be there to act as chaperones. Marie Elena had the sailor hanging on her every word as she regaled him with story after story. He did not listen, as he could only look into her eyes and remark upon the darkness of their colour.

Here at last, on a ship anchored in the Gulf of Sadness, in the century of his own birth, Lavren Monagas de los Macajuelos is witness to the love he believes could have engendered him; if in a later tale he can prove that this sailor with blond hair and blue eyes returned to Kairi nine months before his birth. That is for a later tale. Now, on the deck under the moon, with the waters of the gulf turning green, red and black, Lavren listens and looks.

'He was a silly man. He just kept talking about my eyes.' Marie Elena turned in her bed and asked for a sip of water. 'Hail Mary, full of grace . . .'

Yes, Lavren would have them like that at the railings of the deck. He has drawn her imperceptibly towards his body. Her chin grazes the naval epaulettes on his shoulder. Lavren is himself suffocating from the perfume of the eau de Cologne. Lavren Undsett pulls the eighteen-year-old Marie Elena towards him. She tilts her head and he bends his to kiss her on the mouth. Marie Elena Monagas de los Macajuelos, convent girl of the Nuns of Cluny, chatterbox, dreamer of dark secrets, is silenced. If she were to talk about what was happening to her, she would say that it was disgusting. Such effrontery! Remember the age, Lavren! But no. Lavren would have her yield. He who can know the openness of her heart and the silence of the sailor's, yields her, his own beloved muse, to him; as he would have yielded himself to the sailor, Lavren Undsett, on the fifteenth step of the staircase in the Hotel Colombie, because he wished to taste him, the man to whom his muse and mother had given herself. He wished to protect him from the small boys and girls and the elaborate courtesans on the first floor. He could bring it about, instigate it himself, her romance and her yielding, and be there to witness it. He has them make a promise. The sailor is leaving the next day. They will write to each other.

Marie Elena is chaperoned back to the house at No. 18, Cipriani Boulevard. Lavren Undsett is chaperoned by Lavren Monagas de los Macajuelos back to the Hotel Colombie.

The promises were still wet upon the sailor's lips, her kisses still wet upon his mouth and cheeks, the eau de Cologne for Lavren still to smell upon the naval epaulettes, for the betrayal that Lavren Monagas witnessed in Room Ten on the first floor of the Hotel Colombie. It both shattered his illusions about lovers, and by a strange twist, made him desire betrayal as a part of love. His guardianship of Room Ten was not successful – as far as Lavren's tale was concerned, for whom does one believe? Lavren Undsett spent the night with a notable courtesan and had his kisses and promises stolen from him, mere hours after he had given them to Marie Elena.

The next day, Lavren Undsett's ship sailed. No letters followed and Marie Elena had a broken heart, thereby cultivating the intrinsic belief of Monagas women in the distrust at the heart of all love.

History takes over from Lavren to heal the wounds inflicted by his tale. Lavren dreamt that his father was a nordic sailor who went away to live in a castle of ice on the edge of a fjord. 'Don't be a silly boy, look at your eyes and your skin the colour of olives.' Marie Elena smiled knowingly.

Yes, history took over from Lavren. It was to nurse her broken heart some years later – when Carlos Agostini was still calling at No. 18, Cipriani Boulevard as a hopeful suitor, Immaculata was still the stigmatised art pupil of Monsieur Cazabon, Uncle Anatole was still inundated with dust in his attempt to solve the pigmentation problem and Aunt Clarita, a newcomer to No. 18, who had come back from Bolivar after losing all her money on the horses, and was now scared of being buried alive when she died – that Marie Elena went to her first dance in months at the Casuals Club on the Savannah.

What they called the First War, or the 1418, thus relegating it out of memory and experience to a medieval period, was over. Josephine was down by the wharf. 'Cric.'

'Crac.'

'Master Lavren, is true, yes, Chancellor say, "You sacrifice your lives." I went down myself by the wharf the day they come back on the ship them, to meet Miss Dolly other boy, not the one who get decorate and kill. They had put up arches for the fellas, triumphal arches of ferns and flowers, and if you see white people! Pappy! Down by the wharf, you would think all of we is one people. People dress up in their best, you know. But it not last long. The boys like all the white fellas; them Planters' Regiment went "For King and Country", as Chancellor say; "You sacrifice your lives." If you see how the man speak sweet. Mistress Marie Elena as she was at the time, Madam, your mother, Master Lavren, was friends with his wife, Lady Chancellor. If you hear how the man speak sweet so, and then what you think? Is so it is, is so English people and them is, sweet, sweet talk and then a good stab in the back. They does take the food from your mouth, the glory from your heart. It not last long, no work, Master Lavren, them same fellas! If you ask me I don't know why they went. It not them war, is them blasted white people killing each other for what? For what they have too much of already, if you ask me. Anyway, people line the streets and police band play "Land of Hope and Glory", "Rule Britannia", and then people start to cry when they play "Home Sweet Home". It was fête for so. But it finish that Sunday afternoon when bottle and stone fly in the air down under Victory wing, Memorial Park. Big Sunday afternoon and razor in the crowd to cut your skin. People say enough of that, "We doh want no Englishman . . . Cipriani!" Was a creole, you know, they had some good apples in the basket, you know, Master Lavren. "We doh want Major Rust to make bassa bassa here. Cipriani!" The waterfront workers take this country and pelt it in their face. Wages and Work and Rights. This place change. They dance their dance but the place change. From now so, things different, people not want English to make bassa bassa here for all their sweet talk.' Josephine put down Marie Elena's bowl of chicken soup at the bottom of the stairs to the turret room, and she sat down and she said to Lavren, 'Put it down for me, all that I tell you.'

And he does. But he returned to his tale that is continued in the Casuals Club on the Savannah. Marie Elena trembles with excitement and Lavren trembles with fear, because across the floor is the apparition that is to transform his beloved muse and mother. He dreamt again, a recurring dream, that his father was a nordic sailor who went away to live in a castle of ice on the edge of a fjord . . . 'Don't be a silly boy, look at your eyes and your skin the colour of olives.' Marie Elena sipped her chicken soup.

Auguste de Boissiere was *haute aristocracie* from the Versailles Cocoa Estate; no more de Lanjous, no more new blood, creole with creole, cousin with cousin. He brought silence and forgetfulness. Auguste enters the tale, and immediately Lavren's skin begins to dry and peel off the tips of his fingers. Immediately the palms of his hands and the soles of his feet begin to crack. Immediately his ears begin to tickle and he scratches them with cuticles of cotton wool twirled on a matchstick, to placate the aural orifice and its industry of wax which dries and falls, sprinkling the lobes. Immediately new smells enter the world: Palmolive soap, vaseline hair tonic, Capstan cigarettes, soap mixed with cigarette smoke and shit; aromas that pervade the rest of the century, rising out of the houses of Kairi to seduce and tantalise the polymorphous imagination and sexuality of Lavren, hermaphrodite and last of the Monagas de los Macajuelos. Loneliness, silence and yearning entered the world. Here at the foot of the stairs at Casuals Club at the corner of Queen's Park West, at a pre-carnival dance . . . already downtown is knocking about to tamboo-bamboo and the bamboo for the tents is being put up on Wrightson Road, Docksite, for calypsonians to sing. Through sepia and the corruption of moths Lavren surfaces and reaches the foot of the stairs where Auguste stands, son of a planter, last of the planters, in the days of the last of the plantocracy. Out of the hills of Tamana comes the dream of ancient tales, and within those tales, the dream and nightmare of the witchbroom. Here is the last of the plantocracy to go up into those hills to plant cocoa and be defeated by the insistent entanglement of the fungal parasite brought in the wind troughs from Saramacca in Surinam, the witches' broom. His silence and remoteness was like magic, it drew her and tantalised Lavren. Will he be Lavren's father? If not, who then? The Holy Ghost? Hence his interference with the golfball of Mr de Lisle, the foot fetishist. Lavren, hermaphrodite, immaculately conceived? What a wonderful notion! Paternal origin, only in the realm of the paternity of paternities, the eternally absent God the Father.

Auguste has a face shaped like a heart, chiselled at the cheekbones; cupid's bow are his lips, the gentlest finger in the world has pressed a dimple into his chin, his nose is like Alexander's. The planter's son is drawn to the travelling doctor's daughter, Lavren's muse and mother. Lavren's fingers slide over the vaselined hair, like Rudolph Valentino's. She is animated in a waterfall of pearls and crystals dropped to her low waist, cascading to just below her knees in panels of silk. 'I've asked for you, I've asked who you were. I've asked to be introduced to you,' he said quietly.

She will answer, and in the not too distant afternoon, not long after the honeymoon, he will grow silent and hardly speak, and this will draw her always to think there was something there, something therefore for which Lavren in his turn will yearn. But at this moment, at the foot of the stairs in Casuals Club, she is Lavren's immortal muse, as he so slowly lifts the veil of sepia from her face to reveal a face as smooth as silk, a cheek of damask, her brow a dome of alabaster with one small curl in the middle, the mass of thick black hair collected into a net snood, pearled with jet, to rest at the back of her head on the nape of her neck.

'You shouldn't have been asking other girls to introduce you to me, you must know they wouldn't.' She smiled. 'They would have you for themselves.'

He smiled. He had said his piece and now left the rest to her. She cancelled her dance card a second time and waltzed the rest of the night with him, made to believe he loved dancing, and with her most of all. He played butterfly in the band, with her that carnival, Mariposa, throwing confetti from the lorries and going with her from house to house for the carnival balls, and soon they were secretly engaged in the year of the franchise, and she thought only of him and being his wife and taking his name and bearing his children.

At the gate of No. 18, Cipriani Boulevard, Lavren witnessed the suitors who called for his muse and the stigmatised artist, Immaculata. The veranda always received Carlos Agostini and Auguste de Boissiere for cocktails at six, and supper at seven. Lavren must be content with melancholia, and at night, the silence of his room at the Hotel Colombie. Lavren Undsett has sailed, leaving only the memory of his betrayal in Room Ten on the first floor. Lavren cannot undo history. His tales are destined to follow Auguste de Boissiere. He too will change his name to Monagas de los Macajuelos. The engagement was given out, jointly with that of Immaculata and Carlos, and invitations for the wedding were printed at Pereira's. Lavren cannot undo his destiny, but was it true or was there another whom Marie Elena keeps secret and will never tell and not even the Holy Ghost and all the force of Mr de Lisle's golfball can alter? Remember Marie Elena never did like true stories. They didn't make good tales.

On the day of the wedding, Uncle Anatole found out that someone had used the tar-brush. 'Way back,' he said solemnly to Ramon. Lavren is able to corroborate this information at the end of the century from a letter discovered in, of all places, Scotland. Ramon did not tell Sou Sou, lest it darken the day and the celebrations. He surfaced from beneath the gulf into his visions afforded him by his peculiar nature which allowed him to levitate between genders to know the sorrow of women and the yearning of men. He levitates between races, a creole in a creole world.

Time is jumbled in the excitement of the wedding of Auguste and Marie Elena, Carlos and Immaculata in the old church of the old capital, San Jorge de Monagas. 'Look him there,' the staring faces shouted, as Lindbergh brought the first airmail service to Kairi, allowing the Pope to be invited to the wedding where the new world had begun, and where the streets echoed with the cries of the crucifixions that had taken place along its boulevards, and where the very first Monagas were buried. Time is jumbled in the carnival imagination of Lavren, as he jumps to the calypso, as the skies above Kairi trembled to the rumbling and tumbling in the atmosphere of the Graf Zeppelin which appeared in the skies with the comet of ancient times to herald the marriage of Auguste and Marie Elena, Carlos and Immaculata, whose wedding is shot in sepia, filtering through palms and jalousies. The bells of the church rang out, mixed with the rumbling and tumbling of the zeppelin and the echoes of the crucified in the strains of the *Salve Regina* . . . in this lacrimarum vale.

THE TALE OF THE HOUSE
IN THE SUGAR

'BOY, WHEN COCOA WAS KING,' the old planters reminisced. Witchbroom had strangled the cocoa, cast its spell once and for all over the central cordillera. Prices fell on the world market. The Demerara shutters were brought down on the offices of the Monagas Import and Export Company, down by the wharf and the old lighthouse near the old fort. Auguste moved with Marie Elena from the ancient cocoa hills to manage sugarcane estates on the plains, following where labour was the cheapest, down in the gully among the barrack-rooms where the ancestors of the indentured lived as indentured still. King Cocoa was dead. Long live King Sugar! The colonial economy was sucking the orange dry, said the history book written by the Third Most Intelligent Man in the World. No one seemed to know who the first and second most intelligent men were.

The century rumbled yet again, though the graves on Flanders' fields had hardly sunk. Those who had played havoc with people's lives: ancestors of buccaneers, pirates, conquistadors, governors, slave owners, rulers of the Raj, who had shunted the great continents of the world into this necklace of islands to plant cane, now tore themselves apart for money, race, blood, the supremacy of white skin, blond hair and blue eyes. There was a lunacy which ignored the innocent, choking in showers of gas, shovelled into graves. Capital! Filthy lucre!

While the century rumbled, a train clanged along the line to the sugarcane factory down by the Cipero river. Other trains clanged along to the concentration camps of silent Europe. The stench from the factories and the concentration camps flowed to Embarcardier, the sugar depot on the Gulf of Sadness. All this was happening when Lavren was conceived in the house in the sugar. Was it passion, and therefore a mistake? *O felix culpa*, O happy fault (not the mistake of a perforated condom, never used), surely not duty? Yes, the Pope's injunctions, the natural law, the rhythm method! The house was bursting at the seams. Children, just like that, to Marie Elena and

Auguste: Luke, the Evangelist; Gabriel, the Archangel; Leonardo, the Inventor; Elena Maria (mirroring her mother's name); Paris of Unsurpassed Beauty and George the Usurped . . . and many others. Lavren hallucinates them even before birth, but does not know all their names, only these last ones in the last days. The mosquito wire was torn from the windows and not replaced, letting in Anopheles and his retinue of flies with germ-furred legs. The house was bursting with children and the painful cries of the last baby, George the Usurped, who suffered from dysentery, and who already, even before Lavren had poked his head out of the birth canal, had sensed Marie Elena's preoccupation with the miracle that lay beneath her heart.

History interferes, as it always does, and now with Lavren's birth, events inaugurated his arrival.

This archipelagic rosary of the Caribbean trembled with the noises of the old world. The seas were infested with the iron barracudas and sharks which surfaced in the Gulf of Sadness like the caravels of the conquistadors that had crammed the entrances to the Bocas. The evil eagle of Capitol Hill now crouched to spring and spread its wing of rule from where its neck and beak rested on the peninsula of Florida, sipping on the waters of a bitter sea, stained with blood, ringed with the tang of the sea grape and manchineel, twisted in sepia and indigo. It sought its prey. Its claws crushed the movement of people. Old flags were to fall and a dose of Uncle Sam's dollars was a good purge . . . *rum and Coca-Cola . . . mother and daughter, working for the Yankee dollar*, calypso say.

Uncle Tom went cap in hand to meet with Uncle Sam, but not before he was well taught and educated at Queen's Royal College on the Savannah (not the family bed), or at the College of the Immaculate Conception on the main street, Fredericstrasse, which the plantocracy had put up long ago in the time of Elena Elena to educate their own (letting in a few mulattoes, bright black boys and coolies, to fool), to carry on the stupidness of the judiciary and the Colonial Office. The proverbial schoolmasters did their business for them, an education in licks and beating books. A few got through the net. They were exiled from the official histories, exiled even from the memory of today, our own dear Black Jacobin. At these schools they learned to play the game of cricket, the colonial game.

These masters, out from England, held in their hands the fragile brain of the Third Most Intelligent Man in the World, who would push against the door which the British Foreign Secretary held open, and call that Freedom. But the time was no respecter of events, and soon the cycle and treadmill came round again, turning like the old waterwheel in the plantation yard at Speyside Tobago, overgrown with pink coralita. But Lavren jumps, starts on one thing then goes to another. Calypso say: *Brownskin girl, stay home and mind baby* . . .

George the Usurped screamed and screamed, so that Marie Elena gave him to the shoulder of Josephine and would have given him to the servant's breasts had they not been black, and had the sugarcane company not deposited seven pints of cow's milk on her doorstep each day from the dairy where the grassy fringes of the verge petered out down by the black galvanize barrack-rooms in the gully. She weaned her children on to the company's milk.

'Girl, take the child.' Marie Elena handed over George the Usurped, and then rested herself in a hammock on the veranda, cradling her womb and her seventh which floated in the amniotic sack peacefully, putting the last touches to the faculty of the imagination that would imagine all time from the beginning of the new world. She swung in the hammock and cradled her womb in the peaceful rest brought about after the trauma of George's birth.

'These will put you straight, my dear.' Dr Adolph Kruger handed Marie Elena the brown bottle of mixed hormones.

'I feel absolutely perfect, as if I've been shaken into place. As if someone had taken the puzzle and given it a shake and it had all found its perfect symmetry.'

Josephine had taken George the Usurped as she had taken all the others, the children divided and straining between mothers, cradling them from birth in her black arms, those arms empty of her own children left for grandmothers, aunts or neighbours to mind. 'Neighbour, you go take the child?' She left her children to that intricate network of illegitimacy spread through country and town. They were succoured on the vine of stalwart and stoic grandmothers whose faces look and arms reach from a previous era of servitude and rebellion which left some of them regretting, with the deepest remorse, their own blood by their own hand killed and left in a ditch. *Brownskin girl stay home and mind baby* . . . Calypso sing . . . *I going away in a fishing boat and if I don't come back throw way the damn baby* . . . In the twilight by the beach, calypso sing again . . . *All day all night Miss Mary Ann* . . . *down by the seaside sifting sand* . . .

Josephine lifted George the Usurped to her shoulder, allowing him to cling and sit on her fat belly, full of her own child. 'Is so I find myself. I wonder if I will ever say the truth.' As she looked at her madam swinging in her hammock, she knew that they both had reached their time, but that the birth of the child in her madam's belly would be an occasion celebrated and fêted with lace and broderie anglaise, trimming a christening robe woven by silkworms, passed down since when. She said, 'Madam, I go have to take the day off to have this child,' sounding almost guilty, always pleading, knowing her right but not being able to take it yet.

'You won't take too much time, will you, Josephine? You know what it is with all these children and the boss. You know I couldn't cope without you.' Marie Elena continued to swing in her hammock, dragging her alpagat feet on the pitchpine floor. 'It's so hot, Josephine, bring me a glass of nice cold lemonade.'

Lime trees grew behind the house in the sugar, a cure for scurvy long time. The extravagance of gables and turretted verandas reached out of a gravel yard splayed with the shadows of the tiptop flowering of the palmiste, like the plumes on the Governor's hat – *The Governor tall, tall, tall, He peeping over the wall.* This was a ragged reminder of opulence, high ceilinged with bands of fretwork like lace draping the curlicues and cornices, rotting. Here was the remnant of a folly, born of a long-ago dream of grandeur. Materials had been brought as ballast for ships: bricks and stone from England, marble from Italy, limestone and coral from this rosary of islands, slate from Wales, timber and shingles from Canada, cast iron for balconies and the railings of verandas. It was into this old house with the backstairs falling down, the Demerara shutters swinging in the wind from their rusty hinges, and the mosquito wire torn out, that Lavren was born. History interrupting all the time. And that new music . . .

War and news of war; money in the coffers of the merchants clinked, *rum and Coca-Cola.* Calypso. Up on Calvary Hill above the shimmering Belle d'Antilles, where Taffy was crucified and the Blessed Virgin Mary of Laventville looked down on the shanty towns, hallucinated in the blue air, tumbling down to the Gulf of Sadness, the first pingpong is picked out on a rusty dustbin cover. Lavren is stirred within the womb of his beloved muse and mother, Marie Elena. He is stirred by the first pingpong, pingpong, pingaling ping p'ding, and is tempted by the sound that was to transform the world's music, to be born early and become a douen escaped from limbo to jump up J'Ouvert morning. But Marie Elena held him beneath her heart and cradled him as he took that music down into his imagination, and began to learn that all which would last here in the new world would come from beyond the gutter, full up with dirty water; would come from the villages burning kerosene lamps, would come from beyond the bougainvillaea hedge, from the black galvanize barrack-rooms down in the gully where the grassy verge merely petered out.

Lavren, like John the Baptist, leapt in his mother's womb, not to the felicitous greeting of the Blessed Virgin Mary, or the presence of the messiah in her womb, but to the sound of an oil drum, a steel pan, from which the imagination of the poor had transformed the greed of capital, the new El Dorado, oil, into the music of liberation. This would outlast everything. Lavren leapt to the music of oil drums and sang in his imagination, the lyrics of the calypso. He learned to tell the long tales that Robberman and Pierrot related out of imaginations tempered and burned down in the cauldron of an oil drum, fashioned for music on the slopes above the city, still this harbour of Spain.

Lavren rocked in the womb of Marie Elena as she swung backwards and forwards in the hammock scraping her alpagats on the pitchpine floor. 'Josephine, shut the window. I'm going to come inside because of that noise in the barracks.' Lavren leapt to the sound of the tassa drum like King David to the tambourine and the tympanum. In his imagination he was almost already a child on the sill of the Demerara window, listening to the coolie wedding music on a Sunday afternoon. He didn't want to go inside. Torn between Marie Elena and the world, he longed to be born and lie on the shoulder of sweet Josephine.

The world beckoned to him. At first no one noticed, but his companions were already waiting at the bottom of the gravel road. His first companion was a little Indian boy who held his distended stomach, which was burnt the white of fish-bait. He had heard of the birth to come. 'Tell that coolie boy to go from the bottom of the gap. What does he want?' Marie Elena asked Josephine.

'He say he come to play with Madam baby.'

'Nonsense. Oh, Josephine, such a pain. What is this child doing to me? I must lie down. It's not a kick. It's more like a lash. If you could imagine it.'

'Lie down, Madam. Take it easy.' They could both see the little Indian boy going away with a switch in his hand which he used to swipe and lash at the hedges. 'Hi! Hi!'

'Oh, Josephine, you'll have to call the doctor before you go.'

'Yes, Madam.'

On the morning before Lavren's birth Auguste sat longer than usual on the latrine seat, because of the pungent perfume of the wild white lilies with the yellow centres which grew in the seepage by the tania patch manured by the washing-up water and Josephine's pee. The perfume of the lilies was stercoraceous. He enjoyed it because it was his own shit and urine, though he would never have owned this to anyone in the world, but all the family knew in their hearts that both their parents in different ways were expert scatologists. Scatology was the science of the Monagas de los Macajuelos. The past, the present and the shape of the future since the beginning of time on the Savannah of the Monagas at Aracataca had been divined by the shape, texture and smell of turds.

This morning it was not just the lilies manured by Josephine's pee but something else in the air which immediately made Auguste think of the child in Marie Elena's womb. He wondered about that child, the way it kicked and moved, and thought that it must be going to be quite different to any of the others. Marie Elena, though almost middle aged, seemed to look and feel as if she were a young girl having her first child. 'It's these mixed hormones. They're wonderful.' There was something which both excited him and frightened him, but it puzzled him because he did not know what it could be. The texture, smell and size of the turds told him this child was going to be quite different to any of the others. He had had a dream as it kicked one night in bed that it might be a ballet dancer. The thought disturbed him, unless of course it was a girl. He was so accustomed to sons, bored with them, he could not imagine a little girl. He had the feeling it was a girl. He hoped for a girl, if the truth was known, though he did not talk about these things to Marie Elena or anyone else.

'You know, there was an Indian boy at the bottom of the gap this afternoon, said he wanted to see my baby. And you know I felt such a pain when I heard that, not a kick but like someone lashing out inside of me. I hope nothing is the matter.' Marie Elena looked at Auguste for reassurance, knowing though that he could never take the birth of babies. And certainly he looked more unsure of this one than ever, despite the hormone pills.

'I will see that Ram makes sure that little boy does not come up the gap again, dear.'

'And then the strangest thing was that little Brunton girl. Her mother phoned and said she's noticed Lydia has been getting ready for the baby ever since I announced the birth. She's been making all these dresses for the baby, clearly thinking it is going to be a girl.'

'Well, she would. Just another doll for her. I saw her just now coming up the gap with her dolls all sitting up in her pram.'

Lydia Brunton, with skin as white as a swan's, wanted him to be a girl. She vowed in her little heart, as she sat on the front steps of the house with her dolls Elizabeth and Margaret Rose, called after the Windsor princesses, tucked up in their perambulator in cotton and broderie anglaise, that if this child she had so long awaited, the nine months' gestation seeming like an eternity, were not a little girl whom she could add to her collection of dolls she would do her very best to make him into a girl.

The first contractions came immediately after lunch and Marie Elena said to Josephine, 'That's it. It'll be four hours. I'll phone Dr Kruger and tell him to come in three and a half hours.'

Josephine went down to her room to change and pack her clothes in her grip to go by her mother to have her own child. 'Josephine, don't leave me.'

'Madam, you know I must go. Let me drop this child and then I go come back.'

'Soon, Josephine.'

Josephine went with her pain and her secrets. She went down the side of the house so she wouldn't have to pass Auguste pacing up and down in the front.

Marie Elena called the children and told them to go and play with Uncle Peter's children, and she held Elena Maria close to her large stomach and let her feel Lavren moving inside of her. She let little Elena Maria hear the heart beating. But she particularly wanted Elena Maria out of the house, because she did not want her to hear the pain of the birth. 'Will you suffer? Will you die?' she cried.

'Run along, darling.'

The children dawdled and whined about leaving. George the Usurped bawled the place down and Marie Elena had to send the young nurse with him, since Josephine had gone. The children wished to take all their playthings with them. The Evangelist wanted to take his chemistry set because he was in the middle of an experiment and Leonardo wanted to take his cages with all his animals. He left the house with a parrot on his shoulder, a squirrel in his pocket, the agouti and mongoose in cages on his arms. He got Paris of Unsurpassed Beauty to help him, reluctantly, as Paris didn't like anything dirty which would spoil his looks, and was scared the animals would shit on him. Anyway, Paris was still obsessed with being a horse ever since his nervous system had been shocked by coming upon Auguste's horse when he was four; he had never seen one before. He continued to want to be a horse and would stray away from the others when they were playing and start to eat grass on the verge of the road. The Archangel used his bike rather than his wings and went flying down the road with his butterfly net over his shoulders, and Elena Maria took her favourite book *Black Beauty*.

Soon the house was silent, except for Lydia talking to Elizabeth and Margaret Rose. She set up doll's house on the front steps and brought her wickerwork chairs and table set, and a little porcelain tea-set for the dolls to have tea while Marie Elena was in labour. She sat alone keeping watch, and all the time that she played on the front steps she could hear Auguste pacing the gravel yard, crunch, crunch, because he could not bear to go inside and be with Marie Elena. Marie Elena lay on the bed, called the Savannah, and recited the Five Joyful Mysteries of the Rosary as she waited for this seventh child to appear and alter the reality of their lives.

As Marie Elena lay there, Lavren's other sentinels kept watch: the Indian boy with a stomach burnt the white of fish-bait. And, in the little house at the bottom of the gap by the bamboo patch, two little black girls were telling stories about Brer Rabbit and Tar Baby. They too had heard of the baby coming and had one ear cocked for the first scream. Lavren would not want for playmates. They came out to play under the orange trees to get closer to the house. 'Now, away you go.' Auguste shooed them away, but they slunk back when he turned his back. They played under the orange trees and the Indian boy held his burnt stomach, waiting patiently.

Josephine cross over to the other side of the sugarcane-factory yard, beyond the secret garden with the pond, the poisonous lilies and the staircase leading nowhere, beyond the sugarcane fields and the gully where the barrack-rooms huddled; beyond this colonial compound and indentured skein of traces and rutted roads with their secret ditches of massacre and murder, the burial ground for untimely ripped babies. She cross over the road to the villages of unpainted, weathered board-houses which rose up precariously on stilts, with small verandas you have to mount to by a new steps. On each step a mixture of newly painted tins and rusty tins filled with earth, growing ferns and lilies, shook in the breeze. Under the house was sweep clean with cocoyea broom. The veranda ledge lined with more tins of ferns and lilies, and on the clean pitchpine floor was the shadows of the seed ferns and lilies. A varnished door, set with panes of coloured and cut glass, opened to a new linoleum floor buy last Christmas, and the lace at the window buy last Christmas too. The new paint on the walls fade where the family photographs, frame in passe-partout, hung a little too near the ceiling. The varnish stain on the morris chairs was cracking with the heat on the arms, and on the small table at the centre of the cluster of chairs a crocheted doily mat and a coloured-glass vase of waxed paper flowers make for last Christmas, when everything was make new for when the family came and they give the ham on the bone to the parang singers bringing in Christmas, singing 'Manzanares' and 'Maria, Maria, Maria, Maria Magdalena'; and they drink out the sorrel and cherry-brandy wine, eat black cake and sweet bread.

This is a small house make new each Christmas-time with hope, dignity and a little Christmas bonus if you lucky, and everybody put in a little bit and the women draw the sou-sou-hand of savings if they lucky that month, to buy bright new things; some toy for the child and a new material for the seamstress to make a new dress to walk out Christmas morning to church. Into this place of hope and faded Christmas things Josephine come by her family to have the assistance of the women in the village to have her child in dignity. No one foolish enough to ask who the father is. Josephine's secret. People know better than to ask questions which could unravel a completely new tale. One of the women buried the navel string under the pepper tree in the backyard.

Josephine had a boychild who astonished the village with his green eyes, sandy hair and skin the colour of cinnamon. Still no one foolish enough to ask who the father is. After the pain which was like the pain woman does bawl with when she making baby, Josephine get up right away because she know she have to go and see after Madam and she baby. Quick quick, she give she baby a suck, and she will have to see how she could make it home in the night to suck it some more, when all day she will have to be minding Madam new baby. 'Tante, take the child and make sure Millicent, the little girl down the road, help you when I gone.' She turned to Millicent. 'Millicent, I want you to help Tante with the baby. You have to bathe him, but make sure the water not too cold not too hot after you boil it on the coalpot. You must press the little clothes I have in that grip on top of the bureau. Madam give me the clothes she throw out. And you will find a piece of flannel I bring. I know Madam not going to miss it. She buy a set of new things the other day and she sister bring some more blankets and little coats and bootees for the new baby. I wonder what Madam make. I sure is a girl. Madam want a girl bad. I know the boss want a girl. Well, I has a boy, a fine boy. I wonder if he ever go see him. The boss don't want any more boys.' Tante watched Josephine and the young Millicent and wondered when this stupidness going to stop, but remembered when it was even worse, and women were dropping baby right there in the canefield like the Indian women them even today. Women make baby, drop baby and can't even remember the father them.

Tante say, 'Child, don't worry about the boy, and if that man, the boy father, come, I go give him one lash amd make him understand he going have to give you some money to mind the child.'

'Don't worry, Tante. I don't think the father go come here.'

Josephine walk out early from the little board-house to make sure she catch the early morning market bus to drop her at the bottom of the gap.

*

While Josephine was having her baby in the small board-house with the women from the village ministering, Marie Elena lay in the silence of the house on the hill above the canefields that whispered their own secrets in the voices of Hindi, incomprehensible. These voices were led by the mantras of the little Indian boy with the burnt stomach. His mantras were to spare Lavren the pain of the century. Marie Elena whispered her own prayers, the Five Sorrowful Mysteries of the Rosary, and ejaculations to Saint Gerard Magela, patron saint of safe pregnancies. Auguste continued to walk up and down the gravel yard outside. Lydia served tea to her royal dolls. The other children, as we know, were up at Uncle Peter's and Aunt Leonie's, eating sugared almonds. Elena Maria was being lured beneath the house by Uncle Peter to see his winemaking and then down to the bottom of the garden to see his prize capons being fatted up for the Christmas table. She had to sit on his lap while he stroked her knee and told her to keep their secret from everyone else.

Then Nurse Sturgeon came, sent by Dr Adolf Kruger. She stood above Marie Elena in her starched white cap and nurse's uniform, a private nurse for the Monagas births, bristling with silver safety-pins, a thermometer which gleamed with the mystery of its mercury and a pair of scissors she had newly sharpened to snip lint and flannel, snippets of hair and the umbilical cord of this last of the Monagas de los Macajuelos. Nurse Sturgeon gleamed with cleanliness and moved about the room backwards and forwards and to the empty pantry with crispness and efficiency. She was not a servant. She was a nurse. But she could smell the absence of Josephine and her own fair-skinned mulatto yellowness gave the house a malarial aura as she assumed the power of the house. She would have liked to have Josephine to boss and fetch. 'Madam'; she would still call Marie Elena 'Madam' in spite of her imperious way, 'where is that black woman who works here, your cook?'

'Josephine? She's gone to have her baby. But she promised she would be back as soon as she arranged for her mother to look after the child. She'll be here in a day or two. She's probably like me about to deliver her infant.'

'Well, I hope she makes it back as I won't be able to stay more than a day or two.'

*

Lavren lay beneath Marie Elena's heart listening and wanting to jump out into the world the Indian boy with the burnt stomach was calling him into. The gravel road was lined with a procession up the trace by the dairy. It was a pre-natal procession of women, as if only yesterday they had disembarked from the *Fatel Rozack* beneath the saffron clouds over the Gulf of Sadness, older women and young girls carrying bowls of saffron and paprika rice, their faces veiled and heads shrouded in the orhnis, swathed in muslin, Hindu women, chanting their mantras, going down the gravel road under the window where Lavren lay beneath Marie Elena's heart. Lavren wanted to be born to walk in these processions.

The house began to shake with the mantras and the song which Lydia on the front step sang to her royal dolls. The house shook with the singing of the little black girls in the house by the bamboo patch, 'There's a brown girl in the ring, tralalalaa. There's a brown girl in the ring, tralalalaa. She tastes like a sugar and a plum, plum plum . . .'

Lavren, still in the stillness of the amniotic bag, followed with his memory the women to the edge of the pond that supplied water for the sugarcane factory and was infested with alligators. He saw the women throw the rice into the water, imagining the Ganges and leaving in a circle of stones a lighted pujah of sweets and flowers which burned down the congealed ghee butter.

The pujah was for the child kicking to be born, whipped by centuries of pain. The voices of that prayer was the voice of Madoo Krishnasingh, the voice of his son Ram, his daughter Leela, his wife Prabwatee. The voice of that prayer came from Lavren's future, from the Indian boy with the burnt stomach the white of fish-bait, raw like fish-bait, no pain like this body, which howled from the barrack-rooms to say: *No salaam, baas, no more, salaam, mam sahib, no more hoe to jook the ground in the yard, no more arms to slash and cut down cane in the field, to brush the tall grass round the house, to weed the furrows, to plant ratoon, to load cane on truck for the factory, no more hands crushed in the machinery.* The voices jangled with the bracelets of the women, they smelt of incense and burnt cane for the canefields like a pyre on the Ganges. *No salaam baas, no salaam, mam sahib. No more crossing the kalapani, no more crossing the black waters. Coolie people is people, is people self.*

Lavren was born into a fever of riot that was beaten on drums down in the barracks and mingled with the violence of the people's own frustrations, living ten to a room with dysentery, typhoid, malaria, hookworm and malnutrition. A fever gave ague to the sugarcane as the strikers burned it, field after field, from Debe to Tarouba. A fever ran under the ground where the blood had been spilt once in 1884 and the police had fired on the Hosein Rioters and killed and wounded, and would have killed and wounded more, but for the need of more and more indentured labour in the fields from Picton to Malgretoute. Into this violence of geography, when the only tenderness was the voice of Lydia comforting her royal princesses on the steps of the great house, and the little black girls in the house by the bamboo patch singing 'Brown girl in the ring . . . tralalalaa', the yard echoed to the pacing of Auguste on the gravel. Into this fever came the stamping and marching feet that had started in 1937 with the smell of burning flesh in Fyzabad. A trail of blood ran down Hangman Alley, where Indian men hanged themselves for tabanca, the sorrow of unrequited love. This fever was the fever of the world, the lines of whose horizons were written on with the smoke from the funnels of Dachau, Auschwitz, Treblinka. Lavren was born screaming into a world which crowned its beauty with the petals of a mushroom opening over Hiroshima and Nagasaki. Lavren was born screaming into a world at four o'clock in the afternoon as the iron trucks clanged into the siding and were shunted into the factory. Sirens blew their scream of steam over the horizon of canefields and barrack-rooms and weathered board-houses in small villages that would become enslaved and indentured to his imagination for the rest of his life.

'You have a daughter,' Dr Adolf Kruger announced as he drew the head and top part of the torso showing its potential for breasts, navel still umbilically attached to Marie Elena's womb. The girlchild trembled to the steel drums in her head that trembled themselves beneath the mango trees in Laventville and Morvant looking over the swamp and the Gulf of Sadness, the city beneath the silk-cotton trees, all under the smile of Our Lady of Sorrows at the top of Calvary Hill, *Pray for Us . . . rum and Coca-Cola down point Cumana . . . mother and daughter working for the Yankee dollar.* Calypso announced the birth of the last of the Monagas de los Macajuelos.

'A son,' corrected Nurse Sturgeon as the little penis, erect with the shock of new life, astonished both the doctor and the nurse, as well as his mother. Her cry made Lydia drop her dolls so that they rolled to the bottom of the steps of the great house, throwing her royal tea-party into disarray. The Indian boy held his stomach in pain and the little black girls stopped singing. Marie Elena, still stunned with the exhaustion of giving birth, could not be blamed for thinking that she was being told she had given birth to twins. This was a double ecstasy which would have given a double joy to Lydia who had not bothered to go for her dolls at the bottom of the steps, but was now in the gallery off Marie Elena's room, peeping through the jalousies.

'Twins!' She could not believe her ears. She would have to make room in her pram for a fourth. She had anticipated one to sit with Elizabeth and Margaret Rose, but two! She could not believe her luck. She blinked with astonishment as Nurse Sturgeon snipped the umbilical cord with her newly sharpened scissors and handed the bloody screaming infant to Dr Adolf Kruger, who turned it upside down and smacked it twice on the bottom, although it was already screaming with the longing to be put back inside his beloved's womb. Marie Elena stretched out her arms for her twins. Where was the second one? Twins? Where was the girl, for this was surely a boy? Nurse Sturgeon brought the basin of warm water and together with Dr Adolf Kruger, washed off the blood.

Dr Adolf Kruger examined with his expert fingers the toes, fingers, ears and respiratory apparatus of the nose. He soothed the wound where the umbilical cord had been snipped, and marvelled at the perfection of the infant. He cried out, 'Perfect, my dear, perfect. You have a perfect infant, my dear,' turning from the ablutions and smiling at Marie Elena, while Nurse Sturgeon cleaned up the mess and wiped up the blood from the railings of the bed and floor. It was at this moment, in the very act of examining with his expert fingers the number of ribs, that he again felt the potential for breasts in the infant, the very slightest protuberance. He turned again to Marie Elena; 'Perfect, absolutely perfect, nothing to worry about,' all the time caressing where the breasts would grow. Dr Adolf Kruger, almost mesmerised by the sensations emanating from the infant, felt his soapy fingers slip between the infant's legs and into the crack between the legs which he at first thought was the anus, and then thought, Oh, no! It did not have the tightness of that orifice, the texture of the tissue, not fluted as the rose of the anus is . . . this was, but surely it could not be, for here was the penis unmistakably in his fingers, the serpent which needed baptism, still erect with the shock of the world. He allowed his fingers to linger there as he fingered ever so gently, as a doctor does, and the infant looked up at him with that face of adulthood that infants have on being born, prophesying their own being and becoming. At this very moment, Dr Adolf Kruker realised he had witnessed a miracle.

This was the incarnation of a mythology. Stories told centuries ago on the Hellenic archipelago were now becoming a reality in the archipelagic rosary of the Caribbean, into which the billowy ships had come, bringing rosaries, chalices, typhoid, Holy Communion, smallpox, the blood of Christ, swords and crosses. Suddenly the birth of Lavren surpassed the virgin birth, the immaculate conception, the leaping of John the Baptist in Saint Elizabeth's womb at the greeting of the Virgin Mary. Dr Adolf Kruger extricated his fingers from the crack. It opened and closed like the soft petals of a purple rose and decided to keep the secret to itself. He had thought he should sew it up, but the sweetness that he saw on the infant's face and the sweetness it gave to him, filling the room with the fragrance of the eucharist lilies which had been brought from Aracataca, where they had first appeared in the Convent of the Immaculate Heart of Mary, when Gaston had seduced Clarita with tamarind balls, decided him against that course of action. 'Here you are, my dear, one whole and perfect child. You could not want or ask for more. The best of two worlds.' Dr Adolf Kruger winked at Nurse Sturgeon, who left the room scandalised by the event.

'These white people think they could do anything, yes. I never see thing so in all my life, and I midwifing now for years.'

Marie Elena pondered the words in her heart and kept it a secret. Only when she was alone did she gently lift the diaper with her fingers, and feel for herself the astonishing evidence.

Auguste had heard the screams of birth and the announcements of perfection from the latrine outside, behind which the wild lilies grew. He had an attack of the runs. The prophesying, labyrinthine intestines of the Monagas de los Macajuelos could not maintain their regularity. The actual birth of Lavren threw the whole system into confusion; it was impossible to judge anything by the size and texture of the turds when there was only a continuous flow of putrid water whose stench mixed with the perfume of the lilies, to announce to the entire neighbourhood that what had been going on in the houses of the Monagas de los Macajuelos all these years was pretty shitty. Auguste realised at once that there was something out of the ordinary. But when he went to stand at Marie Elena's bedside, all he saw was what looked like a normal healthy little boy. Though this bored him, he was relieved. Marie Elena decided to leave things to time.

Once the entire mess was cleaned up, Marie Elena got on the phone to Aunt Leonie to say that all was fine and that the other children could return. The Archangel flew, carrying Leonardo, followed by the Evangelist and Elena Maria, still suffering from the shock of having her knee stroked for the tenth time by Uncle Peter. They dragged George the Usurped and Paris home with them. This took some time because George cried all the way and had a tantrum lying down in the road, and Paris kept straying to the verge to eat grass.

Lavren pauses to say pardon, excuse me, if he has given to the announcement of his birth, the birth itself and its aftermath, such a chunk of time, such a number or words and lines in this Carnival Tale, 'The Tale of the House in the Sugar'. He intends by leaps and bounds to carry you to the very end, to 'The Tale of the Last of the Houses' where he first heard of his birth from Marie Elena. She had not told it in quite this way, but then she is not as open a person. She would never have mentioned all the blood and mess, would never have told you about the secret place he carries between his legs.

Josephine returned to the house, and Lavren screamed when he first saw her because of the loneliness on her face. He screamed because he knew he would fill up that loneliness with his love and that she would give her heart to him. She would give him all the love she missed giving her own child.

Ramon, Lavren's grandfather, died soon after Marie Elena came to see him with the news of the baby. 'Should I bring my baby to show you, Dad?'

'No, dear, and move away, you are taking up the air. I can hardly breathe.' When she turned away he took a last snatch at the air which was left and died, knowing that the world was going to be a different place.

Sou Sou covered all the mirrors in the house for luck. It was a luck which did not last. She took to her bed the day Marie Elena brought Lavren to his grandmother's house. She died alone, even refusing to see Father Sebastian, the parish priest. 'He is a saint, yes, but he talks too much.' She turned to the priest, 'Go and say a mass for me.' Before she closed her eyes in death, she pulled Marie Elena's sleeve and said, 'Look to that baby; what've you brought into this world?'

Dr Kruger, Nurse Sturgeon, and Lydia kept the secret from the world for ever, according to 'The Carnival Tales of Lavren Monagas de los Macajuelos'.

Now, Lavren runs the risk of a jam. There is too much to tell. His nature precipitated catastrophe after catastrophe, such misunderstanding, such incestuous and miscegenatious mistakes. He must compress. He must select and he must, after all this time, devote 'The Tale of the House in the Sugar' to his miraculous self and to his love for his beloved muse and mother; both centre stage, as it were, and the others but attendant lords and ladies. But there is Josephine and the fabled children who come to play and bring the world into the estate house. The epic of gilded cruelty, the tales of Josephine, the cries from the indentured barrack-rooms, the whispers of accusation which hide where the woodlice eat away at the house: but for these, which must be told, Lavren must explain how he, above all others, could tell these tales and has to tell them in this preposterous fashion, as if everything turn ole mas. Anecdote must become single sentence, and the full flow of this time of change and newness be told in such a way that balance is maintained and this part fit its proper place. But balance is difficult for a child tingling with the music of steel drums and inspired by the Holy Ghost, Robberman and Pierrot. But he will try! History interrupting once again.

The radio told of other events. 'We will have to pay for this.'

'Dear?' Auguste sipped another rum and soda.

On the BBC, Hiroshima. Later Nagasaki.

Then the christening, for example! Dr Adolf Kruger came in the morning to perform the circumcision. But really! Who had ever heard of Saint Lavren? Saint Lawrence, yes, a proper saint barbecued on a gridiron who asked to be turned over to the other side when he was finished on the side he was lying on. If you wanted a name beginning with L, that would be a name. But Lavren – there lies a tale. 'Why Lavren, my dear? There's been no name like it in the family before,' Auguste asked one evening where he sat at the far end of the veranda in the cloud of a linen suit sipping rum and sodas. Marie Elena did not answer, as she sat at the green felt of the bridge-table. In that silence of twilight, when the palmiste in the yard whispered their own fate, Marie Elena's thinking and the reading of Auguste were interrupted by a scream from the barracks. 'They'll kill each other,' she said.

Marie Elena shut it out, her thoughts languishing in the past, knowing that Josephine had Lavren, rocking him to sleep in the bedroom. She played patience, knowing that just at her lap, in the drawer which she could pull out if she wanted (and did sometimes when Auguste was out at a fire), were the portraits of her nordic sailor with the blue eyes who had enchanted her on the balcony of Government House. This thought reminded her. 'No fires tonight, dear?' He did not answer but continued to read Kipling.

'Darn good chap.' She continued to play patience.

Yes, she could take out the portraits of that other Lavren and could remember back before the honeymoon and before the wedding and before she had seen Auguste at the other side of the room at the Club on the Savannah; before that time, her first night out, her début in the dress she had had from Aunt Sissy in Paris. She languished in the memory as she played patience. 'You have the brightest black eyes and I can see myself in them.' She remembered the first Lavren, her first love. She lost her way with her patience, staring at the cards pondering her next move, or that time so long ago. Lavren. The name could now ring out in the house for the rest of her life. Lavren. Lavren. He would be her lover. What a strange lover. In him she could have both lover, daughter and miraculous boy, her little treasure.

'Isn't that child asleep as yet?' Auguste asked. 'That darn woman puts him to sleep for hours.' That darn woman was his Josephine, on whom he liked to use his charm at the table when Marie Elena would invariably criticise the meal and he could praise it. 'How is your son, Josephine?'

'He fine, boss, getting to be a big man like you, Sir.' Josephine turned to go into the pantry with the vegetable dishes.

But the child Lavren was getting too much attention. Everyone was always drooling over him. Boys and girls loved to pick him up, bounce him on their knee, hug him. It was all one could do to get Leonardo to give him up, playing in the boys' room with all the animals. He flew around the house on the Archangel's wings and the Evangelist stared at him as if he was an experiment. They had to watch Paris who would have had him eating grass. Elena Maria, because she was the only sister Lavren remembers and would have got harnessed with him more than the others, tried not to make a fuss of him. Anyway, she could leave him to Lydia in the daytime. George the Usurped was the only one who hit him continuously. He pushed him out of Maria Elena's lap, pulled down the cot railings so that Lavren tumbled on to the floor screaming for Josephine. Poor George the Usurped, he was the victim of the green-eyed monster for the rest of his life. He forced a marble down Lavren's throat one day in an attempt to choke him, but he only smiled and the marble slipped right down the gullet and astonished Josephine the next morning. She brought the shitty diaper to Marie Elena to see the miraculous orb which the child had passed in his stool. What did the future hold? Poor George the Usurped, he could no longer be a baby. Lavren was the baby. Lavren, everyone called for Lavren.

And he grew fast, shooting up before anyone knew. People were always saying, 'Oh, how you've grown!' and, 'Isn't he just like you, Marie Elena?' She smiled, knowing the secret of her own little new daughter, her own little lover, her own self, her own reflection when they sat together and he watched her do her hair at the magic dressing-table with its cut-glass vials, silver boxes and silver-backed comb, brush and mirror. She would let him try a little lipstick on his cupid lips and Chanel No. 5 behind his ears. This was the time when her shoes were always missing and Lavren would be found halfway down the gap teetering on Marie Elena's stilletos, hat on, and carrying her shopping basket. It was still a time of fun. In the evenings he sucked his thumb and Josephine told him stories, while Auguste sipped rum and sodas, Marie Elena played patience, the boys played in the long room and Elena Maria read her favourite book. She was always reading and she never went to school. She would never leave the house in case Marie Elena died. Her friends were Marie Elena's old aunts who taught her embroidery and how to sew. But, as we know, she liked to play tennis. Marie Elena tried to get her to be friendly with Immaculata's daughters, but they were like film stars and spoke with American accents because they had gone to school in Philadelphia, and drove a convertible Chevrolet with a running-board and smelled of cigarettes which they were always smoking. Remember Giaconda, who had lips of carmine. They ate steak and wore very bright lipstick. Elena Maria was not like that. When she wasn't playing tennis she was in bed with a book. Maire Elena wondered what would happen to her. 'Children grow out of things,' she thought.

In the papers the first reports. Jews. Gas. Death camps. Mounds of dead. Ashes. The smell of burning flesh etched on each horizon.

It was such an eventful time that Lavren was almost not noticed. A number of things were not being noticed. It was fine to have a baby who was a hermaphrodite, just about. Already Auguste was thinking of him as a girl and forgetting that he had only dreamed he was. But for a young boy, an adolescent, this was another question, and no one dared think of adulthood. Monstrous! Marie Elena tried to keep him as a baby as long as was conceivable and sociable. But there were all the other distractions; a holiday, because Marie Elena was tired, and they went to Barbados and heard the whispering casuarinas whispering their fate like the palmiste in the yard. The end of Empire. They had to come back suddenly, because Leonardo had decided to experiment with flying. 'That child does not know fear.' He tried to fly off the roof of Immaculata's citadel and, instead of gliding over the flamboyant trees, skirting the hill Cazabon had painted and surveying the town in order to divine from a height where water might be found in the place of no water, Naparima, he crashed just below on to the pitch drive. The Holy Ghost, a spirit often represented by the semblance of a dove, picked him up and saved him in spite of a fractured skull, all limbs broken, and a suspected broken spine. But he got up in a dream one night and went for a pee.

The doctor said, 'Thank God, he can walk.'

Leonardo terrorised the household with his plaster-of Paris arms and had cages hanging from every point of the ceiling with some wild animal or the other. Paris had given up being a horse and spent his solitude collecting butterflies with the net the Archangel had passed down to him, because he had now grown up and was in love with a beauty from up the islands who thought she was Marilyn Monroe. He went to work in the oilfields on a bicycle, with a hot thermos of soup Marie Elena had specially made for him. Marie Elena became an expert on oil wells.

Chiney never had a VJ Day, calypso say. War pass. Carnival come. Lent. Cricket, West Indies playing MCC. August holidays. Rainy season. Dry season. Christmas, and the years go by. It was no wonder Lavren was forgotten.

Childhood was a fever. It killed off the babies in the barrack-rooms.

The pitch road is humming. When the humming stops, Lavren hears the stamping feet. The marching of stamping feet. Conversations in the drawing-room. 'They're marching up to the General Manager's office.' Auguste sipped.

'What can these people want? What can they want?'

'Mummy, Mummy.'

'Fyzabad. It will be Fyzabad all over again, 1937 all over again.'

'They'll have to call out the regiment.'

'Shush, shush, my child. It's nothing. People have to do what they have to do. Shush, my child, my child.' Josephine breathes her blackness over the small Lavren, growing below his mosquito-net with his own secrets. She breathes and she brings the world beyond the yard and the pitch road into his dreams. She brings them as close as the yellow palm of her black smooth hand which strokes his hair and soothes the fever on his forehead. 'Shush, my child, my child.'

Lavren quietens and grows beneath Josephine's blackness, her breathing of ginger and vaseline; he grows and listens and the capacity created by the Holy Ghost, Mr de Lisle's golfball and Josephine so close, so close, makes him pay attention to the story she tells while he hears the stamping feet, marching feet, bare black feet, slap, slap, slap on the pitch road right through his dreams, and the palmiste, before it was cut down for the Princess Royal's salad, whispers: *the end of Empire, the end of Empire*.

'Mummy, Mummy!' He woke in a hot sweat to their voices.

'Blasted coolies this time. They'll burn the place down. Like those niggers in '37.' Burn the place down! Fire! Fire! Fire! Auguste is out fighting fire, fire from Golconda to Tarouba. 'And they burn the policeman.'

'Mummy, Mummy.'

'Shush, shush, do do, petit popo, shush, my child, my child.' Josephine falling asleep, herself the whole day working, and they not sit down to dinner yet, more drinks and they calling for more drinks and they don't know she have children to go home to. 'Shush, shush, do do, petit popo.' The stories get mixed up in Lavren's imagination, the story of fire and tenderness and the voices in the gallery laughing, and Josephine breathing, telling her story and mixing her dreams and sorrows with Lavren's.

'Don't go, Josephine. Josephine, tell me a story.'

'Shush, shush, do do, petit popo . . . I have a boychild like you, Master Lavren. I have a boy like you, home by my mother and I not see him since last month end. Madam say I can't get the day off and she don't let me bring him here and put him in the room downstairs. Sleep, child. I have a boy like you, Master Lavren.' Josephine smiled, knowing Lavren's secret. 'He soft and pretty like you. He not big like you, not too big yet, but he getting strong and soon he go get limbs like yours, Master Lavren. He's going get big, fat smooth limbs. He going be smooth and full out. I going feed him strong with dasheen, yam and eddoes, nice pelau rice. I going cook good food for him. I have a boy like you, Master Lavren. He going read book. Madam say she going give me some old book all you throw out. He going go to school, but Madam say I can't bring him here. I can't bring him here to play with you. Must be she frighten you get black, or is something else. That is a story Master Lavren. Shush, do do, petit popo . . . sleep, my child, your mother calling me.'

Lavren fell asleep to the story and dreamt. 'Mummy, Mummy.'

'What, my pet?'

'Mummy, Mummy, there is a black boy in my bed.'

'Where, where, my pet?'

'He climbed through the window.'

'What has Josephine been telling you? Frightening you, speaking Congo to you again. Let me tell you a story: there was a king and queen who lived in a fine castle . . .' *Congo Congo Congo.*

When Lavren woke from this babyhood into childhood, he woke from a dream in which both stories were entwined. He woke from a dream in which he had been both boy and girl, changed and interchanged from one to the other by Lydia, who arranged him in her perambulator in broderie anglaise, or on the back veranda of the two little black girls who lived down the road in a dolly house. When Lavren awoke, the noises of change were out there beyond the hedge and down in the gully, in the barrack-rooms, beyond the gully in the villages and the board-houses. He remembered Josephine's words, 'People have to do what they have to do.' The Indian boy with the burnt stomach was growing ahead of him, beckoning to him.

There were two worlds. Marie Elena's story in a fine castle and Josephine's boychild who could not come home. It was a lonely world caught between the two. He listened out on the Demerara window for the next procession, Hosay with tassa drums. On Sunday afternoons when all the windows of the house were shut he went down to the bottom of the gap with Josephine to peep and wait for the decorated wedding car with bamboo and tissue paper in all the colours of the rainbow looking like a Hosay self, to pass. The bride and the groom were dressed like a sultan and his princess with gold in their noses, a little boy, a little sultan, between them, and Josephine said: 'You see the little boy, he go stop them jooking in the night. He go sleep between them.' Lavren wondered about jooking, but Josephine would not tell him more yet. All the cars in procession, with the front car carrying the loudspeaker for the Indian music, which always sounded to his ears like 'hana ca jani', disappeared down the gravel road in clouds of saffron dust, dissolving over the canefields.

Lavren took all the stories down into his loneliness and there he began to learn a way to write the Carnival Tales and to swim beneath the Gulf of Sadness. He read the history buried in the sea, not the history of Eleanor of Aquitaine and the Princes in the Tower. He took into his loneliness the sad story of Josephine's boychild and wanted to go for a walk with him. The world had shrunk, and but for the stories of Josephine, the Indian boy with the burnt stomach and the black girls who sang *tralalalaa*, there were no doors into that world, but only windows to sit on and dream, and those dreams became nightmares as he heard the marching and the cries. All the time from the windows he could see the canefields burning. Into the canefields rode Auguste on a chestnut horse. Then he was tired when he came home and sat in a linen suit at the far end of the veranda, sipping rum and sodas.

'Daddy, Daddy.'

'Stop whining, be a little man.' Lavren ran to the lap of Marie Elena and attached himself to the hem of her dress and stared, sucking on his thumb, at the stranger in white linen who continually denied his nature. He watched him as he sipped rum and soda with ice clinking in the glass.

Marie Elena had grown accustomed to finding her shoes missing and would send Josephine to the bottom of the gap to collect them, under the orange trees where her hats were often found hanging from the branches in the orchard. Her scarves and dresses were found in the black cave under the trap-door where the ironing was done. She had become accustomed to her Chanel No. 5 evaporating, her eau de Cologne disappearing without trace. At fist she suspected the maids who cleaned the rooms and didn't stay long. Some were even wrongly accused of these disappearances and fired. Then she realised it was Lavren, because he smelt so sweet all the time. He smelt just like her. 'He even smells like you,' Auguste said. And this was to cause confusion and bacchanal later on. While Marie Elena was accustomed to these things, she and the rest of the household had not grown accustomed to the disappearance of Marie Elena's lingerie: panties, petticoats. Not girdles, they were too big, though one did disappear once. There were pieces of jewellery; for instance, the gold pendant with the opal at the centre, and the earrings which had once been Sou Sou's and had been passed down to her by Elena Elena. They were reputed to have come from Aracataca. Some say they might even be the earrings Gaston gave Clarita when they were eloping over the Gulf of Sadness from the port at Guira. Though, of course, all that jewellery is now supposed to adorn the black Virgin of Tortuga, La Divina Pastora, the miraculous madonna. History, history! Too much history, Lavren thought. How does she remember it?

Each day the house trembled with all the children flying or running about or else creeping around the house looking for the missing things in the ceilings where the parrots lived. They searched between the pitchpine floorboards, in every crevice and behind every jalousie. Lavren ran to Josephine, who laughed and picked him up and shooed the other children away from her, particularly George the Usurped, who always wanted to tap him on the head. One day, Marie Elena was so beside herself that she even said, 'Wait till your father comes home'. But she could never bring herself to tell him and thus initiate a lengthy flogging with tamarind switches picked freshly from down the gully. The day would come for such punishment.

The turning point was when the rag doll was found. Lydia had been there that morning and Lavren had spent the day under the orange trees having a tea-party dressed as one of Lydia's dolls. He wasn't a baby any more. He was ready for First Communion. Why was he still playing with dolls? She could not resist this live doll. Because her dolls were as real to her as people, she gave them toys to play with and because Lavren was one of her dolls, she gave him a doll, a rag doll. The Archangel grabbed it away from Lavren and flew around the yard with it. It seemed almost as high as the palmiste. He threw it to Leonardo who gave it to the parrot on his shoulder to hold in its beak. Even Paris of Unsurpassed Beauty was forced out of his solitude by the play. Lavren ran behind each one and fell on the gravel. They teased and called 'Rag doll, rag doll,' until that hurt as much as the gravel on his grazed knees. George the Usurped tapped him on the head and Elena Maria told him he wasn't a girl, that she was the only girl in the family. Only the Evangelist did not play, but stayed in the old servant's room and conducted unknown chemistry experiments, and no one knew what it was he was doing.

'He's like your Uncle Phillipe who always wanted to invent something,' Marie Elena said.

'I'm the only inventor,' shouted Leonardo. 'I shall invent a new world.'

'Yes, my pet, yes, you will.' Marie Elena willed her Leonardo on.

Josephine came to the rescue and made the yard-man get the rag doll down from the roof of the house where the Archangel had dropped it. It was sodden with dirty rainwater because it had got caught in the spouting. Josephine put it to dry on the windowsill of the servant's room and Lavren spent the afternoon with her, learning how to sew. He made a little doily mat and gave it to Marie Elena, who hid it in case the boys or Auguste saw it. The secret was getting out, the secret that everyone knew. Maids, who were two a penny and didn't survive long (either they didn't survive Marie Elena or if they got away with her, didn't survive Josephine), would say: 'Boy, you just like a little girl, better Madam had had a girl.' Lavren would blush and bury his head in Josephine's lap.

'Look, girl, go and do Madam work, you hear; leave my child alone.'

'Your child?'

'Yes, my child. Look, girl, don't answer back woman older than you – what your mother teach you?' And these maids scuttled off with hand-brooms and dustpans to do Madam's work. 'Come, Master Lavren, let we go in the garden to pick some flowers to make flower vase for Madam. When she come back she go like it and say what a lovely child you is.' The only one, as the years went by, to arrange flowers more superbly, was Immaculata herself, who also had a hand in this changeling child, having him to stay with her in her blue citadel overlooking the gulf. There she taught him how to paint and to begin keeping a record of his life, like she did with her diaries. He used to come home crying.

'She bleeds so much. Why does Aunty Immaculata have to bleed from her hands and feet and through her belt at the side?'

'Don't worry, dear, you will learn in time.' It was during Lent in particular that he couldn't visit his favourite aunt.

'Is she a saint? Could I become a saint?'

'Don't worry, dear.'

The rag doll had alerted the boys and Elena Maria. Lavren was never allowed the rag doll in public and Lydia had to hide it in her pram when she came to take him out to play. He fast outgrew the dresses she had made for him, so now they used bits and pieces of old mosquito-net and leftovers from Elena Maria's début dress.

Then came the day when Elena Maria, Marie Elena herself, and Immaculata with the help of Aunt Leonie, cut the pattern to alter the black lace dress. Snip, snip, snip like water it flowed off the varnished dining-room table on to the pitchpine floor and settled like black lilies, which Lavren and Lydia picked and hid under the mattress of the pram. In the evenings, when the lights were dim and sometimes went out completely, and Marie Elena had to work by kerosene lamps, the black lace dress was pinned and left to hang in Elena Maria's room under the portrait of angels set in battle array. It hung over a petticoat of aquamarine satin, so that now the black lilies flowed over translucent water and clogged Lavren's dreams. He longed to wear the dress as much as he longed to see Marie Elena in it, as much as he longed to become her, to be loved by Auguste whose silence became more and more complete.

Soon the day came when Immaculata came from her blue stone house overlooking the little town of San Andres near the Gulf of Sadness, driven by Giaconda in the Chevrolet with its roof down. They had come out at dawn to go to the market in Princes Town on Savanna Grande where blood had once flowed in the streets. They stayed for breakfast which Josephine had laid on the large linen tablecloth. The ashtrays were laden with butts stamped with carmine kisses by cupid lips and the house smelt of perfume and cigarette smoke. In this haze of excitement, school for Elena Maria and Leonardo was suspended. Lavren had his own little desk made from an orange box, where he first learned to write and to practise the telling of the Carnival Tales all on his own in the gallery while the palmiste whispered: *the end of Empire, the end of Empire.*

The women talked of the dances at the time of the house in town, of the suppers and dances at Government House, and Marie Elena was sad that Elena Maria could not be presented at Government House to make her début. Uncle Ramon Junior had said: 'What for? She'll only meet a bunch of coolies and you know what.' Even if the Governor was still an Englishman and they hadn't put the Chineyman in as yet. Anyway, he would be okay, because he was Catholic. His wife's sister had taught catechism in the village where Lavren made his First Communion when he nearly fainted and choked on the host, even after practising swallowing it with Marie Elena playing the part of the priest. It was at this time that Lavren had his first vison of the wings of the Archangel Gabriel behind the altar curtains. Lavren, like his muse, digresses.

Lavren was allowed to lie on the bed and watch the trying-on of the black lace dress. Luckily, Auguste was out in the canefields, otherwise he would have been ordered out of the room with all the women. Josephine came to peep at the door. 'Madam, you looking sweet, sweet for so,' and there were laughs and screams and Lavren was delighted and ran off to tell Lydia. But no sooner had the black lace dress been folded away in white tissue paper and put in the drawer with camphor balls and cuscus grass brought from Dominica by sloop (the latter to offset the lamentable odour of the former, which was a necessary defence against moths nesting in the lace, and over the years making a meal of it), no sooner had this been done, than the black lace dress went missing.

It was after lunch, two o'clock in the afternoon, when Auguste had already gone back to the canefields on his chestnut horse, and Marie Elena had fallen asleep reciting the Five Sorrowful Mysteries of the Rosary and was snoring so loudly you might have thought there was a pig in the house. Josephine had washed the wares and was combing out her hair on the steps of the servant's room. Even the barrack-rooms were silent in the heat beating down on their galvanize roofs and walls, making ovens of their rooms. Woodsmoke rose from the board-house villages into the haze of the heat, and the only sound in the distance was Lydia playing her piano gently so that her mother could sleep. If Marie Elena sounded like a pig, Lydia's mother shook all the bungalows along the gravel road above the golf course.

At this sleepy time, when it seems there will never be any more water in the world, Lavren let the black lace dress slide out of the white tissue paper, scattering mothballs all over the floor downstairs, so they flowed out into the garden. The perfume from cuscus grass hung in the heat. The straw of the cuscus grass got caught in the lace and in Lavren's hair. He crawled into the dress, emerging at the top like a chrysalis from a cocoon, the flare of the skirt like the wings of a butterfly. His naked body tingled beneath the lace and slipped like a fish in water below the turquoise of the satin petticoat. Lavren entered a dream as he dressed and undressed several times and walked the length of downstairs in the black cave without much light under the house, in the silence of two o'clock in the afternoon. The house creaked, expanding with the heat and the miracle of his sex. The only light which existed filtered through the latticework. Lavren was transformed or uncovered to himself, as he felt for the first time, in the heat and the silence, his young body slipping between the slide of the satin and the rustle of the lace. Then came the first emanation of juices, as if he were a flower yielding pollen to butterflies and bees, and syrup to hummingbirds. The juices seemed to rise from all three orifices, and his breasts tingled as if tickled, pricked with pins or pinched with the tips of sharp fingers, so that all at once, beneath the tent of lace and satin, his gender flowered in all its glory, blinding him, and at the same time yielding visions which had first come when he was hit at the back of the head with the golfball. In the midst of his pleasure he saw the Indian boy with the burnt stomach, as raw as white fish-bait, and he heard the cries from the barrack-rooms. He was swimming beneath the Gulf of Sadness, between the skeletons and ruined barques and picking up the skulls of exhausted Amerindians. Almost by coincidence he learnt how to evoke the visions of the past. The black lace dress was his fetish, became his charm, his talisman. It worked like a mask, like a masquerade. This was mas. This was carnival.

This secret meant that he could see all the other secrets brushed beneath the carpet. Knowing himself as different, he could understand all difference. He could accept it, seek it. Two o'clock in the afternoon became his hallowed time. Then the catastrophes of mistaken gender occurred. Boys mistook him for a girl and then discovered their own hidden desires. Girls were tricked and discovered their own hidden desires. 'Those hormone tablets,' cried Marie Elena. Between the Holy Ghost and Dr Kruger's science, there was no knowing what would happen.

The dress was allowed to hang with Marie Elena's other dresses and there was no pretence again. Lavren was known to take her things to become her, so she thought, so that Auguste might love him as he loved her, but in fact he was further rejected by Auguste, because the confusion of feeling which Lavren created in others, he also created in his father. The cause of the profound loneliness the Monagas men, and maybe all men, suffered, was because they could not accept their desire and passion for each other. Hence mythology produced Lavren, who had to be both girl and boy in order to love and be loved.

But the black lace dress as fetish, charm and talisman, has been a secret kept by Lavren till now as he sits at the foot of Marie Elena's death-bed in the turret room overlooking the Gulf of Sadness.

It was soon after Lavren's confirmation, when his new shoes squeaked all the way down the aisle, when he was desired by both the Syrian girl across the aisle of the church and the creole boy in the pew next to him, that Marie Elena decided in her heart of hearts that this could not go on. She landed on the wonderful idea of using all the material of invention at her disposal, which had been imported into the new world with the paraphernalia of the church: cassocks, stoles, maniples, surplices made of lace, chasubles, copes of flowing silk. A desire for these could be instilled and distract from lace dresses. He must start by becoming an acolyte. These dressings-up had to stop. Lavren had held pantomimes at the window for an audience in the barracks, to the accompaniment of Mantovani's interpretation of Beethoven's 'Eroica' which was played at full volume, blaring over the trembling canefields, and angering Auguste. If something was not done at once, things might get as bad as Margarita and Quentino in the house in the cocoa.

He was constantly being seduced by his cousins and other playmates who mistook him for a girl, or so they said. It was precisely the continuing of that syrupy feeling which Lavren had felt between his legs when he wore the black lace dress under the house which would not end, but had only now started. This decided Marie Elena on a plan with the help of a parish priest, an archbishop, an abbot and a monastery of monks. It did seem as if there was something this clerical panoply could bring about. 'Father, you must do something.'

'Yes, my dear child,' said Father Sebastian, who was reputed to be a saint. 'I detect a natural instinct for piety and devotion, a natural way with the liturgy.' And indeed Lavren developed, like no other acolyte before or since, a particular grace of movement that had old aunts and uncles as well as young boys and girls going wet between their legs or swooning in the aisles. He was beloved of priests, archbishops, monks, and was chosen to carry the papal nuncio's train which was almost a mile long. He was beloved of him too. But he did not give up the black lace dress, the source of his visions, his two o'clock in the afternoon talisman.

Lavren noticed that the blue veins beneath the white skin of Father Sebastian were like the blue veins that ran in white marble. At this time, instead of Chanel No. 5 and eau de Cologne being the potions in his games, Lavren chose holy water and a collection of the relics of the saints. A prize was a piece of Maria Goretti's flesh – she had died for purity rather than have sex with Alesandro, and together with Dominic Savio had been instantly created saint by the Pope in Rome. These innocent Italian teenagers were to be heroes and heroines to distract all from the gyrating hips and legs of Elvis Presley and teenage romantic love rocking round the clock. Lavren found that his passion for the liturgy was matched only by his passion for the Hollywood screen. It was indeed a convenience to possess the institution of confession, so that purity could be restored as instantly as it was lost. The cathedrals of the big screen, Rivoli in Coffee Street, Empire on Penitence Hill (called so because it was so steep), Globe,

Radio City, Gaiety and New Theatre were all cathedrals of the big screen, monuments to passion: Marilyn Monroe, Jane Russell, Gina Lollobrigida. All were grist for the mill of fantasy when he was tempted away from cassocks and surplices back to his black lace dress. Then the visions started again. Lavren would slip into his fetish of lace and sink beneath the Gulf of Sadness.

Lavren digresses and is himself seduced by his own re-creation of childhood and early adolescence. That syrupy feeling made him forget his Carnival Tales. He was brought up with a jolt. On the radio, BBC News: Suez filled the house. For the first time in his life Auguste and Marie Elena quarrelled. Auguste nearly pulled the house down and Marie Elena went to lie on her bed after dinner, to quieten her hate for Anthony Eden. Somewhere, inside that story, Lavren learned to hate British colonialism and imperialism. He listened to the news more. Yes, there was Dalip Singh who had cut his wife into little bits and drowned her in the Oropouche Lagoon. There was Boysie Singh who lured his victims out to the Gulf of Sadness and strangled them. He read newspapers, but the news dominating the papers and the radio was self-government and independence and the arrival of the Third Most Intelligent Man in the World.

Even carnival was second to this. Even Marie Elena, trying to suggest fantasy substitutes as she had always done in the past when she dressed Lavren up as a sugarcane-company milk-bottle, or one of the Pope's Swiss Guards at the Vatican, and even as Peter Pan in Kensington Gardens, because he was her Peter Pan, could not blot out the news. All pupils at school had to say an extra rosary per day against communism which the Third Most Intelligent Man in the World was bringing into the island. 'Our good negroes wouldn't want that,' Marie Elena said at dinner. The Irish Archbishop prayed thirteen times in the year on the Laventville hilltop shrine against communism. Nuns who had been tortured under communism in China were brought to speak in schools to terrify children. Sermons were given on the persecution of the Church in Russia. The invasion of Hungary was a theme of the sermons and the Fatima devotions, and the overtaking of the world by communism was preached from every village pulpit. Communism was afoot. More than ever you could not trust what the coolies or the intellectual negroes would do. 'The ones with the beards who look like monkeys,' said Leonardo, beginning to take an interest in re-creating the world in his own image and likeness, as Marie Elena's God had once done.

And from up the archipelago the clamour rose: *Fidel, Fidel, Fidel!*

Lavren wished with all his heart that great events didn't happen only in Hungary, China and Cuba. They didn't, but in the house in the sugar they were not discussed in that way. They were a 'Darn nuisance, another fire on the canefields, anothe strike in the oilfields.' Monkey Cedric, Marie Elena's brother, hadn't been able to get his cars off the ship at the wharf because there was a strike. Increasingly, Marie Elena could not get a half-day girl.

'Madam, girls not going to want to work like me, you know, they want real work, Madam,' Josephine said.

'Real work? What do you mean, real work?'

'People want to better themselves, Madam.' Josephine knew she would stay until the end, whenever that was, and it seemed to be coming. The world seemed to be coming to an end.

Auguste grew more and more silent, and already the first signs of amnesia were there. His mind was filled with the tonnage of cane, the planting and manuring of ratoons, labour problems. These plagued his daylight hours. His nights were entwined in the nightmare which was still witchbroom, the loss of his father's cocoa estates and the consequent loss of position and money. Hence he was working for English people in the sugarcane company.

Marie Elena became eschatalogical and, like a Christian of the early Church, felt heaven was nigh; but it was a strange combination and mixture of things, for it sounded as if there would be a private heaven for the Monagas family alone. Since most other people were excluded from good society on earth, Lavren could not imagine why they should be included in heaven. Hell was obviously where everyone else was going to go. Even Lydia was an Anglican heretic. The Indians were pagans and the black people were 'our good negroes' to Marie Elena. So maybe there were two heavens, since they had to be one for the women of the Legion of Mary and the one or two black priests.

Two o'clock in the afternoon, which was Lavren's hallowed hour, the time for the black lace dress and that syrupy feeling which could be absolved by confession on Sunday, was sometimes renounced for the privilege of spending siesta with Josephine. 'You not dressing up today, eh, Master Lavren? You growing out of that or what? Or you frighten the boss or one of the boys find you in your mother's clothes? Is all right, you know, you could come here. I understand.' And it was on one of these occasions that Lavren discovered more things about Josephine. She could see that he was growing up: 'What they teaching you in school, boy? Let me tell you a few things, because I does hear the boss and Madam talking in the night when I clearing away the wares, and the way they does talk I can see they don't understand one damn thing in this place. So long they living here and they don't understand. I wonder if you go understand. Let me show you these pictures. Fetch me that album there, let me show you a few things.'

Lavren fetched the album from the windowsill which served as a shelf. Josephine brushed the dust off the cover and sat herself on the edge of the black-iron bed with the fibre mattress. 'Come, come and sit. Let me tell you a story.'

'Like when I was small?'

'You still small, you small in the head.' Josephine opened the photo album like an enchantress opening a book of legends. 'I collecting these for some time, since you small. Watch: you know that man? You does read the papers, but you does know what you read? Anyway it better you don't understand what they does say in these papers. The papers only own by a set of white people up town. But is the picture I like. This is my man, you see him, a healthy-looking man, yes, if you hear him speak. I hear him speak down in town and down Fyzabad. Buzz, Uriah Buzz Butler.'

'Daddy says he's a lunatic.'

'You have to be mad to live in this place. You have to be mad to change it. He start to change it.' She turned the pages: 'He bring us out of slavery, he bring us out of Babylon to the land of Judah. This man is our Moses and with he we cross the Red Sea coming through the desert into the land flowing with milk and honey. Is a great man, yes, no lunatic. Your father more a lunatic – don't tell the boss I say that.' Josephine turned the pages of the album and there were more pictures of the big man and Lavren remembered the bandstand on the promenade in San Andres opposite the school by the Church of Notre Dame de Bon Secours where they used to play: black boys, Indian boys, coloured boys, Syrian boys, chiney boys.

'Darling, do play with them at school but don't bring them home for tea.' Marie Elena ran her fingers through Lavren's hair. She remembers the day he came home with concussion because he had bumped into a black boy. Marie Elena thinks that might have reactivated the damage done by the collision with the golfball hit by Mr de Lisle. 'Their heads are so hard.'

Tea, what tea is that? Cocoa tea? Bang bang, on the company school-bus, whitey whitey cockroach . . . blackie cockroach, chiney chiney never die, flat-nose and chinky eye, coolie coolie come for roti half-past two. All rhymes spilled out, children of the Motherland, 'Land of Hope and Glory' marching on the promenade: boom, boom, the bells toll and the King is Dead. Long Live the Queen. Cinema, film of the Coronation in the Rivoli Coffee Street, scrapbook with Lydia, cut-outs from the *Illustrated London News*. Events were a contradiction and a confusion, a real carnival, ole mas. The reel of film was going backwards rather than forwards.

Here was his beloved Josephine, and she was now showing him the picture of the man they called at table: 'Communist . . . think of what they do to those poor nuns.' Another special rosary for the conversion of Russia. Here was Josephine, proud of her people.

'This is the man, Master Lavren, brightness. You hear your father have him on the radio. He does listen to him and then he does get drunk because he can't cope with what this bright man telling all you. Your father does pretend he understand, and because he drunk he does like to disagree with Madam, and Madam only praying. All you go have to pray. Massa day done.'

The teachers said they had to pray, communism coming in the land just now, torture like in China, 'Hail Mary full of grace . . . now and at the hour of our death, Amen.'

'You hear him, Master Lavren. He gone in them place, up in them university. He learn the things they learn and he go beat them at their own game. He is my man. Madam have me here still like is some kind of slavery. Is because I black.'

'Josephine, Josephine, are you down there? It's nearly four o'clock. It's nearly time for tea.' Josephine picked up her dress and poked her backside in the air in the direction from which Marie Elena's voice came. At the same time she smiled at Lavren, a smile as big as the continent of Africa with all its gleaming ivory.

'You see what I mean?' Then she lifted the window and said, 'Coming, Madam, will be right there, Madam,' and to Lavren, lowering the window: 'Blasted slavery.'

Lavren hung between Marie Elena and Josephine, and he hung between their schizophrenic selves: Josephine's rebellion and her servitude, Marie Elena's religion, love of God and her oppressive regimes. Lavren hung between them, swinging here one time and then there another.

The altar games had in fact started earlier, even before Lavren became a proper acolyte. Altar games were in the afternoon after school when George the Usurped was practising to be an acolyte but decided that he was really the priest, so Lavren would have to be his acolyte. This was George the Usurped at his most tender. George displayed invention in the adaptation of towels as chasubles, mosquito-nets were flowing copes. Auguste's press was raided for ties to be stoles and maniples, and where else to be the altar but the dressing-table, covered with the already hallowed vessels of Marie Elena's toilette. The bathroom cabinet, emptied of toothpaste, brushes and Auguste's Andrews' Liver Salts, was unhinged from the wall above the basin to be the hallowed tabernacle and place of the real presence made visible, hidden in Coca-Cola in a wine glass and a Crix biscuit on a chosen silver salver from the cabinet when Josephine wasn't watching what they did with Madam's things.

Innocence can be the best form of trickery. And it was through this innocent play that Marie Elena saw to it that Lavren now became as equally seduced by the sacerdotal fantasy as he was in becoming her, in her black lace dress. Increasingly, Lavren was spoken for when asked by uncles, aunts and visitors to the house, 'And what will this little man be?' They doubted their own eyes in giving such a definite ascription of gender, but preferred to trust in pants and shirts rather than their own fancies, which dressed him in a skirt. Marie Elena always answered for Lavren:

'He will be a priest.' It was proclaimed, ordained from the time of innocent (innocent?) childhood and was to lead, dare we suggest it at this stage, to a bizarre and sorry conclusion.

The old estate house could hardly stand up to the fervour and passion of what was going on inside it. Auguste absented himself. 'Your father is not a demonstrative person,' Marie Elena said. The house first started trembling at dawn, shaken by alarm bells and the vigorous stirring of Andrews' Liver Salts with a silver spoon. Auguste came down the corridor to administer the daily dose (his one contribution to the morning ceremony) to whichever child's turn it was, after having administered the effervescent laxative to himself, the constant stirring of the bowels making sure that there always would be some movement to read the signs of the times by. Then there was the queue for cold showers.

Josephine had been up at four o'clock ironing khaki pants and white shirts. Bakes, cocoa, scrambled eggs hurried and indigestible, so that all could (especially in the month of May) huddle, kneeling around the conjugal bed and bed of births as big as the savannah, hung with the mother-of-pearl crucifix and murmur, falling again back to sleep and adolescent dreams, the 'Hail Holy Queen Mother Mercy Hail Our Lives Our Sweetness and Our Hope . . . the Five Sorrowful Mysteries of the Rosary – the First Mystery, the Agony in the Garden': squeeze your eyes ever so tightly till those green pools come, and in the midst of that hallucination meditate and contemplate on the Garden of Gethsemane, the chalice which would not pass away.

Marie Elena led off as clear as a bell, giving example of devotion. Lavren followed every gesture, every raised eye to heaven, every downcast eyelid to his/her humble self, modelling himself and his responses on her with every modulation of tone and emphasis of meaning. But out of the mouths of the others could come the greatest variety of response, depending into which prayer they happened to wake into. Lavren would often be distracted by Leonardo's invention, eliding the response to the Hail Mary with, 'Holy Mo . . . gd pray for us sin . . . ow and . . . the our . . . death . . . Amen.' Such was the cacophony which cast its spell upon the day and absolved any subsequent misdemeanour.

All this while the day outside had started much earlier and was alive with women, barefooted in hitched-up skirts, heads bound against the morning dew and covered with old faded brown trilby hats, processing from the barrack-rooms a good distance behind their husbands and men, leaving small babies and children to be cleansed for school by slightly older children. All was fine on earth and with God in His heaven as the house on the hill woke to prayers in the month of May and the women processed to the canefields behind

God's back, back of Barackpore in the baking sun which had now risen in the sky.

The house on the hill could not at times hold this passion and spell, and the pitchpine planks would suddenly split and let in shafts of light in some of the most inconvenient places, making its insides visible to the world, and then Auguste would have to send a man up from the yard to nail down the wood. Sometimes, the galvanize from the roof would fly off and had been known to hurtle through the air and cut ordinary working people in half. It was as the gospel says: 'Out of the mouths of babes and infants . . .' Lavren's prayers and devotions shook not only him but the world which merely petered out along the gravel road where the grassy fringes of the verge gave way to barrack-rooms and some of the most painful crucifixions upon the mango trees. 'These people have no respect for life.' Lavren began to pray for the stigmata, for the five wounds to pierce the palms of his hands, to nail his feet and to pierce his side just beneath his appendix. He slept on the bedsprings, shunning the mattresses and ancestral linen. He knelt at night before the open moonlight-flooded skies hearing all the time the breathing of interrupted sleep in the barrack-rooms. His secret places were not sought for the rehearsing of Marie Elena's life in the black lace dress, nor for the powers of his talisman, but for the silence and hiddenness in which he could strip himself for the Third Sorrowful Mystery of the Rosary – Jesus is whipped and spat upon. His reading was *The Life and Times of Catherine of Siena*, and one night he had his second vision: when the statue of Notre Dame de Bon Secours came from the church in San Andres and entered his bedroom. She stood over him holding the baby Jesus, whose sandal was falling off in accordance with the iconography of this particular representation of the virgin mother, Theodokos.

It was at this time that the passion and spell of the house on the hill affected not only the roof and walls of the house, but also the foundations. Then there were the disturbances in the entire hemisphere, brewing up the tail-end of a hurricane in the Orinoco delta, and whipping up a storm from the west which came up the Gulf of Sadness from the Serpent's Mouth, following the very route of the Great Navigator's first voyage of arrival. It created havoc with the barrack-rooms. It destroyed them to such an extent that the company were forced to build alternative dwellings, though meanwhile hardship was more exteme as the labourers continued to live in half a barrack-room, flooded and damp, breeding Anopheles and his malarial eggs. Marie Elena and Lavren continued to pray, and the more they prayed the more destruction and havoc were perpetrated by the western wind until every saman tree on the fabled golf-course had had its branches wrung from it, and the pond rose and flooded the course. Alligators crawled up to the front-door steps, and though this was like the flood of Noah, there was no ark and no blessed rainbow and no new covenant.

The havoc created was worse than the storms of Auguste's temper during the Suez crisis, which used to send Lavren's beloved Marie Elena to her bed to lie beneath the mother-of-pearl crucifix, fingers manacled to a rosary, and Lavren after her, to lie and stroke her face. The havoc created was worse than when Auguste threw the food out of the window because Marie Elena had cooked it and not Josephine. These were untypical displays of emotion by Auguste and revealed the extent of his repression of passion. There were still the storms of independence and the speeches every night on the radio by the Third Most Intelligent Man in the World at the University of Brunswick Square proclaiming, 'Massa day done.' This storm created by the prayers and passion of Lavren in his first quest for sainthood, continued until every mango tree was uprooted on Hangman Alley. All the barrack-rooms were completely destroyed and the sugarcane company was obliged to build new dwellings, not the best, but better. Lavren's prayers culminated with the sugarcane strikes. His rosaries, instead of keeping away the dreaded communism, seemed to give added strength to trade-union leaders.

While change was marching through the land, Lavren was marching in its ranks below the windowsills of the Demerara window and himself/herself looking up at the house to blow it down. It creaked and swayed and more galvanize flew off its roof and planks of pitchpine split. But it stood as all the houses have stood, wreathed in witchbroom and full of ghosts.

The old man from Muruga Road met Lavren on the march and so did Josephine's son. Josephine waved from the window under which the rabble passed marching towards J'Ouvert. Lavren marched down the road, taking the hand of the Indian boy with the stomach burnt white as fish-bait, and marched down the road with the black girls from the house by the bamboo patch. Lydia waved him goodbye with tears in her eyes.

Lavren pressed his ear against the perforations of the radio to hear the lowering of the Union Jack while Auguste and Marie Elena snored. The Evangelist had left long ago, following his own experiments. The Archangel flew the roost and became an expert in divining oil, a gift which he inherited from Clarita of the first house. Leonardo continued to invent the world, which eventually swallowed him up. Paris, in his solitude, went on a pilgrimage to the Holy Land. George the Usurped sulked at Lavren's *coup de famille*, and Elena Maria, in the longest tradition of the women of the Monagas de los Macajuelos, made babies on the orders of the Pope. They dispersed, fleeing and fragmenting the family in their fear and guilt, their obsession with pigmentation. They missed the roti, pelau, hot pepper, steel band and calypso and continued to speak Congo: everyone does on the island of Kairi, even if they have fled as far as the antipodes. In the extremity of their fear, they preferred their exile and their loneliness, like the loneliness of the houses of Kairi.

Because of Lavren's reckless praying, his visions, penances, his transvestism necessary to express his full nature as a hermaphrodite, and because he had taken part in the marches and his prayers had destroyed the house in the sugar, he was committed to the asylum at Saint Ann's. 'You have to be mad to live in this place,' Josephine said. He was visited by priests and nuns who continued to seduce him with Gregorian chant. Eventually he was rescued by Immaculata, who took him to live with her in the blue citadel overlooking the Gulf of Sadness. He was now a young man, but even at this age, while eating gigantic guavas under the guava trees, wormy guavas as big as moons which he used to scrape out and fill with brown sugar, gorging himself on the fragrant confection, Lavren was kissed as if he were a woman. Then he had to remember the vow of chastity, hardly lasting between one confession and another, forced on him by the nuns and priests in Saint Ann's after he had made love on the island of centipedes, again mistaken for a young girl in the darkness of the night.

Avoiding the occasion of sin he lived with the stigmatised Immaculata, helping her with her orchids, learning how to paint the changing skies, and beginning to record the history of the Monagas de los Macajuelos when he was not bandaging his aunt's hands, feet and side, mopping her brow of ruby drops of blood. He also spent part of the day in the black lace dress, which brought his visions. Lavren continued here, in the blue citadel, until the death of Immaculata relieved her from the pain of the stigmata. Then he moved in the last days to the bedroom of Marie Elena, his beloved muse and mother, who in her very old age, had reconciled herself to the extravagance of her miraculous prodigy in the turret room overlooking the Gulf of Sadness.

THE TALE OF THE LAST HOUSE

THE RAIN continued to fall, as it had fallen all this week and these months of the rainy season. The swamp became one with the old rice-fields and flooded the plains of Kairi where they lay, a watery waste between the mountains of the continental cordillera and the ancient riverbed of the Orinoco. It was said in Aracataca that it had been raining for forty years without stopping. No one had returned from there for nearly half a century, so that people were convinced that the magic which could transform their lives was no longer to be found on the ancient savannahs of the Monagas, where the first de Lanjous had come in search of child brides with their baskets of pearls as dowries. If there was any magic left in the world it was to be found in the masquerade of history, a history whose calamitous waste had produced the possibility of a new world. But this, only by the repeated creation and simultaneous destruction of beauty, the grasping at the ambivalence of nature in the masquerade of cruelty and horror, transforming it out of darkness into a sunlight of music and colour: Carnival! By the second night, this beauty was abandoned and destroyed, burned down into ashes; the same ashes that are collected on the banks of the river, and signed upon the foreheads of the faithful on Ash Wednesday morning. The old rituals, the old formulae, still take hold of the imagination of Lavren, as he writes the last of his 'Carnival Tales of The Houses of Kairi'; his life has shrunk to the repeated turning of this square of a manuscript's page, and ministering to the deathbed needs of his beloved Marie Elena, mother and muse of history. 'With all this rain falling, the world has indeed become a lacrimarum vale, a vale of tears,' she said, turning in her bed, turning the leaves of her prayerbook.

Josephine was too old to mount the stairs to the turret room of this last of the houses of the Monagas de los Macajuelos. She came at the usual time with her trays and left them at the foot of the stairs. Lavren carried the bowl of chicken soup up to the turret room. This

226

was the only diet that could be digested by Marie Elena, the only food to pass her lips, except the wine that is the blood of Christ and the bread that is His body.

Father Sebastian, though old, can still mount the stairs, because he is a saint. He sees it as his Golgotha, mounting as he mounts the steps of the altar to the sacrifice of the mass. It is a joy. 'My daughter, open your mouth'; then he says on her behalf in Latin, *Domine non sum dignus . . .* and she moves her mouth in English.

'Lord, I am not worthy to receive You into my house, but only say the word and my soul shall be healed,' the formula taken from the rich man in the gospel of the New Testament which lies on the table next to Marie Elena's bed. This abject prostration of spirit is repeated three times before Father Sebastian puts the host to her lips. Since returning from Saint Ann's, Lavren can no longer be an acolyte to these liturgies of Holy Mother Church.

'Why aren't you answering the responses, dear? You knew them so well.'

'You know I can't remember them.' He wanted to tell her that he no longer believed, he no longer had the passion which was hers. Lavren knew he could not communicate these understandings to her, so old, so fragile. He felt that not only would his words break her heart, but her body would collapse and there would be no heart to break. While she knew in her heart of hearts that he had lost his soul, she preferred to delude herself that he was making the responses to Father Sebastian's supplications. At moments like this she would hallucinate him at the foot of the altar, robed in the vestments for his first mass, after she had received his first blessing and kissed his consecrated fingers, which had the power to accompany his words and change bread and wine into the body and blood of her Lord. *Introibo ad altare Dei . . . Ad deum qui laetificat juventutem meum . . .*

Lavren says: you see that the magic of the old is still vibrant in the metaphor for transforming and understanding the new.

The rain had been falling since the funeral of Auguste, so that Lavren wondered if he should visit the grave to see whether the dirt which covered it had been washed away and the coffin exposed where it lay in the family plot in Lapeyrouse. He put away his manuscript in the drawer of the desk belonging to Auguste and went down to the bottom of the stairs to fetch the tray with the bowl of chicken soup that Josephine had left, she herself falling asleep at the foot of the stairs.

Lavren knew that the understanding which had come with the death of Auguste had left him in a place of solitude. That place was with his square of manuscript, at the desk of Auguste, at the foot of Marie Elena's bed overlooking the plains of Kairi and the Gulf of Sadness. He had seen the history of the new world from here.

Father Sebastian came each day with the viaticum. The last days were near. He did not understand this last of the Monagas, this archivist and recorder of myth. He would rather this young man had hidden his nature in the asylum than attempt to follow this neurotic epistemophilia, to discover the source of passion, the history of cruelty, and the development of fungal diseases in the cocoa plant: witchbroom.

'Don't break your mother's heart, my boy.' The priest patted his shoulder one morning as he was leaving the turret room. Lavren smiled. He did not want to talk to theologians; there were no secrets held in their words any more. And, ever since he had given up the idea of being a saint himself, he had become bored with sanctity. Besides, he was mending a broken heart. Auguste had gone, with his silence and the dry skin peeling off his hands. After his fiftieth reading of *The Ascent to Mount Everest*, Auguste had put the book down on the ledge of the veranda and decided not to remember anything that had ever happened any more. From then on he depended absolutely on Marie Elena to remember for him.

Marie Elena had not as yet taken to her deathbed, and so could pretend to the world that Auguste was still active by doing everything for him. He had long ago given up speaking in her presence, though she reported many conversations and secrets they shared when they were on their own in their bed. Lavren, because of his love for his mother and muse, had to believe her, give her the benefit of the doubt, but he had serious misgivings about these reports. They had not shared a bed for years because of the damp which had come up from the swamp and entered his bones and lodged there, to irritate and stiffen with arthritis, limbs as twisted as the mangrove in the swamps.

Auguste decided to forget everything because he could not bear what was happening to the world around him. Particularly, he could not bear the way the savannah was being destroyed, parcelled up and sold off. So that when he looked up from his fiftieth reading of *The Ascent to Mount Everest* and gazed out over the savannah, where Pablosito the Second was going to build a supermarket complex, he said, 'Sell it yourself.' He had remembered trying to grow sugar and cocoa and how he had had to fight the froghopper and the witchbroom which entangled the ancestral plain. When he looked upon this plain and savannah to which he had returned for his retirement, growing pangola grass and rearing pigs for Pablosito the Second, his heart was not in the selling of the land for houses. He did not have the stomach for the bargaining and the business. Left to him, he would still be in the Tamana hills with his little cocoa-crop; he would not have moved into sugar if his wife had not continued breeding children in a Catholic way.

Marie Elena took over the selling of the land, though Pablosito the Second continued to address all the business correspondence to Auguste, which impressed Marie Elena. Nothing wrong could be said of Jeansie's son, caretaker of the family fortune, the fortune which lay right here below the sea-level of the Gulf of Sadness.

While Monkey Cedric and Ramon Junior (Marie Elena's brothers, fabled uncles) had been busy selling motorcars, tyres and batteries and drinking too much rum, being mayors and senators to make sure their business would be safeguarded, the land, the family land, lay fallow. Though when the family passed it on the modern highway they always pointed out where the pot of gold was buried. Then the Third Most Intelligent Man in the World, deaf to most things but his own aggrandisement, having lost his way in pride and folly, and written his history of the people, said he would confiscate all land that was not being used. So they rallied. The old blood rallied: the descendants of Count Lopinot who had come with his loyal slaves, Roume St Laurent with his ancient mother, Rose de Gannes de la Chancellerie, Marie Louise de Lapeyrouse, Eugene Vessiny, Anna de Noirmont, Catherine de la Boisluisant, Jacques de Verteuil, and the long list of the 'de' this and 'de la' that, all the rag-tag-and-bobtail of the *haute aristocracie* who came from Grenada, changed their names on the way over and became nobility overnight. They all rallied with the blood which had overseen the growing of cocoa, coffee, bananas and sugar. The names and the sound of the names trip off the tongue of Marie Elena, and enchant by their very music the imagination and memory of Lavren.

They now owned all the newspapers, motorcar firms, car-accessory services. They appointed themselves director of this and that and formed the new conglomerates of this and that, publishing newspapers, canning milk imported from Argentina, while the Third Most Intelligent Man in the World thought he had given power to the people because, indeed, Kairi was swimming in oil, the new El Dorado, the economic miracle which Muhammad wrought in Libya and Saudi. The foreign bonds were being bought and money for the people was being banked abroad in Switzerland, laundered in Panama, hidden in the Bahamas and Jersey by O'Hara, the bosom pal of the Third Most Intelligent Man in the World, and the papers said he did not know anything about it. The Minister of Transport imported hovercrafts to speed across the Gulf of Sadness to solve the traffic-jam problem. The Minister of Education imported schoolmeals from Luxembourg, the percentage-cut tucked into their own pockets. The Minister of Health was made President of the World Health Organization for running the most deplorable hospitals in the hemisphere. The Third Most Intelligent Man in the World put a television and a ghettoblaster into every home for the people (his people once) to listen to American evangelists and savour the advertisements for a way of life no one could really afford. Each minister had a swimming pool and heated Jacuzzi. Black limousines created traffic jams in the centre of town on Friday afternoon when the parliament sat, encircled with corbeaux in the sky. The Chief Inspector of Police imported cocaine for the children and gunned down the youth in the hills; the ganja burnings sent everyone into the seventh heaven. They had had no other example, and fell themselves into the illusion, *folie des grandeurs*; drunk with whisky, so much whisky drunk that even rum prices had dropped, swinging in their hammocks in their island condominiums on Gasper Grande. Lavren listens to rumour and reads the newspapers.

When all this was going on in a bacchanal *Danse Macabre*, the sons and daughters of the indentured generation bought up or mortgaged themselves to the land on the Gangetic plain for their sons and daughters, grandsons and granddaughters, hiding the money under the mattress to send the child to become a lawyer and doctor up in England self. The enfranchisement of the enslaved was moneyed by the Third Most Intelligent Man in the World, Party Politics, Party Patronage, the best village show you ever see, so that the Monagas with their entrepreneurial cousins could sit and sip rum punches and laugh on their verandas and on the deck of their yachts and on the jetties of their island homes and console each other: 'Boy, life good, eh?' They thought they had never had it so good, even though, 'Boy, I never see so much coolie, nigger and cro-cro in my life. You never know, you might have a coolie living right next to you.' They even had coolie lawyers now, though Marie Elena continued to tap her wrist to indicate the permutations of colour as if she were in Dessaline's Haiti, obsessed with octaroons. Some of the Monagas began to legitimise what Monagas l'Diable had done a century ago, fuck with black people. Lavren jumps ahead. He leaves his life and love for history.

Before the glut and the greed, when the Third Most Intelligent Man in the World said he was going to resign and never did, the poor burned the streets and went from the hill overlooking the city out into the canefields to meet with the other poor, to come back into town like another Canboulay. They filled the streets like it was carnival. The army was playing *To Hell and Back*, had practised their jump-up in Sandhurst and didn't have an inkling what they would do when they took the town. The Indian major said, 'Boy, I didn't know what we would've do.' Then the Deputy Prime Minister sat in the Third Most Intelligent Man in the World's chair till he came back from the airport where he had gone, pretending to desert the sinking ship and caught him redhanded.

'Who ent like it could get the hell out of here.' Lavren is engrossed in the newspapers and their version of the truth.

During those times, Immaculata's daughter, Giaconda – aching with a sorrow for the passing world which had encroached upon the citadel of blue stone overlooking the Gulf of Sadness, so that the orchids no longer bloomed as they used to, and Immaculata, bleeding more profusely than ever, had not written an entry in her diary for the last five years and the pages were turning yellow on the windowsill – decided that she would stay put when her husband suggested they should flee to Miami as the shouts of 'Power' broke through her siesta, penetrating even the walls of the citadel which Carlos Monagas de los Macajuelos had built.

'Darling, we must leave, otherwise these niggers will burn us,' Giaconda's husband urged.

'I can't leave my mother in her bleeding with the five wounds of

Christ. And my children? I can't look after them without the nurse.'
While the streets were full of the power of Black Power, Fortune,
the nurse of Giaconda's children, continued to shell pigeon-peas,
wash diapers, lay table, wash wares, and in the afternoon go into
the streets of San Andres and jump up and shout 'Power'. Giaconda
said, 'I hate those monkeys but I can't do without my Fortune.' She
was thinking of her nurse, but mentioning that prophetic name, she
meant that she could not leave the citadel of blue stone. 'Fortune,
how can you go with those savages?'

'Savages, Madam? They are my people.'

As Lavren writes, he smiles at the irony of life, as he sees the
windows flapping in the wind, the overgrown garden, the broken
statue of the Blessed Virgin Mary under the calabash tree, the rotting
orchids and the stumps of rose trees killed off by batchacs. The ruin
of the blue stone house, the domain of purity, the tomb of
Immaculata, the house of funerals, now a brothel, a house for all
the young beti in town.

'Child, we ent have no fortune now,' Giaconda, the last of
Immaculata's daughters, said as she dug up the last of the anthuriums
she had planted under the mango trees behind the orchid house in
the days when she and her fiancé walked in the garden and kissed
on the night of their engagement so Lavren and Monkey Cedric's
children could see. Lavren remembered her dress the colour of lapis
lazuli, a cloud of tulle over a thick water of satin.

Lavren is weary, weary with history. History in one sense, as it was
once written, was also dying. News and rumour had come to the
last of the houses on the plains of Kairi, that the Third Most
Intelligent Man in the World was dying. He had not been seen for
months. Josephine brought the rumour into the turret room by
saying, 'Madam, if you see corbeaux in the sky, there must be a big
death in the place.' It was from this time that Marie Elena decided
to pray for the Third Most Intelligent Man in the World and the
salvation of his soul. He had turned out not be a communist after
all, and really what would happen when he went nobody liked to
imagine. The colonial structure had been kept intact, and even
though there was the show of banishing the Americans from their
base with the rhetoric 'Massa Day Done', the dollars still kept coming
in payment for keeping Uncle Sam's backyard in order. Those

rosaries, Hail Marys and *Pater Nosters* must have worked their miracle. Lavren had to hold himself back because he could already see the future. Marie Elena wondered whether she would die at the same time as this milder descendant of Jiminez, Batista, Duvalier, Samoza and his closest neighbour in Grenada, who spent his last days identifying unidentified flying objects and practising the occult, while prisoners were tortured, and languished in the fortress above the jewel of the Caribbean and, further into the future, when the innocent and good were to be butchered.

Marie Elena can hardly digest the chicken soup. For years now there has hardly been any coprolites to analyse which could indicate the future. When she got up off the commode and looked into the porcelain bowl, she could barely perceive a stain at the bottom of the bowl, and there was little she could make of the watery stool. 'There is no future. Darling, empty this bowl.' No other member of the Monagas family would admit to interest in their shit, except of course Lavren, but s/he is not to be counted; given all that you have read, there is no need to explain. Lavren knows there is secret scatology going on. You can guess who the closet shit analysts are. At all corners of the universe there is some Monagas or the other turning round and looking down into the lavatory bowl in the morning after breakfast to see what he or she, or s/he (not that any have admitted, yet, to this ambivalence) . . . Lavren would suggest, give a clue, no no no . . . don't worry. All shall not be revealed. But why not? Given all that has been said, this would be a little thing, so why not? The biggest shit analyst in the world is, of course . . . guess who? You may, dear reader, wish to write this off as a whole load of shit, but if you analyse it you will see what Marie Elena saw the morning she asked Father Sebastian to anoint her body with the oils of Extreme Unction.

She had formed the opinion for some time that there was no future left. There was what the theologians wished to fob you off with, and that was her only hope. But there was no future in this greed, this folly of cross and sword, no future in this *folie des grandeurs*. There was no future in this elevation of pigmentation, this obsession with large houses and grand gardens, no future in the accumulation of things which had taken such proportions as to send several members of the family to the Saint Ann's madhouse until they could learn to stem their desire for more tea-sets, sofas, dishwashers, necklaces, bracelets, stocks and shares, yachts, condominiums, children, servants, motor cars, transatlantic cruises, shopping malls, valium, gin and tonics, an everlasting list of consuming materialism, which had devoured the Monagas de los Macajuelos since the time of the very first Monagas who had ever taken a pirogue from Guira on the shore of the continent of Bolivar, who had killed a python that had swallowed a cow and who had then eaten both the python, called a macajuel, and the cow.

While Lavren meditates on these matters and as Marie Elena tries to dredge up the past, Josephine continues to be messenger with the news of the man she thought was bright, but had changed her mind about in her old age. 'Madam, they say he dead. They can't see him and no one moving in the house and the police won't even allow the ministers and them to go in. Anyway, they say the ministers 'fraid him. 'Fraid what they go find. Is only corbeaux in the place. And you know what, Madam, they say a lot of people going deaf. Must be spite.'

'Josephine, the poor man. How can you talk like this about him, and he is one of your own people? I pray for his soul, poor man.'

'Is our people, yes, but he ent do one blasted thing in the end, that is what I say.'

'Josephine?'

'Madam?'

Before Auguste had died he had wanted to give everything away to the poor. But Marie Elena told him, 'My darling, what we've got? What would the poor do with these things?' One morning, when Marie Elena was detained in the office with a man who had come to buy six lots of land and insisted on giving her the money in cash, brought in a brown-paper bag: 'They keep it under the mattresses, you know; these coolies always have money. You see their children, they're lawyers and doctors.' Auguste had got the ornaments and crystal and monogrammed tea-sets out of the cabinet. He wanted Josephine to pack them into boxes to take for the poor who lined up outside the bank and the market, in the little town where they sell oysters and the Hanuman House is now a pharmacy and television crews come to make films about the Indian novelist who once lived there. Auguste always gave money to the beggars in his old age. When Marie Elena remembered this she decided she wanted the women of the altar society and the old women who arranged the flowers for the parish priest Father Sebastian to come up to the turret room. Father Sebastian brought them in his car with the acolyte, because he knew he could not depend on Lavren to act as acolyte even at this last moment of his mother's life.

Marie Elena's memory was in the faraway past. The recent past, yesterday, last week, didn't interest her. Her interest in the present was myopic, except for her growing concern about the Third Most Intelligent Man in the World. It didn't extend beyond the door of the turret room, and since she didn't get out of bed much she did not go to the window and look out over the Gulf of Sadness, which might have jogged her memory into a full flow of historical recollection.

As it was, the distant past came in fits and starts, which accounts for some of the fragmentation of Lavren's narration. Some of course is his inexperience and some of course is this new fashion which he is a little open to. But in all seriousness, he would argue that what you are reading is in the most appropriate form for this material. He hopes critics will agree with him, but he knows when a country bookie comes to town, some little colonial boy, as they will inevitably think of him, they will want to link him with the Indian novelist, their sole point of reference: so that they speak of 'before the Indian novelist there was nothing and since the Indian novelist there has been nothing'. While digression is the very life and soul of his muse and mother Marie Elena, Lavren must stop on this sort of critical dissertation here at the foot of Marie Elena's deathbed. His mind moves to publication as he nears the end of his endeavours and he thinks of critics, publishers, bankers, agents, distributors and of course readers, but too, bookshelves, the shelf-life of a book. libraries, school lists, translations into Japanese, Chinese, and a host of other considerations which, unhappily, he will have absolutely no power over. You write a book and it might very well stay in the bottom drawer of Auguste's desk. Well. Writer's syndrome.

Marie Elena has been lying here, dying and shuffling her tarot pack of holy pictures in a hope that she can fix things to be just so, when she goes. She can of course do nothing about the insomnia of the Evangelist, or the hyperactivity of the Archangel, always flying hither and thither. She can do nothing about the to-be-pickled heart of Leonardo, or the solitude of Paris of Unsurpassed Beauty. She thanks God that Elena Maria's menopause has at last arrived, and she hopes that by now George the Usurped believes that she loves him as much as any of the others and that he was never supplanted in her love by Lavren. Though at the time, she had fallen head-over-heels in love with this last of her babies, this wonder of creation, this combination of all that was male and female, all that was good and bad, this little legend, her Peter Pan, Marie Elena's baby. And then there are the others whom Lavren cannot remember. She too has no memory of them but all were born by the will of God, according to the Pope's rhythm; these too, she can do nothing for.

'Darling, my glasses,' Marie Elena turned towards her bedside table with the paraphernalia of her religion: rosary beads, the bottle of Lourdes water, the mother-of-pearl crucifix. He too, as we know, had his little altars which included in their paraphernalia for veneration a piece of Maria Goretti's flesh for purity. There are her books of theology, her goldleaf missal, her Book of Hours. The old catechisms have been metaphorically thrown out of the window. Now she has the new biblical theologians of the United States, the popularisers since the Second Vatican Council, when John the Twenty-Third threw open the windows of the musty, dusty rooms of the Vatican so that the gusts of wind lifted the black soutanes of the cardinals in their red hats, and showed all their ancient and dirty secrets with which they used to terrify the minds of the faithful. Now the fresh air has let loose upon the world a new breed of charismatics and Catholic evangelists, trying to compete with the Born-Again Christians, the Evangelists, Gospellers of the Radio Waves and the Television Tubes, who keep many in this archipelagic rosary of the Caribbean well tied up to Uncle Sam. *God and Uncle Sam and His son Jesus Christ Rule − OK, and the President.* This new theology is near to her, her new-found library.

'You've got your glasses on.' Lavren poured Marie Elena a fresh glass of water to take her pills. There were pills for circulation, there were calcium tablets and little dots of white to be placed under the tongue when she went upstairs (which she hadn't done for months) to placate the angina attacks. There were Nitroglycerin Transdermal Systems to be applied externally on adhesive poultices, a polyester laminate film which she placed beneath her heart. This touched Lavren. He had lain his head there when sucking at her breasts, dry dugs now (remember the old blind hermaphrodite, Tiresias, who could see everything), so full and comforting then, before he was weaned on to bottles of cow's milk, delivered free to the door by the sugarcane company. Here she is again, cured by the mysteries of modern medicine, as she had been shaken into place by the miracle of Dr Kruger's brown bottle of mixed hormones.

As Lavren watched her shake the contents of each vial and open each little plastic box, from which to extract her daily dosages and place them in a compartmentalised plastic tray, he meditated on the mystery of mortality rates and the accumulation of wealth. Death, this final separation, could be manipulated with money and drugs. In these enlightened days she was on Herb-Lax, A Pure Natural Herbal Laxative, not that there was much to clear out with a diet of only chicken soup. Maybe some of the idiosyncratic designs in the recent stools was due to the cumulative use of these laxatives. She was on Isorbide and Cardizem. Lavren is back to his old tricks of falling under the spell of names, the sound and music in words. But maybe the real future wasn't what she was seeing. Maybe it was being altered by the use of drugs, the way the seasons were being altered by the interference with the ozone layer. Maybe this was why they were having so much rain, and the rumours from Aracataca had begun. Whatever was causing deafness and the increased consumption of sugar in the population had nothing to do with the ozone layer, or Marie Elena's drugs. Or did it? Marie Elena Monagas de los Macajuelos and the Third Most Intelligent Man in the World became twin stars in the skies over Kairi.

Lavren had chosen to place himself at this point in time, at this particular end of the world, at the end of his world, at the end of Marie Elena's bed at the end of the century. Who would now inspire him when she had gone, help him fill up the other squares of other manuscripts? Maybe, there was no other manuscript and no other story but this one. Maybe, from now on books would be sold with blank pages until each person felt inspired to write their own story. This idea of the writer, the one with the muse and the sensitivity, the class, the breeding and the connections, would be discarded for ever. The writing of books would be something libraries and bookshops went out of their way to propagate, because the silence and solitude of empty pages would be too much for people to bear as they watched the world slide off the edge, as the people of Genoa had watched the Great Navigator slide off the horizon, never imagining the new world. Did she imagine a new world? She had her heaven, the medieval idea. What would he do, left up here overlooking the Gulf of Sadness? He wished now it had another name, something more cheerful. Perhaps he could rename it and call it by its old name, Mar Dulce, the Sweet Sea, or the Freshwater Sea, alluding to the discovery ('Discovery?') by the Great Navigator. The lake, the gulf guarded by the rock Soldado in the Serpent's Mouth in the south, near the bay of cedar trees, and The Dragon's Mouth in the north, near the island whose name was the music of chac chacs, was sea water mixed with river water.

Maybe, with a new name and a host of different words and characters, a completely different story could be told. Or, with the same cast, a completely different story. He knew that to a man, to a woman, they would all wish to refute this history of the Monagas de los Macajuelos. 'Refute nancy story?' Josephine said. All he could answer in his defence, was that from where he stood, that was how it looked, not that he always stood quite in this position. 'Is nancy story, Master Lavren, not so? I should know,' Josephine chuckled.

'Have you given Father Sebastian the message, and where is Josephine? Can she get up the stairs today?' Lavren helped Marie Elena on to the commode with more than a little apprehension as to what the forecast would be on this day, the day of Marie Elena Monagas de los Macajuelos' death. The radio droned: ' . . . daughter of Sou Sou, granddaughter of Elena Elena, great-great-granddaughter of Elena, and others in the mists of the plains of Kairi and the forests of Tamana, mother of . . . ' Organ music followed, and Lavren realised that the radio was on for the BBC news, but they were listening to the death announcements instead. The deaths were read out alphabetically and Lavren and Marie Elena listened with awe, Marie Elena on the commode with her still commodious hips, the girth of Sou Sou, like the old queen with the girth of the world. The organ music droned in the silence of the turret room overlooking the Gulf of Sadness: 'Marie Elena Monagas de los Macajuelos, wife of Auguste Monagas de los Macajuelos, mother of Mark (known as the Evangelist), Gabriel (known as the Archangel), Leonardo, Elena Maria (Gross), Paris, George and Lavren, and others whose names have been forgotten and so not reported to Radio Kairi. Marie Elena Monagas de los Macajuelos died at the family home on the plains of Kairi near the Baie des Crabes on the night of 8 December, Feast of the Immaculate Conception of the Blessed Virgin Mary, in the year 2000. The funeral of Marie Elena de los Macajuelos will proceed from the house of mourning to the Cathedral of the Immaculate Conception and thence to the Lapeyrouse Cemetery. Friends and relatives are cordially invited to attend, flowers and messages of condolence to be sent to the family home on the plains of Kairi.'

'My God, they've got it all wrong. They can't kill me off before the good God wants to take me, and they've got the year wrong; what year is it anyway? What is this, a prophesy? Does it matter? Who'd be concerned with my age?' Lavren helped Marie Elena to wipe her arse. She loved Josephine, but such an intimacy could not be allowed with a black woman. Josephine could empty out the commode afterwards, after the ritualistic examination of the stools for signs of the dwindling future. The Monagas de los Macajuelos were secure in their past. 'Not much here now, not much longer to go. These words you're writing, this book. I see something about that, but it's not clear. They're not going to kill me off yet. I still have things to do in this world. I wish to have a bath this morning.' This was new. Lavren had been sponging her in bed with warm water, boiled and brought up by Josephine to the bottom of the stairs. A bath would mean several buckets of water, hot water. Auguste and Marie Elena had failed to moderise this section of the house. Its very dereliction went well with the fiction of Lavren who writes of the end of things, the last things, the last days, the eschaton and the coming of a new age that cannot yet be glimpsed. Lavren would not be able to allow Josephine to bring up the buckets on her own, or at all, though she would insist in giving a hand in spite of her high blood-pressure. The boys in the yard would have to give a hand.

Lavren went down to oversee (a last ancestral act) the filling of the buckets and the procession to the upstairs bathroom with the murals of anthurium lilies painted by Immaculata. Lavren did not enjoy this role of overseer, and he gladly handed over the supervision to Josephine who had four pots of water boiling on the stove in the kitchen, and two others on coalpots outside by the dead lime trees. This felt like old times.

Lavren wondered if Marie Elena would have time to die today and be buried by six o'clock this evening, as the announcement on the radio had prophesied, though projecting it all into the next decade. Was this art or life? Whether art or life, Lavren would be arranging it. He wished to arrange her death so he would be there, and it would be given the importance and significance that he wished his beloved Marie Elena, muse and mother, to have. The announcement of the death had been premature, projected into the future, and though he found that artistically interesting, it was not quite his fault (well, you know what he means); it was the Radio Kairi people who had got it all wrong. The place was falling apart with the death of the Third Most Intelligent Man in the World. Apart from that, he wanted the rest of the day to go according to plan, if he could fit it in today. The cables had been sent and the Evangelist, the Archangel, Leonardo, Paris, George and Elena Maria were all arriving by plane this afternoon with their spouses, as were the children, grandchildren, and great-grandchildren of Marie Elena. Those other siblings whose names could not be remembered would be there if they got the news, everyone was sure. They were coming from the four corners of the world. Most of Marie Elena's contemporary family had gone before her, and no one was clear what was going on in the antipodes, so Lavren left them out. It was too far anyway for them to make it on time. Lavren had wanted the Pope to come, but he had only recently been, and since his predecessor had been to Big Mama's funeral in Macondo it was thought unwise for any other pontiff to try and attend another funeral of such magnitude, on the continent of Liberation Theology in this age of the Condom.

Maire Elena would never have tolerated this kind of intimacy when she was younger. She never liked showing her body, but in the end forgot to bother about it when the effort to resist became too much.

Lavren lowered her into the ancient porcelain bath which had been in the house for centuries it seemed, at least artistically. 'There, there we go, easy does it.' He wanted this to be a perfect moment, after he had got the water to the absolutely correct temperature.

Marie Elena Monagas de los Macajuelos had shrunk, except for the Monagas hips. Her shoulders had caved in. Her face had sunk beneath the cheekbones. She hated her neck, which she tried to cover up, saying it looked as if she were turning into a turkey. They had grown to have different ideas about things, but their love remained. It was with exquisite tenderness that Lavren scented the water with tonca beans. After lowering her fragile body into the warm balm, he soaped her sagging arms, the thighs under whose loose flesh he could feel the bone. He soaped between her toes, which even on this day of her death tickled and created an indescribable sensation which she had kept a secret most of her life. It was like the secret that Immaculata had kept from her husband and the world about the sensations that could be created when her ears were licked. She had refused to remember when she had first noticed this delight, but had felt guilty about it till the day she died. Marie Elena did not feel guilty about her toes, and it was something she could do herself if she wanted. She smiled as she looked up at the ceiling decorated with Immaculata's watercolour mural of anthurium lilies. Either the day seemed to stand still (with hindsight) or, with the omniscient power belonging to Laven, was made to stand still, or because of the unique quality of the time it seemed as if they had been at it for ages, or rather that time had not existed at all and they were for ever in the eternal moment when he let his soapy hands slip along her arms and along her legs. His hands slipped along her legs to the mystery of that place he had not been to since his birth. She lay back with her eyes closed as he felt the opening where his head had been, the small tender place that had dilated to his coming.

The morning broke with slatted sunlight beams through the jalousies into the ancient bathroom with the old porcelain bath and the white wickerwork table with the jug and basin; walls the softest pink and green of Immaculata's watercolour murals, which created sensations of trickling water in her orchid house. Marie Elena let Lavren have his way with her as he let his finger slip into her vagina, soaping the hair there, which was grey and not fresh as a young girl's. The smells, mixed with the tonca beans and the soap (her favourite lavender), were extraordinarily like saltfish, but also reminded him of herself when he played with the crack between his anus and the base of his penis. He was of her and partly her. There was no insistence and rush in this washing of her, no intention, but sole sensation, as he soaped her breasts, the wide nipples where he had sucked and the creases under the heaviness where they dropped when not in a bra. He returned to her back and down her spine as he sat her up in the bath, feeling, slowly feeling how much he was going to miss her going, the final separation of her death. He had lived with its possibility, all through his fiction, his own truth, his own way of seeing things, written at the foot of her deathbed, almost joking at her going and her way of going. Now it seemed it would be impossible to live without her, or for anything to go on without her. At the bottom of her spine he moved to her anus and the fluted orifice from which the way to divine the future of this world, this family, had been excreted. He realised they would have to do this again when she had died and this body here in the water, in his arms, was a corpse. They would take her to Mr Samaroo's and do it all themselves, and he would find her the next day arranged in a coffin, the very best, but he would have had no place in their arrangements. Therefore, he was taking this liberty now.

Lastly, he poured some water from the jug that stood in the basin on the white wickerwork table and washed her hair, getting her ever so slowly and tenderly to bend her head backwards. He had watched so often as a child when she washed her hair, dried it and set it in pins. He wished to do this for her for the last time. He wished to be there, to exist in the scents and the beauty of her dressing and her boudoir. To be her, in the dressing of her. He let her drift in the water as he went to the jalousied door to collect the freshly laundered towels that Josephine had fetched from the linen cupboard at the foot of the stairs and left hanging outside the bathroom: 'Master Lavren, I leave the towel for you.'

'OK, Josephine,' he had whispered, not wishing to break from his ritual, from the liturgy of her body, from their communion. He felt a lump grow in his throat as he saw how old she was, how near her dying and her leaving of this world she had loved and controlled for a century, giving to Lavren the power to control the unfolding of the past centuries. He lifted her to the side of the bath, held her wet body against his chest, allowing them both to rest there for a moment. They had not spoken. He did not know what she was feeling; Lavren was without words for what Marie Elena was thinking or what she would say. This was their communion, their last rites. Later, Father Sebastian would anoint her and she would be prepared for her last journey across the plains to the church near the Gulf of Sadness where the crowds would come to venerate her going. He might fancifully have wished her cremated at the side of the old river, but that was not appropriate. (Cremation was being considered for the Third Most Intelligent Man in the World: a special crematorium was being ordered from America though still no one knew what they might find in the house with the darkened windows. The radio said.) Then they would bury her in the grave where Auguste was buried, and they would shovel the dirt on her, accompanied by the recitation of the Fifteen Mysteries of the Rosary.

But now was a time when he had her to himself, and she did seem unusually peaceful, allowing him to towel her, each limb patted with the newly laundered fluffy white towel. All his life he had approximated to being her, to perform these intimacies which were hers, as she performed them in the privacy of her room, always so concerned with covering her nakedness. It now seemed the greatest privilege.

Once she was towelled he guided her to the chair at her dressing-table, which had been moved into this ancient bathroom. He put a fresh towel over her shoulders and lap and combed out her hair as they both looked into the mirror and saw themselves reflected there. He threw open the windows with the jalousies, and the keskidees (which other birds would be there at this appropriate time?) were chattering and asking their question in the almond trees. What is he saying? *Qu'est ce qu'il dit?*

Lavren had arranged the dressing-table the way it had been when he was a child and used to sit at her side and the room was drenched with Chanel No. 5, or on some afternoons, eau de Cologne. This was indeed the altar of his life. He had fished out the doily with the embroidered forget-me-nots in blue and pink in a coronet in the middle. At the centre of the dressing-table was the cut-glass powder-bowl, to the left, the oblong silver hairpin box embossed with silver scallops, to the right the round cut-glass cruet with silver top. The silver-backed brush, hand-mirror and comb were laid out as they used to be in 'The Tale of the House in the Sugar'. Now he was her arms and her eyes as he brushed her hair and pinned it up, dipping the comb in a glass of water and combing each strand and twirling it as she did when she had the hairpin, opening its clasp between her teeth, and he watched her concentration so that he knew exactly what to do, exactly what to feel. He tied the head of set, curled strands with a Pierre Cardin scarf he had once given her. Together, they imagined how it would dry and, unpinned, be a nimbus of grey, a coronet for death.

Their hands moved as if they were the same hands to the table for the Pond's Cream, which she scooped with her old finger, and he helped her bring it to her brow where there had been no lines before; now he had seen creases appear almost without knowing when. The cream did little but soothe and remind her of when her brow had been smooth. 'Here, put this one to your cheek,' he whispered and guided her fingers to the cavity below her cheekbone. She smiled shyly.

'Oh, my neck. It's terrible,' as together they stroked what she called her turkey, upwards, imagining there was still time for a facelift. He stood behind her lifting the skin, giving her the illusion. 'I can't let anyone see this. Poor Father Sebastian, to have to see me this way, and poor Miss Metivere and Leela, poor girl.'

'You look wonderful,' he encouraged. 'Powder?' He guided her hand and lifted the heavy cover of the cut-glass powder-bowl. She scattered powder over the shiny mahogany dressing-table top. Lavren left the imprint of his fingers in the pink dust as he tried to rectify the heavy cut-glass top of the powder-bowl. Then she dabbed, missing the exact spots she wished to powder, her cheeks, the tip of her nose, the sides of her turkey. Lavren smiled, almost chuckling with a kind of amused affection for this very old woman, his mother and muse. The giggle brought tears to his eyes, of sadness and of admiration, sadness at the inevitability of her passing, and admiration for her stoic survival and effect upon her world in spite of the grand illusion, the folly of grandeur. He would have her this way for his fiction. He would have her this way on the prescribed morning of her death, which has already been announced. He would have her this way on the morning she was to descend to meet the parish priest Father Sebastian and the women of the Altar Sodality and the Legion of Mary. He would have her this way on the morning she would give all to the poor. He would have it this way. She was a grand lady.

'Now, what am I to wear?' He threw open the door of the mahogany press that had belonged to Sou Sou, with its carved panels of vases of English flowers. 'I will wear blue, blue is the colour of Our Lady and my best colour.' She who had divined the future by an expert analysis of the stools that passed through the labyrinthine intestine, inherited from the Monagas who killed the python and became known as 'de los Macajuelos', had been from the moment of her birth the focus of the family, soothing her brothers so they could sell more motorcars, producing sons, a daughter who was almost a replica, a hermaphrodite, an Evangelist and an Archangel, and many others whose names have been forgotten; she who was beloved of archbishops and abbots – who had brought the mysteries of the immortality of the soul, the incarnation, the transfiguration, the resurrection and the assumption to the children of the villages, so they could know salvation through transubstantiation and the infallibility of the Pope in Rome – had shrunk to this world of the turret room, her dressing-table and what she was to wear.

She wore the blue seersucker because it was hot. At one time he had imagined her in the black lace dress. It was a fancy. She had opals in her ears and on a pendant that hung from a gold chain, both belonging to Sou Sou. Lavren had slipped her silk stockings over the loose flesh of her legs. Her white shoes were manacles on the bones of her feet. He crowned the nimbus of grey, which had set just the way she wanted it, with an invisible grey hairnet sent from Harrods in London's Knightsbridge by Lolita her favourite neice, daughter of the tragic Clemence. Last was the lipstick that Auguste thought looked like yolk of egg because he was colour-blind. Then with the guidance of Lavren's hand she shook the vial of Chanel No. 5 and sprayed perfume behind her ears and on the inside of her wrists, rubbing them gently together. She would not bother with a bag. Instead, she carried a fan showing a triptych of the hanging gardens of Babylon, the fan that Sou Sou had given her and Elena Elena had unfurled when she visited Archbishop Gaspar Grande de los Angelicos to complain about the shortage of altar wine, long, long, long ago, and had worried that transubstantiation was not taking place because the Archbishop had ordered the wine to be watered down.

In this way, Marie Elena Monagas de los Macajuelos, last of the great matriarchs of the continent of the new world, descended on the arm of her ambivalent child, her Peter Pan, her little Lavren, once thought to be the love child of the nordic sailor who continued to live in portraits hidden in the drawer of the bridge-table. He did not look appropriate, he knew. He should look like Auguste or any of the others who had not yet arrived. But this morning she did not notice his bright shirt and unironed pants and old leather sandals. Once she had thought, 'Oh, he is an artist, he was always like that.' But not today. 'He's just a child.' She needed all her concentration to make it down the stairs to the drawing-room, where she had not been for over a year. Josephine waited by the pantry door. She waited for this last visit of her Madam to her drawing-room to order and serve tea. The day would need more than twenty-four hours to fit in all that was to take place. By now the others should be arriving by plane. There was lots to do before then.

She sat on the couch and looked out on to the veranda and beyond that to the lawn with the bird-bath which Auguste had erected after it had been given as a gift by Paris of Unsurpassed Beauty because he knew his father loved birds. Josephine had the water boiling on the stove, the Braganza tea-set had been laid out, first brought to her to open and take out of its case just as she had always done as a little girl when she saw the gift of the Count and Countess de Braganza as a gift to her on the day they had anchored their yacht in the harbour of the Gulf of Sadness. This was how Lavren had first seen her, setting out the tea-set on the veranda of No. 18, Cipriani Boulevard. It was laid out on the mahogany table with the cucumber sandwiches, which were folded in a damp linen napkin and placed in one of the silver entrée dishes. The tea was in the fluted silver teapot, and the china laid, the white and gold monogrammed tea-set that was soon to be given to the eldest grandchild, had she been the eldest? Which one was she?

When Father Sebastian arrived with Miss Metivere and Leela, Josephine would bring in the tea when Lavren indicated. After tea would be the dispensing of all the wealth to the poor from the contents of the cabinet, as Auguste had wished. Tea was always served at four o'clock.

Even though there were to be sandwiches folded into a damp napkin and arranged on a silver entrée dish when they were taken from the Frigidaire by Josephine, Lavren wanted there to be guava jelly, Crix biscuits baked by Bermudez, and a great big piece of yellow rat-cheese from Naipaul's Grocery, where Marie Elena preferred to cash her cheques rather than go to the bank. Josephine disapproved of some of Lavren's arrangements. 'Master Lavren, you going to give the Father priest and them his ladies that old piece a cheese Madam does grate for she macaroni pie when one of she boys come?' (Not that Marie Elena ever grated it herself, but would get Josephine to do it; but Josephine was accustomed to talk as if her own labour were the labour of her madam, the schizophrenia of a servant, the last of the servants.)

'You know they call them domestics now?' Marie Elena said,

turning to the arrangements at the table, then back to her view of the garden. 'And they all have them, all the government ministers and their wives. They have them dressed in the whitest cotton, with starched caps and aprons my mother would have envied.'

'Master Lavren, Madam like thing just so, you know.'

'I know, Josephine,' Lavren smiled and put his arm on her shoulder, 'don't worry, nuh, but you see this tea, this is the last tea we going to have in this house and it have to have guava jelly, Bermudez Crix biscuits and a big piece of rat cheese like we used to get in the chiney shop long time. You remember? Otherwise Mummy can't talk, and tell her stories.'

'The last tea, how you know these things, Master Lavren? Madam does talk a lot of stupidness about death and thing, don't listen to she. You hear what I telling you, Madam don't want to dead now. Madam don't want to leave this world at all. She only want to pretend. You see Madam there, she would like to go through with the whole thing, the last tea, the Father priest blessing, holy mass, the requiem them. Madam would even go in the coffin self and drop she in the hole Lapeyrouse, but you see when the prayers and thing finish, then she want to be right back where she belong in she bed up in that room calling out, "Josephine, Josephine, bring me a bowl of chicken soup." They had to be must kill so many chicken in this place to keep she happy, I think the Minister of Agriculture, Farming and Fisheries say in the papers they have a shortage. They importing chicken from China, they say.'

Lavren smiled but continued to arrange the cheese and the Crix biscuits.

'Cheups, Madam correctly knows that when she get to heaven there not going to be no Josephine, and when I meet she up there we go both be sitting on equal throne. That is why Madam don't want to die. She trying put things right with this poor people business. I done tell she I want the bed when she giving things away.'

Lavren looked at her and thought of the equal thrones. He saw a future, when he was old and dreaming of his sweet Josephine the day she came back from the dead.

One morning, in the future, when he got up in his house by the sea and walked on to the veranda in his dream, Josephine was sitting in the rocker looking out to the sea. She was wearing her work-dress and she looked sad. In the morning light she looked like one of the Irish bog-people or one of Van Gogh's pickers. She was very black and her skin was smooth and shining. 'Josephine.'

'I come back,' she said as she turned from the sea to look at where he stood in the doorway. 'I lonely.'

'Lonely?'

'Yes, heaven lonely, boy.' She turned again to look at the sea. 'I was lonely for so, boy,' she said again, without turning to face Lavren, who continued to stand in the doorway and to stare and listen to his sweet Josephine. Then she turned decisively and stared at him. She looked very old, as on the day she died and her face was crumpled and had caved in, because she died without her teeth. Then she began to change in front of him and began to become young again. She glowed in the dawn, and brought a warmth to the damp veranda in the house by the sea. Lavren looked out at the sea, and when he looked at Josephine again he noticed she was not alone. 'I bring them with me.' She had noticed his surprise and offered the explanation. Josephine was surrounded by a group of black women who were administering to her and stroking her skin, smoothing it all over with their hands, as if they were moulding clay. She became younger and younger as they moulded her. Her hair became straight and black like a Spanish woman's hair. Her figure became slim, and the women smiled as they stroked her slim waist and hips, so that she was no longer the body of his sweet Josephine. Her face changed, and they remoulded her nose. They stroked her all the time and stroked her between the legs all the way up the inside of her leg, and beckoned to him to come and stroke her and to put his hand against the hair that grew between her legs. Lavren was scared to put his hand over her vagina, but the other black women took his hand and put it there and he remembered how he had been taught to make love with her when she was much younger and he was a boy, and she looked herself with her big hips and fat backside and her big flat nose, and he had found her beautiful. He wondered at her coming to him in this way, in a dream. He wondered at the meaning of dreams and really what it was that he desired. The women all looked like Josephine. Then they walked into the sea. 'This is what they do we, Master Lavren, so we could stay in heaven. You see my skin. It going white.'

Lavren stood before her and watched her grow pale and white, grey and then die again. He stood looking out to sea and he wept for her death and her eternal loneliness. He wondered how he could change it.

But now Josephine was fussing round the tea-table in all her blackness, as if she was as young as ever. Every now and then she would stop and stand back from her arrangement of the table and say, 'Blood pressure, it getting me, yes.' Then she wiped her brow as if she were in some other past and she mused, 'Madam go like how I do it. I pick them vanda orchid early morning before dew gone. Is a wonder I don't have fresh cold right now, the things I does do for Madam.' She paused, and looked at Marie Elena on the couch. 'The things I do for all you, Master Lavren, and you talking about last tea and Madam going dead.' If Lavren didn't know Josephine he would have thought that she was just being sentimental, but it was what Lavren had known all his life, that between the two women there was an allegiance which history had shackled them to, and they had made out of its inequality a kind of partnership. They had run this house together for almost a century, a madam and her servant. Josephine, being born in the family and having lived with Sou Sou first, and then taking over from her own mother Celestine, was of course more than just the half-day girl or a woman who had come to the back door and asked for work. Josephine was family. But Lavren also knew what that meant. It meant of course that she was no family at all and that the boundaries were absolutely clear and there was no romantic eyewash about where Josephine could put her foot and where she couldn't. Josephine knew her place.

Yes, Josephine, his sweet Josephine who had bathed him, dressed him, wiped the shit from his arse, paying no attention to it because she didn't know how to read the signs in coprolites. She was not versed in the science of scatology, in the study of shit. She had left her own children for him, bringing stories of her boy into his bedtime stories. 'You think Madam go go just so and leave me, Master Lavren, and leave me? What will become of me, Master Lavren? You go take care of me? The boss gone just so, and before that he forget everything. I done tell Madam I want the bed. I wonder if Madam know, Master Lavren, why I wants that bed? I know you know, and I know enough of all this business of yours to know that if you didn't know you would've imagined the whole thing. Well, you don't have to imagine nothing.'

Josephine sat at the tea-table where Marie Elena would normally sit. 'Well, my child, why don't you sit and have some tea? Let me pour you some tea. Have a scone, a cucumber sandwich, and let me tell you the story of this place.' Josephine was not playing. Lavren knew when she was merely mimicking his mother and muse, Marie Elena. There was another tone in her voice as she sat and began to pour tea for truth and not pretend anything, but to be the madam of the house.

The mahogany table was covered over with the best damask linen which hung almost to touch the floor and seemed to Lavren like an altar cloth, and the tea-things were like the holy vessels for the liturgy. Josephine, priestess of history, was not going to let the chance pass, particularly as she had her Lavren there as acolyte, as he had been acolyte to Marie Elena. She leant and touched his hand as Marie Elena might. 'Another cucumber sandwich, dear?' Josephine enunciated with all the elocution and etiquette that had been inherited over two hundred years of British colonialism when it had come with its lime juice, tea and cucumber sandwiches, and 'Ha ha, ha,' on the balcony of Government House. Lavren helped himself to Crix biscuits and rat cheese. Josephine picked up a minute cucumber sandwich with the tips of her fingers and inserted the morsel into her mouth and then pressed a linen napkin to her lips to wipe away the crumbs. 'I see this whole ceremony from over there by the pantry door for nearly a century, and I decide right now that before it all come to an end, I going to sit down right here and have a cup of tea. I going to sit down right here and tell you a story, Master Lavren, in case you didn't imagine it yet. This is the story of the bed that I tell Madam I want when she giving things away.'

Josephine sat up in the chair Marie Elena had been accustomed to sit in at meal-times, before she had retreated to the turret room overlooking the Gulf of Sadness. The afternoon was bright and a flock of keskidee were singing their questions for Josephine in the old and dying almond tree and Lavren, like the birds, wondered what she was saying, what he was saying, as she embarked on her tale of the bed. When she drew herself up in Marie Elena's chair she could just see the tips of the mountains in the north above the rooftops of the houses, which were closing in and clambering up to the last of the houses of the Monagas de los Macajuelos. Lavren sat where he always sat, at the right hand of Marie Elena, and now at the right hand of his sweet Josephine. 'I always say you is my child, you is my white child, you is the child I leave my own black children like my black self for, to come up in this house where the good Lord will that my mother drop me right there, on the kitchen floor in the house where your grandmother live in the town by the Savannah, long time.' Josephine spoke, all the while looking at Lavren and reaching out to touch his arm, the way Marie Elena used to reach out to touch his arm when telling him the stories which have filled his head all his life; the stories which tasted of Crix biscuits, guava jelly and rat cheese. He was nibbling the cheese at this minute and feeding Bermudez Crix biscuits, rat cheese and guava jelly into the mouth of his sweet Josephine, who was now telling her story as the century closed and the house crumbled and the lime trees were dying in the backyard.

Long time now the cocoa had died and the witchbroom had cast its spell over the fortunes of these houses of Kairi. 'Cric,' Josephine began her tale.

'Crac.'

'I know about you. I know the kind a child you is, the kind of child you was. I know it since you is a baby and I wash you in the bath-pan out by the tank where the boys find the dead cat. You know, I never shame of you, I just say is so the good Lord make you, just like a man and a woman at the same time. But as I watch you grow I think it over, and I think you really confuse about who you really is and so you decide to be your mother and your father at the same time. But then you is who you is, and I don't know if you go believe me when I tell you that at times you father the boss used to think you was my child and I get confuse too. You remember I wasn't at your birth, because when Madam make baby with you, I was making baby too, and Madam never let me bring the baby in the house. Of course the boss ask about the baby. I think he want to see the baby. He want to check out the colour of the baby skin and see if the baby have eyes like he, or if they gone green with the mix-up, or if they dark brown like yours, Master Lavren. Is a funny time we live in, yes, Master Lavren. Is a funny world we make, but I keep the promise I make to Madam, never to bring my child in she house. But you know, Madam funny, yes, because she insist I get the old baby-clothes and take for the child, like she know something, the same clothes all you children wear. So he grow, yes, he grow like you in your own clothes. But is the bed I coming to. I know Madam will give me the bed because she can't take it with she, that is what I say. You can't take it with you, things, you have to leave them right here when you pass over. The bed, I want the bed. You see the board-house I build up in the village, I make the bedroom to the exact specifications so that the bed could fit in.'

All the time Josephine spoke, they each, Lavren and herself, were nibbling on the yellow rat cheese and licking their fingers, which were covered with the guava jelly. The damask linen tablecloth was covered with Crix biscuit crumbs. The cucumber sandwiches folded in the damp napkin in the silver entrée dish were going stale because the napkins had been left open and the napkin was almost dry from the hot air coming off the savannah. Lavren and Josephine were drunk with the tea and the nectar of the guava jelly. They were drunk with the story of Josephine which continued to unfold with the patience of one who had unfolded linen sheets and made beds all her life for all the family.

'Since that afternoon when the sun was going down and I went in the Madam and boss bedroom to put down the nets them, I decide that I would have to keep this bed to die on. You know, Master Lavren, how the boss always compliment me cooking, how he always say, "Josephine, that was a fine meal," was a real gentleman, the boss. That is what suprise me, Master Lavren, so that me . . . I was a big woman then, well, yes, big like Madam self, and the boss come in the room and I was just ready to pull down the mosquito-net. I go speechless when I feel the boss right near me, like his cheek is right there on my neck and he only breathing and I could hear a train passing down in the gully taking cane to the factory. I think of so many things at the same time. I think that Madam not coming back for an hour or so because she teaching catechism down in the village. All that time I not even turn round to face the boss, but I standing up still trying to pull down the mosquito-net and, Master Lavren, the boss have he hands right up my backside and the next hand undoing all the front of my dress and pulling down my apron. I feel so hot I can't hardly breathe. I never tell the boss anything in my life. I never cross him. Madam tell me she never cross him either. You know when I was lying on the bed my head kept knocking against that crucifix Madam have hanging from the railing of the bed. I want to pray, yes, but, Master Lavren, I always liked the boss and I let him take me right there on Madam bed. You know I never look at his nakedness. I keep my eyes close the whole time till the boss tell me to go downstairs and tidy up myself.'

When Lavren looked up at Josephine because he had been building little mounds with Crix biscuit crumbs all the time she spoke, listening entranced by her story and by the truth of her imagination, he saw that she was crying. He knew that not even he could tell that story as she had told it. When he looked at her she was staring over the savannah, and without putting the napkin to her cheeks she was allowing the tears to roll down her face, and she cried for the loss of herself in that far-distant afternoon when the sun was going down. She cried for her son whom Madam never allowed in the house. She cried for the boss whom she had nursed when he had already forgotten the distant afternoon, and she cried for her madam whom she had never wanted to betray. 'I had really like the boss, you know, Master Lavren. He was a real gentleman, but you know it really surprise me how the man put his hand right up my backside.' Josephine looked at Lavren and together they both laughed and laughed and laughed. They laughed so loud that it woke Marie Elena, who had fallen asleep sitting on the couch where she had waited after Lavren had helped her with her dressing and toilette. She had not heard a word of Josephine's story, but had all the time been dreaming of the arrangements for her funeral which she hoped she would not miss.

Marie Elena had long decided that she would be buried in the same grave as Auguste. It had become her responsibility to manage the plot behind the railings in Lapeyrouse in which all the Monagas had been buried. She had had it weeded and fresh pebbles brought from the beach at Pointe Baleine to be laid. She had made sure the various crosses and monuments were resettled after each of the burials, and it was she who was responsible for the inscriptions on the monuments. She had directed the undertakers, Samaroo, who had served the nation for more than a century, to undertake the inscription she had written for herself. She had no intention of leaving to anyone, in the emptiness and desolation that was to follow her death, the job of looking after the words which would speak to history of how she was to be remembered to any passer-by who dropped in to look at the ancient monuments of the Monagas de los Macajuelos. She didn't feel she could even entrust this task to Lavren, particularly not with his tendency to exaggerate and to see the marvellous and extraordinary in the most ordinary occurrences.

She awoke from her reverie on the couch and turned to the dining-room table and saw Josephine and Lavren sitting having tea and laughing. 'I don't know what you two are laughing at. It's no fun when you don't even have time to go to your own funeral, particularly when it has been announced before your death. Can I have a cup of tea?'

Lavren felt now that there would not be time for all the arrangements he had made. There was the tea to be had and the dispensing of the riches to the poor, as Christ had asked, and though the Pope had not been invited to come again to the new world for a funeral, the Archbishop, who had got wind of the funeral arrangements and had been fooled by the announcement on the radio, rang to say that he personally was coming to the parish church on the plains to officiate at the solemn obsequies of the last of the matriarchs of the Monagas de los Macajuelos, whose mother had founded the Legion of Mary, whose father had founded the Saint Vincent de Paul Sodality for the Preservation of the Poor, and whose brother had given his wealth to the poor and to the Archbishop – much to the anger of those who would have liked to have had some more cash.

The dining-room table with the damask tablecloth was covered with crumbs from Crix biscuits and rat cheese and stained with guava jelly after the telling of Josephine's tale of the bed. Marie Elena was clearly only going to have a cup of tea and would not sit to table. Father Sebastian and the women of the Legion of Mary were late. Lavren could not see how Marie Elena would have time to die, far less be able to be buried before nightfall, or for all the family to arrive with the Archbishop in time for the requiem mass and funeral with the procession across the plains of Kairi to the cemetery at Lapeyrouse.

All the while that Josephine spoke and told her tale, Marie Elena dreamed of her own funeral arrangements and whether she would have time to fit everything in. His mother now appeared to Lavren to have shrunk even more than she had over the last year. In Lavren's mind's eye she always remained his beloved Marie Elena who had lived with him in the house in the sugar, doing her hair and talking all the time to him. So that all his life, he has not been able to get out of his head all the things she has told him, that have seduced his imagination into the writing of his Carnival Tales.

Marie Elena now looked like an ancient foetus or a shrivelled cashew nut. Lavren did not think there would be time for any of the grand arrangements he had prepared for the death and funeral of his beloved Marie Elena. There might not even be time for the giving of everything to the poor, though this would have to be a priority. What would he do when the Archbishop arrived and Marie Elena had decided not to die? His worry was interrupted by a radio announcement declaring with great agitation that the Third Most Intelligent Man in the World had actually died. The stench that had been emanating from the house, forcing the President to leave his house nearby and go and stay by the sea to get some fresh air, made the police decide to break open the darkened glass doors and windows, where apparently they found the housekeeper keeping guard over the putrefying body of the Third Most Intelligent Man in the World. The lawn outside was strewn with dead corbeaux. Even vultures could not survive this death. The tabloids were lurid in their descriptions. The public were told to stand by for further communications. When Lavren told Marie Elena, she uttered the customary ejaculation: 'Eternal rest grant unto him, O Lord.'

Lavren replied as he had been taught, 'May he rest in peace.'

Josephine finished the prayer with, 'Amen,' and then: 'Let perpetual light shine upon him. Amen.'

While Josephine cleared away the tea which Marie Elena had never had, never sitting at the table to eat Crix biscuits, rat cheese and guava jelly to inspire the last of the tales, Lavren sat on the couch beside Marie Elena to try to hear what she was saying, for her voice had almost gone and she was bent double, so that when she lifted her neck to see what was in front of her she looked like a morocoy poking its head from under its shell. Lavren had eventually to sit on the floor and put his ear to her lips to hear what she was saying. She had long forgotten to use the telephones that were installed in every room, so that she could at a moment's notice contact Leonardo, whose to-be-pickled heart she was trying to save with her prayers, or Paris, whose loneliness was only broken when his beloved mother rang to speak to him. She was puzzled to know what they would do when she had gone and had no one to love them. The others who had been forgotten were now phoning from all the different parts of the world, so that Lavren had to hold the phone to her ears and even speak for her to his brothers and sisters, whom he had never met. They had not been able to find love like unto hers in all their wandering in the world. Lavren became the listener for all she had to say to the others, but now he deciphered, from the sounds which came from the depths of her spirit, that she was speaking to him of himself. 'Your soul, what will become of your soul?' While she spoke, she fumbled at the button of his shirt in the middle of his chest, as if to break through to some inner part of him where his soul was located, so she could extract it and repair the damage she had so insisted he had inflicted on it himself. 'Your soul, that is what I care about,' she croaked into his ear, 'not your body or your heart.' And, as if instructing one of her village children in the mysteries of the penny catechism, she asked from the very depth of her bent body and spirit, 'What must you take most care of, your body or your soul?'

He found himself like a dutiful acolyte replying, 'I must take most care of my soul because it is a spirit and is immortal.' She smiled, in her utter vagueness, believing that his parrot-like response showed he had not forgotten her teaching and would in future attend to his soul, having been reminded of its immortality.

After Josephine had cleared the things away from the tea-table, Father Sebastian arrived with the women of the Legion of Mary. While Josephine got Coca-Cola and juice for the ladies, Father Sebastian popped a host into Marie Elena's mouth, almost having to lie on the floor to do it, which was as much as his old age could take. When everyone was settled, Josephine began taking the contents of the cabinet out and laying them on the floor in front of Marie Elena. 'What these things go do for the poor,' Josephine muttered, and the ladies of the Legion of Mary looked crossly at her.

While Josephine showed the treasures from the cabinet, and the women of the Legion of Mary chose for the poor, Father Sebastian decided there and then to administer the last sacraments to Marie Elena. He happened to have with him his little black bag, like a doctor of health, with its stole, cruets of oils and holy water.

Though he could not depend on Lavren to be acolyte, he could grab the opportunity of having the women of the Legion of Mary here to answer the responses for the liturgy of the dying. Josephine exited to the kitchen to wash up the tea things, for she thought that this was all a masquerade. Marie Elena had no intention of dying. 'She not going to die. This whole place go dead before she die.'

The next announcement on the radio declared that the funeral of the Third Most Intelligent Man in the World would be that afternoon. The hurry apparently had to do with the state of putrefaction the body was in. The announcement from the Prime Minister's office, through the State Radio and Television, was that the body was at this moment being laid in state at the Casa Rosada in Brunswick Square. Lavren lowered the volume as the announcer went off the air.

Lavren, like Josephine, did not believe at this late stage of the afternoon that Marie Elena would die, would have the time to die. He was disappointed that they had not been able to have the last of the teas with Bermudez Crix biscuits, rat cheese and guava jelly, and Marie Elena telling the last of her tales, or retelling the tales as they came back to her jumbled and fragmented. This was what happened in the last days. It was this fact which made Lavren think differently from Josephine. Marie Elena was bereft of tales and so could now leave the world.

Lavren would in a minute go up to the turret room to pick up the last pages of his manuscript which he had scribbled on after he had given Marie Elena a bath. He knew that he would have to continue scribbling until she was covered over in Lapeyrouse.

Josephine's belief that Marie Elena would not die was based on the fact that, after all was said and done, she could not imagine a world without her madam, but she also could not believe that her madam, who had lived her life with such a sure knowledge of who she was, would leave the world for the uncertainty of death. Josephine did not put much trust in Marie Elena's medieval theories of heaven and hell. She had her own ideas, and it was logical that she would want to leave this earth and go to a heaven. But as we know, she came back to Lavren after her death, complaining that heaven was lonely.

So while Father Sebastian, assisted by the women of the Legion of Mary, administered the last sacraments to Marie Elena Monagas de los Macajuelos, Lavren and Josephine were absent.

The FM Radio music was suddenly interrupted by a report direct from the Casa Rosada. As soon as the last announcement had been made, people from all corners of the island began coming into town to see the body of the Third Most Intelligent Man in the World as it lay in state in the main entrance to the Casa Rosada. But confusion broke out when it was discovered that the coffin was locked down; while the expert techniques of Samaroo and Sons had stemmed the stench, the people wanted proof that a death had in truth taken place. The announcer was saying that a riot was imminent, with people shouting: 'No body, no votes.' The announcer advised people to stay in their homes, especially because of the heavy rains.

The telephone lines were down as it had not stopped raining. There was a rumour of hurricanes out in the Caribbean Sea which Lavren heard reported on a transistor radio which Marie Elena liked to keep in the turret room, so that she could listen to the BBC News from London, and to the cricket when the tests were being played either in India, Pakistan, Australia, Guyana, Barbados, Jamaica, in England, or right here in her beloved Kairi, at the Oval. The old river had broken its banks and overthrown its bridges. The plains of Kairi were returning to their original and ancient form as the riverbed of the ancient Orinoco. Lavren continued to write for an unknown length of time as the rain continued to fall. He felt comforted in his memory of the rain dripping from the roof of the turret room on to the lower roofs. It reminded him of Marie Elena and her love for the drip of the rain in the cocoa, and Sou Sou his grandmother, telling his mother that she would marry a planter. There were now so many pages that they kept falling off the writing table and falling on to the pitchpine floor. He felt strangely elated and realised that there was nothing more to write. He did not wish to admit to himself that this could only mean one thing and he resisted going downstairs, although it now seemed hours or days since he had heard Father Sebastian and the women from the Legion of Mary with their treasures for the poor leave the house. The house was silent, except for the fall of the rain on the roofs. The Gulf of Sadness was grey, the mountains in the north were not visible.

The hour had passed when it would be permissible to bury Marie Elena. Lavren realised that his fabrication, his design, had not worked. He had not been able to get Marie Elena dead and buried before the setting of the sun. Yet he felt that it was all over and he could write no more of these Carnival Tales. He dared not now contemplate the grandeur and scale of his design and fabrication. He could not bring himself to reflect on the preparations which had been made.

No one could get to the house, since all roads were flooded and the telephones were down. This, together with the crowds who ignored the advice on the radio and were still pouring into the city to see the body of the Third Most Intelligent Man in the World, meant that no one could get to the funeral. This explained the silence. This meant that the entire family from away was stranded at the airport or not even allowed to land because of the flooding of the airstrip, and because they were awaiting a new part for the crematorium, which was not working so that they were unable to go ahead with the cremation of the Third Most Intelligent Man in the World. The news said that the Archbishop had got halfway across the plain and his car had shut down because the engine was flooded. No one was sure where the Archbishop was heading in this terrible weather, but rumour had it that he was going to officiate at a funeral of a person who had not as yet died. The advice to the Archbishop, if he was near a radio, was to return to the capital to attend the cremation of the Third Most Intelligent Man in the World as soon as the part arrived from America.

As Lavren tidied up his manuscript of the Carnival Tales he said to himself, 'This whole thing gone ole mas.' Maybe readers will wonder as the centuries unfold whether he was referring merely to the recent events or to his life's work, this manuscript in his hands.

'Master Lavren, Madam gone!' Josephine was shouting from the bottom of the stairs.

'Gone? She can't go out in this rain. You mad or what?' Then he understood. Lavren dropped the manuscript on the floor of the turret room overlooking the Gulf of Sadness.

When Lavren met Josephine at the bottom of the stairs she was grey. 'Not in the rain, Master Lavren, Madam couldn't've walked nowhere in this world, far less gone out in this rain like the heaven break open and God can't fix the pipe and them.'

'I thought she was dead — then she must be in the house somewhere.'

259

'No!' Josephine screamed.

'Where is she then?' Lavren was rushing down the stairs to the drawing-room where he had left Marie Elena sitting on the couch. The room was filled with the odour and perfume of the eucharist lilies which Clarita had brought from Aracataca after she had been seduced by Gaston in the Convent of the Immaculate Heart of Mary. Marie Elena's blue seersucker dress was on the couch. 'You mean she gone out in the rain naked?' Lavren said, confused by the events which had overtaken him. He would now have to change the end of his tale, 'The Tale of Last of the Houses'. What would people believe? He knew that they would not believe this – so that is why he had wanted the large funeral with the entire family and the Archbishop and the monks and the Abbot and all the women of the Legion of Mary and all the old servants and yardmen. That would have been appropriate to the grandeur and the style of his story and it could have been true. But Marie Elena had decided otherwise. There was no sign of her, except for the blue seersucker dress lying on the couch. He could not believe she had gone for good in her panties, bra and girdle. Later, when the rain abated, Josephine found those under an old rose tree by the bird-bath. Her shoes were found out on the savannah by one of the Indian children when they were tethering their cattle.

Lavren does not quite know how to put this for a secular audience at the end of this century, when scepticism is rife and cynicism is the companion of greed. It is, as Marie Elena herself would say, not a matter for the intellect but a matter of faith. This is what Lavren doesn't quite know how to describe. Josephine believed Marie Elena would never die. She merely wished for the drama of the requiem, not that she quite got into the hole in Lapeyrouse. How can you ask people to believe you when you tell them that your mother has been assumed into heaven body and soul? Lavren wondered why she had to go naked, dropping her clothes off as she floated heavenwards. 'She could've at least have done it in some style. If I'd known I would've dressed her in the black lace dress and the turquoise petticoat. Maybe heaven would've been the best place for them.' But even though she had gone, she had left him his fetish, his charm, his talisman.

The women of the Legion of Mary came back and took the rest of the things, and Josephine got Ram to move the bed for her. She slept on it in peace until the day she died.

The people of Kairi never did get to see the body of the Third Most Intelligent Man in the World. And in the end, they did change their votes. But for what? The same old khaki pants? This petty dictator was eventually cremated and his ashes strewn over the waters of the Gulf of Sadness to mingle with the rest of history. Lavren believed that this was the reason why Marie Elena chose to go to heaven body and soul. She could not bring herself to mingle her ashes with just anybody. But Lavren also believed that she could not bear to have her own going eclipsed. So she played the trump card which God had given her.

Today, there is a stone for her next to the one she laid for Auguste in the family plot in Lapeyrouse. *Marie Elena, Assumpta Est in Coelum*. She had arranged it herself with Mr Samaroo; it had not occurred to him to question its truthfulness in any way, knowing that white people had been doing anything they liked in this place, since ever.

J'OUVERT

BEFORE DAYBREAK, before sunrise, before J'Ouvert, Lavren took my hand and led me into the darkness of the city, this Belle d'Antilles, this city on the edge of the Gulf of Sadness, filled with the bones of those who had died diving for pearls, guarded in the north by the Dragon's Mouth and in the south by the Serpent's. This is the city which grew from the first fishing village of the new world, the first houses of tapia and carat, the first muddy streets under the silk-cotton trees at Mucurapo, where, as the tales tell of the beginning of the world, Clarita first landed with Gaston, Elena Elena went to reprimand Archbiship Gaspar Grande de los Angelicos, who loved small boys and girls: this city at whose wharfside the chains, like those of the Inquisition, imprisoned and tortured a young girl of fourteen in an upper room under the heel of an English governor.

Lavren and I descended into this city in which poison had run its course, along whose avenues and boulevards, along whose torturous alleyways, which had become a grid, a rack, named after kings and queens (Charlotte and George), after governors and admirals (Abercromby and Chacon), blood had flowed. And, upon the trees of these boulevards had hung the black fruit that Elena Elena saw on her last visit to Coblentz Estate, hanging from the gibbet of Picton, before she chose seclusion in the turret room overlooking the Gulf of Sadness from where she saw clouds of saffron and paprika, sails of dhotis and capras, ballooning muslin, Muslim and Hindu indentured to these shores. Here, in this city, she asked that all the crucifixes of Kairi be painted black since she had never seen any white people hanging from crosses in this hemisphere – except where the ochre people, through the analogical imagination of the new world, had hung their executioners and baptising priests on their own crosses in acts of supreme irony. Into this city, Lavren takes me by the hand and says that this is our descent into hell, that after the crucifixion and before the resurrection we must descend into hell for three days

263

and three nights. He snatches here at a fragment of Marie Elena's *Credo*.

I take his hand. I take her hand, and I'm enchanted by his dissembling beauty.

The city is black like the wings of a corbeaux and I know where to wait at the foot of the mango tree against which I lean up a cross which Lavren is to carry this J'Ouvert, by the gate with the bluestone arch over which a frangipani hangs, perfumed like a Magdalen's breast. I wait for the dead to rise from the graves of Lapeyrouse to play ole mas. As we wait, she and I, he and I, pronouns confuse and dissemble, King Carnival's magic begins to work. The first procession I see is the cortège of douens released from limbo, unbaptised babies with their feet turned backwards, small enough to pass under the limbo stick. They are the unbaptised babies of Santa Immaculata returned for the carnival, carrying the uncorrupted body of Aunty Immaculata.

There is no hierarchy in carnival; no colour, no class, no race, no gender: all may cross over and inhabit the other. Mas can come out from any house, any alleyway, up Belmont so, down Dry River, even up Lady Chancellor and St Clair, where the rich come out at last and can pretend to be black. They daub their white skins with shoe-polish, charcoal, mud and molasses, streak their skin with blue and bind their white bodies with greasy chains. They wish to chain and enslave their spirits. They wish to indenture their bodies. Here they can be people from up Laventville. They can be people like people self. They can be black with plaited hair.

And as we walk through the streets, carrying the cross, Lavren is Jesus with a dhoti round his loins, and I, dressed as his muse and mother Marie Elena in her black lace dress and the turquoise petticoat; to be her, so that I could be loved by and love his father, Auguste. We meet up with the inhabitants of Lavren's Carnival Tales come out this J'Ouvert morning to play ole mas and to take off themselves and be another.

Immaculata smiles and is happy in her uncorrupted body, dressed as the Blessed Virgin Mary when she meets the Clarita who feared to be buried alive, daubed in the mud of Lapeyrouse and joining up with a white band from the Champs Elysées Estate, in which Rose De Gannes de la Chancellerie plays Madame La Diablesse with a cow-foot, a big hat and smoking a cigar. Lavren was jumping up and showing everyone the crack between his legs and jumping with Madoo the yardman who was playing Dame Lorraine dressed in Marie Elena's house-dress. Marie Elena was herself there, where Lavren met her by Green Corner under the Globe Cinema and mistook her for his beloved Josephine. She so wanted to be loved as he loved Josephine that she had dressed up in cap and apron. And she so wanted him to be like Jesus.

The city, Belle d'Antilles, the last bead in this Caribbean archipelagic rosary, trembled under the moon and stars of the dawn, with the north star still over Laventville hilltop shrine in the sky, with the moon over the continent of Bolivar, sipping on the waters of the Gulf of Sadness. The comet that had once heralded the witchbroom blazed through the sky. The city trembled to every tinkle of every bottle and spoon in the whole of Kairi, as each and every tamboo-bamboo band from down the centuries came out to play, and Makandal himself descended on stilts from Mount Hololo as Moco Jumbie, Majesty of the Niger. In every backyard under a governor-plum tree each dustbin cover, each piece of iron, played its part in the forge of fire that fashioned out of all this pain, all this passage over all them sea, entangled with sargasso weed, the pure and silver beauty of the slung-round-the-neck pan, tenor pan, pan, ping p'ding, pingpong pan, woman on the bass pan, until the whole beautiful city, Belle d'Antilles, rocked and jammed like a gigantic Hosay from out St James, coming down Western Main Road to meet up with Invaders steel band Tragarete Road, with pan and tassa in unison, together with the old-time tamboo-bamboo. Jour Ouvert!

Lavren took the cross like a Hosay self and stuck it in the ground middle of Brunswick Square where the Third Most Intelligent Man in the World had said, 'Massa Day Done.' Lavren got up on the cross to show himself to the Shango Baptist people them, who the Governor long time ban with their candle and bell and flower in a vase, with the black Bible on the white cloth spread on the ground. And the same Shango Baptist throw off the Baptist and play Shango and possess themselves, the people, with the spirit of Africa walking tall through the streets, turbanned in the saffron clouds over the Gulf of Sadness. And in that congregation were all kinds of people who had come through the centuries to realise, at least carnival day, that they were people, that man could be woman, woman could be man, could be god, could be servant, could be master, could be indentured labourer, could be enslaved, and revel with the rebellion of the jab-jab band coming out of the Morvant hills ladened with dou douce mango tree. King Carnival's magic.

And in that congregation was Paris playing borokeet, a pretty donkey from Venezuela, the Archangel playing bat with his own wings, Leonardo playing drunken sailor meeting up with the Evangelist playing American GI from *To Hell and Back*, and right down the street was George playing baby in a pram with a bottle in his mouth pretending to cry for Marie Elena's love, and all the other forgotten ones played sailor for this carnival. Elena Maria was queen of the band and following pellmell behind her was Mr de Lisle, who was trying to meet up with her to kiss her feet and do any other kind of watlessness because it was big J'Ouvert morning.

After the sermon from the cross, Lavren asked me to help him carry his cross to the bottom of Calvary Hill, where we met Desperadoes steelband coming from their panyard tent on top of the hill. And, as we looked back the city, Belle d'Antilles, glittered and tingled with sound and colour, music, bottle and spoon, tamboo-bamboo, pan-pan-pan, jam-jam-jam, and Lavren thought it took the suffering away, as he met Aldrick, a steelband man, a friend, coming down the hill in his dragon constume with the band from Alice Street. He heard Spoiler the calypsonian say out of hell: 'Tell Desperadoes when you reach the hill, I decompose but I composing still.' This was hell, three days and nights, after crucifixion, limbo, and then with Saint Magdalen in the garden playing gardener, Holy Ghost appearing in pentecostal storm, throwing open the windows and the doors and coming, in tongues of fire.

Coming up from the bottom of the hill, Quentino and Margarita were playing each other, Father priest and Mother Superior, and having a real bacchanal, back to back, belly to belly. Archbishop Gaspar Grande de la Angelicos played the Pope and kissed the ground he walked upon, and those from the house on the plains played Caribs and Arawaks. Clarita, Elena, Elena Elena and Sou Sou played slave girls. Ramon made long speeches playing Robberman, from where Marie Elena said Lavren learned to write things down. Monkey Cedric and Ramon Junior played twin transvestites, because they such men. From on top the cross Lavren spotted the Englishman, Elena Elena's husband, playing the cruel English

Governor Picton and driving Luisa Calderon into the upper room down by the wharf to do with her what he would. But, it was only when he looked down that Lavren saw Auguste, disguised as the beloved disciple John, kneeling at the foot of the cross so that he played at loving Lavren playing Jesus. Lavren looked down on him and said, 'Father, I forgive you because you don't know what you do.'

Lavren stretched upon the cross above the city by the will of his father, played Jesus this J'Ouvert to save people. I help him withdraw the iron nails glistening like skewers of ruby meat. I kiss those hands. I kiss those feet. And here upon this hill called Calvary, upon which a man called Taffy once crucified himself, I take him into my arms and we are our own *pietà*.

Later Lavren played the part right out and Auguste and Immaculata, playing the Blessed Virgin Mary and John the beloved disciple, took him from my arms and played mas again Ash Wednesday, all in white with whitened faces and ash on their heads, like at carnival in Guadeloupe and Martinique, till they end up right down town by the old railway station where Josephine met them and said, 'All you not see anything. I reach Green Corner and I see myself coming down the road to meet myself and when I take a good look again, is Madam self I see is me and she see herself is me.'

Josephine turned to Lavren and I and said, 'Look my boy,' and we saw her yellow brownskin son with the green eyes and sandy hair, Lavren's brother, son of Auguste, his actual child.

I left town the next morning, leaving King Carnival's magic blown by the wind through the streets. I headed for the north-east coast, and when I passed out on the highway, I saw an Indian fella with a burnt belly, the white of fish-bait, selling cascadura on the side of the road. I bought some of the fabled fish. We waved to each other. I had taken off the black lace dress belonging to Marie Elena and I realised that, all along, I was Lavren Monagas de los Macajuelos, the great storyteller.

POSTSCRIPT

YES, LITERALLY, after writing my journal and reading the last of the Carnival Tales, I felt that there was this small, but important part of the story still to tell.

After some years had passed the last of the houses, the small pink bungalow which my aunt had painted on the wide open plain, under a wide sky and squat among the ochre bush below the mountains, had been sold off. An Indian man who specialised in selling hamburgers bought it and used the spacious yard under the almond trees for parking all his vans which blared out in orange and red: HASANALI'S FAST FOOD (Imported).

I had left the museum, as I've already said, and was putting my hand to a little writing, a small collection of stories, in a house I had acquired up Cumana way, beyond the bridge by Rampanalgas. Much water had flowed under the Caroni bridge, some flooding over. And while I still worked for the preservation of old things as reminders, my view of history had been altered. There is the history of the plantation water-wheel, the bit which fitted the mouth, the manacles which clasped the neck, ankles and wrist, the chains which tethered, the muzzle. There is the memory of treachery and cruelty. There is the last barrack-room of the enslaved and indentured, that we can all go and see. Some of the mango trees still stand where the hangings were executed. There is the last great house on the hill. The first huts for the indentured were like these, mud and dung. This was how the Caribs baked cassava. All conjure a past. That is the past. What do they teach us, if, relatively, we continue to organise and structure our world similarly? What does the teaching do if it does not prevent? I found myself looking out to sea, exchanging these seeming clichés for the shells on the beach.

The doors of the house have been ripped away, the windows bang in the wind, the doors of the presses have been unhinged and the shelves with their contents examined.

There is the reversal that happens in Carnival, the collapsing of opposites. Each year the ritual comes around.

One day I went to see Antoinetta and she offered me tea, sitting on the old couch where we sat watching a new television my mother had bought her, in a board-house she had built on squatted land. Some things had not changed but had got mixed up.

There is the putting-down of all this. There is the continual alchemy which the imagination works, and I knew that no words here would have been possible without the poetry, prose, history, painting, sculpture, the mobility of mas, the invention of pan, calypso and the spoken voice which had come out of the yard of this archipelago, and which had invaded my ears, sitting on the sill of the Demerara window.

And − but − there was friendship, which allowed me to come down off the sill and walk hand in hand. 'Pardner, how you?'

While now I spend my days mostly looking out to sea up the road Cumana way, not far from the bridge at Rampanalgas, I remember a more recent past and wish to tell another tale which continues the story of us all, on the shores of the Gulf of Sadness.

Children from in the village had taken pieces of wood which had belonged to the house and built a big swing which hung from some wire attached to a branch of one of the mango trees. It grew on the bank going up the small hill where the house used to stand in a small clearing in the forest, not far from the main road. They had covered the seat of the swing with a piece of old brown linoleum which had once covered the shelves in the kitchen. I recognised it at once.

It has been part of the weave of the house, part of the intricate tapestry which this house had been of old and new, of the past and the present, and a hope for the future. In its fragility and strength, part of a dream for the future. More than a house this; rather, a life. Each plank of wood, each strip of bamboo which had been woven into a screen under the rude Demerara window, each piece of new zinc or rusty galvanize, was part of the weave; part of the story.

This was a house which we had built in the forest on this land near a village, to proclaim a self, a life, and in its weave, I saw the lofty beauty and airiness of great houses; I saw cleanliness of cocoyea-brushed yards in the mornings of villages and backyards, water fetched from the standpipe, flower garden in kerosene tins on the veranda ledge, red, red exhoras. We could all come home to this house. This house was built of every part of us. Each of us who had come here had woven a part of themselves into this house. Into this house was woven tapia and carat. This house housed an ajoupa. It grew modestly with the work of our own hands, climbing on stilts to airy bedrooms which pushed Demerara windows into the green light of the nearby forests, the close overhanging breadfruit trees. This house was cool for the heat of our land, and the ground floor, walls and roof, were built Sunday morning, gayiappe, each one giving their labour, and on that cool floor we scraped out feet, swinging in well-made crocus-bag hammocks, looking up to ferns which grew in pots in the corner and from the rafters of the ceiling. We sat here in old-fashioned morris chairs telling our stories, talking of this land and all its peoples and its greatness. We grew our own food, fished our own fish, fetched conch from the river, and with melangene, okro, pumpkin, rice and peas, and good cashew wine, we ate and drank to our health and the health of all.

This yard had reverbrated with cries of cricket-match Sunday morning with soft-ball, cricket on the beach kinda cricket. The parang band came up the hill from the village into this yard and into this house, filling it with a music which drew in more of our peoples, strumming cuatros in pirogues over the waters of our gulf from down the main, singing an *aguanaldo* and a *joropo* by the River Manzanares of our mornings, sipping sorrel. There was place for all people in this house. A nancy story, yes?

Can you blame us for these dreams? Dreams of the ordinary, ordinary people, long-time things?

In this house we dreamed our future, weaving our past into our present.

This had been part of an old estate. The crop was mixed, cocoa (no witchbroom), citrus and a little bit of coffee, coconuts on the boundary. The old cocoa house was still there for drying the cocoa; the place where they danced the cocoa. The ground between the citrus was stubbled with pineapple, and down the slope a clearing for a vegetable garden.

I had come up the hill. I had known where to put my foot to get a hold in the stones which had been washed away in the rain. I wanted to see where this house had once stood. I imagined it open, its doors and windows banging in the breeze, awaiting new people. I imagined dead leaves by the door, lizards scuttling. There was still the breeze in the high trees, the faraway sound of the river over stones passing under the bridge.

I stood now at the top of the slope by the small mango tree where the anthuriums used to grow under the low branches, and there was a pot of flowers gone wild, breaking the pot to root in the ground. Something in that.

The house was not there. The layout of the house was still clear. The stubs of pillars coming out of the ground showed a plan. It reminded me of a grid which preceded an archaeological excavation. A piece of cleared ground.

I stood filled with all that had been here, looking at the vacant space. It rose before me transparently, so that I saw it and, through its walls, the people of the house. Transfigured by absence. Fully present − a remembered self. Our remembered selves.

This was no ruin, and it did not tell why it was no longer there. It asked a question. It was a question concerning the nature of love, the pain of love. I noticed the shadows tremble in the nearby forest where the light made a clearing.

As I went back down the slope, I could hear the hysteria of the parrots in the forests. Voices, and nearby on the branch of a tree, a keskidee: *Qu'est ce qu'il dit?*

Down on the plain near the gulf, 'Imported Fast Food' flickered in the neon shopping malls to the tune of the long-time calypso, playing in my ear again for the meaning of the time: *Rum and Coca-Cola . . . mother and daughter working for the Yankee dollar.*